From Inside Her Bedroom

Doug Booth

From Inside Her Bedroom

To Linda,
Who steadfastly believes there's good in everyone.
If only…

From Inside Her Bedroom

Five Years Earlier

Clint Evans glared at the woman standing at the very edge of the loading dock through the tinsel-like downpour streaked with sporadic flashes of electric blue, reading the cold, dead eyes of Kim Moon, sneering, tasting his blood trickling across his twisted lips and into the dancing rainwater spilling into his mouth. Once she had been exotic to him: one part Asian, one part Cajun, her skin with its sensual hue and texture of cream pale against the dark silkiness of her cropped mahogany hair and her coal-black eyes. Her eyes were the blackest he had ever seen, as black as the night he would remember forever.

He would survive. Surviving would mean one day finding her and destroying her, humiliating her as she was humiliating and destroying him.

One

Month Six

Clint Evans had never felt lost. He had always known where he was before and after the steel doors clanged shut behind him and that hadn't changed. His five years in prison were informative, a time of learning, of re-education, a time to review his options which were limited at best. At thirty-five he was living in a halfway house with old and new acquaintances he cared nothing about and had ten thousand dollars stagnating in a bank account from his previous existence. Those days were gone forever. He would never again take clients to dinner or invite their wives to lunch soon thereafter.

He did his time. He paid for his one mistake in life, his one serious lapse which brought his fast-paced career to an abrupt end, if not his inherent charm. He was a survivor. Somehow he would endure and get on with his life. Although how he would accomplish that vague ambition he wasn't quite sure. He never robbed a bank, nor did he ever kill anyone. Those weren't his skills, nor did he ever hate anyone or want anything as much until the night she lured him into a maelstrom of violent swirling rain and sudden flashing lights, voices screaming against the wind and vice-like hands crashing him onto the broken surface of the company parking lot. Now he did hate, which he realized was of no particular consequence in his immediate future because even the most dim-witted cop would tie him in to his sense of poetic justice and he'd be arrested for murder. Though, in time, what was done would be undone. Live and let live was the credo of the naïve, the faint of heart and he no longer had one. He had adjusted quickly to the rigors of prison life. After the failed initiation the other inmates gave him space. They left him in peace to harangue younger and more passive newcomers, which didn't mean Clint Evans wouldn't call upon his pent-up hatred to hurt someone else like her.

He knew he would never go back, as he knew he would never again be completely honest. Prison did that to a man. Rehabilitation was a specific term relative to parole, meant to satisfy diligent functionaries. However, once out beyond the gates, beyond the din and the smells of men in close confinement, rehab went to hell and fear of survival took over to guide most men along paths of least resistance. He hadn't worked a hard day in his life. Everything had come easily to him. He was charming, people were drawn to him and prison hadn't diminished his capacity to beguile. Not even the cons were exempt. He would succeed and survive, walking the same path he had always travelled, only this time his clientele wouldn't be six-figure executives and that's what made him different from the others. They hadn't arrested him for compulsive dishonesty. He was arrested by simple virtue of unfortunately being caught and his prison days were over. He wouldn't go back because he knew better. As much as he'd been a good convict, he'd been a good student. He would call upon the skills honed over a ten-year career, marry them with more recently acquired competencies, and succeed.

He adapted to his confined life by keeping vivid memories of her alive, images never usurped by monotonous routine: daily orders to shower, eat, exercise, work and sleep. Lights out meant reliving each occasion, each titillating touch and whisper until each night his dreams took over to be curtly invaded by yet another day of monochromatic grey, single file, yes sir, no sir and may I. How could he ever forget or forgive her? He lived and breathed for her. He always had, though his threat was real, not the hysterical ranting of a condemned man. He imagined finding her, inflicting deep-rooted pain as she had done to him, taking what was rightfully his: his home, his money, his career and the life he once devoted to her. She had walked away taking everything with her, leaving him a paltry sum in his account and a prepaid safety deposit box where he found final divorce papers and a wedding ring without so much as a scribbled note.

His first morning of freedom was strangely uncertain to him. He slept in the dark behind a closed door and stayed in bed without a baton banging against the bars of his cell. He showered alone, and when he made his way to the kitchen he was alone to make a breakfast of toast and jam. He had forgotten how to fry an egg, or had forgotten he could. He drank one coffee from a ceramic mug without the familiar aftertaste of tin lingering in his mouth and sat wondering whether he was allowed to have another.

He wasn't on parole. He had done his time, which he reasoned was the fault of the first con as much as Kim Moon. The lifer had thought to instruct him in the rules of prison hierarchy, conduct and obeisance, the man whose head Clint disrespectfully crashed into a nearby concrete wall. The arresting cop had given him good advice: Do onto others, but do it first and do it right. And after thirty days in solitary with a damaged hand for Clint, and as many in the infirmary for the less fortunate inmate, he was escorted to his cell. The next day in the recreation hall, amidst side glances, murmurs and worry, he confronted the man to forgive him for breaking his hand. He held his breath, forcing his eyes not to betray him until the huge con guffawed and a strategic friendship was cemented with their left hands. The friendship he would soon forget, never the cop's advice or the faded scar.

He was free, with longer hair and a shapeless suit paid for by the system. He had known the precise date of his release and had let his hair grow, assuming any hairstylist could make him look less like an ex-con. He was half-right, however prison life was undeniably etched into the greyish pallor of his face and hands and he determined to erase the social flaw.

After several days spent acclimating to city noises, daylight and people, solitary evenings spent in his room thinking and rethinking his life's plan, he awoke one morning, showered, and left. He had earned a dollar a day throughout his incarceration and took half the amount to buy a suit that instantly felt familiar to him, shirts, ties and shoes. He didn't leave the halfway house that morning; he simply didn't return and checked into a hotel he could afford for a week without dipping into his ten-grand reserve. He would be Clint Evans again, very soon.

He hadn't thought of women for sixty months, doing so would have provoked emotions he wanted to suppress and he hadn't seen her in five years. She would have known to run and hide and he had no means with which to find her. Nor did he consider curb-side relief or escort services, unable to rationalize paying a woman for sex when sex is what they all invariably wanted. He would find a woman on his terms: young, attractive, single or divorced and unencumbered. He would invite her to dinner, enthral her, take her home where she would invite him to spend the night and he would leave her in the darkness of predawn with sufficient cash, credit or debit cards to carry him through another week or longer. He would work primarily with cash, taking one card or the other and never leave a woman without means that would inevitably lead to her embarrassment and his possible undoing.

That was the crux of his plan. The city boasted hundreds of nightclubs, dozens of luxury hotels in the downtown core. Not to mention other cities and vacation resorts, his first priority being not to look like an ex-con in a fancy suit. His next order of business was a day at a spa.

Two

In time Kathy Burberry had learned to become average. She felt ordinary. No one had told her in years that she was special and she had begun pretending to believe in everyone but herself. In fact, she believed in no one. At thirty-five she suffered through endless weeks as a college counsellor, doing her best to advise brain-dead adolescents as incorrigible as her own who attended the same campus and spending her evenings alone, waiting for her husband to return from yet another business trip.

She hadn't worn silk in years, not since he stopped seeing her as a vital, good-looking woman. Ted Burberry no longer regarded her that way. His world was his career. She had the simpler job with more time to raise the children and had unwittingly become "the wife" after eighteen years of faithful and dutiful marriage. Their first was a girl, he'd wanted a boy, and eleven months later she had both, secretly wishing she had neither. Kathy had every right to feel ordinary.

Ted, on the other hand, worked twenty-four-seven, often leaving to catch a midday flight on Sunday or early Monday, returning home very late Friday or the following Saturday and she hadn't once thought to smell his clothes or check his shaving kit after the first time. She had no need. She knew Ted slept with other women and she didn't care. Any other man would have shown the decency to discard the stained shirt and buy another, not Ted who had simply

11

rolled the tainted collar into the shirt and placed it in the laundry bin. He'd been screwing around for years since he first began travelling and at thirty-eight his once slim, athletic build was giving way to encroaching middle-age despite the blue suits and white starched shirts with French cuffs which were no longer tapered and red ties. Kathy wore cotton dresses or woven skirts with jersey tops and was never invited to the twice-annual corporate parties in July and December. Who would look after the kids, if not her, he had asked in defence once too often? His parents were old, hers were dead and finally Kathy stopped asking.

She drove a rusting four-door sedan while Ted drove a late-model Lexus LS supplied by the company. She arrived home each afternoon at 5:00 with her son and daughter, neither one wanting to sit in the front with mom, while Ted sat in bars enjoying a few drinks and, she imagined, most likely flirting with barmaids or bimbos. The two-story cottage on a hill near the shore was comfortable, with an attic Kathy didn't like and no one ever looked into. The living room was never used, the family room had become Kathy's domain over time and the dining room had never seen romantic candles. The kitchen was a functional workshop for Kathy, a place to cook and serve meals she would usually eat alone before washing the dishes and retiring to her bedroom to arrange her clothes for the coming day and read about someone's fictional life that was better than hers. Not so much Ted's, whose expense account allowed for five-star hotels, health clubs, wining and dining in fine restaurants and theatre tickets for whosoever name he would attach to the receipt.

Melissa Burberry was seventeen and had forgotten those happy times in the kitchen with her mother, baking cookies and gingerbread men. She thought her mother was old, out-dated and a bitch for working at her school. Timothy was sixteen, in the first semester of his first year and laughed at his mother behind her back, telling the other college kids how weird it was to know how one of the staff looked in her underwear, often promising he would one day post photos on the web. He had forgotten the sun-filled days by the seashore, splashing water at his mommy and running from towering waves that weren't as high as her waist, and now the two kids had decided their father was no better. At least he was always gone and when he was home he left them alone. He never spied on them like she did. He never told them to do better at school, to finish their meals or to study. He was like all the other fathers. She was the bitch who never took time to understand, always telling them not to stay out late, not to drive with friends and not to drink. Always preaching like she did to the other kids she knew nothing about. Unfortunately, Melissa had forgotten the good years and didn't realize her mother hadn't bothered her for quite some time, not since midway into her last year of high school when Melissa suddenly hated the world and the woman who brought her into it.

Dinner hadn't been a pleasant family hour for quite sometime. Conversation was difficult, a monologue most evenings, until Kathy decided they could eat in their rooms when Ted wasn't at home. With her meal finished she slumped into her récamier, uncertain whether Melissa would outgrow her attitude. The girl would be leaving for university in six months where following the rules wasn't dependent on mood swings. Wherein laid the problem. Melissa didn't follow rules. And Timothy would follow a year later to become a man, she hoped. Leaving home would be their first challenge in life and they would do so without a key to the front door. Each one would return home as an invited guest and would leave the same way. They would work through the summers and upon graduation she would give them sufficient funds to live comfortably for six months while searching for work, a gift from the dead and forgotten grandparents, and nothing else.

Kathy sipped from her wineglass. Of course neither one believed her threat, which would prove to be a rude awakening for Melissa and a possible revelation for Timothy who she was certain wasn't yet into drugs. She was trained to spot signs of abuse, though she wasn't naïve. Of more concern was Melissa who steadfastly refused any mother-daughter conversation, and Kathy wasn't sure at all. Her daughter was rebellious and perhaps the question wasn't so much if, rather who or how many. She took another sip and curled into herself, tossing away the bookmark to continue reading about the woman she wasn't: the woman in stiletto heels, wearing a short silk dress and sitting at the bar with a stranger who used her name, listened to her and told her she was beautiful. Monday wasn't the loneliest night of the week for Kathy, rather the first with four more to follow and possibly by Friday she would finish the book. Maybe one day she would be the lady at the bar and not plain Jane Kathy Nobody with flat hair, sad eyes and no reason to dream.

Conquered by her day, she drifted into sleep feeling desperate and jealous, the beautiful lady and the stranger bookmarked for her Tuesday night alone. The house was quiet and dark. Outside the autumn sky was clear, brilliant with stars, tall trees swaying noiselessly to the rhythm of a gentle wind and the sea was calm.

Three

Jack Caden quickly developed an aversion to big cities. All his life he'd been surrounded by noise, sightless pedestrians, mindless drivers, and in business he had quickly climbed the ladder to a rung where he cared about no one and no one cared about him. What mattered was the deal, all else was subterfuge and everyone knew it. Yet he never thought to escape the melee because he was young and at the top of his game with fewer and fewer rungs to grab onto. His career was a political balancing act and he was unparalleled on the corporate tightrope, never worrying that one misstep would be his ruin.

Bayville was a big enough town with a small town flavour and being at the ocean rapidly altered the slanted perspective. His transfer to the coast had come as a complete surprise and at first he argued the decision. Now he was glad. The seashore was bringing him a sense of peace and well-being. He discovered life by the ocean was slower, quieter, and friendlier with fewer expectations. He was accepted for whom he was, not for what he was, which was entirely foreign to him. He began where he left off, at the top, never looking down, envisioning that one day he would find the girl of his dreams and live with her by the sea. Until then he would live day by day.

He was urbane, exuding a certain edginess most women found disarming and erudite without being pretentious. He was toned, tanned and knew what he wanted. He was indefinable, intriguing, young and alone. Saying no to him required intense concentration and no one did, except one who had been his downfall, the love of his life who deserted him when he needed her the most. He'd been burned once and his fear of rejection was real, afraid he might make the same mistake. This time he would be certain, though life was too short not to find true happiness, not to share love with someone special. In business he was unstoppable, aggressive and unequalled. In love he'd let himself become susceptible to warm flesh and tender words, though no longer. This time he would search beyond the sparkle in her eyes, feel beyond the heat of her body to find the chill in her heart. Until then he would wait without regret.

He gazed out over the harbour front from his high-rise vantage. Another Friday night scene seeming less peculiar than the first time he witnessed the end-of-week crowds strolling to bars and cafés, not running home to ruts, enjoying cocktails and talking, not rushing through traffic to the next red light. The time was 4:55: Happy Hour for the young, he thought, 5 à 7 for the bons vivants and a perfect time to end a week and possibly meet someone new.

Four

On Eileen Aubergine's twentieth birthday she received the gift of a lifetime. She had recently graduated at the top of her class with a degree in design and her days as a waitress and part-time model were over. She had dreams and aspirations. She wanted to travel, to see the museums of the world. She wanted to order espressos in French and sit at quaint café-terrasses to sketch lovers kissing and promenading hand in hand.

She was a romantic. She loved art and was selected to intern at one of the city's best known galleries. She was ecstatic, determined that one day she would own the most renowned gallery and service clients from around the world. In the meantime she would help organize exhibitions, deal with French tourists, go for coffee, look appealing and no one ever objected to her short skirts and tight sweaters.

Not long into her third month a man she didn't recognize came to the gallery, a connoisseur and respected client invited by the owner to a private after-hours unveiling of a promising unknown artist. He was elegant and charming, completely ignoring her as he examined the oils, sipped expensive cognac and spoke with the artist. He acquired several of the canvases, a fact which would greatly enhance the value of the remaining paintings in the days to come by his name alone, and before leaving he asked that the girl in the corner be the one to visit his home in order to achieve a sense of colour and ambiance prior to the completion of the customized frames.

Eileen arrived precisely at 9:00 after being coached by the owner as to what the client would expect, what she should expect and, above all, not to jeopardize the business. What he didn't tell her was where to look for the buzzer on the towering brick pillars on either side of the wrought iron gates or about the cameras. The gates swung open with an eerie slowness. She had never seen a mansion before, let alone be invited to one. He greeted her at the main entrance as he would a familiar acquaintance and escorted her through the rooms of his home where he was considering hanging the various pieces of artwork. She noted the details of colour, texture and furniture style and when they were done he thanked her for her time, requesting that she personally take charge of the delivery the following Saturday.

The week passed quickly for her and Saturday morning she was ready. When she arrived the gates swung open and she drove to the service entrance. The day was bright and warm, a cool breeze gently disturbing the heated pool water and parasols scattered across the patio. He greeted her by name, ordering his staff to unload the van. He invited her to join him by the pool for coffee and cake where she could explain what she had done and, when each of the paintings was ready for hanging, Randolph Kimberly and Eileen went inside to oversee the staff. When they were done he invited her to stay for lunch. She wanted to decline, remembering her boss' warning her not to jeopardize the lucrative account. Yet, she accepted. They spoke about art, travel, the theatre and business, Eileen explaining matter-of-factly that one day she would own the city's finest gallery and he didn't laugh.

He hadn't laughed in a long time. His wife had died unexpectedly a few years earlier when he had lost interest in business and most other aspects of his life. He asked what

Eileen was doing for dinner. She answered that she was celebrating her birthday alone because she didn't have much time since graduation to meet new friends. She was ordering in pizza or Chinese and had a special bottle of wine. She planned to watch a movie and go to bed early because Sunday was the gallery's busiest day. Then her heart all but stopped, her face blanched and the crystal wine goblet fell from her hand.

He was fifty, and lonely. His wife, whom he continued to love deeply, had been taken from him in her relative youth. The proposal was simple: He wanted Eileen to be his wife as a matter of practicality. He often entertained and constantly felt like a party crasher in his own home. He liked Eileen. He was attracted to her and had considered the reasonable terms of a mutually beneficial agreement over the past week, a prenuptial he had signed in his mind that morning.

Once wed, the couple would travel quarterly to wherever she desired, she would be free to pursue her career, to gain experience which was no substitute for money, spend her weekends onboard his yacht and he would treat her well. She would be free to divorce him at anytime without contest and they would sleep most nights in separate bedrooms. She would enjoy a living allowance for clothes, a car and sundries. She would receive a monthly annuity of ten thousand dollars, indexed annually and sweetened by a signing bonus of fifty thousand and a lump sum payment equal to all annuities anytime she wished to divorce him after her thirty-fifth birthday or upon his untimely death. In return she would learn gracefulness, tact and refinement. She would plan dinners and attend each of his functions, which would help her career. She would be a faithful wife in every way, yet he would understand if she chose to see the early morning sun rising beyond the windows of her private boudoir. He liked her body and her

19

smile.

She didn't know what to say or how to react. He was older than her father and he understood her distress. She would have a full week to decide, unbothered by his phone calls or impromptu visits to the boutique. She agreed, completely flustered, and before she left he gave her a complete tour of the mansion and walked with her to the wharf. A week later she returned. Her sacrifice would be young love, which she had tried on several occasions and didn't rank highly as one of life's priorities. And she didn't know; he might be a good lover. He was wealthy, attractive and had probably bedded hundreds of younger women, women who had never loved him and she could divorce him at anytime. The annuities alone would amount to millions whether he saw her reach thirty-five or not and, more importantly, her career would blossom. He was important, his dinners were social events and she would be the centre attraction.

He greeted her reservedly, walking silently with her to the pool area, waiting. Eileen took a deep breath. They were thirty years apart. In fifteen years she would still be young and beautiful. He'd be sixty-five. How handsome would he be then with tubes in his nose or hobbling on canes and would he care about her being faithful? She sipped her wine.

"Yes, Mr. Kimberly...Randolph. I will marry you, and I agree to your terms."

"Thank you, Eileen. I was hoping you would." He slid an envelope across the patio table. "Inside you'll find a cheque for sixty thousand dollars: the signing bonus and the first month's annuity. I expect you to live here until the wedding which will be in September. Do you agree?"

She gulped. "Yes, I do agree."

"Excellent. Now...stand in front of me and take off your clothes. I want to watch you swim."

She bent forward, placing an open palm over the envelope which she swept coolly into her purse. "No, Randolph. I'm sure you'll understand a short grace period. You'll have to wait until Tuesday when the cheque has cleared. I'll come by in the afternoon to sign the prenuptial we discussed, not before. Not that I don't trust you, I do. The truth is at the moment I can't take a chance that you won't like what you see and change your mind while I'm standing naked, dripping and vulnerable. When your lawyer has gone, and I have a signed copy, you can watch me to your heart's content."

Kimberly chuckled quietly. The girl was smart and beautiful. He agreed, inviting her stay for dinner. Tuesday the document was signed, Eileen was substantially better off and she stepped from her shoes, unbuttoning her cotton shirtdress and pushing her panties to her ankles. She stayed the night, drove to work the next morning in a pristine BMW and not long after the couple married in a private ceremony. Eileen didn't invite her parents to the wedding who, eighteen years later, still hadn't discovered truths about her husband or lover.

Five

Clint Evans' second order of business was to buy a book on etiquette and reacquaint himself with good manners. For so many years he had eaten hunched over, elbow to elbow with society's lowest common denominator, using his fingers or eating his three-a-day of processed or dehydrated and tasteless food with plastic spoons and forks. The knives and napkins were never touched: the knives were useless against the cowhide-texture of meats and slice-resistant breads and daring to use a napkin and not the back of one's hand or sleeve was tantamount to smiling in the shower area. Prison was where he had learned to read deception in the eyes of men, his sole protection against what he could not hear or see behind him.

He spent several evenings alone in his hotel room, eating in front of a mirror with a complete place setting, critiquing his every move and posture, speaking with invisible waiters and paying the bill discreetly with imaginary cash without over-tipping. The last thing he wanted at the moment was a credit card and with each room-service dinner he limited himself to one bottle of French wine which had always been his favourite in his previous life. He was moving on.

He was becoming familiar with the city, reconnoitring high-end and mid-range hotel bars, the airport, popular watering holes and café-terrasses annexed to the hotels. His days began at noon, ending with a late dinner in his room

22

until the first day he felt ready to venture out and over the past six weeks his wardrobe had expanded in accordance with his newfound prosperity. He had more tax-free money in the safety deposit box for working four nights a week than he once earned in three months of sixty-hour weeks. Life was getting good and his plan was improved upon daily. He had a map, divided into zones which would keep him from screwing up, a listing of upcoming conferences slated at various hotels and he was just beginning.

He kept no diary or agenda, adopting the precaution of sending the suits, shirts and ties worn on the weekend to the cleaners. He wasn't going back. That's all he knew, especially for something as easily overlooked as a lipstick smudge or a strand of hair. And every Monday morning, after leaving the cleaners, he ate breakfast alone before a five-minute shoeshine.

He believed his out-of-pocket expenses were reasonable, given the lucrative profit margin: two-hundred dollar dinners and a dollar slipped into the vending machine in the men's room of her hotel if she didn't have one in her purse. The first one he remembered, and whoever was currently the last, not the others. For the most part his workload consisted of businesswomen staying in five-star hotels, women who knew what they were doing for whatever reason. Students were a different breed. They equated an extra glass or two of wine and a handsome man paying for a hotel room instead of a backseat or bathroom stall with sophistication, the distinction of a four-star lost on anyone staying in a crowded and noisy dorm.

Both types were equally profitable. He knew from his past years of business travel that Thursdays and Sundays were best for meeting businesswomen, discovering quite by accident that Fridays and Saturdays were ideal for students and the younger nightclub crowd. His oldest thus far was in her late forties, divorced, supposedly successful, and

23

dragged down with grown kids who didn't know where the front door was. The youngest was twenty, like stepping back in time when conversation and technique didn't matter. Leaving her had been a toss up, common sense taking over and forcing him to leave. A lesson well learned. Business was business. Live and let live, maybe for some, but, above all, do unto others.

He was amazed by his rapid success. He had expected to get by reasonably comfortably week by week, not exceed his wildest dreams. Though sidewalk cafés began closing for the season and he anticipated a modest downturn. Students were never his focus. They were extracurricular, overtime work, fringe benefits and a way to hone his skills. Soon they would move indoors to campus lounges or bistros where he didn't belong, where he'd be spotted as a predator and not a travel-weary businessman looking for companionship or the premature widower lost and alone in a strange town.

He left his hotel after his first week of lessons by the mirror and moved into a one-room bachelor apartment which he paid for by the month. He'd been free for nine weeks and not a night went by that he didn't think of her, always finding time to hate her despite the time-consuming research, preparation and increasing workload required to launch his career. And as much as he hadn't planned to supplement his income with senior college girls, the experience had given him food for more thought. He would put them aside until spring and continue with his core interest group while discovering the best places to hunt Friday and Saturday nights. He hadn't stepped into a nightclub in years and the ineptness would show. He would start with smaller clubs early in the week, not very late and without the expectation of increased earnings before graduating in the shortest time possible to the most popular nightspots. He would require a different approach and dress code, something sophisticated and not at all flashy. He wanted to convey a smooth, easy-going exterior, calm and confident, not his mindset. He wanted to be seen, not remembered.

He was no longer the pathetic man forced to lay prostrate on rain-soaked asphalt so long ago, humbled by the court and dehumanized each of the 1826 subsequent days. He was no longer the fallen angel. His life was turning around.

Six

Ted Burberry arrived home at 1:30 PM Saturday to a clean house. He was ninety minutes late and didn't apologize to the wife. Such was his job. Kathy shelved the book she finished the night before, envious of the beautiful lady who had found romance with the stranger who couldn't live without her by the final chapter. She had found love, the man of her dreams, and Kathy chortled a "yeah, right" to herself, believing life wasn't stranger than fiction. Life was crap. He hadn't called to say he'd be staying over, waiting instead to call her mid-morning to confirm his connecting flight was about to depart. She tried to remember the first time his thoughtless had made her angry, and couldn't. Neither could she remember the last time they went dancing or to dinner or anywhere without the kids.

Timothy hadn't come home from hockey practice and would spend the afternoon at a friend's house for band practice. At first she had wanted to discourage the boy, when he would inevitably come home defeated and bruised, knowing one day he'd be cut from the team. Then she gave up when increasingly her words fell on deaf ears. She wasn't worried for his well-being. She realized no one ever suffered from an occasional head-butt. She knew intuitively the kid would never be a star, on the stage or the ice. He was wasting his time. He was an average student, an underachiever and gangly. He couldn't read music and was better suited to being the team's water boy, though his father took a different approach. Music got the kid out of the house and hockey was all about bonding. Boys needed to bond, not to say he had more confidence in the boy's future than Kathy, he didn't, which was his principle reason for agreeing to the wife's no-return-after-college rule. Ted simply preferred not having the kid around and his sister was no better. Neither one would amount to much: a family ill-conceived.

Melissa put on airs she couldn't afford, acting as though she was attending a private girls' academy and not a regional college. She was constantly at the mall spending money her paternal grandparents insisted she needed to get by; reminding her parents that two-hundred a month was insufficient for a girl her age. Somehow she always found bargains, designer clothes at half price, imported shoes and jewellery which Kathy had trouble believing was costume. Clothes and jewellery her father had never seen.

Ted didn't say a word to Kathy after his distant "hello," dropping his bags and coat and running up the stairs to the en suite bathroom. The wooden seat crashed into the lid of the tank, resounding throughout the house, the muffled sound of his relief following seconds later as the loud splashing noise diminished to a quiet trickle amidst the agitated soufflé. By the time he finished his suitcase lay unopened on the bed and Kathy was in the kitchen. He tossed the week's clothes onto the floor, never certain which article went where, except his suits and ties. Then he joined her. Kathy had set the table for him at noon; she served his meal and continued preparing dinner for the family, waiting for him to say something, anything. She didn't know what; maybe that her hair looked nice because she had styled it differently, or that her jeans and sweater were sexy, or that he noticed the new make-up which gave her skin a fresh and lustrous glow even she could see.

He said nothing, waiting until he finished his meal to

27

chuckle. "The steak was a bit tough, Kath. I suppose I should have eaten in-flight. And, talking about flights, I'll be in Chicago in a couple of weeks. The big guy's called us in. He didn't say why and we have no agenda, so we're all assuming he's about on schedule."

"The announcement," Kathy said, taking his plate.

"That's about right...and you know what I'm thinking."

"Don't get your hopes up. Five others are thinking the same."

"Two have less than four years, one's set to retire, one's useless as teats on a bull and the other's a corporate go-boy."

"He wouldn't be the first CEO to like a go-boy and, really Ted, who isn't a suck at your level. You'd jump as high or higher if not jumping meant losing your job or giving up the promotion."

"I don't jump."

"Everyone jumps for one-fifty a year, plus car, plus travel, plus golf games, plus parties, plus whatever."

Ted took a deep breath. "Kath, I don't jump and you have no idea what I go through to get all those pluses you're so happy to take advantage of."

"Yes, Ted. You're right. I'll remember the next time I take my limo to the garage and before I buy a dress for the Christmas party. And whatever did happen to my golf clubs? Gosh, I must have left them wherever you didn't take me last time."

"Don't be annoying. You hate golf and there's nothing wrong with the car you only drive to and from school."

"Or an eighty-thousand dollar Lexus that stays parked all week at the airport."

He pushed away his chair. "That's my perk, not yours. You're not the one stuck on planes for hours each week, delayed in airports, missing appointments, eating restaurant food and missing his kids."

"Missing what kids? Do you see any kids here? No, you don't. So I guess they miss you as much. And don't get so defensive. You fly First Class, the company pays for your elite lounge memberships, and" she looked at his midriff, "let's not talk about restaurants."

"Hey, you know what? I'm glad I came home. I don't get this much strife from my clients." He paused. "Listen, I've had a bad week. Thanks for asking, and don't bother waking me when they get home."

Increasingly he'd been thinking of not coming home at all, completely fed up, but her dead father had been an excellent lawyer and the marriage contract was one thing Ted wanted to forget. The old man never liked Ted, never trusted him and had threatened legal proceedings if Ted didn't do right by his daughter. Leaving sooner would have destroyed him financially. Her father, despising Ted for what he had done, made certain Ted would forfeit any claim to any future home along with half his income and savings was he ever to leave prior to Timothy's eighteenth year. The house, however, would remain Kathy's irrespective of his timing. The alternative would have been a rape charge and, at the time, Mr. and Mrs. Burberry agreed.

He was between a rock and a hard place, where he had been for years. On the other hand a man could dream, and he did. His promotion was a certainty, the single worrisome caveat was that being away kept him sane and the promotion would keep him at the house most nights with a wife and kids no one at Chicago Corporate knew anything about. He didn't know how he would survive, or whether Eileen Kimberly would let him. On the bright side, with the promotion, he could afford to lose half his pay if doing so meant getting rid of Kathy along with the hangers-on and living a life that made him happy.

"Ted…"

"What?"

"I'm wearing a new outfit and make-up. Thanks for noticing. Always nice to have a man around the house."

He didn't look back. "News flash, Kath. You're wearing jeans and sweatshirt. Call me when supper's ready."

Kathy folded her arms across her chest, letting her thoughts drift, ignoring the fact she might absolutely despise him. Dinner was ready at 6:00. Timothy was the first to leave, Melissa followed and scarcely a word had been spoken. The kids didn't care about promotions and budgets and Ted couldn't feign interest in a garage band created for the sole purpose of disturbing neighbours, a miserable athlete or a girl who thought "daddy" was a synonym for rich and stupid. He hadn't been her daddy in years and he watched his first biggest mistake walk out the door behind the second. Such was life, he mused, and he pushed himself away from the table and went to his office.

Kathy cleared the table, did the dishes and went to her favourite nook off the bedroom with her glass of wine. She pulled a book from her shelf and when her toes touched the stack of papers on the floor by the corner of her récamier she kicked them over, cursing. She was home alone, thinking that what the kids in her scattered reports needed was a good kick. She would finish the reports on Monday. She would cancel her appointments and finish the reports in her office, eat lunch at her desk and drive home to another thankless week alone.

The woman on the book cover was dressed in a black silk peasant blouse and bodice, jodhpurs and riding boots. With one gloved hand grasping the reins, her other was poised to thrash the lowly fellow easily gripping the horse's bridle and smiling at her with a devilish smirk. He was a rogue, a daring highwayman in tight-fitting pants and a billowy blouse fluttering in the gentle breeze. He was tall and tanned, handsome and unafraid. Ted had never been a rogue, never adventurous. At one time he was a collegiate jock, the team captain. Now his idea of danger was arriving late at the airport or bringing home one bottle over the limit and Kathy delved into a century gone by to learn more of the widow and the dashing scoundrel.

Seven

Month Five

Melissa's graduation was five months away and the girl showed no interest whatsoever, having declared emphatically weeks earlier that she would not attend. Nor did she attend her high school prom several weeks after a recognizable change in her character, during which time she retreated from her friends and spent the summer alone at the house. She became increasingly withdrawn, not going to parties and not going out with boys. Ted didn't see the problem; Kathy did and tried talking with her daughter, thinking the worst had happened and how her own life would be so much simpler and happier had she gone to the clinic instead of her mother.

Kathy practiced what she preached to other parents. She never invaded Melissa's privacy, never jimmied the feeble lock to her diary, checked her knapsack or asked the doctor for a private consultation after the fact. She did, however, monitor her daughter's computer activity each week, verifying several parental safeguards and birth control had been part of Melissa's daily programme since Kathy's uncertainty. And Timothy was no less respected or monitored, despite being much less of a concern. He wasn't popular with the girls. He couldn't dance, sing, play sports, be witty or do anything else to charm a young girl. He was a loser who wouldn't listen to his mom or anyone else and a week earlier Ted confiscated and locked the boy's camera phone in the safe, giving him a much more basic model to prevent further misuse.

Ted was furious returning to the house near midnight on the Friday, yanking the wide-eyed kid from his bed and throwing him across the room while enumerating all manner of drastic punishments. He would do without his computer and credit card for three months. He was off the team and the band could do without him. One more word, Ted threatened the boy, and he'd find himself at the police station and without a home sooner than he thought. Adding that the first time he discovered the boy's room locked, he'd kick in the door.

Melissa stayed in her room smiling, laying in bed, noting the event in her diary. Her brother was a pain. None of the junior girls liked him. He was a geek and totally weird. She inserted the key into the lock and laid the book on her night table, waiting patiently for her mother's "goodnight." When the house was quiet, the dim light from the hallway filtering into her room at the base of her door finally darkened, she went to her knapsack to retrieve her other computer and the 750ml bottle of premium vodka. In nine months she would leave for university, able to do whatever she wanted with no doubt she'd earn twice as much as her father in her freshman year. So what did she care about not coming home? She sipped her vodka before undressing and pushing apart the skirts and blouses hanging in her closet. The shopping bag on the wall hook had "Christmas – Stay Out" printed in bold characters and over time she had labelled several similar bags to befit various occasions. When she was dressed she put on the headset, took another sip and entered her password. The time was 11:59. Her mother was so totally lame.

Ted came to bed earlier than Kathy expected, though they hadn't been romantic in months. He said goodnight from his side of the room, muttering something under his breath about the army or trade school and fell asleep. Kathy remained lounging in her nook, engrossed in the final pages. The mounted widow in black had succumbed to the devilish rogue, his sunburnt and chiselled body impossible to resist, his smile beguiling, his gallant manner captivating and alluring. Her sad and desperate days were at an end. The sun had set and she would awaken to a new and wondrous day.

Kathy woke that Saturday morning hugging the book to her chest, her blanket drawn to her shoulders. She lay pensive, remembering the violence and rage of the previous evening. She hadn't intervened partly because Ted was right to defend her and partly because she wanted desperately for her life to change, and something did change. She made a decision. The mounted widow had convinced her. She would no longer be envious of historical romance characters. She would no longer wear clothes that made her invisible, or sensible shoes, and if the kids at school wanted to laugh behind her back, let them.

Ted had already left for the final foursome of the season and she had no idea about the kids. She padded into the bathroom, locked the door and stripped away her flannel pyjamas, curling them into a ball and tossing them into the receptacle by the sink. She wanted to bathe, unable to remember the last time she had, or the last time she had luxuriated in warm scented oils. So she showered instead and sat at the vanity to dry and style her hair, cream her body from head to toe and open her towel in front of the mirror. She certainly wasn't drop-dead gorgeous and would never walk a runway, though neither was she a dog. Her breasts were firm, her stomach only a little rounded, and her ass, she thought, wouldn't take long to look great in a thong with a little hard work. Thong, she thought, for whom? She had thrown them out years earlier along with her garters, bustier and desire. Ted seldom saw her naked over the past several months and, on the rare occasion he did, he showed no interest.

She went to her wardrobe wrapped in a towel and determined. She had never worn the silk blouse and skirt in the ten years since buying them and she would wear pantyhose, she decided, because she had no stay-ups and her underwear was sexless, purely functional. A couple of spoiled kids and a visually impaired husband were not ideal incentives. Now they would just have to get used to it and as she dressed she planned her day. Her meeting with the principal on Monday to discuss banning cell phones in classes and hallways was secondary. Of primary importance would be the pre-class coffee in the teacher's lounge and telling them "yes." For the first time she would join them for a Girls' Night on the town. She wasn't completely satisfied, impatient to see how she would look by day's end. More importantly, she had taken the first step. She had always believed in dressing for the job and was realizing maybe she'd been wrong all along, about a lot of things.

She knocked at Timothy's door. Trying the handle when he didn't answer, the door opened easily to an empty room. She called his name and when he didn't respond she went to the garage where she found him holding the separated neck and body of his splintered guitar and looking disconsolate.

"Next time you think to take a picture of your mother in her slip to show your buddies, you might think twice." She smiled. "I hope he hasn't done the same to your computer. Anyway, by the time I return your card I'm sure you'll have found something you like better than hockey. He's taken your equipment to the mission box. Your skates included." She saw the look. "Don't say it, Timothy. He won't like coming home from his golf game and I won't stop him. Oh, and by the way, give me your house key. For the next three months you'll go out when I say you do. And where's your sister?"

"Who cares?"

"Where is your sister?"

"In her room, I guess."

He threw her the key which she let fall to the floor, staring at him. When he finally thought to correct the rudeness she turned and strode away, forgetting him. She knocked at Melissa's door and no answer came. She knocked again, calling her daughter's name, rolling her eyes and shaking her head as the footfalls came closer.

"Your brother's grounded and you're not to give him your key or have one made for him, which would mean no computer or card, phone or shopping sprees for you. I'll be gone for the day and when I get back I want you here for dinner, which you're going to help me prepare."

Melissa grimaced. "Like...no." She scrutinized her mother from head to toe. "My God, mother, you're not like a teenager anymore. What do you think you're doing?"

"I'm going shopping and doing things I've neglected for a very long time. And...like...yeah, you'd better be here when I get home."

"Mother, you can't be serious. What if someone from school sees you? Your skirt is like way too short and, God, your cammy shows through."

"Thank you, Melissa. For a while I forgot I had breasts. It's nice to finally remember and, maybe if I we bump into each other at the mall we can do lunch...my treat. What do you think? We'll be like sisters."

"Like...no. Duh."

Kathy coughed out a laugh. "Don't forget what I said." And she walked away.

The November day was brisk. The firs hadn't lost their colour and were deep green against the bright blue sky. The first snowfall wouldn't be long in coming, then Christmas, another new year and with it would come a renewed Kathy

Burberry, she promised. The dowdy counsellor had passed on, urged into a long-sought reality by a mounted widow in black. Her day would be interesting, fun, her evening even more so and if he didn't like the transition he could go to hell and take the kids with him.

She had always been her father's special girl, yet not until recently did she realize he'd given his most precious gift to her years before the fatal crash. She whispered a thank you to her dad as she drove from the property and onto the winding country road toward the ocean. The seas were angry, which she thought was amusing because she wasn't. She was excited, invigorated and for the first time in a very long time she was anxious for Monday morning.

Eight

Jack Caden was maintaining his stride and beginning to fit in. He hadn't changed his thinking about big city living, gradually learning to regard people differently. Being at the coast was a large part of his redefined outlook on life and he began spending most weekend days by the ocean. Prior to his transfer he hadn't allowed himself time to relax or adopt a hobby. His previous life was all about money, about being the best and he realized he must make changes. He wasn't athletic, sports were out and he certainly wasn't about to start surfing for two reasons: he would loathe being seen as a novice and he hated being cold.

During the summer the water temperature never rose above sixteen and in November four or five degrees was the norm. However what he had come to enjoy was watching the action and taking pictures from the boardwalk, particularly of girls gliding to shore and later changing from neoprene suits into sweaters and jeans. Apart from a few glaring jocks nobody seemed to mind. In fact the girls would often smile and wave and the hobby occupied his mind most weeknights as he cropped and enhanced the best photographs he would later print and frame.

He enjoyed his time alone. His job allowed him to meet plenty of women and his apartment building catered mostly to professional singles, none of whom ranked highly enough to consider as a long-term girlfriend. He wasn't in a hurry to make another mistake. He had managed to train his mind and body to slow down, take life easy and enjoy. He kept his fingertip on the shutter release, capturing a few dozen shots of the young woman leaning against the rear panel of her van. She was posing for him, being coy and he would have been tempted anywhere else or had she been five years older. She looked about twenty, ready for a good time or free meal, but when she raised her camera with a mischievous curve to her lips he waved at her and left. He didn't need complications in his life, nor did he want to search for another boardwalk.

The shoreline was sandier than most along the coast, a favourite with surfers and he could imagine the hundreds of bikini-clad bodies tanning along its length during the summer, hopefully a divorcée or two or someone as lonely as he. He was anxious for summer, regretting he hadn't arrived in town before early September, and whether he came alone or with a newfound love he didn't care. Eventually he would find the one he was looking for, the one who would define his life and his future.

He liked his temporary apartment well enough, never thinking of the white walls spotted with amateur photographs of girls he couldn't touch or bring home as a home, and he hadn't stood on the balcony for a month. Weekends at the beach were his one escape thus far and he didn't look forward to four months of cabin fever. Walking to his car he scanned the hillside across Ocean View Road, wondering at the homes and the people who lived in them. He wondered whether anyone was watching him through a mounted lens, following his every move or what he would see looking down.

The drive into town would take thirty minutes, nothing compared to the daily hassle of midtown traffic he once knew, so why not? He had no one to indulge but himself and he deserved. He had money for a good down payment and was good at what he did. He had no vices and didn't live beyond his means. The ocean air made him feel alive. He was a different person by the sea. He could leave work behind and be Jack Caden, not merely another face in the crowd.

Nine

Kathy Burberry arrived home at 6:30. Ted had been home since early afternoon wondering what was going on. Timothy spent the day in his room ranting and Melissa came back well before the dinner hour, eager to tell her father how her mother went out dressed as though she had a date or something. Kathy greeted both of them matter-of-factly, not oblivious to Melissa's eyes darting expectantly from one parent to the other, waiting for her mother to remove her new cape and her father to go ballistic. That didn't happen and she wasn't so certain watching Kathy call out to Timothy, ordering him into the kitchen, and when he shuffled in dragging his heels she told him to go to the car and carry all her bags and boxes into her bedroom. Then she turned to Melissa with the same instruction.

"I said now, Melissa. Get going, unless you want to spend three months at home with your brother. And when you're finished you can set the table in the dining room and start dinner. Your father and I need a few moments alone and we don't expect interruptions. Go."

The girl looked at her father who offered no solace. He had his own problems. He was in for a repeat of the previous night, this time with the wife and not the kid. He jerked his head towards the door and Melissa pushed herself from the chair. When she was gone Kathy shrugged her woollen cape from her shoulders, draped it over a chair and pulled away the matching cloche.

"Nice coat…nice everything, and a hat. Nice touch."

"It's a cape, and the hat's a cloche."

"The kid told me you were going on a date."

"I went shopping."

"Yeah, she said that too." He studied the outfit. "Should I be jealous? You're wearing some pretty fancy stuff, Kath. What's up? Are we going through a midlife crisis thing? Did they get to you last night?"

"I don't understand the "we" part and, no, not more than usual."

Timothy marched past, followed by Melissa who couldn't believe what she was seeing. In a single day her mother had metamorphosed into an older sister and more boxes and bags from exclusive boutiques remained in the car.

She said, "I need to see you in the bedroom. Please bring me a glass of chardonnay and a full box of garbage bags."

His brow furrowed. "For what exactly?"

"For the past ten years, Ted." She reached into her handbag, retrieving a brochure. "I told the salesman I'd be at the showroom Monday night. I chose a red one and wrote him a cheque for ten thousand. He didn't want the rust-bucket, go figure. So when you get back next week you can take the thing to a scrap yard."

"An MX-5, a two-seat sports car a month before Christmas! Are you insane? What about your frigging kids?"

"Don't you mean what about your kids? You're the one who wanted them, or you wouldn't have been so stupid. I was satisfied with the first one after you knocked me up, but then you needed a boy…and for what?"

"Hope you have enough in the new purse to pay for it. I'm not."

"I do, and for everything else. I don't need you for

41

everything, Ted. Actually...I'd be hard-pressed to imagine why I need you at all. " She stopped talking when the boy and girl came through. "I'll see you in the bedroom."

Ted came in as the third parade of novelties was put on the bed, issuing the kids from the room and slamming the door. Her side of the closet was empty, clothes piled on the floor and the wife had never looked so good. She was taller by five centimetres, her black slacks were cuffed, the dark tweed jacket was open to show a belted red vest over a ruffled white blouse and the crowning touch was her cropped auburn hair. The blonde ponytail was gone. He looked at the bed, then to her, watching her sip the wine.

"What's going on, Kath. I don't need this right now. I'll have enough on my plate with the promo. I don't need a divorce."

"Why not? At least you'd get the house, or part of it anyway."

"Where's this going?"

"I'm not divorcing you, Ted. I'm leaving myself. Say hello to the new me. The old one won't be back, not ever."

"And how much did the new you cost."

"So far, two month's salary plus the car."

A deep red washed over his face and his mouth dropped open. "So far, what does that mean? You can't be serious about any of this. You spend your life in a frigging cubicle for pity sake. What the hell's going on here?"

"I did spend my life in a cubicle, not anymore, and from now on I'm going out for dinner with the other women at school once or twice a month. Sometimes they do a weekend trip and, when they do, I'm going with them. You'll have to arrange those weeks accordingly. Oh, by the way, if you're interested, I'm wearing a thong. I bought a whole drawer full along with silk teddies, camisoles, silk blouses, short skirts and dresses, the whole nine yards. Remember when you could run nine yards, Ted. And I'm done with one-pieces. This is next year's beachwear and we're vacationing where I can wear them, or I'll go alone." She paused, sipping her wine as she reached into a bag. One bikini was a skimpy Rio with tiny triangles. "This one is for the backyard and Christmas in Miami with your folks." The second was a handful of strings and the third was a slingshot thong. "These are for Myrtle Beach, where I won't have any problem being seen alone."

"Not in front of the kids."

"The French do, and so do the Italians. Or don't you remember your eyeballs falling into the sand. So, yes, I will and the kids be damned. I'm not ashamed of my body anymore and I won't be the only bare ass at the pool. You haven't looked at me for over a year, Ted. Maybe now you will and, if you don't, I know someone else will."

"And what does that mean?"

"It means I'm tired of not being seen. This morning I looked in the mirror and pretty much liked what I saw. The thing is: I'm the only one who knows. People do judge a book by its cover, which is why no one ever looks at me, including you. Imagine no one ever looking. Now they do, believe me, and not just men. I'm not finished Ted, not by a long shot. I joined a club and I'll be putting in fewer hours at school, so the kids will have to start bussing and you're going to start taking taxis to the airport. The Lexus stays here. Hell's going to freeze over before either of those brats gets into my convertible."

"No."

"Yes, and I expect you to pay more attention to me. I don't expect hot romance, that's gone forever. Truth be told, I can't even imagine a reasonable facsimile." Her grin was snide. "Not to worry. I'll use the three minutes doing something else and the next time you refer to me as "the wife" use an adjective, because I will leave," she emphasized, "and not with them."

"You're pushing, Kath."

Kathy sipped her wine, thinking she was about to say too much, a reasonable facsimile was all she ever had after Timothy. He had nothing else to offer.

"Tell the kids I want them to change for dinner, unless they don't want to eat, and you do the same."

"Why?"

"Because I'm not changing. Now go make sure she's not burning the water and tell the other one to bring me another glass of wine. I'll be out after I've hung my clothes and arranged my lingerie. Lingerie, Ted, not underwear, real lingerie."

He inhaled deeply, blowing a long, hard breath. "This isn't good, Kath. Whatever's got you so pissed, you'd better get it under control."

"You're wrong. It is good...for me. And I'm not under your control or anyone else's. I'm in control, of myself, Ted, and thank you for not noticing my hair, something else I'll be doing more often."

Ted should have said he loved her, wanted her, or ask her for an impromptu fashion show. He didn't. Instead he walked from the room, shunning the wife, the very person who could have saved him.

Ten

When Kathy came out an hour later, Melissa and Timothy were seated with their father at the dining room table, scrutinizing the wife and mother they didn't recognize. They had never seen her wear shoes in the house, let alone three-inch stilettos and designer clothes. The kids ate quietly, speaking when spoken to. Ted, on the other hand, didn't know what to say. When dinner was finished the girl cleared the table and went to her room, Timothy was told to wash the dishes and not be seen until morning.

Kathy poured a digestive and went into the living room to scan the stereo for Latin rhythms. Ted stayed in the kitchen where he poured a two-finger deep scotch, grimacing at the empty glass as the amber liquid burned his throat. He was at a complete loss. The next twenty-four hours would be an eternity and he hated the thought of sharing his bed with her. He poured another and went into his office. He couldn't join her, he had nothing to say and any effort to apologize or understand would seem insincere: a stopgap measure until he could get the hell away from them for another workweek.

For whatever reason, her poutiness could not have come at a worse time. He was leaving early Monday for Chicago and his acceptance speech was far from finished. He joined the company fresh from university, working his way up to Regional Sales Manager and finally after   years of hard work and hundreds of weeks away from home he was being rewarded. On January 01st he would take over as Divisional Manager and she had already spent his increase in one day.

He closed the door, reclined and put his feet on his desk. He needed the extra money. With Melissa gone he'd still have Timothy in the house for a year while Melissa lived on campus with money Kathy hadn't wanted to spend on home renovation. He unlocked his drawer and stared at the bottle, another part of his life over which he was losing control. For once Kathy was right. He should have walked away from her the day she told him she was pregnant, but then she was beautiful, risqué and young. The sex was heated with passion and she never said "no" whether at the beach, at school or the drive-in. And she dressed the part, exuding sensuality in short skirts, tank tops and thongs at the ocean. Then came the wedding, Melissa, and Kathy put her degree on hold to become a mother. But she was wrong about him wanting a boy. What he wanted was his life back; the boy was another mistake, one that wouldn't go away

They were young. They should have travelled, seen the world and gone clubbing with friends. Instead they lost their friends and stayed home, still struggling to break even when Kathy returned to college two years after Timothy, the same year he got his first company car, began travelling and began having affairs. Kathy graduated with honours when Melissa was eight, by which time Ted had made a name for himself, learning to equate success with money, money with travel and he began travelling more frequently which didn't diminish when he became manager of the northeast region.

He couldn't remember the number of times he'd cheated on her during the first couple of years he travelled. At the beginning he simply enjoyed the attention and being risqué the way he once was with Kathy, being with something untried and different. Then as the kids grew more demanding, and Kathy proportionately inattentive, he saw less need to be home and four-night weeks became five and five often became six.

He didn't mind that his expense account had as much to do with his amorous success as his charm and good looks. He believed the perk went with the job and he doubted whether he would have married Kathy on his own. She was far from his first. In fact she was the last of many. She had come to his frat house party to end the school year, and she did, big time. She was younger than the other girls and ready. They found a room and that one night led to several dates over the summer until she told him in August, when he was introduced to her father one month before her eighteenth birthday. The civil wedding happened a few short weeks later and he returned to school to finish his degree on a tight leash, working evenings, weekends, and taking money from both families he would have to reimburse. Kathy didn't return. In March she had her baby for the simple reason she hadn't taken precautions and he'd been paying ever since.

Back then one summer seemed like a lifetime and he hadn't so much as taken her to a hotel room. Their time together was spent at the drive-in, the beach or the lake until summer came to be viewed from an entirely different perspective. He peered past his reflection into the blackness beyond the panes of his office window. The promotion wasn't a moment too soon. With half his upgraded salary, company car and expenses he figured he could endure the extra financial burden of divorce for a year or so until both kids were gone, most of their higher education funded by their dead grandparents.

He poured a fourth, locked the bottle in the drawer and took up his micro cassette to finish his speech.
*

Kathy curled onto the sofa wanting to dance, anxious for Monday morning to speak with the ladies and drive home her new car. Timothy watched television in his room and

Melissa lay on her bed waiting for midnight.

Kathy wasn't tired. Her day was exhilarating, a renaissance long overdue. So many men had glanced over their shoulders at her and women smiled approvingly as she passed them by. She hadn't felt sexy in years. She hadn't felt naked in her clothes since her rapid conversion from carefree teenager to increasingly depreciated mother. She had missed out on so much for so little in return. Ted wasn't her first boyfriend, during high school she experimented with several boys until he came along to capture her heart with ardent kisses and sweet words. Now he was distant and cold, never home and, when he was, he never looked at her. She snorted, sipping her drink. She hated the thought of going to bed. He hadn't touched her in such a long time, and what was the point? At one time they would sleep naked; he would pull her on top of him and tug at the strings of her thongs at the beach when he thought no one was watching. Now he slept in his underwear, she wore pyjamas and the last time was so comical they both decided the effort was too great and went to sleep.

He was in his office, working, though his toothpaste never fully masked the pungent smell of liquor on his breath. She didn't have a home, she realized. She was running a boarding house where the kids lived rent free, did nothing, and he dropped by on the weekends to pick up his golf clubs. His promotion would change everything. He would work more from home with a nine-to-five schedule and be gone once or twice a week for meetings with regional managers apart from quarterly meetings at HO.

They would divorce within the year, she decided smiling. She was young enough to start over and she would. Ted would never adapt to an office routine or dinners at home most nights, let alone dealing with the kids twenty-four-seven. The entire notion was implausible. There was more to life than money and he wouldn't take long to figure it out or regret that he hadn't. And who would fill the inevitable void? Or how would he go from ignoring her on the weekends to ignoring her all week, exchanging occasional five-minute phone calls for entire evenings? He wouldn't. Divorce was a certainty. By then Melissa would be at university and, given the choice, Kathy was certain she would stay away permanently. Timothy was another matter. He knew his options. He just didn't believe them, although he would soon enough. His choices were simple: get accepted to a university or get out. Either way he was leaving and not coming back. There would be no home.

If Ted walked out first, she would get the house, which she would sell and buy a luxury condo down by the harbour. In addition, with his promotion, the alimony and child support would be close to seventy-five thousand the first year, enough for tuition and living expenses until the first failed course and her parents' fund would remain hers. If she left first, she'd lose most of the house and along with the alimony the education fund would be used per her parents' request. Either way, she'd be free of each one in turn and well on the road to a full recovery.

She strolled into the kitchen, filled her snifter, took off her shoes and padded quietly past Melissa's door. She looked over to the office without expression before climbing the stairs. In her bedroom she pulled a new camisole and tap pants from a hanger, walked into the bathroom, closed the door and watched herself undress wondering how a another man in her life would see her. Monday would be her first day at the gym, in her new car, in her new mindset and Monday night she would sleep alone between fresh satin sheets.
*

In town Clint Evans' nightclub skills had come round quickly and the decision to spend his weekends clubbing was proving worthwhile. His income doubled. He continued working Thursdays and Sundays, aligning his expenditures with the evenings' anticipated revenues and increasingly curious he hadn't yet been mentioned on the nightly news. He suspected the older women travelling on business didn't care. Married, single or divorced, he gave each one a memorable experience, which is what mattered most. He came through for each one, watching them fall asleep like babies without a care in the world. Many suggested getting together once or twice more, or exchanging numbers for future encounters and he assumed they later accepted the loss of bank cards and cash as the cost of doing business. Embarrassment wasn't an issue. They all willingly climbed onboard and neither husbands nor boyfriends would ever discover the indiscretion or loss, which was his impetus for deciding to no longer limit his earnings to cash-on-hand and a few hundred on a card which might never be noticed. The younger ones, the ones in the clubs, were easy, anxious to be wined, dined and romanced, anxious for someone else to pay and he did. He had no doubt each conquest was afraid to tell her friends or parents and Clint became much less considerate of them, leaving them with empty purses, miserable hangovers, considerable credit card debts and lessons learned.

By Monday most weeks he was exhausted. He never thought for a moment he would have so many beautiful women in such a short time. He discovered his true calling too late in life to save him from prison and, certainly, from her. If he ever once imagined in his wildest dreams, he would never have married her and even in his most vivid and haunting memories of her he couldn't remember why he did. And she hadn't come cheap.

She had a brain which she used as Chief Accountant at the electronics firm where they both worked, modulating every facet of her lithe and exotic body to her advantage at quitting time, happy hours or parties. At work she was all business from her sensible pumps to her straight cropped hair. She wore pant suits and jackets with silk blouses by day, after-hours décolleté or sheer blouses with embroidered bras and daringly short skirts or dresses hugging every curve. Outside the office she was a coquettish tease: tall, lean and sexy, desired by all who saw her. Lying or walking she moved in a sultry and provocative way most woman could not and reading any man's thoughts was an easy matter, for her and for him, and women were often no less candid or exempt. He'd seen many attractive women fall prey to her seductive charms. The first few times, he remembered, were intriguing. Then she stopped inviting him to the party, never making excuses, never apologizing.

She was a year older. The two met at work, married a year later and spent the next seven years together until the fateful night the police waited outside the loading dock when she was a week away from her thirty-first birthday. He never stopped thinking of her, images of her standing on the loading dock, protected from the rain, her slender form illuminated by headlights and the clear blue of police strobes. He knew right away and she wasn't the least bit remorseful, her expression mocking him. He did his best to stare into her eyes, to defy her; desperate to show his hate as the cops dragged him to his feet and hurried him from the pouring rain to the cruiser.

He'd risen to the top of his field, the most successful Technical Account Manager in the company, headed for a top management position and she set him up. That was the deal. She would testify against him in court and lose her job, when the entire scheme was her invention. For six years she invoiced clients for high-priced electronics never delivered, products fenced without names or handshakes to be sold in stores or on street corners he knew nothing about, products replaced with cheap, imported copies until one client thought to hire an independent techie and the police waited until he left town on business to arrest and interrogate Kim Moon. Strangely, the evenings they spoke together he didn't notice the slightest telltale inflection in her voice, which was the most unsettling, not that after his arrest and conviction she immediately filed for divorce, sold the house and left the city.

Yet she went to prison with him, concealed in his darkest thoughts. The girl at the bar was twenty-four, tops, and spent the better of an hour looking at him. Whatever she called herself, she'd be something generic by midnight and by 1:00 AM she would leave with him. By 1:30 she'd be in bed, by 2:00 she'd be in love and by 3:00 she'd be begging for more. Then she would sleep, purring softly, and by 9:00 AM she'd awake with a monstrous headache and find herself a few thousand poorer, which would likely keep her away from clubs and him for the next few months. She was cute, she'd be fun and he'd forget her in the morning. He had to. He hadn't forgotten that once he was a nice guy.

*

Melissa's cell phone hummed her awake at eleven and she waited until eleven-thirty for her mother's nightly expression of good wishes which didn't come. Like why did she even pretend to care and what was with the wardrobe thing? She was freaking out with old age and clothes wouldn't make her any younger or beautiful. She was a mother, a housewife and guys didn't want that. They wanted young, tight and sexy. They wanted smooth, pink skin, not tonnes of make-up and someone else's leftovers. Her mother could pretend all she wanted. She hadn't been laid in a year because her husband was a cheat and a loser, getting laid on the side because he was afraid to ask his wife for something different and they were growing farther apart each week. Booze wasn't the only thing her father kept under lock and key. He was so banal and now he was climbing the stairs away from his beloved Eileen locked up so lovely and naked in his drawer. He deserved getting caught and she wondered what else he did when he travelled, whether he had ever visited the Midnight Rhapsody site for a sneak preview. How sick would that be?

The band of light at the bottom of her door went dark. She wriggled from her bed and pressed an attentive ear to the wall separating her from Timothy's room, hearing not the slightest sound and went to her knapsack. The house was quiet. Midnight was her favourite time of day: the quiet, the darkness beyond her room and the freedom. She poured a shot, sipped from her glass, stripped off her clothes and went to the closet. Christmas was a month away and she would wait a while longer to wear the red and white velour bra, matching skirt, panties and elf hat. Tonight was naughty schoolgirl night: white thigh-high leggings, ultra short pleated skirt, ruffled panties, push-up bra and a sleeveless shirt knotted under her breasts. The final touches were the bright red lipstick, horn-rimmed eye glasses, dark wig and contacts.

At 11:59 she sipped her vodka once more, typed in her password and leaned forward to greet her first visitor. In two years, minus family vacations and holidays, she had logged fourteen thousand hits with fifty regulars who paid to see more than a short skirt or bra strap. She had amassed a small fortune from a career she began quite by accident, surfing the web for bathing suits and innocently linking onto sites where girls posed with less or nothing and charged a fee for anyone to admire them. Then she remembered the three of them in the dark, their cruel jeers and Midnight Rhapsody was born.

She first needed another computer with a web stick to bypass her mother's surveillance and began studying one site, then many, imitating the girls in the videos until she was ready. Her first night was clumsy. She had no liquor and nothing to wear but pyjamas, her mother's lipstick and sunglasses, posting headshots and images of her bare shoulders and making a few hundred dollars in the first month. She slowly became more popular and with success came more money and the urge to be more daring. At the end of six months she had different costumes, she had read books on acting and her skill had improved. She wasn't going on eighteen; she was twenty-something to anyone watching her and by the end of the year she was going live every night between midnight and 2:00 AM.

Midnight Rhapsody was an instant success in ten-minute increments for fifteen dollars or twenty minutes for twenty-five, doubling her fee by mid-summer. In the last year alone she pulled in thirty-five K for her videos and eighty-five K for more provocative live performances. She also began drinking, though never enough to ruin a good thing. She found a source not far from her school: an older man down on his luck whose payment was his own weekly bottle and throughout the summer months she kept him on her leash by never telling him to stand from his spot on the sidewalk. She enjoyed being seen and desired, no matter by whom or where.

Requests came in each night for her to do increasingly more and in the New Year she would with higher fees and more eroticism. It's what she wanted to do. When she went to bed each night she wasn't tired, she was turned-on, excited and anxious for another midnight. The thought of attending university was ludicrous to her. Brain surgeons didn't make the money she could earn in a year working full-time, but she would go and her parents would pay, whatever their reaction to her decision to enrol in Arts and study acting. And she had other plans, thanks to her first love and his two friends.

From Inside Her Bedroom

She didn't have a boyfriend, though every guy at college did try to hit on her at one time or another, either jocks or wannabe jocks and she knew all too well about jocks who would brag about doing the number one stuck up bitch in the school and that wouldn't happen again. University would be different. She would have relationships, albeit not at school. She wouldn't be a nun for four years. Sex excited her beyond all else and being the prettiest girl and Virgin Princess at school was difficult. Definitely she would have relationships, without love, and she would be the one in control. Her parents hadn't loved each other in years, nor would they ever again. She could see the mutual dislike in their eyes. Love was archaic, a desperate synonym for release, so was virginity which she guarded until her final year of high school when she willingly gave herself for love, not the tainted memory of his laughter and deception. Release is what counted, urgent release, the physical, not the ethereal romance of novels and she would continue to do exactly that: offer release.

She would sublet her dorm room, attend class and remain aloof. She would rent a condo for one persona and a full-time studio for the other. Midnight Rhapsody was here to stay and Melissa was along for the ride. She would hire a videographer or become her own, and no one would know. One thing was certain: she would never return to Bayville.

Eleven

Jack Caden woke Sunday morning feeling good; better than the weather until he drew back the curtains. The sky was dark, smudged with unstoppable black-grey clouds rampaging toward the coast without the slightest shadow or glimmer of light breaking through. Battleships in the distance appeared passive at dock, unmoved in the violent waters of the bay, the black city streets below glistening and the colours of once vibrant storefronts were muted and sombre.

He hadn't watched television in years, not since the nightly news became repetitive, the anchors lacklustre and entertainment pedestrian. His stereo was his all-important link to the world and the forecast was bleak. Welcome to the coast, he thought. He wouldn't see the beach or smiling girls anytime soon. The depression was slow-moving and would take through Tuesday evening to move into the Atlantic. The time was 11:40 AM and he wasn't hungry. So he poured a glass of wine and lay in bed waiting to fall asleep.

*

Ted Burberry woke early out of habit, ignoring Kathy out of habit who was murmuring softly in deep sleep. He saw the weather and cursed. He hated flying in bad weather and instinctively knew the system wasn't abating anytime soon. He remembered the last time he damn near died and she hadn't given a moment's thought to his harrowing experiences. The week was a trip from hell, as though his family life wasn't bad enough. He was covering for the southeast manager who was on vacation and unreachable. The problem was a simple misunderstanding at the Tampa docks which no one wanted to entrust to a novice sales rep and Ted the Reliable volunteered to re-establish goodwill.

He reserved First Class seating to Tampa, though once at the airport the flight was cancelled and passengers rerouted to Orlando on a delayed flight from hell which he should have recognized as a precursor to the week and, subsequently, always wondered whether the pilot soiled himself. The return flight was no better and the interim events would have broken a lesser man: He missed his lane exiting the airport, driving something resembling a hearse and he drove until he thought Christ might come back to greet him personally before he found the hotel whose restaurant was closed and he was on the road once again searching for food.

The next morning he decided to invite an old acquaintance to breakfast who, he was informed by a distressed receptionist, had died in his sleep earlier the same morning. En route to Tampa the port authority called, delaying the meeting by a day, to which he congenially agreed, pressing end and spitting out a string of invectives. Moments later a car burst into flames a few hundred metres in front of him on I-75, creating havoc as the driver cut three lanes and skidded to a panic-stop amidst a cloud of dust and flying pebbles on the soft shoulder, managing to exit and run like hell before his vehicle exploded. Checking in at the hotel twenty kilometres north of Tampa he had the day to himself and planned to have lunch and spend the afternoon relaxing at the pool, letting the cool water and hot sun revitalize him, abruptly changing his mind when he saw the two-metre black moccasin curled under the driver's door of his hearse. The thing was another portent, Ted backing away as slowly as his legs would allow, transfixed for an eternity until the serpent slithered away and disappeared into the pool. He checked out without a moment's thought, changed hotels and saw the client early the next day, which was dark and ominous, before driving directly to the airport and flying home in coach.

Moments after achieving altitude he knew what was coming when the pilot instructed all crew members to take their seats. Ted's aisle seat was at the bulkhead, facing the flight attendant up close and personal and the young girl seated at the window began whimpering and wiping away inaudible tears. The girl between them was indifferent, worried about her own longevity. He tried distancing himself, wanting nothing to do with either dilemma, but the attendant's voice was inescapable. He was strapped in. The look was at once humorous and unforgiving until Ted took the first girl's wet hand, feeling his being crushed to a pulp and fleeting moments later the girl between them nudged him for a bag. She no sooner pressed the stitched rim to her mouth before throwing up into the bag and over Ted's extended arm as he did his best to avoid touching her bare midriff. When she finished she thanked him and quite literally left him holding the bag until the landing which would make any frequent flyer believe a novice co-pilot was at the controls. The girls gasped, Ted reclaimed ownership of his hand and exited the plane and airport into thirty-centimetres of snow. The short distance to the house took over two hours and, when he arrived after an eighteen-hour day of difficult negotiations, a delayed flight and nervous kids, Kathy was asleep and he closed his office door. She seldom waited up and Monday's trip would be no different.

The final draft of his acceptance speech was ready. He wouldn't be effusive. He would thank everyone from the CEO and outgoing Divisional Manager to his team for their confidence, guidance and support, acknowledging that any one of the five other candidates was equally qualified. He was honoured as much as he was surprised and he would not let them down.

*

Kathy stayed in bed, planning her day. The windows were coated with raindrops and translucent condensation; the tall firs in the distance were a colourless backdrop swaying reluctantly amidst the tempest of swirling and howling winds: a perfect day to stay at home with loved ones, play games and drink hot cocoa.

She sighed deeply. First she would sort the garbage bags by what she would and would not give to the mission. She would prepare her breakfast, shower, change into another new pantsuit and go to the mall for her satin sheets. She would treat herself to lunch, have a manicure and see a movie. With her afternoon gym classes, Melissa would have to begin helping more with dinner and Kathy couldn't think of a better time to start. Whatever came next would come. The mood in the house was already morose because of her son's lack of esteem and need for peer acceptance, of which she would deprive him for three months for having caught her in an ordinary polyester slip of all things. Why couldn't he have waited until the summer to photograph her at the ocean wearing her Rio? At least then he might have said "hey, that's my mom," proud of her, or waited until she might have worn one of her newly acquired silk camisoles. Instead he chose to humiliate her and the other kids thought of her as an old lady in a housedress, which was one reason she was anxious for Monday, she had to admit, even more so for Tuesday morning in her bright red MX-5 convertible.

Her first bubble bath in so long could wait until Monday, when she would be alone, locked in her en suite bathroom. She would have her car, she would know when the ladies planned to go out and she would slip between satin sheets

59

wearing a beautiful silk teddy, or nothing at all. The sheets would be hers to luxuriate between, a weeknight pleasure. Weekends were better suited to percale, sensible underwear and tearless regret.

*

The girl didn't blink an eye when Clint Evans pulled her dress slowly over her head and pushed down her panties. Then she was on him like flies on sticky paper, insatiable until liquor and sleep took her over.

He didn't sleep. He never did. He could sleep all day and, truth be told, he preferred looking at them, particularly the younger ones. She was twenty-six, old enough to know better and in a few hours she would hate him like all the others, though he did suspect some would forgive him, desiring his prowess once more no matter the cost. She was petite, proportionate, good-looking and physical. She was also tempting, but waking her would be dangerous. She would want more of him right away, then breakfast, lunch and his phone number.

He had no problem with the "more" part. The problem was the female psyche and the phone number. Young, single women rarely had sex for fun. For them, whether tender or heated, sex was an audition in the hopes of being recruited by Mr. Right. Older women possessed a more carnal attitude, especially divorcées. They merely wanted to get laid, hopefully by an upgrade and didn't care what his name might be. Businesswomen believed they wanted diversion and diversity, when what they truly wanted was possession of or domination over a phallus. Cheaters simply wanted attention, a divorce or the chance to relive the ever-important audition.

He did sleep with a few he might have stayed with under non-work related circumstances, but he came to understand the supply was endless, separated by quadrants on his map and days of the week. He pulled at the covers, gazing at the details of her nude body one last time. One day she would find her Mr. Right if she was fortunate enough to keep her looks after sliding off barstools and into bed with so many different men, someone who would never know she'd slept with an ex-con or countless others who preferred paying her bar tab to being with a hooker.

He chortled quietly. He was, in fact, the hooker. He took three hundred and a titanium card from her purse, not needing her address, phone number or driver's information which would likely have given him her PIN number. He'd found the actual number in her bankbook along with her balance, amazed how women could generally be counted upon to carry personal codes and SS cards in their purses. He looked at the crumpled designer dress and panties on the floor. In a few hours she would leave the hotel looking like a bedraggled tramp, judged by any and all who would see her. Abandoned bars in the early hours were lonely, dirty, desolate places and the reluctant patrons were no better.

He took a final look, not sure who had done whom, closing the door behind him and pulling down the brim of his hat as he walked to the elevator. Coming to the lobby doors he slowed his pace to a stop, belting his coat, thinking of the girl in her mini dress and bomber jacket, her legs bare, trying to brace herself against the foul weather. His day would finish within the hour, as hers would begin. If she was lucky her insurance would compensate her, if not she'd be in debt for a year. He was pleased, despite being thoroughly exhausted and wanted nothing more than his bed. Sunday nights and Thursdays were the worst, often twelve hours or longer and being in top shape for the more articulate and savvy business type, young or old, was primordial.

Twelve

Monday's weather forecast was predictable: the day would be a bitch and began with the one laying beside him. She hadn't come home Sunday until dinnertime with more bags and attitude, telling Melissa in the flattest voice he could imagine to start cooking dinner or find another place to live, reaffirming that the girl and her brother would be bussing to school in the morning and Ted would be going to the airport by taxi. From then on she would need the larger Lexus for groceries during the week, shopping for the family, taking the kids to the doctor, the dentist or whatever other weekly chore he took for granted. Or, she suggested in the same flat tone, they could begin doing groceries together on the weekends or Friday nights and everyone could share in the housework as well. Ted was livid. Melissa hoped he would say something to put her mother in her place, which he didn't, and Timothy just wanted dinner in his room.

After dinner they went separate ways like strangers sitting at different tables in a restaurant and within a few hours Melissa understood "goodnight" and "sleep tight" were endearments of the past and somehow she hated her mother all the more; whereas Kathy thought the bedbugs could bite all they wanted. Ted spent an hour in his office preparing his papers and came to the bedroom to lay out his clothes for his next trip.

Kathy was in her nook reading, sipping her wine and ignoring him, engrossed in the story of a woman who, after so few days of turbulent passion, had waited twenty-five years for her one true love to return, never knowing whether he had survived the tragedies of an endless war.

Twenty-five years, she mused sipping her wine, not a frigging chance. No man was worth a lifetime alone. Their bodies sooner or later drooped, hair fell out, youthful bravado diminished to the rudest form of nonchalance and once shared passion would inevitably become spontaneous moments alone for a still young and beautiful woman after she put out the lights. The author had to be kidding. At the end of each week she wouldn't wait twenty-five minutes for Ted, she thought, studying him peripherally. When had he begun tucking his undershirts into his briefs? He looked ridiculous and what ever became of his once tight ass. She wanted more. In a few weeks her stomach would be flat, her breasts firmer and there would be no question as to where her ass was. It would be on the mind of every man she passed.

By the time she slid under the covers Ted was asleep and she faced away. When she awoke alone, she hurried to the garage. He hadn't taken the Lexus and Melissa was behind her.

"We can take his car. He won't know and, besides, you have to get to school as much as we do."

"The cars stay here, both of them. I'm taking a taxi and you're taking the local bus with your brother, so get used to it."

"I won't go. It's pouring."

"You are going, unless you want everyone to know you're sitting in your mother's office this afternoon for counselling."

"I'll run away."

"Don't bother. Wait a few weeks until you're eighteen and walk away...with the clothes on your back and none of your grandparents' money, which you won't need if you're not going to university. And don't think you'll see anyone running after you. This house isn't yours, it's mine. So are your credit card, phone, laptop, bed and clothes. You're a boarder, and an expensive one. So watch your mouth and get dressed."

"You're like a real bitch. All the girls on campus school think you're a…"

"I know who thinks what. Now apologize to me or I'll cancel your card before you spend another dime."

Mother and daughter faced off.

"Like, I don't need your money. I've got enough saved."

"Yeah, right, enough for four years at university. Dream on."

"I do. And, anyway, I've decided to study acting."

Kathy was openly taken aback. "Don't be stupid. You'll either drop out or be kicked out. Actors do as they're told, you don't. You're incapable of taking direction. Now apologize." Melissa sniggered, swung around and stomped away. "Oh, Melissa, darling, one more thing before the bus comes. You will repay any amount charged to your card until I call the bank this morning. You're cut off. Also, say one more word and you'll be going to school in whatever the mission gives you."

Melissa's reaction was the one Kathy expected: none. Before the taxi arrived the kids went to meet the local yellow and brown bus and Melissa couldn't have slammed the door any harder. Her rain outfit was meant for show, never intended to be utilitarian and was undergoing its first real test. Kathy stood at the window watching them, reading her daughter's mind as Melissa stood immobile and seething, rivulets of rain funnelling from her stylish nor'easter to her shoulders, cascading down her front, her mid-calf boots splashed with mud. If only she had said "mom, I'm sorry. I'm the real bitch," Kathy might have relented and driven the Lexus. But the last word wasn't always verbal.

Timothy knew better, keeping his mouth shut in the hopes of a reprieve from the parental judicial system, though he did insist meekly that rain ponchos were for geeks. His jeans were half soaked and Kathy couldn't imagine how his sneakers and socks must feel. His nylon shell was zippered to his neck and the hood of his sweatshirt had moulded to his empty head like papier-mâché. Kathy chuckled despite herself. What mother wanted to admit her son was the village idiot?

The wind had diminished somewhat, though the rain continued pouring down and the landscaped ditches lining the sloping driveway were shallow brooks of agitated water. She arrived at school at 8:15 and went directly to the teacher's lounge. Her rainwear was the cause of instant chatter: knee-high rubber boots, a full-length rubberized trench coat and matching wide-brimmed fedora, but not until she removed the rainwear did the real excitement begin. Her hair was so different, her shoes were high-heeled pumps, her A-line skirt came to a full hand width above her knees and the embroidered detail of her camisole showed between the lapels of her linen blazer. What they couldn't see were the garters attached to her thong and sheer nylons. She felt sexy and feminine, in control and for the first time in ages she felt naked under her clothes. Who was she, they wanted to know and what had she done with Kathy?

That Kathy would never be back, she answered, deciding not to tell them about the car. The updated version had arrived and future updates would be frequent. They couldn't believe the transformation, delighted when hearing she would join them for a night out. Darlene and Sheila never believed she would. Michelle was the one who persisted. She saw something in Kathy the other two did not. She saw herself and empathized.

Kathy's day began precisely at 9:00 in increments of

one hour unless some unfortunate soul preferred hearing his or her name broadcast from the dean's office reminding said student that he or she should report to Ms. Burberry as soon as possible and by noon news of old lady Burberry was all over the campus. In the cafeteria Melissa was disgusted and dumbfounded that her mother would come by her table to humiliate her and Timothy said "no way" when some of the seniors asked him to try again.

The boys who went to her office were awestruck as she sat in front of them with her legs crossed, immediately disconnected and fantasizing about what they couldn't see. To the girls she was no longer an old woman who, like, didn't know anything at all. She was "whatever" and suddenly the interviews became friendly exchanges, not invasive probing and none of them could understand Melissa's abusive attitude. Her mother was way cool, not like theirs, and when each one asked Ms. Burberry whether she would attend the graduation dance in April the answer was a categorical "yes." When they asked what she would wear she answered "nothing quite as drab as this."

Her day ended at 4:00 and Timothy answered when she called home to ask whether they had done their homework. Melissa was appalled, refusing to speak with her mother who then told her son to activate the hands-free. Melissa would cook dinner for her brother and her homework would be done by the time Kathy got home from the dealer, unless she wanted a complete sweep of her room and loss of privileges which would include permanent cancellation of her credit card and phone. Kathy would dine out before her 8:00 PM dealer appointment and be home by 9:00.

Her single regret was the torrential rain. She had wanted to wear a thick sweater and short skirt for her first run in the MX-5, settling instead for admiring glances from the men in the restaurant and the car salesman. Suddenly summer was too far away. She wanted the ocean, her bikinis and beach towel. She wanted to tan and be seen tanning in Miami, at Myrtle Beach or the Caribbean in the spring, alone. Melissa would turn eighteen in March, though she wouldn't be staying home by herself anytime soon. Kathy didn't trust her. In her finest dreams Melissa and Timothy would spend a month doing chores for Ted's aging parents in Miami. The reality was that the Myrtle Beach vacation had been planned and paid for in advance and warmer waters would have to wait.

The MX-5 fit her like a kid glove and the bright lights in the garage instantly reignited the showroom lustre; Ted had wisely chosen not to argue when instructed to move the rust-bucket to the side of the house the previous day. The house was dark with loud music coming from Timothy's room and nothing from Melissa's. The kitchen light was the first she flicked on. The dishes were done and stacked with a note taped to a glass, advising anyone who cared that Timothy was the one responsible. She made a mental note to check each plate and utensils before storing them and went to his door to say goodnight and thank him. Anything else he might have expected didn't happen, but when she began closing the door....

"Mom..."

"Yes, Timothy?"

"I don't know." He paused. "Some of the guys who saw you at school, they said you were, you know, pretty hot stuff. And the girls, they were like asking me if you were really my mother or whether I was adopted or something."

"You weren't adopted. Goodnight."

"Mom."

"Yes."

"I'm sorry. You know, for the picture thing."

"Thank you, Timothy, however your apology comes a little too late. The damage is done. Imagine if I showed all the girls who come to see me a photograph of you in your briefs. Family stays in the home, Timothy, like Vegas, and you're in your room for the duration. But I do thank you for the reviews and the dishes. Goodnight."

She closed the door gently, stopping to listen at Melissa's door before going to the kitchen to pour a glass of wine. In her bedroom she undressed piece by piece, hanging her jacket and skirt, pulling away her camisole and standing in front of the mirror to examine her body. When was the last time she saw herself standing in garters and real nylons? She couldn't remember, nor had she started aching, though she did feel the occasional twitch in her abs. The pain would come and the results would follow. The hour-long workout was her first in a long time and her personal trainer promised the sessions would become increasingly arduous and effective. By spring she'd be runway material, he said, possibly exaggerating, which didn't prevent her from hanging on every word. She giggled, sipping her wine, and began stripping for herself in front of the mirror in her closet. She kicked away one shoe, then the other, undoing the clasps at one thigh and peeling down the silky nylon. Then the other leg, raising her foot to the bench and stretching from the top of her leg to her toes. Her panties were last and she bent from her waist to the floor, watching, studying her body.

She couldn't remember when she had last seen another woman in the nude. At one time, before Timothy, she and Ted would watch blue movies or rent adult videos, stopping abruptly and then he began travelling, sucking up to his boss and screwing other women. She stood, studying the confident and apparently hot woman in the mirror. She had been as discreetly shocked by the other women at the club wearing jeans and sloppy sweatpants as they were to see another member sitting on a bench undoing her clasps and peeling away nylons. Neither did Kathy expect to see women as uncovered. She didn't know. She hadn't kept up with current trends. Why would she? She had no reason, deciding she would from then on and needed no one to tell her that she would look all the sexier and appealing on the beach in her diminutive bikinis.

She began her bath, throwing in scented pearls and wrapping herself in a short silk kimono before changing the bed. The satin sheets and pillow cases felt smooth, sensuous and cool to the touch. She laid out a satin chemise to sleep in and took her wine into the bathroom. The water was steaming, her body instantly glistening with oil and she inhaled a deep breath, appraising her body and thinking of summer, the beach and how she would be seen by others. She didn't have a single blemish or imperfection a few months at the gym wouldn't erase. More importantly, with the kids gone she would have the summer to lounge privately on the patio in her slingshot. The ladies were going out Thursday night. They would meet downtown at 7:00 for dinner and drinks; she would be home by 10:00 and wouldn't see Ted until Saturday. In fact, knowing Ted would be at the house more often following the promotion bothered her. She had adapted to being a weekday widow and increasingly believed Ted's new job would hammer the final nail into their marital coffin. They shared nothing in common except a son who would never amount to much and a self-absorbed daughter.

She was excited about the next morning, driving her MX-5 into the schoolyard, wearing another eye-appealing outfit and letting the students imagine whatever they wanted. She was excited about dinner with the ladies and felt strangely sad she had waited so long to join them. Perhaps she was wrong to punish Timothy. She possibly should have rewarded him for yanking her so abruptly from her domestic doldrums. And maybe she would. Yet, as quickly as she had thrown herself into the whirlwind, she realized one conspicuous element was missing: she had no one close to share her renaissance with. Her mother was dead, her neighbours were friendly at a distance, she didn't have a sister and Ted wasn't interested. He certainly wouldn't call, not after the fiasco about the taxi and the bus. Anyway, he'd be out drinking with the boys in strip bars, each one assuring the other he was a shoo-in or looking to get laid.

She eased herself deeper into the water, her face aglow behind a clear mask of minute beads, relishing the sensation of heat swirling in and around the contours of her body. She didn't feel thirty-five, she had no visible signs of motherhood and her skin was smooth. Slowly she stood, looking into the full-length mirror, palming away the residual thick film of oil. She could easily pass for thirty. She towelled herself dry, padded into the bedroom and slipped into her chemise before going downstairs to secure the house. The lights of both lower bedrooms were turned out and all was quiet. She poured a nightcap and returned to her room.

The French woman in her story died after waiting twenty-five years to live happily only a few years longer. So tragic. She and Ted had wasted most of their eighteen years together waiting, watching Melissa and Timothy grow from babies into loving children into disparaging, unappreciative hateful young adults. And the man in the sad story would live out his remaining years alone, contemplating his errors, regretting life the way Kathy was regretting hers, living vicariously through the pages of novels, seeking comfort in the misfortune of others or adventure and intrigue in the imaginations of period writers.

She closed the book, finished her tequila and climbed into bed. The sheets were heavenly, arousing against her skin, something to share with a torrid lover, though content in the meantime to lie between them alone. She closed her light and pulled the sheet to her shoulders, the elegant texture making the quilted comforter outdated and unfashionable. Tuesday after school and gym class she would return to the store and buy a duvet. She lay staring into the darkness: so many changes in such a brief time, her changes, no one else's. Ted would never change and she wondered when and where she would stop as she let herself drift contentedly to sleep.

Thirteen

Tuesday Kathy awoke into another world where the sky was threatening and loud. The air was heavy with a cold dampness that would penetrate anyone ill-dressed and chill them to the bones in seconds. The rain would end later in the day, or not, made all the more miserable by the lateness of the season. Snow was overdue, December was a week away and she hadn't been as thrilled about going to work in ages, partly because of her car, partly because of her Italian ankle-strap shoes, kilt skirt and Shetland V-neck sweater accented with an obsidian pendant. Her lingerie was a matching set with garters and nylons which she decided would be easier to put on after gym class and more feminine than stretching and contorting into pantyhose.

She stood watching for the local bus to arrive. Melissa hadn't spoken with her since the previous morning and she was snubbing her brother at the stop. She was a senior, one of the prettier girls at school and she was in for a major letdown. University wouldn't be a small regional college. She'd be mixed in with hundreds of good-looking girls from bigger cities who would treat her like a junior. Kathy shook her head, wondering how fate had given her two such extremes: Melissa was a beauty, albeit full of herself and reasonably intelligent. Her brother was the beast: awkward and not at all smart. He was standing with his both hands shoved into jean pockets, his head encased in a sopping hood, a second pair of sneakers would be hanging in the garage that evening and Kathy imagined she could hear his bones and teeth rattling in concert with his spasms. When the bus did arrive Kathy checked herself in the mirror, closed up the house and left, chuckling softly when passing what looked like a yellow and brown prisoner transport a few minutes later.

*

Melissa was furious seeing the red soft top pass them by. Her mother was the cruellest ever. She was old, worried about getting older and thought selfishly about herself. Most of the other girls lived closer to school and walked or drove their own cars. There was no reason she couldn't have driven in with her mother and let her geeky brother take the bus, sitting in soaking clothes, shivering, trying to look cool when everyone on the bus thought he was a jerk. She didn't sit with him. She was hugely humiliated, although not for much longer.

Soon she would be leaving home, counting the days to her graduation, her gateway to the freedom of summer and her acting classes. She had no intention of attending the graduation ceremony or dance, irregardless of the growing number of boys stacked in a blind bid against one another. They were immature eighteen-year-olds who'd be paying for her evening with money they hadn't earned and she was leading them on, playing their game. Her ruse was a simple one, knowing each one was a serious aspirant to getting into her pants and declaring a major victory. She had told each one to come up with a perfect après-dance agenda which she would eventually and casually reject one-by-one, save one testosterone charged male whom she would select and wait until the eve of the dance to frustrate. The coup would be two-fold. She would ridicule the boys for what they were and what they wanted, while demonstrating to the other girls that she was the most popular amongst them. On the brighter side, none of the girls were virgins and the boys' disappointment would be short-lived.

She had formulated another decision as well and began advising her preferred clients to dial-in New Year's Eve from 10:00 PM to 2:00 AM on a first-come, first-served basis. Anyone still hopeful at 2:01 would be disappointed. Whether or not her parents would think of her as a woman in three months, on December 31st a select few would see her as one and would forever be devotees of Midnight Rhapsody. Her parents would be out celebrating until the early hours and she had turned down several baby-sitting requests. She no longer needed the pretence and she certainly didn't need the aggravation. What she needed was a wider audience, practical preparation for her acting career and greater earnings. New Years would run four hours in ten-minute segments on the quarter-hour for a fee of one hundred dollars per hit and her fans were eagerly waiting.
*

Ted positioned himself at the round table by the CEO with his fourth coffee in hand. His presentation was always slated for Tuesday mornings, which he understood was meant to stimulate the other managers and encourage novice sales reps. He had presented that way for years and this Tuesday would be his last. In January he would chair the year's first meeting and present on the Monday as Division Manager. However this wasn't a general meeting. He and the five others were expounding on regional successes and failures to the CEO and the outgoing DM, some fearful of their jobs, others confident of their futures.

Thursday was golf day and in the evening the CEO would host a dinner, bidding farewell to one who would be missed and congratulating his replacement, the newest Division Manager. Then they'd get drunk, stumble to their rooms and leave the next morning to be home with family by midday Friday. And Ted was no exception for practical purposes, although he seldom went home on Friday. Nor

74

did he pick up girls or women in bars. He hadn't flirted in twelve years, which didn't give him any more reason or desire to return home to Kathy and the kids. He hated the thought of being at the house, but what he did have, 600 kilometres and one hour by air from the house, was a thirty-eight-year-old de facto wife who travelled as much as he did and to whom he had made a deeper commitment than the bonds of marriage. Her commitment to him was a tubal ligation.

*

Eileen Kimberly was attractive and sexual, diplomatic and successful, and she travelled with Ted to the twice yearly corporate events. She didn't need him, nor did he need her. The relationship had begun as a question of convenience and want. They each excelled in good jobs and allowed for similar travel schedules, they each valued time alone, never once complaining about the other's absence and both were legally married to others. However, to Ted and Eileen, they were each other's real spouse and about to celebrate a twelfth anniversary at a time when what had once been convenient and fresh was threatening to undo them.

They met at a cocktail party when Ted was frustrated with his home life and needed more than a quick fix. Kathy wouldn't be completing her full-time studies for another two years and he was footing the bill as well as feeding two more mouths and paying for baby sitters. He and Kathy hadn't socialized at all since the wedding, restrained by Melissa and then the most unwelcome news he could have imagined. Each night in the house which wasn't theirs was an insight into hell as Kathy studied and he role-played mother, part-time sitter, cook and dishwasher as well as taking care of himself. His one real vacation was the mid-year golf tournament in whatever sunny destination the CEO would choose and several years would pass before he could afford a mortgage, despite being the best sales rep in the company.

His first inclination was to refuse the client's invitation. Attending the party meant delaying his flight by another day, arriving home Sunday, exhausted. By not attending he would risk a negative impact on his career. The client was an important key to his annual business plan and he accepted knowing full-well Kathy would be furious. He arrived fashionably late towards the end of the cocktail hour looking relaxed and refreshed after a day in the hotel spa and went to the bar thinking to leave after the meal and a single digestive for the road. Then he chanced to gaze into the mirror behind a row of staggered bottles lining the bar and saw what he believed must be the most beautiful woman in the city and the attraction was immediate. The host was also her client and gladly seated them together with a sly grin, realizing they were both single and commenting that Ted was always at the right place at the right time.

They spoke endlessly, danced and left together. They found a quiet after-hours place, tossed a coin to choose one neutral five-star over the other and drove to her hotel for a change of clothes. They spent the night together. The next morning he delayed his flight once more and she did the same. They spent Sunday together in bed, restaurants, cafés and museums, sharing secrets and intimacy. She was in a marriage of convenience, a contractual business transaction transcending popular vows. She had married a then recently widowed man thirty years her senior, the very year Kathy promised to love, honour and obey Ted.

Kimberly didn't love her. He never would and she didn't love him. He was physically fit and wanted her youth. He was distinguished looking, wanted a beautiful woman by his side and he was wealthy. He loved her body and wanted her in the time he had left to enjoy her, having unabashedly declared he hated the thought of aging and refused to spend his declining years with an old woman. He was kind and generous, never demanding and never once reneged on the contract. He had no family and never wanted one. He wanted her and was willing to pay to keep her close by. Then one lonely night she saw the man watching her through the mirror.

Ted worked exclusively in the northeast where Eileen operated art galleries in four cities. Over the first year he had no difficulty arranging his itinerary in order to spend time with her; the complication was in the quality of their time together, limited each week to Friday nights, Saturday mornings and Sunday nights. His work began to suffer and he was told by his then manager to justify each night away with corresponding business, which would have meant less time with Eileen and the plan was born.

Ted ate humble pie and admitted to Chicago Corporate that he'd been burning the candle at both ends and that life with his fiancée was suffering, suggesting that he return to a four-day travel week and work Fridays at home like the other reps. The manager agreed and over the past eleven years Ted's schedule seldom exceeded a four-day week. Soon after he and Eileen purchased a home by the ocean, eliminating the need for hotels and rental cars, effectively eliminating the company's need to know or care what Ted actually did on Fridays while he was entertaining by the pool or sailing into private coves and romantic moonlit evenings at anchor.

He was with her most Thursdays through Saturday mornings, frequent Sunday nights and once each month they shared an entire week. She was slim, she worked out, she cooked culinary delights and he never questioned her marriage. She wore designer clothes and met him most nights at the door in silk. At the pool or on the patio she wore skimpy bikinis, thongs or nothing at all.

And then there was Chicago Corporate whose moralistic

ladder was difficult to climb for a single man. The corporate culture took a dim view of employees indulging in lascivious behaviour. Marriage, family and balance were all-important. Had they ever known of his interlude with a teenager, the resulting baby and secret marriage, they would have found any reason to dismiss him. Had they ever discovered he stayed away from home intentionally to fornicate with a married woman, they would have fired him on the spot.

Eileen preferred a simple wedding, nothing ostentatious, attended by close friends and regretted with a smirk that Ted's manager and CEO were both on vacation off-shore that particular week. They did however send gifts, insisting Ted bring his bride to the company Christmas party, which he did and Eileen Burberry was a big hit. She also joined him each year for the summer golf getaway, subsequent Christmas parties and their yearly vacation left him hungry for every part of her. What wasn't to love? She was hard to leave and harder to think about during the long weekend hours and days without her, knowing all the while she was with her husband. However over the years old Kimberly's interest in social functions had waned, many of his one-time colleagues having passed on, calling upon her less often as fitness and well-being increasingly seemed needlessly arduous and the relationship rarely went beyond platonic friendship.

Eileen had done well for herself as the owner of successful art galleries created with the help of her annuities. She lived on a magnificent estate with her husband and shared a beautiful seaside home and yacht with Ted. She didn't look much older than when they met, nor would she look her age whenever she decided to cancel her contract with Kimberly, though the anticipated due date had come and gone. With her future annuities and a one-time cash settlement payable at the time of divorce, or in the event he

expired first, the seaside home with Ted would be on an island somewhere they could swim the waters year-round. Either way, she truly would be Mrs. Eileen Burberry.
*

Ted's day was done. His presentation was applauded, his accomplishments were acknowledged as he would have expected and he left with the others for lunch while, half a continent away, Kathy's co-workers were oohing and aahing over the MX-5 from behind the sweaty windows of the teachers' lounge.

Clint Evans was just climbing from his bed. Sleeping at night anytime during the week was impossible and his irregular eating habits were taking a perceptible toll. He was eating his breakfast at his favourite diner at the end of his workday, lunch after seven hours of sleep and dinner at 9:00 or 10:00 somewhere downtown. His off-days were the same, somewhat annoyed he wasn't escaping prison routine entirely. He found that he needed order and discipline which gradually became self-discipline as much as he needed to breathe fresh air and mingle with people. At the same time agility of mind and body were equally important and he decided to join a health club to bring his body back to prison-hardness and the acuity to his mind which he feared might succumb to complacency. He was investing too much thought and effort into his career not to continue succeeding.

The weather hadn't let up: one thing he hadn't worried about in prison. He didn't like rain or the colour grey and beyond his window everything was monochromatic grey and depressing, taking him back to the rows of incisions he had carved into the wall over his cot, the same cot that concealed his stainless steel toilet without a seat. He remembered encircling the incisions of his first thirty days spent in solitary, the first time he'd vomited and the jeers of the other inmates who quickly suffered along with him. He remembered his suppressed feelings all those years, always afraid of discovery, fearful his surrender would ultimately lead to weakness he could ill- afford while others, discreetly or not, achieved contentment and well-being prior to raising their cots.

Yet he was anxious for snow, the whiteness and the fresh smell of winter, if not the cold. He thought he might learn to ski, get away occasionally from the concerns of business to relax by a log-burning fire with someone not too old or too young. He was doing exceptionally well and deserved a respite if anyone did.

*

Tuesday evening Jack Caden stood by his window, an alternative pastime to strolling along the boardwalk, peering through the lens of his newly acquired telescope at the monotonous passage of the red and green running lights of silhouetted navy and coast guard ships. He decided objectively at dinner that he was lonely, certain his forlorn mood was an extension of the weakening depression moving out into the Atlantic and not self-pity. Business was good and romantic opportunities were endless, but mixing business with pleasure was a potentially dangerous cocktail of failed love and broken dreams and he didn't need anyone's love that badly.

He had no idea why she had acted so callously or why she abandoned him when he was at his most vulnerable. He didn't miss her. He missed the idea of her. He missed the intimacy of touching warm and familiar flesh heated with passion, falling asleep, waking together, steaming showers, hot baths and candlelight dinners when they would hold hands, giggle, laugh and plan a future together. Still, she was gone and he was reduced to viewing colourless ships through drab night skies and photographing women half his age changing into their clothes at the beach. He wanted more. He wanted her, any her who would want him for who and what he was. Thursday night at the Casino Hotel was Ladies Night and, if he didn't succeed, he would resign himself to spending the rest of his life doing his job.

In bed he thought of the beach, the boardwalk and the homes dotting the hilltop, asking himself why not. He could meet a woman at the casino, marry her, move into a dream cottage by the sea and live happily ever after. He chortled, coughing out his nightcap over his sheets. That would never happen. The woman would certainly leave him at the altar after promising undying love and devotion. What was it about him that made her do it? She never said and he would never know. He would live out his life as a lonely and weathered old man, dying alone with no one to mourn his failed existence. He fell asleep with a deep sigh, loosening his grip on the old-fashioned, unaware his brow was furrowed and his lips were pinched tightly together.

Fourteen

Tuesday Kathy came home from the gym, prepared dinner with Melissa, ate by herself and retreated to her room to imagine herself in a different life. Wednesday the local yellow and brown bus arrived under a bright blue and artic sky, the kids left, she debuted yet another outfit, spent an hour with her trainer in the afternoon and went home to cook a meal with her daughter, biding her time. What she wanted more than anything was Thursday night.

Thursday morning she left before Melissa and Timothy, not wanting anything or anyone to spoil her day which ended early so she could train, go home, bathe and change into the sexiest ensemble purchased the previous weekend. She couldn't contain herself. She was going out with the ladies, feeling the excitement of a first date. She told Melissa to order in and gave her thirty dollars. She told Timothy she might consider allowing him to spend New Year's Eve with his friends if his good behaviour continued until the 31st, reaffirming clearly that New Years would be an absolute exception and any misconduct afterward would incur even more severe penalties.

She was ready. Her silk dress with an oriental collar was short enough to stifle even Melissa's trenchant criticism. She hadn't worn pantyhose all week and the nylons attached to her panty garters were a shade of smoky blue. Flurries were in the forecast, her woollen coat was knee-length with a Napoleon collar, oversized buttons and her high boots flared at her knees. Melissa stood agape, wondering what could possibly come next and she didn't wait long. Kathy's pièce de résistance was a wide-brimmed cartwheel chapeau with plumes on either side. Timothy sank into the sofa and Melissa stood wide-eyed as her mother walked from the room without a word and into the garage. She was insane, Melissa said under her breath. Timothy simply shrugged, thinking of New Year's Eve.

*

Jack Caden felt good, lucky enough to first try his luck at the casino and later watch the world go by in the lounge of the Casino Hotel with a cocktail after a mid-evening dinner. From his high-rise perch he could see the glittering neon in the distance, a short walk along the harbour front in the fresh night air amidst the winter's first dusting of intricate snowflakes: a postcard evening requiring a light topcoat and a brisk walk.

What remained of the unstoppable winter in the city would likely not be so pretty. The season was often harsh and bitter, long-lasting northern blizzards making city life intolerable in a matter of hours, squalls and whiteouts in minutes. Few were ever prepared. Kids went to school without gloves, their heads bare and their feet covered in summer sneakers. Women wore high-heeled leather boots for fashion that would stain with salt or abrade with coarse sand. And men were no less disrespectful of the season since affordable jeans and faded tee-shirts had become acceptable in virtually every venue from demolition derbies to art exhibitions.

But what Jack did want was to see winter by the sea, particularly Christmas, and no doubt by himself.

*

Clint Evans was prepared for work, pleased with his updated routine of training and focus. What he derived most pleasure from wasn't the sex, or control over weak, love-starved women. Although sex with beautiful and willing women was undeniably a good thing, they were all about money. He was a businessman, a broker. Had he been born a woman he would be a whore, an escort or a call girl. As it was, he wasn't even a gigolo. He had no desire or need to see any of them again or to pretend they were real. There would be others.

*

Throughout the previous three days Ted scribbled pages of notes, knowing very well the CEO would expect him to step in quickly and take responsive action to ensure a smooth transition. One thing was certain: the gofer would soon be gone.

After a few with the boys at the nineteenth hole, he did his usual once again: He went to his room and had a few more alone while he called Eileen to share his mounting excitement. Ending the call she wished him luck with his presentation and he spent the next hour before dinner practicing his speech. He decided he would arrive at the restaurant precisely on time with his cocktail in hand. He couldn't resist smiling. He was ecstatic. The evening would be the highlight of his career. He couldn't remember being as happy a single day since the moment he saw Eileen's inquisitive eyes exploring him through the mirror.

Fifteen

The three women had already politely refused one round of drinks from a table of hopeful businessmen before Kathy arrived. Girls' Night hadn't begun any differently from past nights, though each one suspected correctly and delved deeply into their closets for the silkiest and shortest outfits they could find. Each one wanted to be a step above that night in particular and they were, thankful Michelle had drawn them into the innocent conspiracy when seeing the woman gliding away from the hatcheck counter towards their table in the lounge. Kathy stood 1.73 metres in her stockings, in her stilettos 1.8. Add a short oriental-styled silk dress, cropped hair and a body taking shape and her colleagues weren't alone in their admiration.

Kathy looked feminine, sexy and nothing like a college counsellor. Even her friends watched her cross her legs and not long after she ordered a tequila and soda they pressed her to know everything: whether she was leaving Ted, did she have a lover, did she want one or did she only have weeks to live? Since Monday she had gone from lovely and new to wow to drop-dead gorgeous and they wanted to know why. Even the students were talking about her and not long after she was seated the waiter announced a second offer of complimentary drinks from yet another group of wishful dreamers.

At dinner she ordered salmon and a glass of chardonnay. She was serious about the redefined Kathy and answered all their questions with a single "no", adding "but, yes, if Ted doesn't get his act together I will be divorcing him very soon and finding a lover or he'll be the one with only weeks to live. I have to believe someone will like this." She discreetly pulled at the hem of her skirt to show Darlene and Sheila the delicate butterfly clasp attached to her stocking. Then Michelle wanted to see, her lips forming an exaggerated pout when Kathy shook her head and told her to sit down.

The ladies faithfully met for dinner the last Thursday of every month and once a season did a weekend getaway to escape monotonous routine, students and being ignored. And now they were four for a ski weekend and Kathy didn't consider for a moment to offer weak excuses. She would join them for the first full weekend after New Year's and Ted would simply have to manage being home Thursday afternoon.

Kathy was elated when hearing the women secretly booked her a return flight the previous Monday, certain she wouldn't disappoint them, and she was deliriously happy when hearing the next night out was December 17th, two days before Ted's Chicago Christmas party. He'd be gone an entire seven days, if not more. They would meet to plan spa time, ski lessons and three-day wardrobes, the three originals chuckling when Kathy commented on the poor bachelors at the lodge.

"That's the whole point of getting away, Kathy," Michelle ventured. "Whatever happens, and you will get lucky, stays behind us when we leave except when we swap stories the next morning or on Girls' Night."

She looked at them quizzically.

"We've been doing this for three years," Darlene continued. "We were so happy for you on Monday…and for ourselves to finally have you with us. We used to speak about you a lot, now we can talk with you."

Then Sheila caught Kathy's attention. "Kath, my husband screws around all the time when he travels, and he travels a lot. I contribute as much as he does but, if I divorce him, I'm the one stuck with the two teenagers and no life. Darlene's husband's a deadbeat. He has a nothing job, he sleeps all day when he's not doing the neighbour's daughter who's too dumb to get a job because she can't add without her fingers and he spends the rest of his time gambling. And Michelle's had about all she can take from her husband who would rather watch porn instead of loving a gorgeous wife. She's at the breaking point."

"The good thing about Michelle's situation is: no kids." Darlene went on. "Sheila and I have a few more years before we're deadweight–free, so every few weeks we get together like this to maintain our sanity and once a season we go out and get ourselves laid. And, trust me, Kathy, we're never disappointed." She eyed Michelle and Sheila. "Keep him till morning or send him back to his own bed when you're done and if he doesn't measure up you'll have all the next day to draw another number. There's no limit to handsome and willing donors, guys out for the same thing we are."

"I can't believe this."

"Believe it," came the chorus.

"They don't know, none of them?"

"We're three women out together, school teachers…b-o-r-i-n-g," answered Darlene, "and he hasn't looked into my closet for I don't know how long. He has no idea what I'm wearing tonight. Does yours?"

"No, he doesn't." Kathy sat back, sipping her chardonnay. "I haven't been done in months." She paused. "I'm in for the seventeenth and the trip. Thank you, ladies." "She smoothed her dress, running her hands to her knees. "I don't know where all this will take me, I just know I'll be in a better place."

87

The evening went on until Michelle asked the waiter for separate bills. The time was 10:00 PM and Kathy didn't want to leave. The evening was the culmination of her week. The next day at work she would see all three women again, but never again in the same light. Or had she finally seen the light? At the moment she didn't know or care. She didn't want to leave and told them amongst an unexpected flurry of kisses and hugs that she would stay to finish her wine, promising she wouldn't be foolish. Michelle was the last to say goodnight, surprising Kathy with the initiative to see her nylons and garters for herself, pulling at the hem of her dress and smugly telling the Darlene and Sheila she wasn't surprised.

While she was with the women everything had made sense. Alone she felt flustered by reason of not being flustered, which made her confusion all the more confusing. Women she had known for years came together regularly for one primary reason: to get laid, to cheat on their husbands and be happier away from their everyday lives. She couldn't believe it, yet she could. The entire evening was surreal, beautiful women her age not escaping into the make-believe world of one-dimensional movies or the worn pages of a novel, rather experiencing living scripts written and directed by them.

The real was unreal and she wouldn't sleep a wink once in her bed. She thanked the waiter who hurried over to pull out her seat. Ted hadn't pulled out her seat since when, nor could she remember the last time he helped her on with a coat or told her she was beautiful. She needed to know, she wanted to hear the words and not from three women whom she suddenly wanted to know much more intimately than talking about little Johnnie's and Jane's study problems. Seeing them seated at the table looking so alluring, she was instantly taken aback. All three looked fabulous, nothing like the nine-to-three school teachers she knew, standing at chalkboards repeating and repeating and repeating into the ears of the walking dead. Darlene and Sheila were vibrant women, each one with different home lives and now she knew each one cheated with the regularity of a utility bill. Michelle, like her, had never wanted children and had recently decided she didn't want her husband. Not only did the women cheat, they planned the quarterly escapades with a fervour Kathy found difficult to comprehend. Yet she could believe every word and understood why.

The lobby was empty, the lounge half-full with hotel guests who didn't want to toss their life savings into a roulette wheel and she went directly to the farthest empty table she could see. In a few weeks she would be with the girls again and she wondered about the interim days at school. They had never given her the slightest suspicion, dressing like teachers, sipping coffee during their breaks and seemingly women who simply wanted a night on the town to talk girl-talk, when each one was getting laid. She had to sort through a barrage of chaotic thoughts, despite being fully committed with no qualms about cheating on Ted. He had cheated on her for years and her time was long overdue. A month earlier she might have thought twice. A week earlier she was in her bedroom reading a novel and dreaming. Now she was sitting in a hotel bar revealing most of her legs, enjoying the glances and not feeling the least bit uneasy. She startled.

"Good evening. I saw you sitting alone. Actually, I meant to say, I hope you're sitting alone and I was wondering if I might join you. I'm sorry. I'm not very good at this. I didn't mean I hope you're alone. I can't believe that you would be. What I meant to say is: May I join you? I was about to leave, not really wanting to, when I saw your friends saying goodbye and I couldn't think of a better reason to stay a while longer."

"That's very kind, however I was intending to have a

quiet after-dinner drink and go home."

"Did you lose much?" He smiled. "At the casino, did you lose much?"

"I don't gamble. I find paying taxes a sufficient waste of my money."

"Copy that. I've never gamble myself. I work too hard for the money, I suppose."

"You're from here?"

"Yes and no. I recently transferred from about as far inland as one can be. At first I was somewhat uncertain about coming here, but I have to say the coast is a great place and so are the people." He tilted his head, the disarming smile never leaving his face. "Enjoy the rest of your evening."

Kathy's mind raced. She was going away in six weeks with women intent on flirting and possibly sleeping with strangers, telling herself she wouldn't mind cheating on her husband. Why not?

"I suppose one drink together won't hurt. Please, join me. I'm not expecting anyone. I came into town to meet my girlfriends for dinner."

He eased into the lounge chair, setting his drink on the table. "My name's Jack Caden."

"Kathy."

"Kathy's a pretty name, and thank you. It's not easy for a guy to approach a good-looking woman, let alone walk away from her with all eyes watching. Not that I do this every night."

"Thank you, Jack...for the compliment. So what does bring you here, if not the lure of riches?"

"I'm too old for clubbing and too young for weekend matinées, so Thursday's usually my night out for dinner and a few drinks." Jack reached for his old-fashioned and sipped what little was left. "Our glasses appear to be suffering from the same severe condition. May I offer you another wine before you leave? I would hate to say goodbye so soon after saying hello."

Kathy hesitated, scanning the room. If she couldn't do this, she thought, what else couldn't she do in January? "Actually I would prefer a tequila and soda. Thank you."

Jack signalled the waiter, continuing when the man left. "Is Thursday a night out for you and your girlfriends, Kathy?"

"Yes, once a month. We choose different places."

"My mind is telling me you're a model, yet you said you came into the city for your evening. So I presume you're a country girl, something I find hard to believe."

She nodded. "I live a few miles out and travel in every day to do counselling at the regional college."

"Important and fulfilling work, guiding the minds of the young."

"You mean frustrating work, trying to find one with a mind." She chortled. "I shouldn't have said that. I know a few do exist somewhere. They just haven't come to me yet. And you, Jack?"

"Advertising, the double-page glossy stuff: girls in bikinis or lingerie selling everything from beer to watches."

"So you're creative."

"I'm not at all. I'm an account manager, though I do get to sit in on the occasional photo shoot." The drinks came and he raised his glass. "I'm struggling not to compliment your dress. Somehow I don't think "out of this world" is a suitable toast. So here's to the prettiest woman in the room."

"Creative and gallant." She sipped her drink. "I'm sure you'll love living here. The city's not too big and the coast is a short drive away. Have you visited the shoreline?"

"I have every weekend until that miserable deluge last week. I envy the people who live by the sea."

"Yeah, it's pretty special. Seeing it every morning before school is reminiscent of the calm before the storm."

"So you're one of them? You live by the sea?"

"Near the sea, overlooking part of Surfers' Beach. You should drive by one day, particularly in the summer."

"In fact, I have. I've walked the boardwalk a few times, envying the people on the hill. Never thinking I'd meet one of them. What a life you must have. Tell me, how do those surfers do what they do this time of year?"

"I have no idea, but they're fun to watch. I get to the beach as often as possible and can't wait for summer."

Kathy brought her glass to her lips with her left hand.

"And to my great dismay, you're married."

She laughed softly. "Mostly on the weekends, the rest of the time the kids are there to remind me."

"Kids would have been my last guess. I would have thought upwardly mobile condo dweller and globetrotter. And Thursdays you're out with your friends for a little R & R and balance away from the daily grind."

"Condo life," she mused dreamily, "that would be a dream and globetrotting is Spring Break with the kids, whom I'm afraid I should get back to before they wreck the place."

"Thank you for sharing part of your evening with me, Kathy. I hope I'm fortunate enough to see you somewhere else another Thursday night or at the beach. I wouldn't mind getting over there once more before winter deals the first inevitable blow. I'll look up and wave."

She smiled, wishing she could stay longer, though she had already surpassed all expectations, had crashed through ancient barriers and didn't trust herself. "One never knows, and if we do the next round's on me."

"I'll take you up on that." He signalled the waiter, signed the chit and sipped his drink. "I wish I could turn back the clock to the moment you came in. I might even come here for dinner next Thursday, on the off chance. May I at least walk with you to your car? I wouldn't feel right thinking of you alone in a public garage. I'll be a perfect gentleman, not to mention being in a casino with cameras everywhere."

"That would be nice."

Jack Caden stood, extending a hand to help her stand. At the hatcheck he helped her with her coat and stood admiring her as she changed from her shoes to her boots. Through the lobby and down the escalator to the garage he held back, wanting to see her again, fearful of rejection, warning himself she was married with a family and hadn't really flirted with him. She hadn't said much and he decided he didn't need the hassle. Anyway, a woman in his life at the moment would undoubtedly conflict with his career.

Kathy maintained the conversation, keeping it simple. He was handsome and toned and helped her on with her coat. He was well-spoken, well-dressed and she wondered what she would do if she were to meet someone like him in January. The car lights flashed bright red as they approached, causing Jack Caden to gasp.

"Somehow I'm not surprised."

"It's new. I decided to treat myself."

"It's not exactly a family car."

"That's right. It's not." He bent slightly and pulled at the door handle. "Thank you, Jack, for a pleasant end to my evening."

"Thank you for making mine unimaginably perfect. I hope we see each other again, being that we have Thursday nights in common."

"I'm sure you'll find someone very soon, someone without luggage and don't leave her alone at home too often. Absence doesn't make the heart grow stronger and turning back time by thirty or forty minutes often isn't enough. We end up turning pages of the calendar, not the hour hand. So when you do meet a special girl, be the gentleman you were this evening. Goodnight."

"Goodnight Kathy. Drive carefully."

As she lowered herself backward into her seat, swinging in her legs, her coat separated showing the laced tops of her nylons, two matching clasps and a hint of bare skin. He couldn't help himself as she waited to straighten her legs and coat before tugging at the hem of her skirt. She hadn't thought to hold the edges of her coat together, the damage was done. So he saw some bare thigh and the tops of her nylons, she thought, so what, at least he was looking and she wanted him to.

She glanced up, smiling, feeling wicked. "I will."

He nodded and stepped away, a wide smile covering his face. The engine purred, they shared a parting glance and Kathy drove off. Jack Caden's charismatic expression stayed with him. He wasn't surprised at the K-A-T-H-Y on her tag, though he felt sorry for her. She was driving to be somewhere with people she had outgrown. He should have kissed her and she probably would have let him. She would have stayed later and he was certain he would fall asleep remembering the glimpse of her pale bare thighs.

*

Ted sat in his Chicago hotel room, despondent. Had he been able to open the window on the sixteenth floor he surely would have jumped and been done with his miserable life. Throughout his career he consistently exceeded all Corporate's expectations and measurements, his figures were the highest, his client presentations the most refined and professional. So why did they give the promotion to the company gofer, the corporate suck who didn't know shit from sugar and never would?

By Wednesday everyone figured out the first three days of the meeting were a virtual lottery. Thursday's golf game served to ease the stress and put everyone at the post-game corporate dinner in a jovial mood, ribald laugher calming to quiet as the CEO stood. All eyes were upon him, anxious for the final few words of what he had to say. Everything else would be preamble to the draw, everyone wanting to know who would be the winner, the next big boss and when the name was finally spoken Ted reached into his suit and continued smiling, preparing to stand and take the floor. He wasn't applauding, focused entirely on his speech until his Chicago counterpart seated across from him stood. Everyone was looking at the gofer, not Ted. He should have heard them calling his name, not someone else's and his mind went blank, one hand mechanically slapping the other as his smile discreetly faded.

He hadn't thought to kill himself at that precise moment, too devastated and not certain he wasn't dreaming. However as the evening progressed toward several more drinks the notion seemed quite doable and, he believed, warranted. He still did. He wanted to die, and would have, if by the end of the bottle he hadn't lost his incentive lying insensate and pathetic on the carpeted floor. He had a wife he didn't love, useless kids he would sell to any gypsy tribe and a girlfriend, ostensibly his wife, whom he did love and couldn't afford. To his credit he did own a tenth of the beach house which had tripled in value, but not the sailboat, nor the car and because of the gofer he couldn't afford to escape a life he despised to begin one he had dreamt of for so long. And how could he face either one? Eileen expected him the following morning. She had made dinner reservations for Friday evening to celebrate his promotion and discuss the next stage of their life. What would he do? Eileen would know he couldn't afford to leave Kathy without losing everything. She was a millionaire, owner of flourishing galleries, respected in the world of art and had many times pleaded with him to leave Kathy and move in with her. He had almost nothing in the bank except his retirement fund, most of his savings having gone to pay his share of the beach house, once so certain of his future, now trapped in a severely stunted career with no social life beyond Eileen.

Without a divorce he'd be forced to live with Kathy for the sake of fifty thousand in alimony, a home which had long ago condensed into a desk drawer in his office and Eileen would have every reason to leave him which would be disastrous. Free of Kathy, she wouldn't hesitate to garnishee his salary, not trusting him to willingly comply. Chicago Corporate would discover his fraud. He'd be jobless and no better off than when the kids were born. He would struggle from pay to pay, relying on Eileen if she would even want him. He was royally screwed.

The promotion had meant everything. He crumpled his unread presentation, tossed the empty 750ml of scotch onto the sofa behind him and crawled to the mini-bar. She would be expecting his phone call and what would he say? He twisted three caps and drained the mini bottles into his glass. The Christmas party was three weeks away. Eileen had bought an elegant gown and they would now be seated with ordinary sales reps and not the CEO and his wife at the head table. And Kathy, with her "I told you so" blasé, righteous attitude and the damned kids who thought he was a loser anyway. Those two he couldn't care any less about beyond the boy's one-fifty and the girl's two hundred each month, giving him nothing in return.

He twisted three more caps and drained the glass. Kathy would have to divorce him.

*

Kathy drove into her garage a few minutes before midnight. In the foyer she pulled one foot then the other from her boots, dropped her coat and chapeau onto the leather bench by the door and went to her bedroom, preferring not to spoil her mood by talking with or seeing the kids. She was thinking about Jack Caden, regretting she didn't stay longer and wondering what memories she would have to cherish or regret in six weeks.

In six weeks she would probably have an affair, a three-day heated romance and she sat on the edge of her bed with her legs and dress the way she positioned them in the car, curious how much Jack might have seen, feeling a deep flush wash across her face. She had no doubt she would spend the night with him if she ever saw him again. She reclined onto her elbows and parted her legs ever so slightly. Oh, yes. He must have liked what he saw and perhaps she would see him next Thursday, without the other girls, or the week after.

She unzipped her dress and pushed it to the floor, crowning the silken folds with her nylons, garters and panties before crawling between her satin sheets. Or as soon as she got rid of Ted and Melissa, she mused, she might find a way to permanently deal with Timothy and ask Jack to move in with her as a boarder. He did say he wanted to live by the sea. She groaned, squirming onto her side, asking herself why not, while one floor below Melissa was entertaining her third spellbound visitor, teasing him with poses that would seem childish and amateurish to her in a month's time.

Sixteen

Clint Evans' first inclination was to take Thursday night off. Nothing was going his way, possibly because he hadn't factored in the twenty-four-hour potential of the casino. Suitable women were everywhere, sitting at tables, the slots or milling around to determine which flashy machine would pay for whatever they were missing in life. Unfortunately, as in the restaurant, they were either in groups, pairs or with men.

Midway through the evening he went to the restaurant to eat alone, drawn to her at first sight. He knew her instantly. He recognized her indefinable aura transcending her great legs and oriental dress few women could wear properly. She was a total package: the haircut, make-up, the way she sat crossing and uncrossing her legs and when she pulled at the hem of her dress he knew he had to spend time with her. She would be good for a few thousand at least, and probably much more. She was beautiful, sensual and naturally erotic and he visualized precisely how she would look in the nude. She would be fun to work with, he thought, or any of her three friends, four being an impossible challenge for any but the wealthiest of men and she was the one. His dilemma was how to separate her from the herd.

He ate his food mechanically, keeping up with them, ordering dessert when they ordered, closely eying their wine situation and when the redhead signalled for the bill he did as well. He formulated a plan and finished his wine, watching her stand, smooth her dress and walk from the room. Timing was critical, not those around him. People were inattentive at the best of times. Put a few drinks in them and they were downright blind. He stood casually and walked to where she had been sitting, pacing himself, dropping the slim vinyl jacket containing his bill alongside hers to reach for his billfold. Then he picked up the wrong one, read her name and went to the cash to pay. Kathy Burberry had ordered a half-bottle of white wine, salmon and sorbet. What he would do next, he didn't know.

What he saw in the lobby did not bode well for the balance of his workday. She was gone, the place was littered with couples and he went to the lounge for a nightcap before making a final tour of the casino, completely taken aback by seeing her again, this time sitting alone, one man sliding from his seat to approach her, another seeming undecided. Clint snorted a snide laugh, bringing the old-fashioned to his lips. Neither guy had a chance. Jerks like that never did. They were too transparent, too eager, a dime a dozen. They never targeted, never adapted their techniques to meet specific needs. She had no coat which meant she was probably a guest at the hotel, which meant possibly staying Friday or possibly she was a frequent visitor. Or she was relaxing away from the din of the casino before trying again. She was no housewife, not dressed as she was unless she was cheating, and if she was cheating she probably lived nearby and wouldn't be in a hurry to get home for whatever reason, giving him the time he needed to either make contact or discover how she would end her evening. Her staying at the hotel would mean his returning the next evening, inviting her to dinner instead of clubbing and the evening would culminate in her bed and in her purse. Leaving through the front doors on foot, he would be tempted to follow her at a distance, from the garage he'd return to the casino and spend Friday night at a preordained club seducing another worthwhile benefactor. Whichever way the evening played out, he would see Kathy Burberry again.

Several hours later at breakfast he sat counting the evening's proceeds: fifteen grand. He hadn't looked at the woman's driver's permit, afraid of what he might see. He placed her somewhere between fifty-five and sixty, being kind. She wasn't bad looking when dressed, yet he didn't take long to adjust the dimmer switch once in the room. She was on vacation, recently divorced and on a winning streak. So was he. He was beaming. He'd never won so much at one time and needed to celebrate, reaching into his pocket to display a thick billfold of hundreds while suggesting that one winner buy another a drink at the bar, which she didn't need. But he was young, she wasn't and what the hell.

She accepted, which didn't surprise him. Nor was he surprised when she ordered a gin shooter. He ordered a straight-vodka and his third didn't make her look any younger, though he was thinking he should get her into her room while she could manage to walk. In the room he took two gins and two vodkas from the mini-bar, emptying hers into a glass and his onto the carpet while she undressed and he went to the light switch. He poured her another double, unbuttoned his shirt, explaining he would take a shower and when he returned the glass was empty and the woman was on her back, naked to her waist and snoring with her chin digging into her chest. Twelve thousand was wrapped in paper bands from the casino, her bankbook had a balance of eight thousand along with her PIN number and he decided three thousand would be an equitable amount for the service he might have rendered.

An hour later he was eating breakfast and remembering the dark-haired woman in the oriental dress. Fanning the bills, he imagined her in bed stretched out beside him, thinking he would definitely pay to spend an evening with her and wondering who did. She didn't seem like a woman who would betray some poor bastard for the sake of a few months but, then, neither did the Oriental Cajun bitch who gave him to the cops on a platter. He would have been out in three years if he hadn't sent the welcoming committee to sickbay or threatened in court to kill her. Thing is, if he hadn't, the three years would have been hell and his education incomplete.

*

Ted woke late Friday morning with a ferocious headache, his lingering stupor allowing him for too short a time to forget he was a failure despite still wanting to die. Soon after he did remember and stumbled his way over to the mini-bar, cursing at the remaining choice of white liquor. All the empty bottles of dark booze lay on the floor and he wouldn't be sober enough to phone Eileen at least until noon and doubted he'd be able to board a plane until the following day. The crippling defeat couldn't have come at a worse time, nor have been a more stinging blow to his pride and career.

He phoned room service to order a mid-afternoon lunch before he forgot, measuring each word, changed his flight to Saturday with as much effort and fell onto the bed. Eileen would understand. She might even be happy, if not delighted. For years she had wanted him to take over the corporate aspect of her galleries, believing his interest in art would soon extend beyond fold-out glossy images of naked women.

In industry he was somebody, everybody knew him, respected him and came to him. In the art world he would be a novice and what did he know about colours, balance, themes and layout? Not a damn thing. Not to mention the girly-boys he'd have to deal with. Then again, he could quit and start over, knowing full-well no one would give him a hundred K to start over at the bottom? And where would that put him with Eileen? Neither was he forgetting his ever-present wife or deadbeat kids. "Kathy, Kathy, perfect little Kathy," he chanted. She could earn double her fifty K in the private sector but, no, she wanted to make a difference by helping kids as hopeless as her own. In one day she spent over a year's salary on a goddamn car, a frigging personal trainer and clothes for no better reason than vanity. She was wearing stilettos in the house and they were eating in the frigging dining room. What the hell was that all about? Melissa was well on her way to becoming a snotty bitch and Timothy would end up on the street with a squeegee washing car windows for a quarter or a cheap peak at some broad's chest or legs.

Ted was oblivious to the several knocks at the door, not the phone's piercing ring that hurled him from an unspoiled life into reality in a split second. He had never looked as terrible in his life, including the morning after he'd heard of his unborn son and had drunk himself into a stupor. The food was tasteless, the wine could have been swill water for what he tasted and nothing short of an endless fountain would could alter or delay his immediate future. He showered, dressed and dialled the number she answered on the first ring.

"Hello, big guy. How's it feel to be the head honcho? By midnight I knew you'd be out celebrating but, hey, we're talking three o'clock here. How did you guys celebrate?"

"Eileen, I'm sorry. I didn't get the promotion. The guy in Chicago's the new DM."

"The gofer won the prize?"

"Yeah, the gofer, and I'm a little pissed, I have to admit. I didn't take the news very well."

"Their mistake and the best news you've given me in a twelve years, sweetheart. You don't need the job, the aggravation or the money. You know that very well, but you won't be home with me tonight."

"No."

"Where will you be?"

"Here, in Chicago, locked in a hotel room by myself and feeling like shit. Phone anytime."

"Good, sweetheart. You should feel that way for not having come home to me right away and I won't be calling. You need sleep more than me at the moment and you certainly don't need them. You need me. Remember that."

"I'll be with you at noon."

"I'll be here, sweetheart."

"Eileen?"

"Yes, sweetheart?"

"I'm sorry. I love you."

"Come home to me, as soon as you can. You have no reason to be sorry or to feel sorry. I'll reschedule our reservation for Saturday. I love you, sweetheart. Enough said." She disconnected.

Ted hated himself, primarily because he couldn't drink white liquor, or wouldn't and he had to phone the second wife.

"Kath, it's me." He breathed deeply, hating what he would have to say. Eileen would always stand by his side to support him, encourage him. Kathy over the years had become a thorn in his side. "So I guess I bombed out again. No tickie, no washie, no kidding and no Divisional Manager. Looks like the Chicago guy knows how to kowtow better than me. Maybe you were right after all. Anyway, Kath, I'm staying a day or two. I'm drunk and I'm going to stay drunk. I feel like shit, look worse and should be home sometime Monday before you."

Ted Burberry hung up feeling desperate.

*

Throughout the day Friday Jack Caden couldn't erase the thought of Kathy, K-A-T-H-H-Y from his mind. For whatever reason, he couldn't stop thinking of her: the way she spoke, the way she held herself, carried herself and her gorgeous legs enrobed in nylon to her titillating garters. He wanted more of her. More than any other woman, he wanted her: an elusive dream and his open palm struck the wall. He deserved. He did deserve, yet he carelessly let her drive away into a winter's night and all he knew about her was her name.

The question was: why did he want her? She had lots of baggage and nothing to offer him that he couldn't find in a hundred different women. She had kids and a husband. She was someone's wife and mother in a little red sports car and a knockout dress topped off with garters. She was out with the girls on a weeknight when her husband was out of town and her eyes lost their sparkle when the time came to go home. Kathy was definitely looking for something, or someone.

*

Kathy finished her week on a high. After five visits to the health club, a modest change in diet and a switch to tequila from sweet liqueurs she dropped a dress size and gained three kilos. Best yet, she understood the smiles between Michelle, Darlene and Sheila. She was one of them, yet she wondered how she would see them or be seen by them in six weeks when she would share a common and unspeakable secret.

She hadn't expected the call, nor was she surprised. If Ted drank at home because he couldn't be somewhere else screwing anyone who wanted a free meal, why wouldn't he drink away from home? Hearing he wouldn't be home until Monday didn't upset her. The kids would eat in their rooms, leave her alone to imagine her first-ever affair and Saturday she would go shopping for skiwear. If Ted thought he was pissed when he called, she could imagine the purple-faced rage when he would hear about her weekend with the girls and see her wardrobe for the slopes. Neither was she disappointed for him. He never shared his excitement with her, never took her to corporate social events and was never proud of her. So why would she share in a perceived failure he couldn't handle?

The sun seldom set in the winter, remaining hidden most days behind heavy clouds until darkness pervaded by late afternoon. She had always thought of the drive home as another thankless household chore, not so since sitting snugly in body-hugging leather seats alone with nothing to see in the rear-view mirror but the occasional headlights and nothing to hear but calming music. Light snow was falling, dusting Ocean View Road, eliminating any delineation between land and sea. Lights on the hill appeared like miniature unblinking beacons and she wondered how much longer she would live there. She loved the new and exciting part of her life which no one close seemed willing to share with her and for that reason she knew a complete transformation wasn't far off.

Melissa wasn't talking to her, which was refreshing in itself and Timothy was intent on redeeming himself which was, in effect, a fool's mission. She seriously doubted she would survive the fifteen months to Timothy's eighteenth birthday and wondered how Ted would react to her decision, knowing instinctively his first thoughts would be of alimony and child support. She would be thirty-six and reflecting over another wasted year. Perhaps lying naked under a complete stranger in January would be her defining moment, her impetus. She didn't know. Would he be a good lover, would she? Would he stroke her naked body with long, gentle caresses, whispering words all women longed to her, or probe her relentlessly with passion, smothering her cries with ardent kisses? God she hoped so.

Surfers' Beach was deserted, the taillights of a single vehicle casting glaring red auras amidst the vast blackness, possibly a surfer lamenting the passing of another season or someone seeking solace from the absolute quiet and the infinity of a darkened sea. One kilometre farther Kathy signalled her left turn, leaving the ocean behind until she pulled into her driveway. The car behind her slowed, presumably continuing on its way to another hilltop home, she thought, not an absolute stranger who knew Kathy Burberry drove a little red car and lived near the ocean.

Seventeen

Ted first went home to Eileen, pallid and distraught. They went to dinner, made love and Sunday they strolled by the seashore holding hands, not wanting to disrupt their quiet mood with troubled conversation. Monday she washed his clothes and drove him to the airport. Neither said goodbye and Monday evening she went home to Kimberly.

Ted's short-haul flight landed at 11:30 AM and when he found himself in the parking lot searching for his car he dropped his luggage and screamed an ungodly sound. Once home he went to his office, closed the door to an empty house and poured a scotch. He should have been a thousand kilometres away, working, managing a young report, somewhere he would be Tuesday and the rest of the week. Thursday evening he would be with Eileen once again.

He brought out his photo album and sat absorbing the dozens of coloured poses of her lounging on the deck of their pool, at the ocean, aboard the boat, in the shower and at work. How could he not want her in his arms? She was gorgeous, without a single flaw and she was witty. Kathy was fooling herself, trying to recapture her youth. She was a mother, married, a housewife and no amount of new clothes or fancy cars would make her viable. She wouldn't be home for another four hours and he had no idea what time the kids got home. They didn't matter. All they wanted or needed from him was their monthly credit limits increased. Relentless blood suckers who clearly understood never to go into his office at any time, for any reason, although when he went to his bedroom with his luggage he closed and locked the drawer.

Normally Kathy would undo his suitcase. He didn't care. He had nothing to hide. Most times Eileen made certain to sanitize his time with her for the sake of peace of mind, not to say he'd be surprised anytime to see an "I love your husband" written in deep red lipstick across the back of his shirts. Eileen deserved more, which certainly didn't describe him. Old Kimberly gave her more cash each month than he earned before taxes in triple the time. Her galleries catered to an elite clientele, she had more potential money listed on her phone's dial pad than he had in all his corporate files and she was beautiful, possessing a love for life he could never equal. Instead, he was gaining weight, drinking excessively when he wasn't with her and hating every moment. Then he saw the shopping bags and swung open the doors to the walk-in closet.

He left his suitcase on the floor, went to his office, refilled his glass, changed his flight once again and phoned his junior sales rep to advise the man he would arrive at the airport later that evening. He couldn't stay. He had to get out, finishing his second drink when his daughter and son came home. He couldn't remember their last happy time together, or when the girl had kissed his cheek or he had bounced her on his knee, for what little it mattered, and the other one was a complete embarrassment on so many levels. Adding insult to injury, when he left the house driving the Lexus neither Melissa nor Timothy noticed and a few hours later Kathy arrived home to the same indifference.

He hadn't bothered closing the closet doors, nor did he leave a note. He must have been furious at seeing her clothes, the customized boots and the skis leaning against a wall by the Lexus. She called his cell, not expecting him to answer and left a message to advise she would be eating out with the kids until whatever day he decided to come home to do the groceries with her, and in the Lexus. She didn't bother asking whether he might be with her for her birthday and their anniversary. Then she called for a taxi and went to the downstairs bedrooms.

The week leading up to her night with the ladies had gone quickly, filled with novelty, yet the seventeenth seemed so far into the future, beyond reach and the thought of enduring another thankless Christmas before her affair seemed impossible. Christmas in Miami never did anything for her. She always did the planning, made the flight reservations, packed for the kids, bought gifts for his parents and did most of the cooking with little time to herself. This year Melissa would help her grandmother. Kathy intended spending time each day at South Beach and, if she saw one other woman wearing a thong, she promised she would do the same.

She thought of Jack Caden each of the four days since leaving him in the hotel garage, each night her thoughts changing to dreamy fantasies. Friday morning she thought she might regard the women at school differently. She didn't. They were typical college teachers who worked hard, went home to dysfunctional families, cooked dinners and four time each year went away to have hot sex with single, free or cheating men. She had wanted to ask how many, partly afraid to hear the answer. Twelve weekends, and possibly more affairs, she mused. No other man had seen her naked body since a couple of weeks before she met Ted. How would she feel and how would she act when facing Ted for the first time?

She did know she would wear nylons and even strip for whomever. All men loved stripteases. Or would he undress her? She would be more toned, possibly tanned and dressed to kill. The girls had played the game for three years. Meeting men was probably second nature to them and Jack

Caden flashed across her mind. What would have happened had she stayed and let her resentment towards Ted blossom or fester? He was good-looking, fit and trim. He seemed genuine, which didn't mean anything. He might have wanted a night in her pants and nothing else, exactly what she'd be getting in January. Yet she didn't believe so and kept him in her thoughts until the taxi pulled up in front of the restaurant.

Later at the house she chuckled. By the time Ted landed on Saturday the dinner and taxi bills would amount to several hundred dollars, but she had warned him about the car. Jack had joked about being at the hotel again on Thursday, knowing she was married. Anyway, Thursday was a school night and how would she explain getting home at such a late hour. She couldn't exactly eat dinner with him, go to bed for an hour and leave.

She finished making the bed and climbed pensively between the sheets. Ted wouldn't be home until early afternoon Saturday and she hadn't strolled by the ocean for several weeks.

Eighteen

Month Four

December's first day was bitter. The kids were gone and Kathy wasn't surprised by how little she was angry with Ted. She was glad he wasn't at the house when she arrived the previous day. No woman needed to know her man had spent a weekend in a hotel room drinking to cloud the reality of his failure and crying. Jack Caden certainly would not.

Winter had set in for the season and with the first snowfall came a thousand-dollar work order for winter tires. Her birthday was on Friday, and the wedding anniversary, a fact she had always held against her father who had sworn to disown her had she gone through with the termination and Ted hadn't remembered either occasion: hers or theirs. She decided he would pay for the wheels. She didn't need a dinner with someone who didn't want her and if she dwelled on Thursday night much more she knew she would soon discover whether Jack had been joking. She wanted to take the day off, go home from the garage or spend the day at a spa or with her trainer, anything but a line-up of stupefied college kids.

Jack also said he might be at Surfers' Beach one Saturday and impulsively she went to her bedroom to gaze out. She could see the boardwalk: a thin ribbon of wooden slats and posts meandering between low dunes and coarse sand. She looked at her watch. She had time and went to Timothy's room for his telescope. A few moments later she knew if Jack Caden was anywhere along the boardwalk Saturday she would see him and might have already if she hadn't been so engrossed in her shopping spree and a New Year's resolution to cheat on her husband, which she believed was a relative term at best. Ted wouldn't start acting like a devoted and loving husband anytime soon, nor would she become a cheating wife. On the contrary, she would be redefining herself with the help of others, conducting interviews in the nude and eventually wishing Timothy's next mother the best of luck. She wouldn't stay married for the sake of screwing four strangers a year until younger men would snigger at her and older men were out of the question. The timing was perfect to put herself out there. The girls and the health club were the catalysts she needed and possibly working in the private sector would be her next step. She had neglected her career for too long, missing out on conferences, exposure to other professionals and cocktail parties.

Jack was a much needed ego boost. He crossed her path at the right time and in the right place to assuage any doubt she might have had, which didn't mean she would sleep with him. He was too close to home. He knew she lived on the hillside and drove a red car. If he wasn't the stupidest man on the planet he'd figure it out. Occasional weekends with men several hundred kilometres away was a different matter, anonymous, and the guys would either be married or contented bachelors: an interim measure she was certain wouldn't last the year while she formulated a longer-term plan.
*

Jack did go to the ocean the previous Saturday and did wave towards the hill. Christmas was fast approaching with the New Year, business would be slowing and he was ready for a brief reprieve. He imagined Kathy lying on the beach, self-assured and remembered her dress and bare thighs. She was out with her friends and was being a little risqué, believing she would never see him again. She was searching for something, so was he and at any another time he might have tried. The timing was wrong. Playful naughtiness would have brought trouble he didn't need and not because she had family. Everyone had family of some description somewhere. She was remarkable, not desperate in a way he found common to all the other women.

He enjoyed his work in spite of the long hours. Although the extensive and requisite research was exhausting and if he didn't take advantage of the year-end to relax, he never would. He wanted to feel the hot sun against his skin, swim in warm water and meet someone like Kathy, someone with a brain who didn't mind being seen as a woman. Staying at home he wouldn't meet anyone. He would succumb to his work ethic and spend the coming year alone photographing other men's women. No doubt if he ever did cross paths with Kathy she wouldn't remember him. The better part of a year would have passed, enough time to take on a different appearance. Each would be wearing sunglasses, possibly hats or scarves and neither would know.

He resisted the temptation of returning to the hotel Thursday night, convincing himself that being at the ocean once more had nothing to do with wanting to see her. He was truly taken with the idea of living by the sea and one day he would.

*

Ted didn't call Kathy once throughout the week. For dinner on Friday she gave Melissa and Timothy the option of joining her in town or ordering pizza, although she didn't trust either one with excessive time alone, having once suspended their allowances for being in her bedroom without permission. Neither one had argued the penalty, nor did they ever discover how Kathy knew. She left the money with Melissa and drove to the finest French restaurant in town where she celebrated her birthday alone, paid the bill and drove home.

She hadn't felt the least bit conspicuous. She was learning, becoming more confident each day. She set the alarm system, went to the wine cooler, quietly climbed the stairs to her bedroom, closed the door and dimmed the lights. The cork shot from the champagne bottle with a loud burst. She poured a little into a glass, then a little more, undressing to her panties and bra and sauntering to the bay windows to stare out across the darkness and a barely visible glimmer coating the sea. She brought the glass to her lips, toasting her reflection, acknowledging the reciprocal smile. No one remembered her special day.

She refilled her glass. The marine forecast was calling for variable skies, southwest winds at twenty knots, seas of one metre or less and an air temperature of plus six: a pleasant day for dressing in leggings, a cable sweater and strolling along the boardwalk in her fleece-lined suede bomber jacket and boots. If he wasn't there he never would be and she would never discover why she cared.

Nineteen

The following Saturday Clint Evans overslept and when did wake he stayed in bed thinking of Kathy Burberry. She wouldn't be a difficult workload. In fact he believed he would gladly pay for dinner and do her without applying the usual fee. He had never targeted a woman long-distance before. This one he did, because he had to have her one last time. She was once a consummate lover, his best and uninhibited without the slightest restriction right to the end when he saw her standing at the corrugated door of the loading dock looking down with her designer legs close together and her arms akimbo with as much emotion as overseeing a delivery.

Kathy Burberry was Kim Moon in every way from her dark hair to her pale legs and Asian dress, only she hadn't married him, lived with him or testified against him. He wanted her once more. Yes, he did. He wanted to see her naked, make love with her and snap her neck. One thing was certain: He would have her very soon and no one would get in his way. He would study her, learn about her, discover who she really was, what she liked and didn't, what she did and when. And then he would know when. He knew where she lived. He knew when her brats left for school, how many minutes later she left and where she parked her car at college. He knew what time her day ended and where she worked out. Matching his schedule with hers when he should have been sleeping was the most difficult part.

He was tired, even though he had come home unusually early. The woman had over imbibed at the club and, unable to undress, had simply fallen backwards onto the bed with her legs open. By the time he'd finished she was unconscious and in debt for five grand. Getting home early after such a long week was an unexpected bonus and he felt refreshed forcing himself from the late morning warmth of his covers, satisfied with the basis of a workable plan.

*

Kathy woke late. The empty champagne bottle seemed as heavy as the night before and she dragged herself onto her elbows, looking into her vanity mirror and letting her head drop into her pillow. She looked awful. The first order of business was coffee and a few tablets followed by a steaming oil bath and a face mask.

Melissa had gone out, escaped more like it, and her brother had his head plugged-in as usual.

She padded to the kitchen wrapped in a short silk robe. Surprisingly the coffee was brewing. More surprisingly the taste was rich, soothing and she was right to think a slice of toast would abrade the night before from her teeth and tongue. The dishes were done and he'd taken the pizza box out to the garbage. He was trying, she conceded, and she knocked on his door to thank him.

"Timothy, by the way," she continued, "how far can you see with your telescope?"

"It's not like for the stars or anything."

"Is it good for looking out to sea? Could I see a ship on the horizon?"

"Yeah, but like why?"

"A cruise is supposed to enter the harbour this morning and I thought I could borrow your telescope to see offshore."

"I don't think so. It's pretty complicated and, you know, sort of delicate."

"Complicated…and delicate."

"Yeah."

"As complicated as a reduced house arrest, say two weeks?"

His eyes brightened. "Serious?"

"Yes."

"Four."

Kathy chuckled. "You mean you like being in here so much you want four more, not two less?"

He grimaced. "What about the old man? What'll he say?"

"Nothing, if he knows what's good for him."

Timothy pulled the plugs from his ears. "Okay, take it, just be careful."

"I don't think so. I'd hate to drop the thing, being that it's so sensitive. Bring it to my bedroom in one hour and set it up by the window, being that it's so complicated."

She closed the door. Upstairs the steaming water tinted her skin and beaded her face instantly, the deep heat from her mask drawing out an involuntary groan. She swayed from side to side for the sole purpose of staying awake, the heated water cascading in and around every contour and she was definitely seeing a difference.

She'd brought her clothes into the bathroom, not completely convinced Timothy knew the number of minutes in an hour. Her shorter hair blow-dried and styled quickly, pulling a camisole over her head and standing to pull on her smallest thong and cable sweater. She wanted her make-up to look perfect. The final touches were snug-fitting knitted leggings and mid-calf suede boots before critiquing several angles and poses in the full-length mirror by the bay windows of her bedroom. She blew out a whistle. Every curve from the boots to her hips was perfectly defined: naked in public and fully dressed. Not the tiniest dimple showed with the tiniest thong imaginable completing the look.

She didn't hear him come in.

"Wow! You going out again or something?"

"I might later for a little while. Do you like?"

"It's sort of weird. It's not like you're fifteen or anything, but, yeah, it's sort of nice. Think the old man's

117

going to like it?"

"Think I care?" She smirked. "Put the telescope by the window, Timothy. I can handle the rest. Thank you."

Kathy watched him setup the telescope and leave, thinking she have been a bit much for the poor kid after so many years of seeing her in polyester slips and frumpy clothes. She waited a few moments after he closed the door to focus in on the boardwalk and scan its entire length. She was nervous, hoping to see him at the shore and leave before Ted came home to rant about her outfit. Noon was moments away. She was starving, her mouth was dry and she wondered whether Jack was somewhere nearby eating lunch or somewhere faraway not thinking of her. She hoped not, or why would she have gone through the trouble? Worse: What logical reason would she have to stay dressed as she was with two adolescents in the house and a wuss husband? She left her room, went to the liquor cabinet and poured a generous portion of tequila without the benefit of soda.

Soon after she was searching from north to south, not caring what ship might be crossing a monotonous sea and saw him on the third pass, appearing close enough to reach out and touch. She sipped from her glass, liking the warmth of the liquor. She couldn't believe Jack Caden was leaning against a wooden rail, studying the hillside, his eyes travelling from one house to another, one window to another from so far away. When he waved he seemed to know she was looking down. Kathy stumbled backward, her mind racing, draining her drink to regain her composure. What if he saw her first? What if he saw the dull sun reflecting off the telescope's lens? She put her eye timidly to the rubber cup. He was pushing himself from the rail, smiling widely and raising his shoulders into an exaggerated shrug. The curve of his lips reversed to a frown, his brow wrinkled. He turned on his heels and began walking north, followed step by step to the midway point.

She folded the tripod, drew her drapes together and closed the door to her room. She returned the telescope, asked Timothy if he needed anything at the store, slipped into her suede bomber and hurried to her car. Not five minutes later she was parked at the north end and walking south. He was wearing an open parka, jeans and dress boots. A camera was slung around his neck. He wasn't hard to look at, neither was she with her gloved hands stuffed in her bomber pockets, her collar up and her head cupped in a knitted aviator's skullcap.

"I didn't think I'd see you again."

He glanced sideways towards the hillside. "So you people can see from way up there."

"Enough to know when the beach is too crowded."

He eyed her from top to bottom. "I have no words. You were seriously gorgeous the other night, seeing you this way I'll have to check a thesaurus. You look fantastic. I'm speechless."

"Thanks. My weekends are a little more casual. Dresses don't quite fit in down here."

"You won't get any argument from me. I can't imagine what the summer will bring. Too bad we didn't meet sooner in life." He took her in fully again. "Don't expect an apology or excuse anytime soon. Pretending I'm not completely consumed by what I'm seeing would be ludicrous, not to mention mortally stressful on my heart."

She giggled, "I'm flattered, but remember not all things are what they seem. The same goes for people."

"That is clearly not the current situation, Kathy. From my perspective, what I see is absolute perfection. I wouldn't be surprised to see you in a studio prepping for a shoot one day. You are definitely model material and I've seen enough of them in different poses over the years to know." He was flirting with her, yet he appeared so calm and casual, she thought. "Can I invite you for a coffee, or a schnapps somewhere to warm you?" He laughed, adding "and a very cold beer for me."

"I have to say you don't look much like an ad exec, more like a swarthy seafaring type. I mean that to sound as a compliment and after a line like that I do hate to say no. Unfortunately, Jack, I really don't have much time. I have errands to run in town and it is Saturday, but I did enjoy seeing you again. I'm sorry." What errands? She had all the time in the world, and yes she did enjoy seeing him. He wasn't there to look out onto a cold ocean. He was there to meet her, to see her and his sad reaction was obvious. What was her problem? What would she do next time or the time after that? She was either committed or she wasn't and saying yes wouldn't get any easier unless she started. In a few weeks she'd be saying yes to getting laid by some guy she wouldn't know, Jack was simply suggesting a coffee together. "What the hell. Let's do it. Listen, I know a quaint little place where no one knows me, somewhere I've always wanted to try, either never having the time or the company."

"I'm the happiest man on the beach."

"You're the only man on the beach and let's be upfront. No dinner, no expectations and we go in separate cars."

"I agree."

"Then I won't be long. Wait for me to pull in front then follow."

Her smile didn't fade as she swivelled from her hips and walked away, looking over her shoulder half expectantly to see his face blocked out by the lens of his SLR. Jack Caden hadn't made a mistake waking to plan his day and hoping for the impossible. She was searching for something. Why else would she be with him on a Saturday afternoon and not her family? Lowering his camera he thought the multiple shots would make an irresistible slide show on his computer and taking his eyes from her as she walked farther away was impossible, his imagination temporarily deactivated. He doubted whether any detail of her body would surprise him. All he wanted at the moment was her, any way she would allow and he followed when the MX-5 drove up without slowing.

*

Kathy arrived home four hours later in the dark with a small bag of groceries, ignoring Melissa's horrified expression.

"Where were you, Kath? I was expecting to see you when I got home and what's with the World War II stripper costume? Don't you think an entire afternoon is a little long for one bag of food?"

"Where was I? No. Where were you...last night on my birthday and our anniversary?"

"I hear you weren't home either."

"I went to dinner, a very expensive one you're paying for and that's not my gift. You owe me for a set of wheels and I want the cheque tonight for one thousand, plus eight hundred for meals and taxis over the past week. You did get the message, I presume, and I wasn't joking. Your car stays here from now on. And before you ask about the skis, I'm flying to Vermont for a long weekend with the girls in January. So make plans to be here and, for your information, this is one of three après-ski outfits I intend to wear. You're also buying Timothy another guitar, since you did smash the other one."

"You've lost your mind woman." He swung on Timothy. "You'll get another guitar, kid, the day you cremate me." Then he swirled on Melissa. "And you, it's high time you stopped acting like a frigging prima donna around here and began doing your share. I swear, young lady, I'll rip off whatever piece of new clothing I see you wearing. This is my goddamn house, not yours, and neither is the money coming into it." He threw out a finger to Kathy. "And you call yourself a counsellor. No wonder you bring in so little."

"Yes, and at the moment I'm wondering what I should call you. Would you care to explain why you didn't come home on Friday or where you were, or why you left on Monday?"

"You can go to bloody hell, all of you. I'll be in my office."

"Take a pillow. I mean it." Ted fumed, halted by Kathy's finger. "Don't dare to even think of saying what's on your mind. In this outfit I could convert a priest or a choirboy and, believe me, I will. You're right, Ted. Things will change around here, starting with you, starting on January 07th and you will be home or these two gems are going to Miami for Spring break and I'm heading to the Caribbean...alone."

Ted stormed out and Kathy turned to Timothy. "You're getting a guitar. Our agreement stands and," she reached into her purse, "here's your phone. This is your last chance, Timothy. One more indecent act and the police will deal with you, not me. And Melissa, no more attitude. I'm doing this for me, not to shock you. Anything you might think matters not at all to me. Keep your snide comments to yourself. I was pregnant at your age, with you. I'm thirty-six, not a hundred and the youngest mother at the PTA. So get used to it or get out. But before you do, cook supper for your brother, don't bother me for the rest of the evening and set the alarm."

She placed the bag on the table, poured a glass of wine and went upstairs to her room. She left Jack at the bistro where the two spent the afternoon enjoying a light lunch and lounging on a comfy sofa by the fireplace drinking hot toddies. She had never sat beside a man so comfortably. She liked the feeling, the closeness, projecting her mind forward to January, imagining how easy the transition would be from neglected wife to some ski bum's fantastic memory. And she would be fantastic. Jack would definitely have lucked out at the ski lodge, now somebody else would. Jack was simply too close and she wasn't prepared to let Ted get off paying less than the maximum penalty because of poor judgement and untimely weakness on her part. She had yet to rethink her future beyond the obvious and satisfying selfish carnal urges and any unforeseeable regret would be unconscionable.

They spoke about Christmas. She was going to Miami. He was staying home. He'd never been to Miami. He had thought of going somewhere, to meet someone, realizing or assuming vacation romances never lasted and since meeting her he had set the bar too high. She would celebrate New Year's Eve with friends, as usual. He wasn't decided, thinking he might book a dinner show at the casino and when he enquired about her upcoming Girls' Night, she honestly didn't know where, which was just as well, she mused, and purposely didn't tell him of the ski weekend. Being with Jack for the entire afternoon fortified her. Touching him and being touched by him convinced her. She needed more from life and she was ready, certain that if he knew about Vermont he would be the man in her bed.
*

Jack understood and didn't press. She was married with kids and despite liking her job she wanted a lot more which didn't include jeopardizing a new relationship or closure with the old. He wasn't much different. He once thought his life was on track, that nothing could go wrong, until he found himself alone.

He did admit to thinking of Kathy often since the Thursday at the casino, and would for a very long time. Committed to living near or by the ocean he didn't see how he could stop thinking of her and perhaps someday, when she was ready, they would meet and make the boardwalk theirs. At that she touched the back of her hand to his cheek, not expecting he would pull her close and kiss her lips. She didn't pull away and what remained of the fleeting afternoon by the fireplace was subdued, Jack thinking aloud in a murmur how the bistro would be a perfect place for any snowy and cold Saturday afternoon. Kathy moaned a dreamy "yeah," crossing her arms and stretching towards the heat and flickering flames.

They left together, pausing in the foyer to don their coats and gloves. A formal goodbye would have seemed silly, an impersonal hug inappropriate, heralding no hope, so they kissed neither hesitantly nor quickly and pulled away, each heart pounding. Words would have ruined the moment. He quietly pushed open the door and watched her disappear between rows of cars and onto the road. He would see her again one winter's day or in the spring. One clear afternoon she would see him standing at the shore and know he was waiting to kiss her once more, to take her in his arms and love her.

Twenty

Apologies from Ted came late Sunday afternoon after Kathy spent her day cleaning the house and generally avoiding him. He wrote one cheque to cover half the restaurant bill and one for five-hundred, what he might have spent for her birthday and anniversary combined, though he did clean his office, his private domain, and closed the door. No way was he paying to winterize a midlife crisis. Melissa was behind her closed door, writing in her diary, Kathy thought, writing about her trashy mother who went into town the day before with her practically bare ass hanging out. She had begun washing and drying her clothes a couple of years earlier, claiming feminine privacy issues and when she did she mixed in the pieces of her costumes from the previous week.

She wouldn't be taking crap from her mother much longer, she wrote. She would bide her time till her eighteenth birthday, let her parents pay for her acting classes at university, her dorm room and her phantom summer job would ostensibly begin the week of her graduation. Business had increased dramatically since her titillating announcement. She no longer needed them. She was independent. On December 31st her business would grow exponentially and over the summer months the current two hours each night would become six or seven hours in her own condo. She giggled and closed the diary, reclining onto her bed and setting the buzzer function on her cell. She was never late for a curtain call.

Timothy was in his room, texting his friends, setting himself up for New Year's Eve and Ted was in his bedroom packing for an early flight, waiting for Kathy to speak, to say anything that would break the weekend's icy barrier. His discomfort was palpable. She knew why and decided not to make his leaving any easier. He couldn't judge what he couldn't hear and her smug silence made him angrier.

"So, Kath, are we good…with the cheques."

"Yes. Actually, I wasn't expecting more."

He exhaled air he hadn't inhaled. "And Christmas, are the old folks set up?"

"Christmas is done. I'm sending the gifts by courier this week. Call them yourself if you need more information."

"No need. Listen, this promotion thing, and the weekend, I don't know how to explain it. I know you're not to blame. You didn't know, but the car, all your clothes and another wardrobe with skis and boots for a weekend we can't afford. This all has to stop. The girl's leaving for university in a few months. I don't know. How did you expect me to react?"

"I spent my money, not yours. I also paid cash. This house has no mortgage thanks to your parents and she's going through her entire four years at university thanks to my small inheritance and what she'll earn over the summer. As for Timothy, if someone's short-sighted enough to accept him, we'll have saved enough by the time he's ready unless you screw up at work. So what's your problem, Mr. Freebie Lexus?"

"Property taxes, food, clothes, vacations, four flights to Miami, four flights to Myrtle Beach for Spring Break, music lessons, computers and phone bills with not enough left over for simple home renovations. Did I mention ski trips?"

"Did I mention I'm paying?"

"This has to stop."

"What you mean to say is: this should have happened long ago. Look, we should never have had the kids. But you got lucky, I got knocked up and we should have named the second one Compounded Error. He should never have happened. Thursday was the first time I went out since I don't know when, I've driven a shitbox for as long and my clothes weren't good enough for the nearly new store. And you, you're gone six days a week wearing eight-hundred dollar suits, living in luxury off your expenses and don't think for a moment I'm naïve enough to believe you're not dipping into someone's candy dish. Is this rocket science, Ted? Something you don't understand?"

"What I don't understand is where we're headed."

"Don't ask me. I'm the new Kathy. You should have asked the old one while she was still around. This me doesn't know you well enough to answer. I possibly won't mind your travel schedule; perhaps I'll prefer you being gone. I don't know. I suppose I will in time, eventually. More importantly, I'm discovering myself and whatever I have to discover about you can wait unless you'd rather tell me who you're screwing and we can cut to the chase."

"This is nonsense. The reason I travel so much is for you and them and this is the thanks I get. So I get home Saturday instead of midnight Friday. So what? When was the last time you saw someone running to the door?"

Kathy smiled. "Maybe she does. Why don't you tell me?"

"There's nothing to tell. And this isn't a good time. I shouldn't have started, what with the HO party, Christmas, the New Year's party down the road and your frigging trip, which we still have to talk about. You should have cleared that with me. You know the first week of the year is critical for business."

"Talk to yourself about it. I'm going. I live with you one day a week, I don't report to you, Ted. You will either be here while I'm gone or take full responsibility. I'm leaving Thursday afternoon until Sunday. Farm them out. Do what you have to do. I've done my time. Kathy Burberry is moving on."

Twenty-One

The conversation ended and Ted went to bed feeling guilty, missing Eileen's warmth nestled into his side. He didn't hate Kathy; he simply couldn't bring himself to like or love her. She was in the way and, once gone, he doubted he would ever think of the kids. They were draining him and Kathy was no better, yet he couldn't afford to leave. She would crucify him in court and she was playing a game he was beginning to understand. She was forcing him to leave, forcing him to make the decision. He did have to go. Eileen wouldn't wait forever. One day she would tire of old Kimberly, divorce him and not be satisfied with a frequent visitor.

Ted felt trapped lying in bed facing away from Kathy, feeling her glare drilling into his back as he listened intently for each page to turn, for the slightest movement, her slightest breath, waiting for her to extinguish the light and come to bed thinking the worst, despising him. He hoped she would read through the night, let him be, and when he woke near 3:00 AM to dress and leave for the airport she was sleeping peacefully on her récamier.

Melissa had fallen asleep barely thirty minutes earlier.

When Kathy woke she lay still, remembering the warmth of Saturday's fire and the kiss. If she left Ted she would be awarded half of what she would gain if he left her, which, according to the terms of their marriage contract, would amount to half his yearly salary until the youngest

129

child was eighteen, the house and half his personal savings. He'd be left with fifty K, a company car and expenses, able to travel and screw around to his heart's content. He'd do fine. So why didn't he stay away when he obviously wanted out? Or was she any better or worse? Why was she staying when she obviously wanted out? She was worth two and a half million, possibly more depending on the coming months. The answer wasn't money. It was the house. Of course she would manage well enough with only a third of his income and savings. She could live very well without it, but she would have Timothy for one more year and her newly acquired lifestyle would abruptly be taken from her. Ted had to go, and one day he would. She thought of telling him at one time, believing the revelation of her true inheritance would make him drop dead in which case she would technically be a murderess. So perhaps Darlene, Sheila and Michelle had created the ideal solution. Perhaps she and Ted were waiting for the same thing: Timothy's eighteenth birthday.

She heard the front door slam shut, swung her legs to the side and walked out into the hallway to see the local bus disappearing down the winding road. She went to the kitchen for a coffee, savouring the quiet and called the dean's office to advise that she'd be arriving late.
*

Jack Caden went home Saturday to change for a dinner out after he finished transferring the file from his camera to the computer. With his slide show on high speed the few dozen shots brought Kathy instantly to life on the screen. He sighed deeply, blowing a narrow stream of air, watching her walk away with smooth, long strides, the way she did from the restaurant into the cold night without saying goodbye, without glancing over her shoulder. He shook his head. Once more he let her slip away when not touching her intimately was so incredibly difficult. He wanted desperately to feel the smoothness of her skin, the soft firmness of her breasts and her buttocks, her warmth and the strength of her legs and her arms, the eagerness of her fingertips and the sweet hotness of her breath. He wanted to believe that one day he would, when she was ready, when she would come to him. Yet he worried. She was searching, without knowing for whom or for what and he might not be close when finally she discovered her truth.

Would she find another Jack Caden in a restaurant or in a bar? Would she be easily swayed by practiced words and tender touches? Would she remember him, think of him and one day search for him? Would he be the one she was searching for? Would she ever love him? Or would she discover her truth too late and never know how much she might have loved him? He didn't know. He couldn't be certain. His one certainty was having discovered her and he didn't want to lose her once more.

Sunday was no better. Kathy prefaced his every thought until at last he sought solace in his work to the point of utter fatigue and drifted into an uneasy sleep to relive her gentle touch.

*

Monday, December 07th, Clint Evans sat in his SUV beyond sight of the house, watching the boy and girl climb the steps of the bus. The girl looked nothing like the mother and the boy just looked stunned. Throughout the previous week Kathy Burberry left her house the same time each day, precisely ten minutes later. Thursday and Friday he timed his passage in front of the house from the opposite direction to see her drive from her garage, wait for the door to close, travel the length of her driveway and disappear from his rear-view mirror. Monday he wrongly anticipated nothing would change. An hour later she still hadn't exited and he was frustrated by not knowing why. Two hours later he assumed she was ill and thought to return another day, until he saw the red MX-5 speed down the driveway. He waited ten minutes.

When he was certain, he drove to the house with the beak of his cap pulled down, stopping the vehicle at the rear patio with the tags facing into the trees and the VIN covered on the dash. The closest window was at the garage and, peering through, seeing the Lexus, he instantly recoiled. With his back to the wall he controlled his breathing. The man should have gone by then and if he wasn't he had probably seen the SUV driving in. Clint hurried to the front door. If no one answered he was good to go. If someone did, he'd be a contractor who had gone to the wrong house.

He rang four times, a minute apart, the sticker warning of central security clear as day. The guy was either gone, in the shower or dead. Clint waited a minute longer and rang twice more. No one was home. He had done preliminary work the previous week. The garage doors were at the far side with windows at the front and rear and partially hidden from the road. The upper and lower front windows were country-style with small panes and open to view, the door was steel reinforced, the garage doors would be locked electronically and the windows were hermetic.

At the rear the kitchen windows were single-hung with contacts and the door was solid. The dining room window was hermetic, the boy's bedroom window was fitted with a contact and a cluttered desk lay directly beneath. The girl's room was equally problematic. Her bed was under a window fitted with a contact and even doing a perfect job with glass cutters and suction cups he would never be a hundred percent certain and certainty was primordial. The upper floor had two large bay windows, neither of which would open and a narrow single-hung window in-between which he assumed was a hallway with likely fewer obstacles. Although he preferred the boy's ground floor room, the bottom pane of the upper window was smaller and would be easier to clean up and repair.

Those were his options and either way he would have to move quickly once inside. The telephone line was at the rear corner of the garage and the utility line ran to the same pole. What he hadn't seen the previous week was a siren, despite having checked the roof as best he could from each corner, quickly circling the house with his face covered while looking for camera lenses. He had found nothing to discourage him and he'd come prepared.

He dragged the extension ladder from the SUV, hopeful he hadn't misjudged the height to the second story. He didn't like heights at all, or the fact that the top rung barely managed to rest against the gutters leaving a full two metres at a thirty degree angle to the base of the window. He cursed a slew of prison words and began climbing, not looking down or up, his eyes focused on his hands. When he neared the top he grabbed onto the gutters, leaned forward onto the shingles and kept going until his feet left the final rung and he heard the scraping sound of metal on metal followed by a loud clatter.

He spread his hands and feet as far apart as he could, arched his body to see between his legs and muttered a less than blessed benediction. Crawling the final few centimetres to the window he fell flat, afraid to do anything including staying as he was. He raised one hand to the window's ledge, then the other, bringing his face level with the bottom of the pane, cursing himself, suddenly realizing she wasn't worth the trouble. He had to stand. He had to see all four corners behind the pane to be certain. Either way he would have to repair the broken glass.

Pressed against the window he examined one side, the other and the centre. He couldn't believe what he wasn't seeing. The window had no contact and was unlocked: impossible! Someone must have nailed it shut from the inside. He put a gloved hand to the pane, pushing upward and the window obeyed. Getting inside would be a piece of cake, unless someone realized the careless faux-pas that evening and he'd be back to square one. He eased back centimetre by centimetre, lying flat, rolling over as cautiously as he could, his heart practically bursting to a complete stop. The drop to the ground was six metres, not easy, but doable. The drop to Ocean View Road was a staggering half-kilometre or more at the bottom of a nearly vertical and wide open slope that would scare the hell and anything else out of any skier.

His day was done. He accomplished what he came to do and he wanted a drink. The problem was getting to it. He lay back, flat, shimmying with painful slowness until his feet touched the gutters, slowing until his knees touched the metal and then the backs of his thighs. He stayed there, inert, his torso rigid, half on half off, his legs dangling in the air, thinking which way to roll and deciding to the left while focusing on the gutters and wondering how he would explain his broken legs to the ambulance technicians. He didn't want to land on the ladder and he weighed too much to rely on the gutters to ready himself before letting go. He rolled, grabbing with one hand and missing with the other, dangling, landing with a grunt an arm's length shy of the ladder and lay motionless controlling his breathing.

His first drink of the day was seldom before early evening, though Monday Clint had a bottle of wine with a seafood platter lunch. He deserved. He also decided to forego his usual reconnaissance of clubs and restaurants for the coming business weekend, thinking he would drive to another city for a complete change of venue. He had too much on his mind, too much to think about, too much to prepare. In twenty-four hours he would learn a good deal about Kathy Burberry, Kim Moon's mirrored image. The likeness couldn't be more staggering or unnerving.

Monday night he reviewed the To-Do list. Everything was set. Tuesday he would watch her leave, yet want her to stay, to see her, speak with her and touch her. That night long ago he would have killed her, strangling the cold, detached expression from her face. Now he didn't think he would or could. This Kim was different. K-A-T-H-Y was different. She would never think to do the unthinkable. He would forgive her, redeem her and love her the way he always had.

Twenty-Two

Clint's Tuesday began at 5:00 AM, believing the wine at noon and the few evening cocktails helped to restore his body from any harm he might have sustained by the jolting collision with the ground. He reviewed his list once more, stopped along the way for breakfast and arrived at Kathy's minutes before the bus drove off. Ten minutes later the red MX-5 left as he finished what was left of his coffee.

He followed her at a distance and when she veered onto Ocean View Road he did a one-eighty. The Lexus hadn't moved. He dragged the ladder from the SUV, slung a canvas bag over his shoulder and climbed. At the top, he stopped, taking a drill from his bag and drilling a hole into the gutter through which he passed the cord he had attached to the ladder. He dropped the bag, made his way cautiously to the window and grinned widely. They hadn't locked it and he made his way to terra firma to store one bag and take up another.

At the Network Interface Device he cut the lock and took a deep breath, estimating he would have fifteen seconds once he snipped the wires. If for some reason he overlooked an exterior siren, he'd get the hell away pronto and devise another way to meet her. He set his chronograph, reached into the bag for the wire cutters, located the ring and tip wires and severed the link to the central security service. The interior siren's shrill sounded instantaneously,

136

barely audible to anyone hundreds of metres away through a forest of trees, he thought without slowing his pace.

At five seconds he was at the top of the ladder, at ten he scrambled through the window, sprawling across the floor, located the screeching pitch and at fifteen he was in the foyer reaching easily to tear away the wires leading to the horn. He was in and sank onto the bench to catch his breath.

The entranceway was large, leading into a living room and dining room which he thought looked more like showrooms. Conversely, the kitchen was expansive with a definite lived-in look and nothing he saw was bargain basement. The Burberrys did alright for themselves. The first door he tried opened into a bathroom. Next was the boy's room, which he searched quickly: marginally neat with nothing electronic, no girlie magazines, no photos of girlfriends, and not much of anything in his desk. Timmy was either gay or a geek.

The next door was the girl's room: pink, with a single wall covered in posters of groups he had no idea about and no electronics, which wasn't surprising on a school day and a collection of stuffed animals. The diary by her bed didn't interest him. He didn't care who the first or last guys were to feel her up or get into her pants. Then he opened her closet to a tight row of short skirts, no dresses, twenty or thirty blouses and sweaters and a Christmas bag telling him to stay out: her gifts for her mommy and daddy. He looked in, chortling, realizing immediately that little Melissa wasn't so little and he searched more thoroughly through her dresser, her desk, under the bed and in her suitcases. The suitcases: a cache of thongs, bras, wigs, glasses and make-up for the quintessential nurse, schoolgirl, secretary or femme fatale du jour.

He was right. Melissa wasn't so innocent. She was a party girl, a naughty girl and, he guessed, an absolute hit with the boys. He made a mental note to learn more about her very soon, resisting the temptation to freak her out by taking a pair of panties from the Christmas bag. He was anxious to see behind the final door, a room he hadn't identified from the outside: Burberry's unadorned and boring office. Where photos of his beautiful wife might have adorned the walls, Burberry had hung awards, group photos of men smiling for whatever reason: job security, placating the boss or impressing the wife. Corporate bullshit at its finest, Clint thought. One desk drawer was unlocked, crowded with pens, markers and useless paraphernalia. The other was locked and he went to the closet where, behold, he saw the sacrosanct safe, a challenge for yet another day. Mr. Burberry had secrets and Clint was becoming increasingly curious.

Next he returned to the point of entry on the second floor, to what he thought must be the family room which was pristine with not a speck of dust or a single scuff mark on the floor, though the next door was pay dirt: Kathy's bedroom, her boudoir where she slept and dreamt of a better life. One side of the walk-in closet was Burberry's which he ignored. The other was Kathy's and he inspected each article, not remotely surprised the woman was acquainted with fashion. She always was. Her drawers were filled with delicate panties and this time he did take a pair, admiring her embroidered bras, nylons and garter belts. She had style and in the bathroom he saw where she showered, bathed, sat, and where she did her make-up. The one place he hadn't investigated was the closet in the hallway and, when he did, he went to her bedroom to remove the bench at the foot of the bed which wasn't enough, so he went downstairs to the garage.

The stepladder was ideal for the task and Burberry had thoughtfully left a flashlight readily available. The access panel to the attic pushed away easily and he peered in. The open area was cavernous and black, something else he didn't like. He threw his loose change into the dark and listened for any sound other than the soft clattering of a dozen bouncing coins. He heard nothing and heaved himself upward, twisting, drawing in his legs and directing the yellow beam to the ceiling, creating an eerie smoky affect. The floor was solid, covered with plywood, the walls and ceiling panelled with drywall which he thought was either overkill or someone's plans not seen through to fruition. Kathy Burberry kept an immaculate home and, whether she knew or not, her attic was no less perfect.

He eased his way out, replaced the cover, returned the ladder and flashlight to their rightful places and went to the kitchen where he poured a glass of wine, made a sandwich and went upstairs to her bedroom. He lay on her bed contemplating Kathy, so beautiful and elegant, sexy and captivating, the locked drawer, the safe and the bipolar girl who liked to play dress up.

Not all was right on the home front. Kathy's clothes were all new, some with tags still attached. A ski outfit hung in her closet, curiously not in his and Clint saw only one pair of never used skis in the garage. The bed was dressed in satin sheets, yet all the other sets were percale. Why was she sleeping alone on a Tuesday in satin sheets and fine lingerie and why would a man lock a drawer unless he didn't trust his family? The safe he understood, nothing else.

The Louis something or other writing desk beside the peculiar looking sofa in the alcove off to the side suddenly drew his attention. One wall was lined with books of every description, romantic and historical novels being the most numerous, the other walls were wallpapered with scenes of another era. His sense was that Kathy was a hopeless romantic, or hopelessly ignored. In one drawer he found an address book, scented writing paper and pens, jewellery in another and he wondered who had actually bought most of the ruby, emerald and sapphire pieces. Kim had always worn jade, diamonds, and particularly obsidian to match her sinister side which he discovered all too late with his head pressed into the cold, wet asphalt.

Another drawer contained a drier, a curler, a comb set, make-up and other sundries important to a woman and apparently he'd saved the best for last. The fourth drawer held one envelope of flight coupons for Miami at Christmas, another for Myrtle Beach in March with confirmed reservations for hotel and a car, and a third containing a single coupon for a flight to Vermont in January and a three-day stay at the White Cliff Lodge. He also found passports, an invitation to a New Year's party and a tiny velvet box. Kathy was going to Vermont in January alone, hence the skis and new clothes and possibly with the women he'd seen her with at the restaurant before he followed her into the bar. And when he opened the box he was honestly shocked. He wasn't expecting to see such tiny bikinis, one in particular that was miniscule, whose top she either misplaced or didn't exist. He hoped the latter and knew exactly how every naked curve would look. What he questioned was when and where she would wear it.

The difficult quandaries were: what to do and when. The resolution was much simpler: He would once again sleep with her, feel her and love her. Kathy Burberry would not escape him. He had gone in blind with no idea what to expect and certainly wasn't disappointed with what he did see and learn. Next he would determine how best to meet her, in what timeframe and under what circumstances. Her work schedule would end in a few weeks and she'd be gone for the better part of a week, after which she would travel to Vermont, possibly doing something he didn't want to imagine and in March she would fly to South Carolina with Burberry and the spawn.

So what were his options and how quickly would he

have to act? He wanted her so urgently he could taste her pungency, smell her, yet she would never want him as an ex-con and manipulator of women. Or could he somehow transform into someone she could love and adore. He didn't know. All he could do was plan and execute the perfect set of circumstances, which he couldn't do from her bedroom inhaling her lingering scent and wanting her. He had to clear his mind, leave her and calculate the outcome as he had done every other day since his release. He would be of two minds. He would delight in the quest, anticipating each stage of the process with fresh strategies and the subsequent invasion of her mind and body would not be detached as with the others. Collectively they were his job and his survival, separately they were quickly forgotten.

Kathy was one, unique, the one he could love as ardently and as eagerly as he once did and ask nothing of her in return. She would be a distinct target, sequestered in his mind and protected from the engine of his everyday existence. He would distance himself at the beginning from the emotional and certain outcome, remaining focused and determined until the timing was right for Kathy Burberry to fully understand the depth of his passion for the woman he would never stop loving and never stop hating.

He looked at his watch, left the drawer open and went to her bed to smooth her sheets and duvet, sweeping the crumbs onto the plate and taking away the wineglass. In the kitchen he washed and replaced them, put the corked wine bottle into his bag, put on his gloves and climbed the stairs to the hallway window where he dropped the bag before returning to the bedroom. He took the three envelopes and passports from the drawer to the office where he first photocopied the detailed personal information, the itineraries, Kathy's flight coupons, and pressed the OFF button with one bothersome question still nagging his subconscious mind. Why would a man with a safe also lock his desk drawer?

He hurried from the office to the garage, searching through drawers and cabinets until he found a set of precision screwdrivers conducive to his the purpose. He knelt under the desk, selected the smallest diametre of hardened steel and centred the tumbler to the flashlight's dim halo. He snorted. Someone else was as interested in the drawer's contents as he and Burberry would have no idea about the amateur's scratches unless he typically got on his knees to insert his key from under the desk.

Clint's expertise gained from years of free time hadn't diminished and within seconds the drawer opened. The scotch bottle was half-full, the glass was smudged from frequent use and the woman captured in the photo album was not Kathy. She was about Kathy's age, a little taller and definitely good-looking, but not Kathy. She had written "Love, Eileen" in stylish script with the thick ink of a fountain pen across the inside of the cover. How cute, he thought? And who was this Eileen, frozen in time? He slouched into Burberry's chair, studying the first photo of the woman strutting her stuff, emerging demurely and naked from a turquoise sea with long shadows preceding her, coated with glistening clear water and long dark hair flowing over bare shoulders. Eileen belonged in a briefcase or wallet, anywhere but a drawer and he searched further with the utmost care without any success. What fool would keep a photo album of his girlfriend in a drawer that any kid with a toothpick could open, or did? Eileen had to be a full-time girlfriend. Why take the risk otherwise?

So Burberry was doing the dirty with Eileen in some Pacific coast paradise while his wife was at home suckling the brats. He chuckled, thinking how he now shared the intimate details of Eileen's body with Burberry. He could also perfectly envision how Kathy would look lying beside him. In another life, she might have been Kim's twin sister.

What he would do with the information was another matter. He replaced the bottle and casually flipped through the pages of the album studying the details of each pose. When he was finished he closed the drawer feeling aroused by the illicit images, jiggled the cheap mechanism until the lock caught, adjusted the chair and left. He was that much closer.

Retracing his footsteps since his arrival and looking for the slightest sign of trespass brought him to the drawer in her bedroom and the hallway window. Crawling out, he hurled everything across the two-metre span of roof to the ground, closed the window and climbed down as gingerly as he could manage. Five minutes later the tip and ring wires were connected, the siren didn't sound and he left thinking of Kathy, Kim and their next intimate evening together.

*

Three hours later Melissa came home with her brother. At 5:00 Kathy walked in and spent an hour teaching her disinterested daughter more culinary techniques. At 6:00 the kids went to their rooms with full plates and Kathy ate alone in the quiet of her dining room, dressed in stockings, an A-line skirt and silk blouse, determined not to give up. She was a vibrant woman and someday someone would notice her. Someone already had and she cried into her napkin thinking she hadn't looked back at him.

What would she do to one day see him in the warm and quiet ambiance of the bistro, one cold and snowy winter's day? She was attracted to him. They were attracted to each other, possibly for the wrong reasons. She didn't know. He was alone, taking his time, waiting to find the ideal woman. He wasn't jumping into another failed romance; while she was planning to give herself wantonly for a night or a weekend to someone she hadn't yet met to either spite her husband or catapult her from desperation into a new existence. What would he think of her then? He had come

143

to her at the wrong time and in the wrong place. Why hadn't he come to her in Vermont? Why hadn't he kissed her again by the fire or at the door? Timothy would turn eighteen in fourteen months when nothing would matter including Ted. Why hadn't she told him so?

She finished her dinner and went to her bedroom, no longer needing to create the heroine's white knight in her mind. At least until January he would be tall, lean and dark with clear hazel eyes and gallant. She wasn't sad. That's not why she cried. She was angry for once being a football jock's summertime interim lay, for being so stupid and that her father's thoughtless sense of righteous propriety had condemned her to so many unhappy years. She was angry because she would go through with her illicit escapade. She would cheat on her husband with a stranger because Jack Caden found her too soon and in the wrong place. He was too close, too accessible and she didn't trust herself not to ruin her life by jeopardizing what she had already accomplished.

Twenty-Three

The remainder of Clint Evans' week went quickly. He decided against travelling to another city. The weather was worsening and the Christmas party season was in full swing. He realized he'd be travelling in a direction opposite to a seasonally high influx of potential single, married and inebriated women who would refuse helpful lifts home with co-workers, take hotel rooms for whatever reason or simply want to let the good times roll, which was his raison d'être above all else and he was committed to that all-important ambition.

His latest reconnaissance of suitable nearby venues was minimal, well below his established norm, though he hadn't repeated a single location thus far. His current logic being that the joy of Christmas and the artificial closeness of friends and colleagues would dull the mind and, very likely, in conjunction with booze, make his festive season the most joyous in five years.

However uppermost on his mind until late Thursday afternoon were Kathy Burberry and what to do about her. He didn't know what he might do with her passport information and what he'd gleaned pertaining to three specific sets of travel dates. He tried creating a specific reason in his mind for returning to the house, a specific need with a resultant value he could justify without the fear of punitive consequences. With snow falling daily he could expect accumulation in the driveway and on the roof. His tracks might not cover over in time and she would know someone had come to her house during the day, or he might possibly be seen by a neighbour who would certainly call the police. At best he would track in snow or ice from his gloves and boots which would mean time lost cleaning unless he slipped from the ladder and broke his neck on the frozen ground. And, whenever she might think to lock the window, he'd be royally screwed. Of paramount importance was meeting her.

Since visiting the house his mind filled with and flushed out countless flawed scenarios, meticulously correlating each action to the objective and weighing any possible consequence against the likelihood of success, each time obliterating the concept and starting afresh. He needed to know everything about her before acting, which he didn't, and knowing her husband was double-dipping wasn't enough. He needed to know more about Burberry and his biggest challenge would be the Eileen woman. The man travelled weekly and would be impossible to follow, which wasn't the greatest issue. His biggest concern was when Burberry would leave home or return on any given week, not to mention the girl with her costumes and Kathy's recent wardrobe. Something wasn't right. Maybe Kathy did know about Eileen, the booze in the locked drawer and perhaps seducing her wouldn't be as difficult as previously thought. He had much to consider over the next few weeks. The one time he could safely meet her alone would be in Vermont, which he couldn't deny was compelling. Yet how would he explain being at a ski lodge hundreds of kilometres away when he couldn't ski, hated the cold and lived so close to her hometown door? He couldn't, not without first contriving to bump into her locally, which was practically impossible in the short time remaining.

No. He would let her go. Being with her again was too important to rush. She would come to him in time, of her own volition. In two weeks she would leave for Miami, New Years was out of the question and she would return from Vermont on the 10th. In the meantime he would put her out of his mind. He didn't want to think about Vermont, about what she might do if, in fact, she did know about the booze and a loving Eileen. Two weekends remained to close his year and the woman at the end of the bar was smiling, accepting his first drink. He nodded once, his eyes sparking with thanks for not embarrassing him with a public rejection. He signalled the barman, ordered another as he pushed his old-fashioned to the edge of the bar and stepped from his stool.

He had discarded his few original suits, his taste becoming more exclusive and expensive. He was no longer a failed Account Manager of a bygone era or an ex-con. He was an executive in all aspects save his credentials, which no one cared about. No one ever asked their doctor, banker or priest how far from the median they'd succeeded, nor would anyone think to impugn a superior calling by scrutinizing poorly framed and yellowing certificates hanging on the wall. The masses discovered the ills of duplicity the hard way: by agony, going broke or going to hell unredeemed.

He extended his hand, introducing himself. The woman graciously proffered her own. He would remember her name until remembering was no longer important, when any name would do. She would survive, they would all survive, though none would forget the torment of shame, the burden of indebtedness and the devil in a tailor-made suit.

Twenty-Four

The anchorman's day was at an end, anxious to escape his blonde bookends for the weekend. He wished Clint "a good one" through the flat screen as though he actually meant what he was saying without knowing what kind of night Clint had experienced or what kind of day lay ahead. In short: the man didn't care, nor would he on Monday. Say something often enough the same way and people will see you as shallow and insincere, Clint thought. Look into the eyes; see what they need or want to hear and you'll gain their trust.

The woman from the evening before had come from a party on one of the floors below, managing to escape the boredom of service awards, speeches and monotonous applause. She hadn't gone expecting to cement her job for the coming year by ingratiating herself with management, nor had anyone nominated her for the best of anything. She went to dance and party, which was to happen eventually in the private ballroom if anyone was left standing or conscious and after making herself visible during the cocktail hour and dinner she was discreetly out of sight and mind.

They enjoyed a few drinks and conversation which flowed from social to quietly unrestrained and uninhibited by the time Clint suggested winding their way to the top-floor dance lounge. He wanted to continue a perfect evening and gaze out over the city's colourful palette of lights diffused by the far reaching curtain of delicate newborn snowflakes. A once in a lifetime event, he enticed. Never again would either one witness such a beautiful backdrop to an even more splendid evening he didn't want to end and they danced until he could feel the weight of her slender body heavier in his arms.

He walked her to her room, took the card and opened the door. Once inside, he kissed her in the darkness, tasting and smelling her, letting his eyes adjust naturally as he held her closely without feeling the need to hurry. She wasn't resisting, neither was he. She had recently arrived in the city. She was divorced and not necessarily looking for love. She was comfortable with being mid-thirties and single, though she wasn't ignoring the calendar either. She had no family, didn't want one and was working on a provisional basis as a claims adjustor for the city's largest insurance company. What she did want was a fresh beginning with someone who would never hurt her, rather love her and respect her, someone whom she would love forever which, of course, eliminated Clint from the running. What was with women nearing the slippery slope of middle-age?

He kissed her again, swept her into his arms, carried her to the bed and laid her down. He sat on the edge beside her and kissed her once more. Her slightly parted lips were full, tasting of raspberries and unresponsive. He waited a moment, watching her breasts rising and falling to a dreamy rhythm. He cupped one, then the other, taking a deep breath and sighing. He reached for the clutch she let drop to the floor. She lived on the far side of town, in a first-floor apartment, her single credit card had seldom been swiped, six ten-dollar bills were folded in half and her bank balance was a paltry 800. She was indeed starting over. He went to the closet. She had come to the party from the office and would wear the same daytime clothes home in the morning.

At the mini-bar he drained three bottles into a glass and

dropped onto the sofa in the dark, perplexed by his quandaries and staring at her. He liked what he was seeing, not what he was thinking. Undressing her would be a simple matter, the rest even easier. He could be gone within the hour, en route to breakfast at his favourite restaurant, thirty minutes if she fell back to sleep. The dilemmas were: Why would he do anything? She was fast asleep, which was the entire point. Or why wouldn't he, when she had suggested a nightcap? She was attractive and half undressed in her little party dress and evening sandals. Because she would want him to stay, and that he couldn't do.

He downed what was left in the glass. Putting her in debt wasn't the issue, or the eight hundred. She was starting over and so was he. She would survive. The real issue was his integrity, his career and long-term success. If he were to make an exception with her and leave unrewarded, when else would he falter? In his profession single-mindedness was paramount.

He reached into her purse, pinched the six bills between his fingers and went to the bed. Despite the lingering temptation to ease her from her dress, to see her and enrapture her, to leave her with lasting memories and a lesson learned, he slipped off her shoes, covered her with a sheet and walked out swearing he would make up the loss with Saturday's workload.

Twenty-Five

Kathy's week passed with miserable slowness. She thought constantly of Jack, never of Ted and had selected her wardrobe for her upcoming infidelity a dozen times. The women at school never spoke of the 17th. The evening was a given and she was certain Michelle would leave her husband in a blink if not leaving meant forfeiting the January ski weekend.

Thick, wet snowflakes were falling steadily, frequent gusts of wind swirling them into violent tempests and the forecast was predicting several centimetres. No one ever went to the beach in a storm and, even if he did, she would never see him. She could barely see the tall trees descending the steep slope behind her home, let alone the beach or a solitary figure. Her weekend promised absolute monotony and she wanted to scream.

Ted called. The airline cancelled his flight at time of boarding. He didn't know whether he'd be home by Sunday or not. He was sorry. He wasn't able to change his flight the day before. The airport was a zoo. He would keep her posted, however conditions weren't promising. He had taken the precaution of booking a room at a nearby hotel and she could call him on his cell if she needed him. She agreed and said goodbye without saying his name or bothering to call the airline for confirmation. Need him for what, she mused. She didn't know. She couldn't imagine why she would ever need him again, once he divorced her.

And she was adamant that he would divorce her.

Maybe she would drive into town, to the bistro. Jack could possibly be there, waiting. Why not? Why wouldn't he be thinking the same thing? He did say "any snowy and cold afternoon" and the weather couldn't be better suited to an idyllic afternoon by the warmth of a fire. She could take the Lexus, meet him, go home with him, make love and hope someone would see the open windows of the Lexus and the keys. Or she could crash the pretentious thing into a tree while she was still sober. Then she could get drunk and forget him, Ted, and them, the ones who hadn't spoken to her all day.

She poured a glass of wine and went to her retreat, again. Why? When what she truly wanted was nowhere to be found in the house. At eighteen she was already a mother, yet her spoiled daughter couldn't boil water and Timothy…she believed once Timothy left she would never see him again. He wasn't going to university. That was her father's pipe dream. He wanted educated and decent grandchildren capable of discerning right from wrong and had made generous provisions in his will for them in the event his death preceded the happy day. Apart from the million-dollar insurance policy and the five hundred she'd made on the sale of her parent's home, her parents bequeathed an additional quarter-million to that end, an equal amount intended for Melissa and Kathy was the sole executor of the joint estate. The total investment had increased in value over the years to not far from two-point-five-million and Ted was none the wiser.

She had repaid her father every cent of the money she borrowed for her education, a debt which wouldn't burden Melissa or Timothy who didn't know of the pending gift. Their education would be paid in full and each would receive sufficient funds upon graduation to live modestly for six months. However, not graduating would result in complete forfeiture of any part of the inheritance, as would any blatant disregard of her father's dream for any reason. At the end of Timothy's second year at college Melissa would be living on her own. If the boy didn't go, his quarter-million would revert to Kathy in accordance with her father's written stipulation.

Intellectual pursuit wasn't in the cards for Timothy. Thinking at any level was a foreign concept to him, beyond his comprehension if not a complete strain. Whatever he didn't see or feel in the now didn't exist. Thank goodness he could see and touch the microwave and fridge or he'd be completely useless, she thought. She told him what to do for dinner, and Melissa. Whether they did or not was up to them. Her evening was planned and the table was set for one.
*

Ted tossed his cell into his briefcase along with the CD containing all manner of confused airport sounds and piercing commands. Reclining into the down-filled futon he reached for his scotch, kicked off his shoes, kissed Eileen and declared the official beginning of his year's seasonal slow period. What with the cancellations, logic dictated that he stay through to the following weekend and travel to Chicago a day or so earlier to guarantee his and Eileen's arrival. The gofer approved the additional weekend expenses as well as the flight penalties and was anxious to see Ted's lovely wife for the first time since the golf tourney.

"I want to puke, right here, right now."

"Sweetheart, I would prefer you didn't. Please relax. It's our weekend."

"My life's shit."

"Thank you."

"I didn't mean you...not you."

"The key word is "my," sweetheart. Do something about

it. Quit. Leave. Get out. You don't need them. They'd be the ones puking if they knew about the galleries and how close they are to losing you. And don't worry about Kathy. She probably wants you out of her life anyway and so what if she nails you to the wall for the house. Until Timothy's eighteenth birthday we'll adjust your income to appropriately modest levels and her little alimony cheques won't create the smallest blip in the portfolio we'll prepare for you. We don't have much longer to wait, sweetheart. Melissa will soon be out of the way, Timothy will follow a year later, Kathy will be happy with her property and who knows if the kids will even stay in school."

"The girl's headed for no good. She's a tease. I know it. She's no different from her mother and I wouldn't be surprised if she's being done by some dope head. She can't be spending all her time at the mall and the other one can't grab his own ass with both hands if he's not in front of a mirror." He paused, sipping his scotch and looking out to sea. "What the hell did I ever do to deserve any of it?"

"A rhetorical question, sweetheart. You know what you did, and you do it very nicely."

"I love you, Eileen. I always have. Why the hell didn't you come into my life first?"

"You weren't ready for me. You had your path to follow, I had mine."

"Yeah, living eighteen years with an old man who pays you to get him off."

"Don't be crude. It's unbecoming and I would have lived with an old woman for ten K a month. And let's not forget he's indexed my allowance by one thousand yearly. This year's monthly cheques are at twenty-eight K for tucking him in before sleeping in my own bed, not that I need them any longer."

"So divorce him."

"I will, sweetheart, the moment you divorce Kathy."

"I'll go to hell before she gets the house."

"It's a house. This is a home. And you know very well when you say house you mean the million-dollar market value. How many times have I said I'll transfer an equal value to your account here?"

"I don't need charity."

"Not charity, a signing bonus. You know how much I want you at the galleries."

He gulped a mouthful of scotch. Status quo, he thought. He would be an employee, working for his wife, living in a home he could hardly afford and sleeping with the boss. He could never buy into the galleries or be her equal, not even with the million from the sale of his house. The galleries would always be hers, never his. He would always be Mr. Her and the thought of being called Ted Kimberly or Mr. Aubergine made him ill.

"It's coming, Eileen. I promise. I can't take much more of this and neither can old Kimberly, but she is not getting the house."

"Don't worry about Randolph. He's fine and he believes in the written word. What he might suspect or believe doesn't matter. He won't contest a divorce when I ask him. He's done alright by his contract, sweetheart. We both have and his current interests are more mundane in nature. I doubt he'll be very disappointed when I go."

"You have no reason to stay with him."

"Yes, I do, and it's not my monthly allowance. You're the reason, sweetheart. Randolph's my insurance you'll leave Kathy. Erase him from the equation and you'll have no real incentive," she stroked his hair, "unless, of course, I get lonely."

"That's not funny. You're my incentive."

"Then leave her. Give her the house. You don't need it. Take the signing bonus and quit your job."

"I can't. She's as frustrated as I am. She's doing all sorts of crazy things, but she knows she'll lose the house if she leaves first and she's right at the edge. It won't take much more to push her over."

"Then push, darling, before she does. You're fighting over a few dollars, not something you want or need, when what you do need is right here. We both know this can't go on indefinitely and don't you suppose she's figured out why you bought the tickets to Miami and Myrtle Beach instead of using your points? Not liking her doesn't mean she's stupid."

The frosted window panes rattled against the wind. Eileen didn't realize that Ted losing the house would also mean losing his job with no alternative but to marry her. Otherwise he'd be destitute. Chicago Corporate wouldn't tolerate a career-long deception they would certainly discover. Or, possibly Eileen did realize and didn't care. He was becoming a pawn, increasingly pushed by one and pulled by the other without the slightest safety net.

*

Jack Caden peered from his window into a blank canvas of pure white. The wind was loud, threatening any who dared to venture out and he understood. He'd fought his way home from the shop amidst the storm's fury none too soon, each breath and every uncertain step worthwhile. An enlarged photograph of Kathy looking over her shoulder lay framed against the wall.

He questioned the need to dine out that evening, yet a joyless Christmas was looming and he truly would be alone. Christmas always had been a depressing time for him, for them, when the loving couple would escape to the sun, laugh and frolic in the waves, take long walks on white sandy beaches and make love on balconies at sunset. He had never loved any woman as much and one day she was gone. He never saw the end coming and now any beach, particularly one, would bring heartache and loathing for what she had done. She had left him feeling empty and abandoned, unsure and untrusting, fearful of starting over, dreading making the same mistake until one Thursday night when Kathy walked into his life.

He imagined Kathy at home by herself, ignored and neglected, hoping she was thinking of their Saturday together. In five days she would be somewhere close to him, in a downtown bar or restaurant and in eleven days she'd be in Miami with a man she didn't love. And then what? It was a matter of time. Eventually occasional Thursday nights would become frequent nights out and sooner or later some smooth-talking guy with a credit card would seduce her and leave her jaded. He didn't do that. He didn't want her to go and he saw in her eyes that she felt the same, though he understood she was fearful of the path that lay ahead. He could hear the disquiet in her soft voice.

He would finish out the year alone, do his job and start another new year. He would see Kathy again, if being with her meant capturing fleeting moments at a time after standing endless hours at the boardwalk, waiting, or spending snowy afternoons alone by a fire in the hope she would remember his whispered words and come to him. He glanced over to her photograph, absorbing each detail of her body and her eyes. She was lonely and she was beautiful: a dangerous combination. He would see her again, before her pain turned to regret. He went to his computer and opened the calendar to January, blocking out each of the Saturdays but one.
*

Kathy spent the afternoon pampering herself. Housework could wait, she was more important. She dressed for dinner in heels, a short pleated skirt and cashmere sweater. She arranged an elegant place setting and prepared a sumptuous meal of creamed soup, filet mignon, steamed fresh vegetables and a slice of cheesecake, starting off with a glass of Côte-du-Rhône: a reward for what she had accomplished thus far at the health club. She had intentionally bought each piece of her wardrobe one size smaller and now everything fit her perfectly.

She hadn't called Melissa or Timothy to the dinner table, each one drifting from their room to the sounds of Pink Martini and standing side by side at the entrance to the dining room, brother and sister, nonplussed. Kathy interrupted her meal, patted her lips and told them their dinners were in the microwave. She expected quiet, they were to eat in their rooms and dim the kitchen lights on the way out. She warned them not to test the waters and barely managed a smile when duplicate expressions showed neither one understood. Waiting until she was alone she returned to her meal, transported to another world.

Ted called earlier to say he'd be better off staying put and continuing on to Chicago for the party later in the week. Going home simply for a change of clothes and leaving again made no sense. He would be home the following Sunday, he promised, and wouldn't travel until the New Year. Big deal, and she wondered who was holding the cue cards. Nor did he mention the kids or the fact that Christmas shopping was far from complete. Yes, she was in another world, another time. She was in Vermont, in January. Snow was falling; she felt a warm glow from the heat of the fire and the wine, moaning with each probing touch. He was tall, dark and handsome. She was the centre of his universe, nothing else mattered but how he might please her. Yes, she would definitely enjoy her January.

She finished her meal and went to her room without clearing the table. Thursday would come soon enough, leading into another empty weekend and she resolved not to hurry the days. Jack might never return to the bistro and, if he did, he would never know what she had done. She felt sorry for him being alone at Christmas. How quickly would she stay with him, given the chance? And how would she feel in his arms, dancing her way into the New Year. Jack Caden. She knew his name. She looked at phone. The time was 8:50. He wouldn't be home. He ate out most weekends, despising the growing sensation of cabin fever. He might not even be in town. So why would she care about what he would think of her weekend away?

She undressed, letting her clothes fall where she stood, slipping into silk baby dolls and satin sheets. Sunday she would drive Timothy into town in the Lexus and let him select his Christmas gift. Jack wouldn't be listed, but 411 would know his number. But then he knew Kathy, he knew Burberry and he knew no man would answer. She was being silly. Of course he wouldn't call. She was married with kids, non-disposable luggage. But they were disposable. She didn't love Ted. She could scarcely be civil towards him and the kids were living the good life on borrowed time. She was resolute in her decision regarding the inheritance. House or no house, she would not give over hundreds of thousands of dollars to someone who didn't love her unless her father's wishes were respected to the letter. Once they dropped out the funds would stop and they would work at summer jobs. In her heart she realized Timothy would learn the hard way without the slightest idea of what he was giving up. She reached for the phone and dialled, immediately wanting to disconnect from the mechanical voice.

The number was local, residential, the name was Jack Caden and she knew what was coming next.

"May I have the spelling for the person you wish to call?"

"Jack Caden, C-A-D-E-N. He lives in city central. I believe the number is new."

"I have no listing for Caden, Jack in Bayville or the environs. Do you have an address?"

"No, I don't. Would he be unlisted?

"I can only tell you whether he is or not." The pause was brief, the clicking of the keyboard annoying. "He is not unlisted. Let me try with a K." The tapping noise was infuriating. "I'm sorry. You might want to verify the spelling and try again. Thank you for calling."

"You might want to verify the spelling and try again. Thank you for calling," Kathy mimicked in a whiney voice, twisting her face into a sardonic snarl. "Bitch!"

She switched off her light and slid under the covers. Why would Jack not have a phone? He was a businessman. And why would he lie about where he lived, or anything else? She snorted, as though she had to ask. She knew why and Kathy Burberry learned a valuable lesson of her own. She had been too eager for attention, too vulnerable and naïve to believe the first man who came along might actually be attracted to her when she had just recently become appealing to herself after two decades of neglect. She thought she was being so au courant, in control, when in fact she went too far too quickly. "Thanks, Jack," she murmured. "Thanks for helping me along." And she fell asleep before the first teardrop blended into her pillow.

Twenty-Six

Clint was right to believe the storm would wreak havoc on the downtown nightclub business, not so the overbooked hotels. His experience over past weeks and months had taught him the meaninglessness of wedding bands often worn by single women as a deterrent and not worn by married women as a sign of willingness. The younger ones with rings rarely disguised the analytical curiosity in their eyes, the quiet rejections or "come buy me a drink" glances, working the room with their eyes as a means of selective reduction. The older ones without rings were no less obvious, their eyes saddened with happiness lost or hope not yet found, searching for adventure or desperate retaliation. Neither was easier or harder than the honest ones who would slash your ego with a single glare or draw you to her pure sexual appeal. To them any subterfuge was time wasted. What was meant to be, would be. Eye contact was what mattered most, animal instinct and carnal connection.

He did indeed make up for the lady claims adjuster the night before and he believed the woman somehow intuited he would love her with ferocious fervour, use her for gain and leave her before another grey dawn, which he did. She might as well have written a cheque payable to, well, to whomever. Who cared? He was very certain she didn't. She went to sleep content and Clint decided the grand in her purse and ATM card would suffice. Part of his education

161

was in discerning what to take from whom, never before considering jewellery and he thought she wouldn't mind since she hadn't worn her ring in the bed, the shower or on the desk.

Sunday morning he breakfasted in the apartment, four K richer plus a ring the size of a small pebble which he had no idea about. His regular restaurant was closed. No one needed breakfast badly enough to defy the weather. The snow hadn't abated and the streets were deserted. He paced the apartment to and fro, not thinking of the coming evening which he was confident would end at least as successfully as the previous two combined. His mind was filled with jumbled thoughts of Kathy Burberry and what to do about her as much as what to do with her.

Returning to the house was out of the question, not with all the snow. Go directly to jail, do not pass go or he'd kill himself trying and deserve nothing more. Seven days of close captivity with a secret drunk, a cheat and a couple of kids who weren't quite right. He couldn't imagine. Kathy Burberry was going to hell for Christmas: a full week of agony when her house would be empty. He inhaled deeply. What couldn't he do in a week? Virtually anything but relive the day before she altered his life and love her one last time.

He had never forgotten her, his sole ambition to find her and hurt her until the moment fate dealt him the cruellest blow. Seeing her again in the bar that night was surreal, hurling him through time and space onto the wet ground where he lay inert with his hands cuffed at his back, looking into the emotionless eyes of Kim Moon.

He had gone to the wrong place at the wrong time and now he couldn't distinguish between hurting her and loving her, which was essential. Without lasting anguish and torment he would find no closure. Seven days and what would he do once inside? What would he learn that he didn't already know? And why did he have to know? He could cajole her into bed anytime he wanted, and that's what he wanted: to have her. He wanted once more to control her, to have power over her the way she had finally manipulated the end of his life. He wanted to injure her, savour her suffering and he couldn't unless she first came to him. Nothing less would give him complete fulfillment and closure, knowing he hadn't begged her to return. Seven days. He clasped his head in both hands wishing he'd never seen her. Kim Moon might one day have been dead and buried in his mind, had she not been reincarnated in Kathy Burberry whom he was inexplicably drawn to when he should have run full tilt to escape her without looking back. He punched the wall. He couldn't allow her to interfere with the last night of his workweek. He would have time enough to create and critique a plan during his off time. She wasn't going anywhere he didn't know about and, if he decided she wouldn't go, she wouldn't.

He looked at the photocopies of her itineraries. Kathleen Burberry wanted out. Why else would a woman purchase expensive ski equipment for a weekend in Vermont? She obviously couldn't ski or the garage walls would be lined with all manner of sports paraphernalia he hadn't seen. The temptation was haunting. He hadn't slept properly in a week struggling with the inner conflict, consoling himself with idle thoughts of Myrtle Beach, of manipulating her into coming to him of her own volition before he would be driven to initiate a chance encounter in March.

Monday he would drive by her home to reconnect with that part of her and use the rest of the week to formulate a detailed plan which he would put into effect a week later. He knew what he was missing because he had nothing but itineraries, a pair of panties and the name of her school. He needed more. He couldn't simply have her for a night, use her and dispose of her like the others because he could never forget her like the others and present-day women were immune to the love-her-and-leave-her broken heart syndrome.

She would expect some well-crafted, plausible excuse and assume an attitude of mutual gain, doing unto Ted as he was doing unto her. He wanted more. He needed her to remember him for a very long time and hate him the way he hated her. He wanted to inflict a pain that would never leave her, something he would not accomplish in her bed or any other he would carry her to. He needed to infiltrate her, understand her mindset, her vulnerabilities and penetrate her beyond the physical.

Twenty-Seven

Kathy never played Christmas hostess to her in-laws. In the early years she was never allowed, Mrs. Burberry commenting on the first and second occasions that Kathy had quite enough in the oven to worry about. Later, the location became the deciding factor: the Burberry's finely decorated home on the hill or Kathy's crowded and loud city apartment. Finally, the old couple moved to Florida, transferred the title of the family home to their son and refused to suffer the horrors of holiday travel. The Christmas tradition would continue, albeit under the sun and Ted willingly agreed.

The aging couple doted over their granddaughter, though Kathy dreaded the annual sojourn. The best she could look forward to was cool civility. She was the tramp who cornered their son and the old lady never missed an opportunity to lecture Melissa on the dangers of wanton play, from disease to the loss of one's "good girl" reputation to one's inevitable failure to succeed, whereas Timothy spent his time at the beachfront villa relatively unscathed. They realized the boy had no talent or affinity for success, nor was he particularly handsome or affable. He was entirely forgettable, which they did most of the year.

Kathy inched her second nylon to the top of her thigh, clasping the garter under a short bubble dress. She stepped into Spanish-styled ankle-wrap pumps and went downstairs, putting Melissa in charge of dinner, Timothy was to do the dishes under the constant threat of once again losing his phone and she walked straight to the garage.

First she would pick up Michelle who had pleaded mournfully for a ride in the red MX-5 and the two would meet Darlene and Sheila at the restaurant. She agreed partly because she liked Michelle a lot. She was also convinced her chances of running into Jack Caden were between nil and nada and he, she'd decided wistfully, would be the one man she would sleep with before Vermont. The thought was outrageous and the women giggled from Michelle's home to the downtown core. Michelle was incorrigible, explaining in fine detail what Kathy might expect. They would arrive at the White Cliff Lodge Thursday at noon, eat lunch and have their first ski lesson mid-afternoon. After dinner they would meander over to the bar and by 10:00 at the latest all four would be hooked up and either heading to the dance floor, the Jacuzzi or a suite. They would meet for a late breakfast each day, sans Romeos, ski, eat lunch, be pampered in the spa and meet up with the guys for dinner.

Sunday morning was open for last goodbyes or lasting memories. Check-out was 2:00 PM and the drive home from the airport would be the longest part of the weekend. They had three weeks to wait and, the best part of all, Kathy knew she wouldn't give a moment's thought to Ted or the other two. At long last she had close friends, girlfriends, and she wasn't alone.

*

At the house Timothy didn't budge when the MX-5's purring motor faded. He lay on his bed waiting for the familiar smell to penetrate the bottom of his door and the noise of Melissa letting the oven door slam shut before he dragged his feet into the kitchen. She never called him, not until she was closing the door to her room. They seldom spoke to one another beyond the occasional, self-explanatory "duh" or "whatever," as though existing in

166

parallel worlds where eleven months apart were light years for both of them, which was fine with Timothy. He didn't like talking, especially with her. He didn't like the way she looked at him, like he was stupid, when she was the stupid one for thinking she could be a famous actress. Increasingly he wondered about her. She wore the nicest clothes of any girl at college, all the guys talked about her, yet she didn't have a boyfriend and everyone knew she wasn't a virgin. The news had carried over from high school and Melissa Burberry was on every guy's To-Do list. He didn't think she was particularly pretty. She was okay, he supposed, reaching for a plate.

She sliced the pizza, took two wedges and left without saying a word, which brought the usual twisted expression and shrug she didn't see. He knew her routine. She would eat supper, return the plate to the kitchen, remain in her room for an hour or so, go to the bathroom for a shower and return to her room where she would stay for the evening.

Lumbering towards the room that would be his cell for another nine weeks with the remaining four slices, he smirked. He would never have a better opportunity. He'd formulated the prank in the weeks since taking the picture of his mother climbing the stairs in her slip. He was curious, the victim of an idle mind and imposed confinement. Melissa was different. She was popular, yet she spent every night in her room and never came out except on the weekends. He hadn't stepped inside her bedroom for years. He wasn't allowed without first knocking and waiting, which was pointless because she would never answer. Nor was Melissa allowed in his.

He would wait for her to return her plate, after which he would do the few dishes, go to his room, dim the light and wait with his door slightly ajar for her nightly ritual to begin. At 8:30 precisely he wasn't disappointed, standing in the hallway to listen for the sounds of the shower's glass door sliding in its track and the harsh running water. Satisfied, he tried the handle. The door moved inward and he hurried into the room to place the micro-cassette under the dust ruffle of the bed by the far wall. On slow the tape would record four hours' worth of Melissa which he would retrieve during her much later Friday night shower, usually the same time his mother went to bed.

Back in his room he closed the door, pleased he had done something worthwhile.

*

Kathy was pumped up. She didn't reveal her little secret to the women. What they might soon share together was one thing, sharing Jack was another matter. She couldn't believe she was sitting with them in a lounge talking about meeting absolute strangers in a few weeks, listening to their preferences, about the men from October, a weekend she might have missed by mere weeks. She was flushed with excitement. She couldn't wait.

"Each time gets better than anything in ancient history, Kathy, much better." Michelle said. "The sexiness, the undressing. The guy's aren't clumsy. They know what they're doing and they're at the lodge for the same reason we are."

"To get laid," Sheila added, "and we're not talking paunchy baldinis. They'll be good-looking, in shape and arrive prepared from everywhere and anywhere. No one wants to start over on night two. It's like sloppy seconds."

"Yeah, and they never scratch themselves or roll off when they're done to snore their way into oblivion." Darlene put in. "They keep going full strength. They want us to wake up wanting more and be there for them the next evening, as long as we're great as well."

Sheila raised her glass. "And we are." She giggled. "Practice makes perfect and this spice of life thing we all hear about…it's true. You'll hate going home and each trip sets the bar a notch higher."

They all agreed.

"I hate going home now. Not that he'll be there, which I suppose should be some sort of perverse consolation."

"Listen, Kath," Darlene went on, "remember the divorce thing. It's not worth the agony. This way I get what I want, so does he when he travels and at home he's either in the john self-serving or searching for the true meaning of the universe. My money's on self-serving. Either way, I'd rather give him a hundred bucks anytime to stop on a street corner instead of wasting my time undressing for a minute-long marathon. Besides, a few years ago when he was gone on business I threw out the queen and bought doubles."

Kathy snorted into her glass. "Tell me you're kidding."

"I'm not. I couldn't take being the reserve unit any longer. Worked like a charm. He even began extending his workweek."

"But you're so young. If you leave you could start over with someone good."

"And I will as soon as the kids are gone in a couple of years."

Sheila nodded in agreement.

"You're young, too, Kathy," Michelle added. "What about you?"

The girls were closing in on home turf and Kathy realized exactly how closely knit the girls were.

"The oldest is leaving in this summer, the youngest in a year and I have no reason to believe an empty house will suddenly make Ted attentive. He doesn't even see me. He'll simply have less reason to come home and I won't contest if he's the first to walk out."

"None of us will contest when the time comes," assured Darlene," and we're pretty much in the same timeframe. Until then we play. Better said, we're keeping our options open, so to speak. We're staying viable and in practice."

"This will be my first time in nineteen years."

"No, darling," Michelle corrected. "This will be your first ever and, believe us; you will never forget your first."

*

Near midnight Kathy phoned Michelle and went to bed feeling completely free of the old Kathy, a phantom bond which she feared might be her downfall. Her aesthetic change was immediate and absolutely stunning; the psychological ensued quickly and was no less remarkable. Although, despite her resolve, when she gazed into the mirror she sometimes felt her inner conversion wavering. Much of that fragility she blamed on Jack Caden.

The girls had changed that condition. She would meet other Jack Cadens who would want her, make her stronger and more determined in whatever she wanted to do. Michelle's "darling" had taken her by surprise, so did the evening's completely candid conversation. No one had ever called her darling. She was always Kathy, Kath, her or mom, never darling, sweetheart or babe. Not even her father had called by any endearment, or her mother. Yet the girls each had special names for one another and she was their darling. What they shared went beyond mere friendship, giving each other what the husbands would not: simple endearments. They were sisters, a fraternity of women who were guiding their futures, not lamenting years past. No one had ever hugged or kissed her as much as at the end of the evening or three weeks earlier. She was one of them, though she did have to admit Michelle was her favourite.

When she dropped Michelle off in front of her home the young woman leaned over so nonchalantly and kissed her cheek, a woman she worked with, insisting Kathy call her once safe and sound. Yet, in the morning, at coffee before the first bell of the day, they would revert to no-nonsense teachers and, her, a counsellor and welcome addition to the sisterhood.

Twenty-Eight

Kathy arrived home after an extra hour at the gym and admonishments from her trainer not to over-indulge. She promised to faithfully run the beach each day, do her crunches and she left him with a Christmas envelope for the good work he had done.

Melissa was setting the dining room table and Timothy was plugged into another world on his bed. She no longer dwelled upon the last time she wanted to hug or kiss her daughter or the last time she wanted to work at understanding her son. Over the years the two had evolved into distant strangers, not the typical rebellious teenagers she might have hoped for and the least effort required to regain any normalcy would be daunting. No, she mused, normalcy would come in time from any effort either one would choose to initiate, not her. She had done her best and a few months would make no difference at all.

In her bedroom she changed into a cable sweater and cords and went downstairs to tell Melissa she'd be gone for an hour. At the door she tugged on her boots, her cloche and swung her cape over her shoulders. Five minutes later she was standing by the deserted seashore staring out across the dark expanse. Saturday's forecast was calling for colder temperatures and snow: ideal conditions for an idyllic afternoon. And Ted wouldn't be home until Sunday acting as though he hadn't done some blonde the night before. So what was stopping her? She would survive Miami by

171

running, sunning in her as yet untried Rio bikini and shopping in exclusive boutiques for something even smaller, something to wear in the outdoor sauna and Jacuzzi in Vermont despite what Sheila implied.

But how would she survive three more months with Ted, beginning with New Year's Eve, an annual tradition destined to crumble like all other traditions? Six hours of not drinking so Ted could once again be the man of the hour, six tedious hours of children, work, career advice and helping in the kitchen. There wasn't a damn thing new about it, except her dress. This year even Ted's witty, scotch-drenched mouth would have trouble competing with the redesigned and reinvented Kathy Burberry in a dress she would take with her to Vermont after making very sure Ted was well aware. Every woman in the house would lavish her with praise, secretly hating her for making them look ordinary in boring black slacks or something equally pedestrian. Not one of them would be a Michelle, Darlene or Sheila and the next day jealous tongues would wag. On the other hand, the men would imagine the unknown according to their particular tastes and congratulate a so-called man who hadn't noticed her in months.

Jack would notice. He would devour her on the spot and want to see more of her. She turned, studying the hilltop homes, her house. Jack wouldn't be at the beach the next day or the day after, and she wouldn't search for him. In a few days she wouldn't care. He was becoming less real, a vanishing memory of fleeting, illicit moments. He was an idea, a motive whose image was kept alive by loneliness, a desire she would soon replace with the very physical and the very real. The marriage contract had no clause regarding provocative dresses, tiny bikinis or trips to ski lodges. Yeah, she thought, Ted would leave sometime soon and if he didn't get the idea before Spring Break he certainly would then.

She didn't want to go home. She wanted a warm fire and strong arms pulling her in close, but she had to clean the house, pack, organize travel documents and suddenly she burst into tears and slumped against the railing. How could she sleep with him, be so close to him or let him see her naked when she loathed the thought that he might one night want her for purely selfish reasons?

She wiped her eyes and her nose, shaking her head. She knew why he wasn't leaving, why he constantly screwed around and she would no longer put herself second to any of his bitches. She took a deep breath of cold salt air, walked to her car and drove into town. She wouldn't endure another awkward evening. As of that moment Ted was in the self-serve mode.

When she arrived home Melissa and Timothy had eaten and she was surprised to see perfectly clean place settings in the dining room. She knocked on Timothy's door first, telling him to be ready at 8:00 the next morning, and Melissa's, opening the door at the first syllable of protest.

"Get this straight. You're going to the hair salon at eight o'clock, your brother's going with you and you will get what I need from the pharmacy without any hassle or your time in Miami will be incarceration, which means no beach, no suntan, no shopping and spending your time with the heartless old hag. Don't believe me? Try me... and next time I say dinner's at the table you damn well do it."

She closed the door more gently than she wanted and went to the kitchen. Nothing stirred. She was virtually alone in a full house and wanted to smash something. She wasn't hungry or angry. Her stomach was in knots for all that was about to happen in the coming months and she felt her eyes welling up once again, her emotions reaching an unfamiliar apex. She reached for a fruit bar, poured a generous portion of tequila and went to her récamier where she sat looking at the bed.

She wanted to phone Michelle, and one day she would. The girls shared an inexplicable bond, a closeness she never would have imagined and she regretted being so angry with them for not telling her, until conspiratorial smiles expressed clear disregard for her pointless objections and they told her to open the Christmas gifts she wasn't expecting. The whole idea was to surprise her, to make her feel part of them. She would know for next year, they each said with a coquettishly meaningful grin. She looked at the small collection of shiny boxes on her dresser: a bracelet, a silk scarf and her favourite eau de toilette.

Kathy resisted shopping for them on the last day of school. The afterthought would have hurt. Instead she would buy each girl something special in Miami which she would give them in Vermont and she was anxious to see them again. She wondered who might have bought Jack a Christmas gift. A one-in-a-million-man like him deserved the best. She finished her drink and crawled into bed, praying for sleep to forget one man and dream of what she might have bought for the other.
*

At 8:30 Melissa was running the shower and Timothy took his time going into her room to reach under her bed. Seconds later he was on his bed, plugged in. The initial minutes were quiet, followed by shuffling sounds he couldn't identify, then several more minutes of quiet followed by sounds he did recognize. He flipped over onto his knees and began bouncing up and down. He was listening to his sister actually doing it, and then quiet. He fast forwarded the tape, hearing nothing but static and rewound to the slurred groans he played over and over again not believing what he was hearing. Then he fast forwarded until he did hear something and pressed play.

"Hi. You haven't visited with me for over a week. Don't you like me anymore?"

"You know how things are. I've been busy, but I must have the best Midnight Rhapsody library. Where I go, you go."

"I hope so."

"What's on for tonight," he paused for effect, "or off? What are you taking off for me?"

"You're so bad."

"Yeah, and I'll be the first one on the 31st. Better not be anybody ahead of me. Give me a hint. Give me something to keep me going till then."

Rhapsody giggled. "Wet."

"Say what?"

"Do you like water?"

"Yeah, I love water. Like what kind?"

"The kind that makes my clothes soaking wet, too wet to wear."

"What are you wearing now? I can only see your head and shoulders. What's with the hat?"

"Tonight I'm Santa's elf, a very naughty elf. I don't deserve to help Santa so he made me stay home in my panties and bra and my tiny little skirt so I won't get into any trouble outside."

"Show me."

Timothy heard a pause, what sounded like her chair pushing back and something being put on her desk, like a glass or something, he thought. He couldn't believe what he was hearing, knowing his sister was in the next room, probably doing the same thing, separated by a few centimetres of drywall.

"Turn around Rhapsody and lose the skirt. You're too gorgeous to wear clothes. Know what I mean. Man, you got to get naked for me."

"Know what? You do have to be one of the first on New Year's. I'd really hate disappointing you and your time's almost up. So check this out."

175

Timothy heard something falling close to the micro-cassette, he didn't know what. "Oh, man, you're like the smoothest thing. Turn, let me see them."

"Santa wouldn't like that, but you know what, he won't be around on the 31st. In the meantime," the total silence worsened the drumming in Timothy's ears until he heard one more indiscernible soft sound near the mike.

"That's good, Rhapsody. Now down, push them down father so I can see a little piece of heaven."

Again the silence was deafening, the tape ending with a faint click and Timothy was about to do cartwheels in his room. His sister was an internet porn star: Midnight Rhapsody. His mind worked hard and he crashed onto his bed. His sister was Midnight Rhapsody, the one all the guys were talking about and she was one door away.
*

Clint Evans picked up the woman partly out of mercy, partly out of fatigue. She was a desperate woman in desperate times and nothing was more desperate than Christmas when the only ones not forgotten were those bearing gifts. She was drunk, lived alone and wanted company. She wasn't old, neither was she young or pretty. She was pathetic, aging prematurely throughout the evening with each drink. Everyone else at the company party had left her, intentionally or not and he took over.

She wanted a man in her life. She wanted a life, a lover and someone to help pay the bills.

What she got was a three-thousand dollar Christmas debt compliments of someone who took her home, dropped her callously onto the couch in her coat and left without the benefit of her love. What he did leave with was her jewel box and lottery tickets. Clint Evans was branching out, despite being increasingly focused on Kathy Burberry and he couldn't prevent the coming Monday from invading his every waking thought or his dreams. He needed to know her.

He needed to know Kathy Burberry and had dedicated his week to that end.

He discovered her snow-filled driveway would be ploughed regularly by contractors, her neighbours were lethargic at best and his primary concern was the window, avoiding the pitfall of overconfidence, believing she or someone wouldn't leave home for a week with a vulnerable window unlatched. He would go prepared and somehow desperate women were no longer appealing to him. He wanted one who was neither hunting nor frail, waiting for the kill. He wanted a woman who would see him for what he was: the quintessential man.

Twenty-Nine

Saturday the taxi arrived at eight o'clock sharp and she wouldn't see the kids until noon. She had the morning to herself. She was fully dressed and the bed was stripped. The doubles would arrive any minute with percale sheets for one, satin for the other and she thanked brassy Sheila repeatedly in her mind. She laughed aloud, imagining Ted's stunned expression Sunday night when he would not only see the twin beds but the night tables between them.

His corporate party was that evening and what would he have thought of her dress swaying across her thighs in front of his bosses. He would never know. He'd never know a lot of things, like what he was giving up to chase after one-night stands or spending infrequent evenings at home drinking in his office and standing sentinel over the sacrosanct drawer she was never particularly curious about. She didn't have to know their names and he made no secret of his drinking. She doubted the reason he drank was even a secret. She was the reason. He was drinking to forget her, the kids and he possibly might have added his nemesis Lester Lamarre, alias the gofer, to the list.

One day she would be curious enough to find out, perhaps with a hairpin. On the other hand the desk was communal property and no law existed preventing a person from opening a drawer with a sledgehammer. The doorbell rang and twenty minutes later she was sitting on the linen duvet of her new bed. By noon her chores were done, the kids were home and she began packing. Ted would be home in twenty-four hours and she wanted to avoid him, not that she was anxious about the inevitable confrontation, on the contrary. If anything, she felt a spiteful eagerness. She wanted to avoid idle conversation which would lead nowhere. Miami wouldn't be a vacation, more like the incarceration she promised Melissa and believing anything else was pointless.

By dinnertime she'd put Melissa and Timothy on alert, assuring each one they were leaving Monday at 10:00 AM, irrespective of what they had or had not packed for the trip and reminding them the computers and cell phones were to remain behind on their desks and in plain sight. By 11:00 she was in bed, feeling victorious.
*

Timothy hadn't said a word during the taxi ride into town, his mind crammed with the words and mental images of the night before, stunned that he was sitting beside Midnight Rhapsody. He hadn't thought of anything else all day, listening over and over again to the tape and trying to visualise his sister taking off her clothes for some sick dude. Taking a photograph of his mother was a stupid mistake. None of the kids wanted to see an old woman in her underwear, but Midnight Rhapsody, yeah, they would, and they'd pay big bucks. He just didn't know how. Her door would be locked and even if she didn't lock it, he just couldn't barge in on her. She'd scream or something and his mother would rush in to ruin everything the way she always did.

He puzzled over the dilemma throughout the day, his mind in a shambles, leaping from one confused thought to another. Something was happening on the 31st with water that he couldn't figure out. His parents always went out to party and never came home early. Maybe she'd do something in the garage with the hose. Maybe she'd wash

179

the cars or something in her bathing suit or underwear or put her webcam on the toilet and take a bath or something, and with that thought his brow furrowed. Her computer didn't have a camera. She had a second computer. Whatever she was going to do, he didn't know, but he was staying home to find out. Being with his friends wouldn't come anywhere close to this.

After supper his mind worked in overdrive, imagining all manner of scenarios and he kept returning to the same plan. He was ready and checked a hundred times that his phone wouldn't give him away. He had eaten a snack and had gone to the bathroom. All that remained was for his sister to leave her room, lock herself into the bathroom and he'd be good to go.

Melissa typically showered at 11:30 on Fridays and Saturdays and her door opened precisely on time. Seconds later the lock on the bathroom door clicked and Timothy waited to hear the water, listening nervously for the sliding noise of the shower door and went into her room. The lighting was dim, nothing was out of place and he dropped to the floor, pushing himself sideways under the bed in black sweats, hockey socks and a black woollen ski mask. The plan was working, with an easy ten centimetres of clearance. As long as his stomach didn't growl or he didn't sneeze or do something stupid he was home free.

He was fixated on his cell's clock. His heart was pounding, his body instinctively tensing when the door opened and he saw her bare feet padding across the floor. She walked to her closet, searching for something. He could hear paper rustling and things being thrown onto the bed as her feet moved in concert with whatever she was doing. He saw the bottom of her robe touch the floor and heard hangers being pushed aside. She stepped in, standing on her toes, reaching for something and, a few steps later he saw her from her hips to her feet, squatting naked, forcing a dark

180

towel into the opening at the bottom of her door. He'd never seen anything so fantastic. He wasn't seeing the sister he hated, the one who ridiculed him at school and called him dufus or deadbrain. He was seeing Midnight Rhapsody. He was afraid to move. He couldn't believe he was watching his sister without her clothes, Midnight Rhapsody, when no one else he knew could afford anything except her free trailers.

When she stood he stayed paralyzed, listening to her dress, watching one foot raise from the floor, then the other. He was insane. His father would kill him. She was again in the closet and he saw her backpack disappearing from the floor. He heard the zipper and the familiar sounds of a computer purring to life as the lighting dimmed slightly. Then he heard her twisting a cork from a bottle. He listened to something being poured and a moment later she put the vodka bottle at the foot of her bed, centimetres from his face. Then she pulled out her chair and sat facing her desk.

"Good evening, Peter. I was hoping you wouldn't make me wait as long as the last time."

Timothy pressed the play and record buttons simultaneously.

"You look fantastic."

"Thank you." She pushed the chair away and stood on her tiptoes, leaning into the webcam as Timothy inched closer to the bottom edge of the bed to raise the ruffle, seeing her perfectly in the full-length mirror by the door. "I wore this especially for you and I promise I'll be even sexier for you in twelve short days." She sipped her drink. "I hope you'll drop by. I'm planning something pretty special for you."

"I wouldn't miss it, but you chose a pretty bad time. It's New Years and not real easy to get rid of the wife."

"Bring her to our party. Tell her it's your first time and I'll pretend I don't know you. Then we can bring in the

New Year together. How old is she?"

"Twenty-three."

"Is she sexy?"

"She was, once." The voice paused. "Rhapsody, step away a little. Let me see something. I'm dying here." Timothy watched her stepping back, bending forward and pushing her ultra mini-skirt slowly to the floor. "Oh, man, that's nice, very nice. Now let me see your backside." Timothy dropped the ruffle. "That is so totally fantastic. How old are you, Rhapsody, really?"

"Almost the same age as your wife. Too bad she wouldn't like me. I know I'd like her."

Her bra dropped to the floor and Rhapsody walked to the door, passing the bed and Timothy chanced to peek. She was reaching for a towel and he hid once more as she pirouetted.

"Fantastic, but lose the towel and the panties. All I've seen for months is your panties."

"Poor you." she paused. "Actually you're right. We've been together too long. You deserve." She went to the computer, adjusted the webcam and turned, stopping halfway across the room before dropping the towel. "Can you see me, Peter?"

"Yeah, it's like I'm with you."

She teasingly pushed her panties to the floor, kicking them away, arching her back and raising her arms as she stood. "I hope you're happy. You're the first."

"At what?"

"At seeing me totally naked. Think of this as a special preview. I like that you can see me naked. Do you?" She reached for the towel, bending from her hips.

"You're killing me."

"I would never kill you. I like you. You're one of my best fans."

Rhapsody pulled in the chair and sat, taking a sip of her

drink and reaching onto the bed. Timothy thought he would
pass out watching his sister walk from the mirror holding
the towel in front of her. The whirring sound was clear.

"What are you doing?"

"Peter, you know what I'm doing and I hope I can finish
for you before your time is up."

"Show me. Drop the towel and stand for me. It'll help
you."

"No. Showing you wouldn't be fair to my other friends,
not until our next time."

Timothy saw her watching a small alarm clock by her
bed, when suddenly her body jerked.

"Goodbye Peter. Sweet dreams." And his sister feigned
exhaustion, pushing away from the screen and dropping the
towel.

Timothy tried opening his eyes wider. He had never
seen a naked girl, let alone his sister, and she was coming
towards the mirror a few mere centimetres from where he
lay. She was dressing, reaching for the bottle and when she
faced away he raised the bed's ruffle. He'd never seen such
a short skirt and finally understood the best way to
photograph her was through the mirror when she was facing
away. If the flash did go off he would simply crawl out.
She'd have nothing to say except "please don't tell mother"
and he couldn't imagine what he'd be seeing on the 31st.

He stayed awake the entire two hours until she closed
the computer, brightened the lighting and reclined to relax
with her fourth drink, tearing away her wig and eye glasses.
When she was done she gathered her costume, tugged the
towel from the foot of the door and pulled her baby dolls
over her head. He couldn't believe what he was seeing or
what she'd done to herself. His mother would freak if she
found out. He'd successfully taken a dozen shots of his
sister. She was so close and lying motionless for Timothy
was increasingly unbearable, believing he would snap in

half if he tried to move.

She disappeared into her bed, the lights went out and he waited, afraid to move. He had to get to his room, to his bed. The urgency was mounting and his face was itching badly. Then he heard the low drone of a tiny motor and moments later her gasp resonated through the bed. No one would ever believe him. Minutes became hours and at 4:00 he strained to hear the faintest sound, reminding himself that he had the advantage over her. He had to get to his room, deciding to risk discovery and New Year's. His sister was a porn star, she drank booze and looking down at her sleeping he saw her in an entirely different way. He always would. From then on he would see her naked and as he went to his bed he had no idea Clint Evans had closed his year to the tune of three thousand dollars.

Thirty

Sunday morning Clint congratulated himself. He hadn't worked four full months, yet he had accumulated not far from a hundred thousand tax-free dollars. Saturday evening was his year-end and he ordered a bottle of champagne with breakfast to celebrate the occasion without allotting a moment's thought to the naïve young woman who might be rummaging through her empty purse, wailing aloud and not because of her outrageous hangover. And so go the spoils of war, he thought, sipping from his first fluted glass.

He was prepared. He was ready and determined. He wouldn't work again until early January and spent countless hours contemplating the best change of venue, certain he would have to leave. If he remained in the same city much longer he would eventually be taken back, a delicate balance of timing and target selection separating him from freedom and the grey shades of hell.

He snorted, grinning perversely. He wouldn't allow anything to interrupt his success. Too much was going right for him and arbitrary retribution by a close-minded system for having supplied a fundamental service was not an option. He entertained his clients, not once disappointing them. He fed them, paid their bar bills, sometimes danced with them and always brought them to fanciful precipices, catering to their carnal whims and filling emotional voids, leaving them unharmed with lasting memories at a cost he believed each one could afford.

Finishing his champagne he left his plate untouched and walked out into the harsh winter's latest storm. He was content. He would move on very soon. He wouldn't wait for every nerve ending in his body to trigger his defences, though what he wanted most at the moment was his bed. Later he would itemize each detail in chronological order and account for each requisite item. He would have one unimaginable chance at success and more snow was in the forecast for Monday

*

Late Sunday Melissa awoke refreshed. She went to the kitchen, made coffee and sat contemplating her strategy which included making her mother and father happy to the least extent possible. Her mother couldn't stop her from shopping in Florida, unless she didn't want a gift. She always shopped in Miami for as long as she could remember, so did deadbrain. Her mother was bluffing and she didn't care. She wanted out and March was Liberation Month. She would be eighteen and free to leave or do whatever she wanted

A few moments later Kathy came in, followed by Timothy. She said good morning to both. Neither one replied, Melissa because she was angry, Timothy because he was seeing his sister sitting naked at the island, recalling every groove and curve. He couldn't believe Midnight Rhapsody was sitting across from him in a plain fleecy robe. He'd watched and listened to her do her thing for hours, and would again in a few days. Until then he had his photo gallery and would try to work out the best possible plan.

Kathy reiterated her wishes about the packing as well as the electronics and walked out, telling them not to expect her before the dinner hour, which, she added, would be in the dining room. She had called the hair salon to delay her appointment, and the spa to begin her day in a floating bath and a massage table. She walked to the garage humming,

186

without mentioning a word about Ted who wouldn't be home for an hour.

Timothy went to his room and closed the door, hesitating to tell his mother for fear of what her reaction might be. He had changed his mind about his Christmas gift. He no longer wanted a guitar, he want a camcorder.

Melissa remained in the kitchen. Her mother was so pathetic. She was middle-aged, acting like sixteen and believing she could live her life over. No guy wanted that, not even old guys. They wanted young and pretty girls with nice, clean bodies, not someone's shapeless or scarred leftovers, especially a woman trashed by someone like her father, the loser of the year keeping booze and a photo album of a naked woman in his desk drawer. Whoever she was, Eileen was the reason he was never home and how pathetic was she to waste her time waiting for a loser who no way could afford her. Whether or not Melissa could recite world capitals or would ever surpass an average grade point, she knew quality. Eileen's lingerie, panties and bras, hats and dresses were off the chart, all imported. She looked years younger than her father, which meant she probably wasn't cheating on anyone and the man didn't even have the brains to scan her into an encrypted computer file.

Melissa went to her room, locked the door and went for the vodka bottle. She would never be like her mother. She would never get old; she would never marry and have children. If anything, she'd be like Eileen whose photo images she had examined with a magnifying glass. Her father's whore didn't have a single mark, dent or bump, not like her mother. That's why he stayed away and Melissa had scanned the coloured images into her Rhapsody computer as proof, complete with dates and places and cute little love notes.

She sipped her vodka neat, thinking of her time with Peter. She had never before stripped entirely for a fan and she liked the sensation. It was a beginning and Sunday at midnight she would do so again, buying more sheer and exotic lingerie in Miami for the few days leading into the 31st. She dragged her largest suitcase from the closet, threw it on the bed and laid out fourteen outfits in reverse order of the seven upcoming days. She hated being forced to buy her mother gifts, finding something she would neither like nor dislike, something safe. She chuckled, covering her mouth before the vodka escaped. Perhaps this year she could give something a little more special: a photo album of her husband's whore. She was obviously doing her best to get a divorce and if he was stupid enough not to give her one after seeing the separate beds, perhaps she would give him one Christmas morning.

She poured another drink, closed the suitcase and dressed. She wanted to see and hear her father's reaction first-hand and waited until she heard the taxi before going to the kitchen for lunch. He came in through the front door, dropped his suitcase, attaché and computer in the hall and went into the kitchen.

"Where's your mother?"

"Hi daddy. Did you have a good time at the party last night?" Was Eileen with you by any chance, she asked silently?

"No, I didn't. Go get your mother. Tell her I'm home."

Melissa slid from the stool. "She's not here, daddy. She went to town for a spa day and her hair. Want me to help you to your room with your luggage?"

"No, thank you. When will she be home?"

"Dinnertime, I guess. Who knows anymore? She's pretty freaked out these days. Maybe you should be hiring a private detective or something."

"Melissa, you watch your mouth. I'm in no mood."

"I'm sorry, daddy. Anyway, I don't think she wanted to be around when you got home. I think she wanted to surprise you with her latest gifts to herself." She grinned, drinking from her milk glass. "She left them in your bedroom."

Ted stood staring at her, speechless. He knew his daughter. She was a spoiled brat and an accomplished troublemaker.

"What's she done now?"

"This time she didn't just think of herself, daddy. She got something for both of you, except hers is a little fancier. You know...feminine."

"Feminine," he repeated. "You don't say. Make me a sandwich and put it on my desk. I don't want to be disturbed until she gets home. When she does get here you knock on my door."

"Yes daddy."

Daddy, he scoffed. The little bitch would sell him for body parts if she could, and her lunatic mother to the white slave trade. Eyes were the windows of the soul and Melissa clearly didn't have one. He gathered up his luggage, climbed the stairs and Melissa tiptoed to the hallway. At the double French doors he dropped his bag where he stood and laughed hysterically. In his wildest dreams he wouldn't have imagined. He walked in, went to the en suite closet, changed into more casual clothes and, on his way down to his office, flung his suitcase into the divided bedroom.

In his office he took a bite of the sandwich, opened the drawer, poured a substantial portion of scotch into his glass and phoned Eileen to be sure she arrived home safely from Chicago.

She missed him and would for the next couple of weeks, though he misjudged her reaction to the beds. She had never wanted to hear about his domestic sleeping arrangements and his thoughtless comments reawakened ancient doubts. She loved her emerald earrings and necklace, however she didn't need trinkets. She wanted him and if separate beds

189

weren't a sufficiently distinct message, she couldn't imagine what was and she expected him at the beachfront property on January 04th.

He hung up feeling dejected and poured a second generous glass. He pushed away the plate, not certain the kid hadn't spit in it or hadn't taken the meat from the garbage. He dialled the combination, reaching into the attaché which he never left vulnerable to prying eyes. Eileen had given him a simple and amusing Christmas card with the monogrammed set of carbon golf clubs. Inside were coupons for ten days of prepaid golfing for two in Myrtle Beach during Spring Break and a promissory note for one million dollars which she would honour if, by the end of March, he committed to leaving Kathy, a million dollars as emasculating as any scalpel. The alternative was worse: Eileen would leave him to a woman who had despised him for years, deprived him of living a dream and condemned him to mediocrity with the slash of her father's pen.

Through his office window he peered out over the frozen lake. The snowfall was worsening and he prayed the morning flight wouldn't be delayed or cancelled. He stretched out, put his feet on the desk, reclined, drained his glass and held the card against his chest. When Kathy came home the sky was black, the sacrosanct drawer was open, the card had fallen to the floor and the half-full plate lay at the edge of the desk. When he opened his eyes she was standing in front of him. Closing the drawer discreetly, he leaned forward ignoring the card.

Kathy eyed the plate. "Not hungry, or is in-flight food getting better?"

"Help yourself. The kid's useless outside of a shopping mall. She'll never survive the real world. Probably the reason she's come up with the ridiculous notion she can earn a living as an actress."

"I saw the clubs in the garage. From anyone I might know?"

"The annual prize from Corporate for exceeding budget."

She smirked. "Or possibly a little something to placate the runner up. And, by the way, I took your black suit to the cleaners today...for New Year's."

"You know I don't wear suits for New Year's."

"You are this year, or you're going alone and I'll go into town by myself, so don't be difficult. We wouldn't want the neighbours talking and I refuse to be seen in the dress I'll be wearing with anyone not in a suit. Got the picture?"

"Yeah, I do, a picture with two small beds in it."

"I know, boohoo. And what's your point, exactly?" She smiled. "You haven't given me any in months, not that I ever expected the galactic explosion I've always heard about, so let's not get overly sentimental. When you decide the wife should get something, give her a call. And I do mean give her a call for something more than saying you won't be home. Make a rendezvous. Wouldn't that be different? Yet somehow I don't see that happening anytime soon?"

"You made all this happen, not me."

"Crap. Don't be an idiot, Ted, or don't think I am. You started this whole thing not long after Timothy happened, when you began forgetting you have a family and I'm not doing anything I shouldn't have done all along. I've ignored myself for eighteen years. Now I'm ignoring you instead. I've never said you can't come along for the ride, because I know you won't and, until the kids are gone, the double beds make sense."

"She'll be out of here in three months."

"But not him, and I'm not sharing a bed for one more night, let alone an entire year. The thought's repugnant and I'll be sleeping on the couch in your parents' guest room.

Explain it to your mother anyway you choose, as long as
you tell her to shut up about it. The last thing I need to hear
is your mother quacking all week about your choices in
life."

"Thanks."

"One more thing: We have to leave tomorrow at 10:00
sharp and I've done all the laundry I intend to. You're on
your own till death do us part, as are they. Melissa can run
you through the process if you need help and dinner's being
served."

"Think I'll pass."

"I thought you might."

Kathy walked out leaving the plate and went to the
dining room wearing a knitted tunic and leotards, her
expression daring Melissa to say a single word. Timothy
was quiet, thinking about his sister and wondering about his
mother whom he wasn't accustomed to seeing in such fine
detail, watching her stand to refill her crystal wine goblet
and walk to the stairs when her meal was done. She wished
them a goodnight, went to her en suite bathroom, locked the
door, showered and changed into silk pyjamas. In bed she
read of love and intrigue, sipping her wine and letting her
mind wander. In a few hours she would be running on the
beach and sunning in something tiny, free of them for a
week and the 25th would be no exception.

Ted remained in his office throughout the evening,
staring blankly beyond the window, not thinking of either
woman, rather of the golf week and one million dollars. By
midnight he was drunk, unresolved, the bottle was empty,
he was hunched over his desk and oblivious to the hard
surface against the side of his head.

Thirty-One

When the quiet chimes of Kathy's alarm woke her, his bed hadn't been slept in and his suitcase hadn't moved from its point of impact with the floor. When she peeked through his office door his upper torso was sprawled across the desk and the bottle was on the floor by his glass and the plate. She felt overwhelming disgust, closing the door and returning to her room to dress and finish packing. When she was done she put her luggage by the front door and prepared breakfast. She went to Timothy's room first. He was dressed, his cell and computer were on his desk, his suitcase and backpack were by his door and he was set to go.

Melissa was also ready. Whatever thoughts had crossed her mind since Friday, she wasn't provoking her mother. She, too, left her computer on her desk with her phone and her backpack was squeezed into the darkest recess of her closet. She had travelled enough with her parents to be familiar with the robotic procedures at airport security and she wasn't taking any chances.

At 9:15 Kathy went to the office, opening and slamming the door shut with a bang that shook the house. Ted might have died on the spot from cardiac arrest or a broken neck when his head snapped violently to the side in response to the violent intrusion. He was disoriented, dazed and alone. His heart was racing, his head pounding and he wanted to be sick. He pushed himself to his feet, checked his watch and screamed out her name, screaming once again in vain when she didn't answer.

He threw the bottle into the wastebasket along with the glass. He scooped up the scattered components of the sandwich onto the plate, retrieved the fallen card and closed his attaché; furious with what he saw when he went out into hallway and living room. Kathy and the kids were sitting, waiting, their coats unbuttoned. Melissa's lips were pressed tightly together, camouflaging a sly grin, hoping her father would explode into a rage any second and Timothy, for the moment, forgot his fixation with his sister's body.

"Not a word, Kriss Kringle, not one damn word. You have twenty minutes to look and smell human. I'm calling two taxis in ten minutes and I won't wait so don't stand around much longer blowing steam."

"We're taking the Lexus and we'll leave when I'm damn well good and ready. You," he threw a finger out towards Timothy, "you get my clubs into the car, the new ones. And you," the finger repositioned to Melissa, "you get me a breakfast." Then he tried staring down the wife. "And perhaps you can manage to clean what's in my suitcase while I pack."

"Get serious. Your clubs are going into a taxi, you can get your own breakfast if you can manage and whatever soiled clothes you need you can either take with you or replace in Miami. You've got seventeen minutes. The road conditions are horrible and I don't trust you with my life, or theirs. We're taking taxis and if you're not ready when they get here you can call one for yourself or drive. And don't forget your clubs because I won't carry them, neither will he." She paused. "I'm calling in six minutes."

He wanted to choke her, kill her, stab her or pummel her self-satisfied face, none of which would be gratifying enough to warrant spending the rest of his life in prison or an institution for the criminally insane. He took a deep breath. "Melissa, would you please make me a sandwich?"

"Yes daddy."

"And Timothy, would you do me favour by putting my clubs by the door?"

Timothy looked to his mother for approval. However stupid he might be, he scarcely saw his father a day each week, he had to deal with his mother every day and still needed a major favour. She gave her approval with a curt nod.

When he was gone, she added with an infuriating grin "fifteen and counting. Let's see how quickly you actually can get to an airport," and Ted went up the stairs resisting the temptation to punch a hole in the wall. When came down the taxis were waiting, the luggage was loaded, he grabbed his sandwich and Kathy closed the door. She climbed into the first cab with Melissa, waiting for any wrong word.

The sky was a grey-white never seen on postcards. Visibility was measured in car lengths and driving required advanced skill. The day was treacherous, no less so for the driver of the dark SUV which came to life as the two-vehicle motorcade veered from the driveway. He followed at a safe distance. The road surface wasn't slippery, however snow has a sinister way of taking a vehicle where it doesn't want to go and he hadn't driven in severe winter conditions for years. The drive was "white knuckle" at its finest and, with no one behind him; he'd be up the proverbial creek if he spun out and all the latest safety bells and whistles wouldn't mean squat if he hit ice or exceeded thirty degrees to the hidden centreline of the road.

The airport was long in coming, but did at last and he lost sight of the Burberrys as the taxis went to Departures and he went to Short Term. The Burberrys arrived with ninety minutes to spare without factoring in delays. And delays were inevitable. What he feared were cancellations or to lose them before he was able to enter the concourse, which he accomplished within minutes of parking the SUV. In fact he was standing well off to the side of the ticket counter before the Burberrys had joined the slow-moving line.

Kathy didn't look much older than her haughty daughter, the boy seemed bewildered and Ted didn't look very good up close and personal. The meandering queue progressed slowly as he sat watching her every step, curve and facial expression. Kathy Burberry wasn't disguising the fact she was going to hell for a full week and he wasn't the only man appreciating her gorgeous looks or wondering at the juxtaposition between her and a man obviously bearing the weight of recent self-abuse. The flight delay was a mere hour and he followed them from the congested line to security where he bid her a silent farewell, knowing he would soon meet her, be with her and control her.

An hour later a general broadcast warned lax passengers of the final boarding call, the flight departed at 1:45 and he went to the restaurant for a relaxed lunch. After all, he was on vacation, a well-deserved vacation at that. He didn't want to arrive at the house in daylight, irrespective of the storm, and waited for the cover of darkness before leaving the airport not far from the time the Burberrys would be landing in Miami: Ted, who hadn't started his week well; little Melissa who wasn't so little and Timothy who was slower than molasses and just as bright. Then Kathy: the increasingly beautiful, exotic and quixotic Kathy whom he would have and captivate in the very near future. He would. He was determined. He was infatuated with her innocence, her freshness and would not leave the city without knowing her intimately. She was, in fact, his barometer of success or failure. The one person who might knowingly or unwittingly send him back to a prison he would most likely never leave.

Driving conditions improved considerably and the contractor had passed by to clear the driveway. Clint Evans drove directly to the rear of the house, stopping by the closest garage window, wasting no time and extremely pleased he'd thought to visit the house the previous week. The nagging thought of climbing an extension ladder and crawling through a half-metre of snow and possible ice to a closed window he would have to break was sufficiently unsettling without the added worry of breaking a leg or his back. With the knowledge he didn't have to, he was doubly pleased. The property was black as pitch and Burberry had never upgraded the windows on the house that wasn't as modern as others on the hill.

He didn't bother peering into the garage. He went straight to work layering the pane with strips of duct tape and placing a hammer on the ledge. He went to the Network Interface Device, took a deep breath, cut through the lock, snipped the ring and tip wires and ran to smash the window, heaving his weight through the perfectly open space and onto a cushion of shards.

Scrambling to his feet he ran to the inside door, halting. There was no sound, nothing, and a guttural "yes" surged from his throat. They hadn't noticed the disconnected wires at the siren. Though what he hadn't expected was the Lexus. His SUV couldn't possibly stay outside for a week. Neighbours might pass by, or the contractor, and alert the police. Somehow he had to find keys to Kathy's MX-5 and his first thought was the closet in the foyer unless she'd given a set to the husband, which he doubted.

He ran. He had to run. His whole body was running on adrenalin and five minutes later the MX-5 was moved up with the SUV snugly parked behind and Clint was busy covering the front-facing windows with black paper. He wasn't finished. An hour later he'd swept up the debris and replaced the broken window, super-heating and painting the fresh putty without leaving the slightest trace.

He was in. He was on vacation. Anything remotely resembling work could wait. He'd done enough. What he wanted was a bath, dinner and one of the several videos he'd rented for the week, although he did bring sufficient paper to cover every window in the house. What remained beyond what he'd already accomplished, he didn't know. He had until the 27th and what else he would do was fully dependent on the coming day and a phone call to the airline confirming the flight did, indeed land in Miami.

He brought groceries, liquor and wine and garbage bags. He brought a change of clothes for each day, his toiletries, and whatever was missing he would borrow or acquire in town after dark. More importantly, he had an entire week without the sense of urgency or anxiety which was usually an integral part of his workweek. Without them he would have failed months earlier.

Kathy landed at 7:15, by which time Clint had bathed in her Victorian tub, finished dinner and checked through her wardrobe. By 10:00 the DVD was ejected, he'd washed his dishes and a plastic old-fashioned filled with vodka lay by her bed. He was right to assume all was not well with the Burberrys. Separate beds were the precursor to divorce. She was the one walking. Married men never bought beds, let alone twin doubles.

He went downstairs to the office, tried the drawer and went to the garage. Once again in Kathy's bed he studied each of the dozens of photos Burberry had taken of Eileen. He was intrigued. She was beautiful, arousing and certainly uninhibited. She was the kind of woman he could love and he made a mental note to learn more about her, chuckling, realizing he didn't need a week. He could leave the house right then and engineer a chance meeting with Kathy a few days after her return with no more effort than placing the album under her pillow and driving away. Kathy would take care of the rest, until he had an idea and went from her bed to the family room.

He knew he wouldn't find what he was looking for in the office. He knew perfectly well how she would look naked, how she would feel to his gentle touch. What he didn't know was how long he would need to erase memories of her once she felt the sting beneath those gentle caresses when he could never forgive her for what she had done.

By the time he finished he'd searched every drawer in every room, every shelf and wondered what he'd missed: nothing. He hadn't overlooked a single possibility, including the box of CDs. The Burberry's didn't have one family album. He returned to her bed. He'd taken a million photos of Kim, each one engraved in his mind, each one a curse which had recently come to life in a hotel bar. He slid under the satin covers, worlds apart from the sanitized cotton sheets and woollen blankets of prison. Kathy was making a point. She was telling Burberry he didn't count, and he didn't.

Thirty-Two

Tuesday after breakfast Clint began with the office, replacing the album as he'd found it. Nothing else of interest was in the drawer and his main preoccupation was the safe. He opened the laptop, spending the better part of the morning searching through files, archives and Burberry's travel agenda, doing a specific search for e-i-l-e-e-n which produced one result.

Connecting to the internet, he Googled the number under residences and came up empty. Trying under businesses he saw the response and reached for the photo album, flipping through the pages until he came to one taken of Burberry and Eileen attending an art exhibit. Eileen Kimberly worked at Las Galerías. He typed in the name, blowing a thin stream of air between his lips when the screen filled with the home page and close-up of Eileen Kimberly. She was no employee. She was the owner of four galleries in as many cities and nothing in the virtual tour looked affordable, including her. He reached for the travel agenda, scrolling through the entire year, each trip ending at the seaside resort town where Eileen lived and worked from her galleries' flagship: La Primera. Ted Burberry had not merely found the pot of gold; he was screwing it like clockwork.

Clint printed the pages and typed in k-a-t-h-y, waited, and nothing came up. Then he typed in b-u-r-b-e-r-r-y, reading each of the several results including the file:

Burberry, Eileen (Wife). He sat staring at the screen, printing the page as he accessed Space Search. Burberry and wife number two lived by the sea in something approaching an estate. He closed the computer and reached for the attaché believing he'd spend hours fiddling with the series of birthdates, phone numbers and other obvious combinations he had worked out over the past week to get into the safe. He didn't. The case was unlocked. Then he remembered how Burberry looked at the airport: as though he'd been put through a meat grinder.

He searched through each file folder sheet by sheet. Burberry had been through a grinder if the empty bottle and flight coupons attached to his expenses were any indication. Then Clint opened the card and slumped into the chair, reading each word of the scented note again, too disbelieving to laugh. Burberry would be spending Spring Break double-dipping. Number two was joining him for Spring Break in Myrtle Beach, bribing him with a million dollars to leave Kathy when they were already sharing a beach house. Ted had two homes, two wives and possibly wasn't being given enough credit. He clearly possessed qualities which weren't fully appreciated. Who paid a million dollars for Joe Average, especially a classy woman like Eileen Kimberly? Clint replaced the attaché on the floor, photocopying one head shot and one close-up nude of Eileen stretched out on a boat that either belonged to them or a friendly neighbour, making a mental note to buy photo-grade paper to copy the others. He put them with her data and went for lunch. He needed a drink in the worst way.

In the afternoon he began with the girl's room, first searching through her desk, cell phone and computer, thinking the lack of pictures unusual for a teenage girl and more curious about her cache of costumes and who was seeing her in them, certainly not the parents. He put the diary aside after skimming through the pages. Some kid had already pushed his way past her pants, which she wrote was disappointing. She no longer loved him and made no further mention of him in the following few pages. He would photocopy the pages to read more at his leisure.

Clint returned the suitcase to its original position and pushed apart the neatly spaced row of clothes, peeking into the Christmas bag and seeing the backpack in the corner, which he opened on the bed, uncorking the bottle of premium vodka and sniffing the contents before connecting her other laptop, losing his mind in a matter of minutes. He scanned the bedroom, doing a three-sixty. He couldn't believe what he was seeing. She was using her bedroom for a porno studio while her mother and brother were in the house. By the time he downed his third straight vodka what he didn't know about the prissy Melissa Burberry and her darker alter ego didn't matter, including her tight butt and the quarter-million in the bank. However he had no doubt what he'd be doing December 31st and for the rest of the day once he finished in the boy's room, curious whether he was as dysfunctional as the rest of the family.

The kid's backpack was empty, his computer, micro-cassette and phone neatly placed on the desk. The recorder had no tape and the phone was missing the memory card. He opened the laptop and clicked directly onto My Documents and Images, finding nothing, searching through each file, stopping at Blank and tapping the touchpad. His day was getting better, or worse. He wasn't quite sure which. He scrolled to the next photo of Melissa and another through to the last of twelve.

He left the screen and went to her room, intrigued by the angle. The kid must have spent an entire evening under her bed taking shots of his sister, unless she knew, which wouldn't be any great surprise. He scrolled backwards through the slideshow, took the computer to the office, burned a CD and went to search for the missing cassette which he found lying at the bottom of the backpack. Bright kid, he thought, and after thirty minutes he rewound. "Kathy, Kathy," he whispered, "no damn wonder you want out. Your husband's a bigamist, your daughter's a wealthy cyber slut and your son's a sexual deviant with the hots for his sister."

He needed a break. He took Melissa's computer and diary to Kathy's bedroom, went to the garage for something to eat and cooked a meal, irrepressibly anxious to penetrate the safe. If Burberry and his spawn had such dark secrets completely unencrypted, particularly the girl, what could he expect to find in the safe? The Midnight Rhapsody videos could wait. He went for his list of presumed codes and sat on the office floor. Midway he heard the beep and by late evening had photocopied his and her blank cheques, bank statements, investment statements, income tax returns, a marriage contract and their wills. He had SS numbers, a copy of the property transfer, credit card and PIN numbers and the ID card required for any future duplicates of the house keys. He was exhausted. He returned each document in precisely the same order, closed the door and circled the correct code in his notebook. Then he went upstairs, showered where Kathy showered and went to her bed to learn and see more of Melissa and Midnight Rhapsody.

She was a little tease who had clearly taken a quantum leap very recently and her brother recorded the event. He reviewed her videos, her December file of performances and read each word of her diary which she encrypted by means of imperfect high school Spanish. Clint's Spanish was near perfect and had no difficulty understanding what was in her mind, her future or her past two years.

Some kid did her at a frat party with a couple of his buds as back-up. Whereas she had expected tender caresses, lying naked together, covered by darkness and hearing the words all naïve females yearn to hear, she heard laughter.

Mission accomplished. The unapproachable Melissa Burberry had been tested and approved for use by others, left to feel dirty and heal her bruises in the pages of her diary. Clint laughed. Girls invariably remembered their first, while boys always forgot who, when and where. In any event, they must have sparked something inside her and Midnight Rhapsody was born soon after.

By morning Clint hadn't slept a wink, struggling to process the incredulous data inundating his mind as he photocopied the diary and transferred each byte from the girl's computer into his. She was a good-looking kid with a decent body, good taste in booze, he allowed, and dumb. Anyone could act smart for ten minutes at a time. The fact was: she'd be a common whore by the age of twenty-five, a drunk leaning into car windows by thirty and the boy wasn't any better. He'd panhandle by day, sleep under cardboard by night and the parents might never be the wiser.

Wednesday he made a hot breakfast to chase away the chill brought on by lack of sleep and went to her family room to begin reading through the plethora of copied documents, already decided he would leave the house before dinner and what he would do. Thursday the stores would close at 5:00 and he would have neither the time nor the cover of darkness, leaving him one shopping day before Christmas.

He had dedicated his time since his release to working at loving women, making them feel special. Now his objective was to make one woman feel special. Eileen Burberry was going to Myrtle Beach, so would Clint and, when Burberry was somewhere loving his second wife, he'd be making love with Kathy, a rose by any other name, and by then he would know her as intimately as her husband and their past would be reawakened or erased.

He left at 4:00, a time when he could expect no traffic. He blackened the head and signal lights of his SUV with shoe polish which he cleared with mineral spirits once beyond the possible view of any neighbour, equipped with Kathy's garage remote and front door key. His first stop was an industrial electronics outlet specializing in security, the second was a home hardware and the third was an IT supply centre where he disposed of his previous days' refuse and the broken window.

Returning to the hilltop home he poured a drink, cooked a late dinner and went to Kathy's bed, watching her daughter's videos, attempting to peer into the mind of a self-made teenage porn star. He couldn't, and not because the videos weren't clear. She was pretty, had a nice body and was probably Miss Popularity at school. She'd been laid once by three guys, which likely wasn't a secret, which also meant a long line of hopeful runners-up, yet she had written of her dislike for the whole physical thing and didn't have a single picture of the next in line with the graduation date highlighted on her calendar. He put the computer on the floor and put out the light. He would spend Thursday walking through the plan, critiquing each step, weighing numerous negatives against uncertain positives and would abort whenever reason took over from his inexplicable insanity. What he was contemplating was crazy, maniacal, making him no better than Burberry or his demented duo.

In the morning he was entirely focused on the first dry run, doing a second from a different perspective and by late afternoon he had moved his gear onto the second floor landing and his equipment onto the worktable in the garage. By midnight the attic was furnished with a rope ladder, a cot and thermal sleeping bag, a folding camping chair and rug, liquor and a case of bottled water, an empty jar for convenience, dried fruit bars and garbage bags, a new computer, pesticide spray and a Coleman lamp. And by the time he fell asleep in her bed he hadn't noticed Christmas Eve had passed him by.

Friday was anything but a holiday. He began the morning examining, his task a veritable charm thanks to the antiquated overhead ducting. He couldn't believe his good fortune and by late Sunday afternoon he had full audio-visual access from his garret to Kathy's bedroom, her bathroom, the upper hallway and family room, the girl's room, the boy's, the office, the entrance and garage. The Burberrys would be home in twenty-four hours and never suspect he would soon monitor their every move. He went from room to room making certain no trace of his week remained.

After dark he moved his SUV to the rear of the house, swept away the dried residue which had fallen from his vehicle Monday and Wednesday and returned the MX-5 to its original spot, replacing Kathy's remote and key. He laundered her sheets, pressed them, replaced them and slept his first night in the attic after uncovering the windows and putting the material by the garage door. At 3:00AM he performed a final check, exited through the garage, reconnected the ring and tip wires, attached the new lock and drove home.

He could not have asked for a better ending to his week. A heavy snowfall was expected to reach its full intensity by the dinner hour.

Thirty-Three

At home Clint Evans felt trapped. He hated doing nothing. He had always worked, even in prison. He always would. The day's weather report was accurate and after enjoying the run of Kathy's house for an entire week the walls of his apartment were closing in. Ironically, New Year's would be a lonely time for him. Any unattached woman with the nerve or need to search for love or free drinks on the year's premier party night would either be pathetic or desperate, big-boned or on the wrong side of fifty, which didn't fit his recently and firmly established criteria.

He doubted he would survive until the fourth when Burberry was scheduled to leave and Kathy would return to college with her brats. Yet he had a great deal to consider, analyze and perfect. From the fourth onward he would hear them breathe, talk and see them sleep. Of least interest was the boy. Kathy was his primary focus, however Melissa had unexpectedly become a very close second whom he couldn't ignore, not to say he hadn't already ODed on her bare backside, the pouty schoolgirl, the naughty nurse, the sultry secretary and the cheeky French maid: turn-ons for the very young or very old. None of which would ever compare to seeing Kathy in a nurse's mini uniform or stripping away her starched blouse one button at a time.

Garters were the real deal, the quintessential turn-on and somehow he didn't believe the kid would realize that before her money would one day run out and her only silk stocking would be the one around her neck: her pimp's silk garrotte. The kid had a quarter-million, a fortune to a teenager which she would easily squander if not properly managed. He chuckled involuntarily. If Kim had taught him anything, she taught him money management and the cops never did discover her offshore investments. At first Kim Moon had mesmerized him with her heated Cajun charm, finally bringing his life to a jarring halt with her chilling Oriental detachment.

He would see Kathy again on the 04th, feeling disappointed he wouldn't see her any sooner. His first New Years in six years and he still wasn't entirely free. They used to have such fun together as a couple, dancing into the early hours, making love and waking to chocolate and champagne served with fine linen and crystal. Now he wanted her never to wake. He wanted her to feel the end of his world, the violent end she once callously witnessed from a distant pedestal of concrete and steel. He wanted her to feel the pain of five colourless years as intensely as he wanted to feel her warmth, her skin, absorb her sadness, bring her happiness and leave her with lasting memories and regret for what she had done.

*

Kathy was tanned pretty well everywhere, and what wasn't could easily be covered with her hands. She ran the length of South Beach six mornings and seven afternoons and bathed in the sun a few hours each day where people didn't stare, where the popular culture was to smile with thumbs pointing upward.

She managed her diet and limited her tequilas and soda. She bought more bikinis for herself and her January travel companions. She bought more dresses and was secretly pleased by Timothy's decision to try another hobby. She looked fantastic, whereas Ted didn't and not because he hadn't teed off enough throughout the week or that Kathy's journey towards middle-age had reversed and his had accelerated. He was furious about the guitar and had spent the weekend fuming. Christmas morning Kathy marvelled at the gift certificates from the in-laws, the briefcase from Ted and the perfume from Melissa, which Kathy exchanged the next day for something less clinical. A gold-plated bracelet from Timothy was the one real surprise, shocking everyone until the ulterior motive unfolded later Christmas day and she agreed.

When the older Burberrys wished their son the best for the coming year, they hugged him warmly. When they embraced Kathy the chill emanating from the invisible film of ice between them wafted across the room to the kids who felt only the hundred-dollar bills tucked into their pockets. The foursome arrived home after midnight, deep in snow, beleaguered from travel, tired and hungry, eating store-bought pizza as they emptied suitcases and filled laundry bags. Kathy was the last to sleep, lounging in the living room with a snifter of tequila to quietly end her day. She would drive Timothy into town the following morning to exchange the instrument for a camcorder while Ted and Melissa attended to their laundry. And the boy was no exception. A new era had dawned.

Mother and son left after breakfast in the shiny Lexus, which Ted agreed to because he needed time alone and his temper had rekindled. He'd forgotten his abandoned suitcase and the empty scotch bottle in the wastebasket. Melissa walked him through the first load and set up the ironing table, leaving him to his own devices and tantrums. When he was done he poured a scotch from the dining room reserve and placed a call from his office. Kathy had refused to buy liquor intended for his private use, reminding him offhandedly that, in any event, he had to drive into town to pick up his suit. She was pushing hard, not missing the smallest opportunity to belittle him.

Eileen answered on the first ring. She was at the beach house. She missed him. She was anxious to see him on the fourth and had little else to say. Her tone was despondent because he was sitting on the fence playing a waiting game, waiting to win a no-win contest rather than deferring to someone with more to gain and nothing to lose. He knew, so did Eileen and so did the other one, he thought. He would just have to push harder than her.

"I rescheduled my flight. I'm flying out this Sunday and you'll have me through to the sixteenth Eileen, twelve days."

"How did you manage that? Is Kathy in a coma?"

"No, no coma. She won't care about Sunday and she'll be in Vermont by the time you and I land here for a long weekend. You haven't been up here for a while. The change will do us good and Sunday we'll fly out together. I plan on spending both weeks within easy travel of the cape."

"We're booked?"

"We are, for midday arrivals and departures. While you're in town the kids will be on their own each day until as late as possible and from early morning the day she gets back. They're old enough."

"Sweetheart, put us in the hotel at the harbour, the one with the casino. At least then I'll have something to do when you're babysitting."

"It's done, three days in a suite facing the bay and I won't be babysitting very long." Ted paused. "She's in the driveway. I'll call you through the week."

"I'll be at La Primera, sweetheart. Goodbye."

He disconnected, wishing he'd stayed in Miami another week or that he had gone alone. He hadn't seen Kathy in her bikinis once, or her tan lines and what clothes she did wear had practically euthanized his mother. Imagining was enough. Thirty-six and acting like a teenager, or someone who was available and didn't have two kids. He couldn't remember how many times his father had asked whether or not the house was safe from partition, or how many times his mother commented on Kathy being a poor example for an impressionable young girl. What he did remember was Kathy giving in about the camcorder and threatening to disrupt Christmas by flying home at his mother's next caustic breath.

Timothy was ecstatic with his replacement gift, a palm-sized camcorder with a 41X zoom and twenty-one hours of recording time, ideal for videoing surfers at the ocean, ships in the harbour or subjects requiring fine resolution. He walked by his father without saying a word and spent the rest of the day in his room while his sister busied herself with laundry and her New Year's Eve schedule. At dinner Timothy excused himself from the table, claiming he hadn't yet done his laundry, experimenting with the more subdued lighting in the basement, in his room from under the bed, all the while plugged-in to Melissa and Peter.

Christmas never happened. Ted went to his office, Kathy went to her récamier and Melissa stayed locked in her bedroom, rehearsing silently for her star performance the way she had each night after dinner over the past several weeks. She was ready and didn't feel the least bit uneasy. On the contrary, she was on a high. She wouldn't work until Thursday. She needed to be completely rested for the four-hour marathon. She put her ear to the door, poured a double shot of vodka, put the glass in her drawer and stowed the bottle in her backpack. She listened again, this time before calling an anonymous friend whom she could always rely upon. He was twenty-six, lived with his parents, was unemployed and liked to drink. Not much else. She first met him in a park, panhandling, and met weekly thereafter, on her schedule. In the summer his price was a 750ml and a lingering peek up her skirt from a sidewalk as she straightened her ankle socks at a park bench or stooped to conceal the bottle in her handbag. In the winter months he was paid with a full litre. She had no preference.

Wednesday she would go into town with her father and, somewhere in the mall would be a dishevelled, poorly dressed man with an identical leather shopping bag. She rehearsed an hour longer, poured the final shot from the bottle and undressed in front of the mirror. In her panties and bra she continued as sultrily as never before, her crowning achievement following weeks of preparation. Pausing to enjoy the moment, imagining her fans admiration, she slipped into her baby dolls and put out the light.
*

Wednesday was status quo. Ted went for his suit and his daughter accompanied him. At the mall he sat in a bar, happy to be away from the house, while Melissa ran errands for herself and her mother. He drove her home without an invitation to lunch and that was the extent of their father-daughter quality time. Kathy wasn't at the house when they arrived and Timothy wasn't very helpful. She had gone out with some woman or something, so Ted went to his office, Melissa rehearsed in her room and Timothy played with his new toy and watched a slideshow he would soon make obsolete.

Kathy phoned Michelle that morning, inviting her to lunch without knowing why. She simply wanted to, she did, and Michelle jumped at the chance to get out before Kathy finished her sentence. And not long after two beautiful women were out cruising the snow-lined streets of town in a bright red MX-5 until finally deciding on the quaint little bistro where Kathy hadn't wanted to sit alone. They spoke for hours, the centre of attention by the fire as Kathy contained her curiosity at how much more beautiful Michelle could be in Vermont. If she dressed like that for a glass of wine and a cheese plate, how enticing would she look in Vermont for a man?

"You're staring, darling." Kathy's head swung around. Michelle giggled. "No one heard."

"I'm sorry. I'm not used to endearments, particularly from a woman."

"Get used to it, especially in Vermont. It's part of safe sex. No one has to remember the other's name unless they want to and, speaking of safe sex, don't forget your trip to the pharmacy. We normally each take a few dozen, so don't rely on your friends. They go fast." She sipped her wine. "I'm joking, darling. Mí proteccíon es tu proteccíon and when we run out we'll always have each other."

"That might be uncomfortable," Kathy sipped her wine, "for the first few minutes."

"Oooh, darling, thank you, I think, but if you do forget, and we always forget something silly, we won't let you down."

"I won't forget."

"How was your Christmas?"

"Running, sunning, sleeping on a couch, resisting the urge to punch out the old broad's dentures and," Kathy held out her wrist, "this is from Timothy, surprisingly. The rest would make you laugh hysterically and make me cry. When I said goodbye to the in-laws neither one had any idea how serious I was. And how were your holidays," she paused, "mi amor?"

Michelle beamed, Kathy blushed. "Thank you. That was Sheila's doing, as in Spanish teacher. And if you think this cutesy stuff doesn't work big time at a bar, just wait darling, and doing lunch together was a great idea. As for Christmas, let's say red and black aren't my colours and I prefer making my own holes in my panties. He got a watch and I cooked dinner for him and his porn-infatuated divorced brother while they were downstairs oohing over some DVD bimbo with big boobs."

"Do you like metallic red?"

"I do if it's short with a bare back and one of us is wearing it in Vermont or for Girls' Night."

Kathy reached into her purse, placing the tiny package into Michelle's lap. "Not bad. I'm impressed. You got Vermont right; the back is definitely bare and short is open to interpretation. Merry Christmas, mi amor."

Michelle drew the slingshot bikini from the box, her full lips forming a wide and breathless "O". "Darling, I love it." She leaned over, kissing Kathy's cheek.

"There's also a cover-up about the size of a Kleenex. I thought of your hair and knew you had to wear red."

Michelle dipped her fingers into the bag, pinching the delicate fabric. "Wow, the girls will hate me."

"And me, if you tell them. So you can't. You'll spoil the surprise. They're getting the same in green and blue. Promise me?"

"I do promise. Thank you, darling." Michelle signalled the waiter, dropping the slingshot on the sofa as she ordered more wine.

"Michelle, you are incorrigible."

"One more word and I'll put this on right here." Kathy put a finger to her lips, shaking her head in silent agreement. When the waiter had come and gone Michelle put a fingertip to her mouth, pressed an ardent kiss into the soft flesh and pressed it against Kathy's lips. Tears welled in her eyes. "It's my nicest gift. Thank you, Kathy."

The response was unexpected, as was the altered mood.

"Hey, I didn't mean for this to ruin our afternoon. Tell you what, next time he'd rather watch porn instead of you, you call me and I'll watch you. Believe me; you're not hard on the eyes, especially in this." She giggled. "In fact, why don't we a have girls porn night? We could buy lingerie and model for each other, watch videos and get drunk."

"Darling, don't ever make that suggestion in front of

214

Sheila. Your feet wouldn't touch the ground until she lands you in the video store. The girl is wild, and sexy. Wait till you see her in whatever colour is hers." She stroked the glittering red fabric. "I do wish I could wear this right now. But I will wait until Vermont. Have you?"

Kathy grimaced, clenching her teeth. "Sort of …in Miami…with the cover-up and sitting at the beach. I was too chicken to go all the way. I chose gold and from a distance you wouldn't know."

"Really." Michelle peered into the fire through the sheer fabric. "Was he with you?"

"Are you kidding? He hasn't even seen my lines."

"What lines? And his loss was everyone else's gain. Wow, darling. Eight days and I can't wait. We've already arranged for substitutes. We're set."

"And I've attended to the needs of my balls and chains. He's coming home early to play caring daddy and won't be leaving till I'm back." Kathy looked at her watch. "Mi amor…"

"I know. Now I wish you hadn't called me. I've had so much fun. Darlene and Sheila are going hate us. They'll feel cheated."

"Then I'll see each one separately and give them the bikinis before we go."

"First of all, there's no time and, secondly, I liked having you to myself. I didn't mean what I said about not calling, so don't you dare. As much as I love them, today was terrific. Thank you, darling, and let's do this again very soon." She swirled her last sip of wine. "And Kathy, when you do leave him, call me, I'll leave with you. I'm serious. I know I should have left already. I can earn triple the money translating or interpreting and I don't have to wait for the longer days of summer. They're already long enough, so don't go without me. Promise me, darling. We can be each other's shoulder to cry on."

Kathy drove Michelle home, feeling sad for her friend, feeling sorry for herself that they couldn't spend more time together. She had expected a big smile and a cheerful "goodbye," what she got was a nonchalant kiss on her lips that was neither fleeting nor lingering and a frown her friend couldn't disguise. Driving to the hilltop Kathy's mind was boggled with thoughts of the ladies, Jack, Michelle, her new sexuality, sensuality and mi amor. Mi amor and darling, she whispered. She pulled in by the ocean. She wasn't ready to go home. What home? What made the house on the hill a home? She could see that Ted was in the bedroom, yet she couldn't push Michelle from her mind, or Jack who hadn't gone to the bistro. Why would he? Saturday was days away and the weather was clear.

She had never gone to an elegant bistro with another woman, let alone inviting someone who was drop-dead gorgeous to join her, someone who clearly had no problem calling her darling. Not a solitary qualm lingered in her mind that mi amor was a "straight" lover of attentive men. She'd worked with Michelle for years, discussing students' problems and needs, including Melissa's. Somehow she would have known and with Girls' Night. Some little clue would have been revealed. She was being silly. She was the one who called Michelle, who gave her a personal gift beyond all others and not retreat from her tender kiss. What the hell was happening to her, she cried? A woman was calling her darling, when Ted never had and Jack Caden never would. And why was she calling a woman "my love" when Jack Caden should have come to sweep her off her feet and carry her to an illicit hideaway. And why had she promised not to leave without her?

She waited thirty minutes or more, letting her eyes dry naturally. She called Michelle from her cell, saying she was parked moments from home and safe. Then she did drive home. In not far from twenty-four hours she'd be dressing for New Years at friends who never called to say hello unless school was involved. She was the local info-psycho outlet, free of charge, or was. No longer. Now she was Kathy, with new friends. She'd flirted in a hotel bar, a bistro and at the beach. She would never be readier and Ted could go to hell. In fact, she would drive him there.

Thirty-Four

New Year's Eve at the Burberrys was subdued, everyone lost in their own time and place. They ate as a family in the dining room, this time in casual dress and Timothy was allowed to party with his friends as long as he was home by 2:00 AM. Conversely, and not out of character, his sister turned down a lucrative babysitting job, preferring to stay home and didn't mind not being invited to the year's best slumber party.

Ted and Kathy were expected at 8:30. Kathy began getting ready at 7:00, Ted thirty minutes later when the wife was finished in the bathroom and, when he was finished, Kathy was dressed and waiting in the living room, adamant he would never again see her undressed.

She was stunning. The midnight blue cocktail dress was décolleté to below the sensuous swell of her tanned breasts which she accentuated even more by a pendant resting between them. Her back was bare, the flared skirt was mid-thigh, she wore no stockings and her matching evening sandals were open-toed. When Ted appeared, his black suit accented with a white shirt and red tie, he lurched forward, his breath cut short, his face instantly purple with stifled rage.

"Get upstairs and change. You're not going anywhere with me dressed like a cheap whore."

She smiled. "Not quite cheap, Ted, more like seventeen-hundred: eight-hundred for the dress, the shoes were four-hundred and the chain was five. Oh, and what you can't and won't see were a hundred. Cheap, I don't think so, and if you ever call me that again I'll bash in your head and throw you and your bed out the window."

His eyes glared. "We're not going."

"Maybe not you…fine. I'll take a taxi, drop in at the party to offer your excuses and go downtown to enjoy myself for the first time." She patted her dress. "Think I'll have any trouble bringing in the New Year? I don't, and what should I tell them is wrong with you, catastrophic diarrhoea brought on by your mother's cooking?"

Then: "Mother! Like what are you thinking? My God. You can't go out dressed like that. Your breasts are like totally bare and you're not even like wearing stockings." Melissa was wide-eyed, standing by her father. "Do you have any idea how fast this will get around? I'll be like laughed at by everyone. Daddy…"

"Thank you, Melissa. I would have preferred awesome, or like totally fantastic. But, hey, they're boobs, nice ones, and, for your information, I had much more of them on display last week at South Beach. Does that put a twist in your panties? And, by the way, ladies don't wear stockings with open toes. Why wouldn't a fashion princess such as you be au courant about that? I'm also quite certain none of your so-called friends who never come over would ever laugh at the dresses they see on seven o'clock trash TV, the ones they can't afford. Now get out of here. And you, if you're staying, fine, if not get my coat and boots."

"This isn't right. The kid's got a point. We'll be a laughing stock."

"You already are, at least in this house. And no one's going to laugh at me. The women will talk about me, sure, and the husbands will wonder what I'm wearing underneath or how often you get laid. Any healthy husband would be proud to see his wife dressed this way. Tell the truth, Ted.

What you're most worried about is not being the star attraction this evening, the life of the party. And, incidentally, how often do you get laid?"

Ted turned to Melissa. "She's right. We don't need your two cents worth. Go to your room and, when your brother leaves, set the alarm and don't expect us before three or four."

"Yes, daddy, I will."

When she was gone Kathy shook her head. "I feel for the guy who gets trapped in her pants."

"Won't be the first time a guy gets in and doesn't get out."

"Your right. The difference being, her father isn't as bright as mine was."

"This can't go on forever, Kath."

"All couples argue, Ted. Didn't anyone ever tell you? It seems we both have to work a little harder for what we really want."

"Meaning what exactly?"

"Meaning, please get my coat and my boots."
*

As soon as they were gone Timothy told his sister he'd be leaving soon and waited for her to take her usual shower. When the bathroom door was closed he removed his boots and coat from the foyer, stowed them in his bedroom closet and hurried to change into his sweats, ski mask and thick socks. Then he yelled from the hallway that he was leaving, went into his room, put out the lights with the door sufficiently ajar to see into the hall and slid under his bed. Ten minutes later her bare feet padded from the bathroom. He was set to go. He just didn't know where, but he had done his arithmetic.

She yelled out his name, twice, from where he could see her feet. She yelled again and disappeared into the front room and foyer. He heard the garage entrance open and slam closed, he heard the high-pitched beeps of the security system engaging and moments later saw her feet. She went into her room without closing the door and he began losing his mind, remembering what he'd seen, viewing each of the dozen photos over and over again in his mind. He heard the rustling of paper, glasses or bottles being moved around and saw shadows reaching into the hall. Then he saw her feet passing his door, disappearing, and heard her climbing the stairs. He inched forward, waiting, hearing water draining through the pipes in the walls, and again he heard her footsteps. His body was pressed hard against the floor, his neck positioned sideways, craning. He dared not blink, catching his breath. He saw her from her thighs down for the second she took to pass his door and moments later she hurried by again, climbing the stairs, stopping the flow of water before hurrying once more to her room.

She made five trips and on the fifth she switched off her bedroom light. He looked at his watch. The time was 9:30 and he was standing behind his door, in the dark, waiting with his heart pounding and his throat dry to see her climb the stairs. When she finally did pass through the narrow field of vision he gulped, catching a fleeting glimpse of what he'd seen over and over again in his mind for days. Whatever she was doing she had thirty minutes left before he would climb the stairs to his mother's bedroom. If she caught him, so what, he'd have the proof, past and present, and she could never explain being naked in their parents' room with a full bath, a computer and booze.

Time stood still. He inched his way to the door, listening intently, pressing his ear to the wall for the slightest sound of running water. Nothing, absolutely nothing. Still he waited, torn between fear, curiosity, wanting to see her naked body and wanting to hide. The light at the top of the stairs went out at 9:45 and he hurried to his desk for water and the first of many sandwiches he'd made during the day.

At 9:50 he was in the hallway, standing amidst the quiet of semi-darkness which was broken at 9:55.
*

Melissa placed the empty champagne bottle on the vanity along with the fluted glass, both in view of the camera. She poured a generous portion of vodka, took a deep breath and swallowed half. She had promised a lot and her fans would expect a lot for a hundred dollars. She had four costumes, dressed in a sheer racer back baby doll and matching panties for her first visitor. The second was a chiffon and satin shirt and thong, the third fan would see her in a micro-mini slip dress without panties and the fourth each hour would be treated to a crystal thong and bra set, each outfit accessorized with a different coloured wig, glasses and contacts.

She swallowed what was left in her old-fashioned, poured a small amount of vodka into the champagne glass, added ginger ale, leaned into the webcam and went live.

"Peter, it's you."

"Happy New Year, Rhapsody. Told you I'd be first."

"Happy New Year, Peter, and you were the first a few days ago if I remember. I hope your sexy wife is joining us?"

"No, we're alone."

"I'm disappointed. I wanted her to see me, and to see her. Could you imagine both of us undressing for you at the same time?" Rhapsody giggled. "I think I would have ended up watching the two of you, watching you imagine you were doing me." She stepped away from the lens and swirled. "I hope the special baby dolls I wore for you will help you forget, Peter."

"That's incredible. Face away from me. Let me see the back again."

"You will because I want to take a bath for you. Would you like to watch me bathing?"

"Damn straight."

"But first, do you have a glass of champagne. It is New Year's you know."

"No. The stuff goes down too fast and backfires the same way. I've got the poor man's sparkle."

Rhapsody held her stemmed glass in front of her. "Not mine. Here's to a fun year together. I hope we see each other often." She sipped the mixed drink once, licked her highly glossed lips and sipped again. "This is especially for you, Peter. Watch carefully and be a good boy." She put down her glass, stepped into the middle of the expansive bathroom, held her hands high and twirled, facing away from the lens when she stood still.

*

Timothy crept step by step to the upper landing, concealing himself in the family room. At 10:00 PM he heard soft music, his sister began talking and he virtually glided to his mother's bedroom door without his feet leaving the floor. Melissa hadn't closed it. She had no reason, she was alone and the room was dark. The walk-in closet was between them and he eased into the point of no return, to the furthest bed, his mother's, and dropped to his knees, biting his lip when she came into view. He braced himself against his mother's bed, aimed the camera and watched.

*

She bent forward touching her toes, asking Peter whether he could see when she knew very well he could. She raised her torso halfway, brought her hands to her hips, tucked her thumbs under the elastic bands of her panties and brought them to her feet, kicking them aside. Coming up, she arched, spun around and faced the camera, crossing her hands teasingly over the apex of her thighs before responding to the man's pleas, bringing her hands caressingly to the single clasp between her breasts, turning away as she let the flimsy top flutter to the floor. She took a deep breath she couldn't believe. This was the defining moment of her career. She had no towel, no muted lighting. He was about to see what no one else had seen before. She pivoted slowly, smilingly, fully at ease.

*

Timothy needed water badly, but he had none and his sister had five minutes left with the twisted dude. She was perfectly framed and he'd mastered the zoom function of his Christmas gift, if not quite the timing. Why she even bothered with school, he couldn't understand. Not with what he calculated. She was making a fortune, at least a few hundred more than her weekly allowance and he could do the same. He could make a fortune as well with what he was seeing and no one would ever doubt what he had to offer was the real Midnight Rhapsody, which was for later. For the time being he wanted to watch her four more hours.

*

He whistled. "You are one hot girl. I can't tell you how much I want to touch you right now. Because of you I have to close my eyes when I'm with the wife."

"You are with me, Peter. Can't you see? No one's ever seen this part of me."

"You're kidding."

"No," she pirouetted, "I'm not, and I can't tell you how much I want to be with a man. Want to know a secret?"

"Yeah, I do."

"I'm a virgin, Peter. No one knows that. Can you imagine being my first?"

"Tell me where and when, Rhapsody. I'm there. Don't even have to ask."

She brought a finger to her lips, pouting. "Peter, I forgot my bath. I'm sorry. Would you like me to bathe for you now?"

"Don't ask, just hurry before I jump through the screen and put you in myself."

She nodded, sipped her faux-champagne and walked to the Victorian tub. She stepped in, put up her hair while facing the lens and eased into the steamy water, turning over, helping her body to float. "Peter, can you see me?"

"Five on five, sweet cheeks, very five on five. Stand for me."

She did, soaping her oiled body from her shoulders to her knees, turning to let him see the growing shield of foam on her back and her buttocks before taking up the flexible showerhead and rinsing herself completely, lingering a moment at the tops of her glistening thighs. The explosion was real. She dropped the showerhead into the water, lurched forward and grabbed for the rounded porcelain edge of the tub to support her convulsing body.

She could barely manage looking into the lens. "Peter, can you imagine me in person? Was I hot? Was my first time good for you?"

"You have to do a live show, sweet cheeks. Your ass is the absolute tightest and those little girls of yours are perfect. You should have a contest with a prize for your most frequent fan, which is me. You know, a night in Vegas or a night anywhere. Hell, get yourself over here and to hell with the wife. I'd kick her out in a split second to spend an evening with you." Rhapsody crawled from the tub, her legs still shaking, not intending to be any more explicit than she had been. "I'll be with you next week, Rhapsody. You know, I'm starting to hate the thought of other guys seeing you but, hey, fair is fair."

"Peter, next time try convincing your wife. I'd like a woman's opinion, really. Can you imagine a three-way in Vegas? I can, with you and your wife. Happy New Year, Peter," and Peter disappeared.
*

Timothy's brain was overheating. As his sister walked to the tub facing away from him, he crept to his father's bed

225

camouflaged by darkness, his clothes and the mask, eager to see every intimate detail of his sister's body. What he had yet to understand was what to do with them, with her, with his sister Midnight Rhapsody.

He knew he needed to hide. Soon she'd be changing costumes in the closet and she wouldn't have much time. Then he saw her leaning forward into the tub, reaching to circulate cooler water with hot and he brought the camcorder to his face, forgetting everything else. He was getting Midnight Rhapsody behind the scenes, the unedited version, and he waited until the last possible moment before scurrying to the far side of his mother's bed and crouching onto the floor.

He breathed into the crook of his elbow in a state of elated disbelief. He heard a chair scraping against the floor tiles. She was once again in the bathroom and he crawled to the cover of his mother's récamier where he could see his sister sitting stark naked at the make-up table, changing her wig and contacts as though what she was doing was completely natural to her. Better yet, his new vantage would give him visual access to the closet. He began filming, frozen in place as she stood to slip into the chiffon and satin shirt, pour a shot of vodka and refill the fluted glass. She stepped into her panties, leaned into screen and went to work.

Part of him wanted to get caught, to see the expression on her face, the other part knew better. He also knew not to leave, not to chance being seen or heard. Food and water could wait. Seeing her was more important and the short distance between his father's bed and the récamier permitted a clear view of her entire stage. He stood and moved closer.

At the end of each hour she started over, each of the four routines changing according to the clients' wishes. Nearing midnight the showerhead in the tub was no longer powerful enough for them, or for her, and by 1:45 fifteen men had seen her strip, bend, stretch, bathe and shower. She padded to the closet, dropping the micro mini-slip into her bag with the other discarded costumes and stood there, apparently not the least bit exhausted or concerned about the hour.

In the bathroom she stood by the mirror, checked her make-up, changed her accessories and reached onto the table for her crystal fall belt and bra, carefully manoeuvring into each piece. From the back she was naked, from the front her breasts were loosely draped with strings of glimmering silver-white strobes and her belt was a single glittering band at her waist with a half-dozen more hanging down to form a tiny, dazzling triangle. She was pleased. She sipped her vodka and connected.

"Hi, I'm Rhapsody."

"Yes, you are. I've been anxious to meet you for quite some time. I love your work and I'm very happy I didn't miss being part of your New Year."

"Thank you. You just made it. What's your name?"

"I'm Clint, and I'm happy to finally meet you."

"Hi, Clint. I hope you like crystals."

"You're a shining star, Rhapsody, a glittering jewel."

"Wow, you must like my work. I think I should do something special for you, to keep you coming back. Do you have any ideas? I can bathe or shower or would you like to watch me get myself…"

"I want to watch you undress, right now."

She giggled, truly enjoying herself. "I'm pretty naked right now, Clint."

"Undress for me, Rhapsody, slowly. Be sexy, feel that you're sexy and when you're finished I want you to stand still so I can appreciate every centimetre of you."

She did. She pushed the strands of rhinestones up over her breasts before unclasping the hooks at her back and at her neck, letting the beads fall to the floor. She brought her hands to her breasts, squeezing gently, leaning forward with a wide smile as she placed one hand over the miniscule triangle while the other undid the clasp at her hip. Standing straight, her painted fingertips pressed softly against the beads, kneading the tender flesh behind. Her other hand rested on her hip.

"Like this Clint?"

"Yes. Now drop the belt and let me see you. Come closer."

"You do like me, don't you?"

"Yes, I do, and in a few moments I'll tell you why. I don't want you thinking I'm another run-of-the-mill voyeur. Turn for me." She did. "Bend over." She did. "Do you have a bench or a chair?"

"Yes."

"Bring it to the camera and sit for me. I want you to imagine you're relaxing alone and no one can see you, not even me."

She dragged the seat from the vanity and sat, first upright, then slouching, then crossing one bare leg over the other, then parting her legs and running her hands down the inside of her thighs. "Is this what you want, Clint?"

"Yes. Don't stop until I tell you. Use your hands as any great musician would on a precious and delicate instrument. Play for me."

"Yes, I will," and she did, her body lifting from the chair in a crescendo. She collapsed, depleted. "Wow."

"Rhapsody, face away from me and straddle the chair." She did, deliberately, unable to hurry, her mind racing. The man was controlling her, directing her and she wanted more. "Now stand, with your feet apart and lean forward." She obeyed. "A rich, handsome man is sitting in the chair and he loves you. He wants you and no one else. He desires you. You're all he wants. Lower your body onto his Rhapsody, and show me your untamed love for him."

*

Timothy was insane. He wanted to run to his room, not to erase the images and sounds of his sister's urgent voice groaning and grunting, her body gyrating and twisting, convulsing as though invisible hands were violently shaking her, but to imagine the hands were his.

*

"Rhapsody...you may stop. I've seen enough. Rhapsody!" She sank into the chair, her body moist with sweat. "Turn and look at me. Relax for me. I want to talk with you about your career and I must talk quickly. Our time is up and you must be quite tired after your long evening. I'm an agent, a very good one and I want to take your talent to the highest level. You're going to be a star, Rhapsody, with my help. Something you cannot do alone. Alone you'll make money in the short-term, which isn't good enough. The big and long-lasting money is in distribution and knowing the right people. We're talking three to four-hundred K a year to start, with no expenses, paid travel, beaches, free resorts and very important friends. I'm leaving tomorrow for Europe and Asia. I'll be returning in five or six weeks." Clint Evans paused. "Can we talk then?"

"Yes."

"Give me your cell number." She hesitated. "It's not like your home number, Rhapsody. And if I have to wait in line to speak to you like this you might miss an opportunity."

"Okay. It's 555-888-2020."

"Good. Thank you. You won't be sorry. And, Rhapsody..."

"Yes."

"I want you ready for an audition. You'll be first choice on the shelves and theatres across the country and overseas by the end of the year. You'll do appearances in exclusive clubs where you can meet your fans, sign autographs and sell limited edition DVDs for thousands each night. And that's only the beginning. You're beautiful, Rhapsody, and don't do anything to change my mind before we talk again. I want you ready, which means I want you rested. I want you to stop doing what you're doing."

"No way, Clint. I love what do."

"You're working too late and too hard for too little money. You have to please your fans, taunt them and tease them. You must constantly work at giving them something original and after tonight's phenomenal performance you can't possibly regress to a chair and a little room. You would destroy all you've worked towards and I won't let that happen. You're too good. Good! Hell, there's no one else like you. Tell them you're taking a sabbatical, that you're creating a production company, exotic themes and costumes. Post a message on your site, promising a performance on Valentine's Day. I can help you with that. Above all I need you rested. Rehearse every night, for me, for your future and get better each time. Don't stop getting better, Rhapsody, and stay away from boys. Know what I mean?"

"Yes."

"Do you have a passport?"

"Yes."

"Are you free to travel? Let's say in March?"

"I don't know, maybe, for a day."

"Not long enough. I'm thinking a few days in Myrtle Beach, in March, during Spring Break, all expenses paid. Can you see yourself being photographed on the beach for your first publicity campaign and your first professional demo shoot? We can discuss your wardrobe in February when we meet. We're talking European lingerie, the best, not the usual sex shop stuff. High fashion all the way and by then I'll have the details regarding your first appearance, something big." He paused. "What's wrong?"

"It's weird. I don't know. I am going to Myrtle Beach in

March."

"Great. Fantastic. We can hook up on the Monday, spend the day together and within a week I'll have the edited version ready for our mutual approval. We can either meet up at your hotel or mine. We can decide later."

"Wow."

"Rhapsody, I hope you're legal. Please tell me you're legal."

"I am legal."

"Sorry. I had to ask. I'm not wrong about you, Rhapsody. We'll talk soon to set up for Valentine's. Goodbye."

He disconnected with seconds to spare and Melissa stayed sprawled where she was. She tore off her wig, walked to the bath, eased herself in and submersed. Sitting, she drained the tub. Standing, she towelled her weakened body, stepped out, replaced the chair and padded to the closest where she added her crystals to her bags, taking time to place the other accessories. She walked into the bathroom, cleaned the tub with her towel, removed the computer, the bottles and glasses and scanned the area for any oversight.
*

Timothy had overstayed his welcome. The closet lights were on, casting a muted glow across much of the bedroom and he fully expected his sister to put on a robe, grab up her bags and get out. She didn't. She gathered her bags together, put them in the corner, accounting for every item and went into the centre of the bathroom where she sat on the floor, twisted the device with both hands and reclined onto one elbow. Minutes later she shuddered, collapsing onto the warm tiles trembling and crying, or laughing or both. He couldn't tell. He didn't care and when she dragged herself to her feet, grabbed up her bags, darkened her stage and the closet, he didn't stop filming until her knees, ankles and feet vanished behind the door.

What he held in his hands was worth thousands: four hours and ten minutes of Midnight Rhapsody. And he was content to remain where he was until he would hear the sound of a car engine and steal into the family room where he had fallen asleep after coming home from his friend's house. He couldn't believe the final performance she gave for his eyes only. That scene alone would bring him in thousands and he sat in the récamier rewinding to where she lay on the floor, his emotions too pent-up. Why did she do it? Why did she use the bathroom and not her bedroom, as though she was laughing at their mother? He froze the close-up image on the screen.

His sister had always acted like a total bitch towards him and he couldn't remember a time when he didn't hate her. Now he saw her in a different light, naked, her body jolted from the bathroom floor and he wasn't sure how he felt. She wasn't Melissa. She was Midnight Rhapsody, a porno star. And what was that bizarre conversation at the end all about?

Thirty-Five

Month Three

Kathy and Ted walked in at 3:30 AM. Kathy drove home, opened the door and waited for him to reach the landing before climbing the stairs with despairing slowness. Her dress was a huge success. The men stared at her constantly as though they'd never seen breasts or thighs at home, at the beach or in strip clubs and she loved every moment. One guy wanted a photograph, another wanted to bounce her on his knee and the attention never ended. The women wanted to know her secret, why and how she had changed so drastically and when she would ever wear it again. She replied: in Vermont and Vegas. She was going to Vermont without Ted and wanted to see Vegas, which began a conversation of double entendre and innocent innuendo lasting through the evening and doing nothing to lighten Ted's mood. For the first time he wasn't the life of the party. He was the comic relief through to the moment the couple thanked their hosts for a perfect evening and Kathy swung open the passenger side door for him.

She noticed Timothy, leaving him as he was with a stale sandwich on his chest, and by the time she came out from her bathroom in tap pants and camisole Ted was asleep. Melissa was finishing her nightcap, lying in bed dreaming of a better life and what Clint would expect of her during the audition. Obviously bikini shots on the beach and

233

something more erotic in a studio. Her website had paid off. She couldn't believe she had an agent. She'd be travelling to Europe, seeing the world and making more money than she ever dreamed of by doing what she wanted to do. Her videos would be professional, seen by thousands around the world and everyone would know her. Clint would hire an acting coach for her. She wouldn't need university and she certainly wouldn't have to explain her motives to her parents, not that she intended to. She was seventeen. She was an adult and one week before Myrtle Beach she'd be eighteen and what could they do to stop her? Anyway, her parents wouldn't know.

She wriggled into the warmth of her bed. Her parents were losers. Her mother was a high school whore, sleeping around to be popular and her father was a has-been jock in a dead-end job. That wouldn't happen to her. Midnight Rhapsody was already popular with thousands of men. With an agent millions would know her: men, couples and women. She couldn't sleep. She doubted she ever would again, she was so excited. She had six weeks to create a routine which would make the wait worthwhile. She threw aside her covers, went to her dresser, cut the legs from her pantyhose and sat in front of the mirror. She had never worn stockings.
*

Timothy waited until the lights in his parents' bedroom were put out. He sat up and reran the final minutes of his sister on the floor. The footage would take him the whole day to import onto his computer, a week, he estimated, to fade in and out from one segment to another once he had a complete copy of the original and he would need several hours each week for the next month to burn enough copies of the sixteen segments and five-minute intermissions to get him started in business. He would save her final scene for last. He would print out a single glossy in his father's office, take orders and deliver them all on the same day. She'd freak knowing he'd seen her on the toilet and the floor.

He tiptoed to the main floor. A narrow band of light shone through the bottom of his sister's bedroom door illuminating the hallway and his first thought was to walk in on her and dare her to scream after telling her what he had done, what he saw and would always remember. A month ago she was Melissa, a stupid sister who hated him. She always had and always would. He could tell. But tonight and forever she was Midnight Rhapsody and he'd seen her as no one ever had. He sat on the second-to-last step, visualizing her, imagining what she must be doing, mesmerized by her slow-moving shadows, wanting to see her.

In the morning when he woke he jumped from his bed, connected the peripheral to his computer and went to the bathroom while everyone slept. He showered, barely getting wet, shaved because he once heard that if he did regularly he might one day actually need to and hurried to his room. His parents wouldn't be up for hours and the import would be complete by the time they sat together for the first dinner of the year. His last year of school would be a joke. His sister was his way out. His way to walk, not run from a family he hated and who hated him. They were a joke: his father pretending no one knew he had something on the side, his mother pretending she was twenty years younger, hello, and his slut-sister getting guys off on the web. He laughed so hard tears streamed from his eyes. Melissa absolutely hated his guts, yet she was his way out. Midnight Rhapsody was his escape and she had no clue.

In the kitchen he made toast coated with jam and poured the first cup of coffee from the automatic coffee pot. When he heard his sister's bedroom door open and close, the bathroom door open and close, he said nothing. When she came into the kitchen wearing baby dolls he was leaning against the counter, waiting, anticipating, laughing as she clamped a hand over her mouth to stifle a scream.

"Nice look, Mel."

"You're like a total pig."

"You're the pig. I'm the one wearing a robe."

"Like, piss off. I'm in no mood for jerk-offs."

"I should get my camera."

"And like do what with it. Mother would totally kill you and put you under permanent house arrest, idiot. Anyway, have a good look, freak. You'll never see anything anywhere near as good as this. The best you can expect is some stupid loser like you who's done it with fifty guys and can't get anything better than you. She'll have brats on her tits inside of a year, like her upstairs and you won't ever be any better than him."

He smirked. "Mel, can I ask you something?"

"What?"

"If you ever left here, you know, if you ever run away, could I go with you?"

"Like, no."

"You're very pretty."

"Duh!"

His lips curled into a mischievous smile, his eyes taking her in from head to toe. "You should be like an actress or something."

"Shut up."

She went to the counter, poured a coffee and took the cup to her room, his eyes following every step she took.

She stayed in her room all day composing a letter to her fans, announcing the creation of her production company and her surprise February 14th performance to make up for her interim absence, asking them to log in closer to the date for exact times and vie for a free and impromptu "see me as I really am" engagement. And Timothy remained in his room as well, continuing to file his sister and store her on his external hard drive.

Kathy woke mid-morning. She glanced over at Ted, shook her head in disgust, got dressed and went to the health club for an extreme workout. Her Latin trainer gave her the once over with a measuring tape and put her on the scale. She hadn't gained a gram and her tone hadn't been compromised. He was pleased, and she was ecstatic enough to treat herself to lunch. She thought about Michelle and hated being alone. Since becoming part of the girls she did hate being alone and particularly liked being with Michelle whom she was certain would join the club once seeing how devoted Enrique was to his clientele.

At 5:00 Melissa called. Daddy was taking them to town for dinner. She could either join them or not and Melissa waited several seconds for the decision. Kathy wouldn't join them. She wasn't hungry and would see them later at the house. Melissa shrugged, pressed end and told her father who seemed equally upset. He needed to get out. He couldn't take another silent dinner. He needed the distractions of a restaurant: being seated, reading the menu, ordering, tasting wine, waiters taking away plates, bringing the next course, the bill, the tip and the drive home.

Kathy greeted them from the living room, quite unwilling to move. She was ensconced with her book, a snifter of tequila and random thoughts. Melissa and Timothy locked themselves into their rooms; Ted went straight to his and was asleep by 10:00. Kathy stayed up. Separate beds were a good idea, albeit still not far enough apart and never would be. She could never go back. She'd gone too far and longed to go farther. She wanted to feel closer to Michelle, to have the best friend she never had. She wanted more time with the other girls, not one fleeting night each month and she wanted a real man in the image of Jack Caden.

Most families had eaten a turkey dinner, watched the

game on TV and spent time together. Her loving brood hadn't cared about a fine meal, and not to save her a full day of drudgery in the kitchen. They weren't interested, and neither was she, nor would Saturday or Sunday be any different. She would go to the gym both days, come home as late as possible, spend her evening alone and go to bed counting down to Monday morning when he would leave town and she would begin another semester of counselling kids whose primary problem was being brought up to believe they were special, that they could do whatever they wanted, whenever they wanted, when in fact they weren't special at all. Neither were their ineffectual parents.

When Kathy woke the house was dark and her book had fallen to the floor from her lap. Months earlier she would have wanted to cry, and might have. Now she had no reason. Her renaissance had begun with new friends, her first temptation, her revamped wardrobe and car. Vermont would catapult her far beyond her past and present dreams and Spring Break would herald the dissolution of her family. Melissa would leave soon after and never return and neither would Timothy one day, whether from university, jail or the street. He wasn't a bad kid, he simply wasn't particularly bright. He had little aptitude for learning, no street smarts which made vulnerable and he wanted everything in life too easily, which would potentially make him someone's dupe. Melissa, on the other hand, would survive as long as she had someone to care for her and, secretly, Kathy hoped she would never meet him, or them.

She wanted to pull the quilt over her head, facing reality instead. She had lost track of time. The sun had come up, the day was bright and clear and her Einstein was already in the kitchen rummaging for food. She listened from the foot of the stairs, heard nothing and went to her room to dress in her bathroom. She would shower and change at the gym and maybe see a movie.

In the kitchen Timothy hadn't moved from the open fridge door, undecided. "Good morning, Timothy."

"Yeah, hi."

"Is the house too warm for you?"

"No."

"Then please close the door. Nothing will disappear before you make up your mind." The door slammed. "Listen, Timothy, I want to see you in your father's office. I want to discuss your future. I think we both realize you're not headed for university. Your interest level is near zero even if your grade point average does improves, which I sorely doubt. You're more likely to spend four years struggling for mediocre results when you can be doing something constructive."

"Yeah, whatever."

She snapped her fingers. "May I have your attention? It's not whatever. I'm talking about choices, about striving or remaining inert." She saw the look. "I'm talking about believing me that any decision you come to will affect your life for a very long time. Make the wrong one and you'll have yourself to blame, make the right one and have yourself to thank. Either way, the choice is yours. No one else will care."

"Not even you."

"I'm talking with you now. If you don't listen to me, no, I won't care. Hear what I have to say, listen, try to understand and I will. I'll also sweeten the pot. Life doesn't get much simpler, but you won't understand the difference if you don't give me some time."

"Why not tell me right here? What's up with the office?"

"Because your sister has ears like parabolic antennas and what I want to say doesn't concern her."

"What about the old man?"

"What I have in mind for you doesn't concern him either.

239

In this particular matter I have full control." She poured a coffee. "So, are you up for it, or not?"

"This is too weird."

"No. What's weird is turning eighteen in a year, dropping out because you have zero academic interest, working at minimum wage and living in the slums. And FYI kiddo, you would earn two hundred a week after taxes, which is how much you're costing me to feed you. You'd be shacked up with a bunch of squeegees, huddled in a corner on a sleeping bag you might have bought or more likely stole or took from a dumpster.

"That won't happen. I've got big plans."

"You don't have plans. You have dreams, which most people do when their sleeping. You don't get anywhere by sleeping. So get real, get in the office and stop trying to provoke me. I'm less inclined each day to invest time in this so-called family, so it's up to you. If you're not beside me when I close the door I'll consider you on your own as of your eighteenth birthday. If you want more schooling you'll have to prove you're good enough. If you don't, I'll expect you to have a job and move out the very same day. I have no intention of living with a ne'er-do-well adult in my house."

"Huh?"

"You'll have thirteen months to prepare, not a day longer." She left him standing and went to the office. She counted to three with her eyes closed and felt a swish of air rush past her.

"I do have a plan, a really good one."

"Tell me." He shrugged, dug his hands into his pockets and looked around the room. "Good plan. Hey, why don't you run to a bank and get a business loan. With such an intriguing plan everyone will want in, including me. How much do you want?" She paused. "You're an idiot and the sooner you learn to correct the fault the better off you'll be.

Listen up. This is a one-time offer between you and me. Tell anyone and the deal's off."

"So what's the deal?"

"You'll be seventeen in a few weeks with a completed grade ten, which makes you eligible."

"For what?"

"The army."

"No way. Those guys are like totally sick."

"Actually they're totally healthy, learning trades, making money and travelling…seeing the world."

"I'd be like in prison or something."

"If you don't do something soon I'm sure you will be one day, right beside big Burt who's going to love sharing a cell with some little boy who misses his mommy." She grinned. "Although I do suppose you would also come out with a trade, if you do come out, possibly a locksmith or a drug dealer."

"That's totally sick."

"And entirely possible. People without jobs and nowhere to live either end up on the street, in jail or both. Then comes the big time, prison, with longer sentences, bigger, meaner Burts and no way out. The army will give you a way out with a livelihood one way or the other, which doesn't mean they want deadbeats." She sipped her coffee. "Timothy, I've put a lot into this family, by myself. We all know your father screws around, your sister's become a snarky little bitch and you're a lost soul which brings me to the crux of this conversation. I've had enough. I'm done. I was serious when I told both of you that when you're gone you won't be welcome any time after without first calling for an invitation: no drop-ins. Melissa is leaving in the spring and I believe you're staying here thinking university is an easy way out will seriously impede your chances of any success, irrespective of your great plan. So here's the deal. Plan one, my plan: Meet with a recruiting officer on your birthday. I'll write you a letter of parental consent. Get accepted and I'll give you a cash incentive. Plan two is not an option. It's a safety net for you. In the event you're not soldier material, but you have demonstrated sincere effort, which I will verify, you'll get the same incentive when you enrol in a trade school of your choice. Do what you want. Be a mechanic, a barber, a French chef. I don't care as long as you do something worthwhile."

"How much is the incentive?"

"For the army, ten thousand the day we sign your enlistment papers. For trade school, ten thousand plus your tuition, room and board for one year. One year Timothy, so don't screw up."

"What if I want to stay here? You can't like throw me out."

"I'm not throwing you out. Being thrown out requires somewhere to throw you from and I'm not sure such will be the case. What I don't have to do is take you with me." Kathy drained her cup. "You've neglected one very important aspect of growing up."

"Like what."

"Becoming a man, and that's how I'm talking to you. Men don't lay around on beds with plugs in their ears. They work. Understand?" She waited. "Do we have a deal?"

"I don't know. The army, it's sort of not what I expected. I could like get killed or something."

"At minimum wage you'll work thirteen-hundred hours to earn ten grand, thirty weeks, and the government grabs a good chunk. The army will feed you, clothe you, pay you, and, unless you do something irresponsible, you'll come out with much more than ten grand and a viable future. Give me an answer."

"Okay."

"Okay what?"

"I'll sign up on my birthday."

"Good. Now listen. This is very important. Do not tell your sister or, not only is the deal off, you'll find yourself on the street along with her. Wouldn't that be nice? The two of you are so good together." Kathy stood. "Nor will you mention this to your father or you'll find yourself in the army without the ten thousand and I won't intercede to help you. Do you understand?"

"Yeah, I understand. I'll keep my mouth shut."

"Good. We're done. You should be happy. You've negotiated an excellent deal."

Timothy stood and walked to the door. "Mom?"

"Yes."

"For my birthday, I'd sort of like my credit card. It'll only be like a couple of weeks early and I want to see my friends."

"Not a chance. If you've forgotten why you're being punished, that's your problem. Think of something else."

The response was quick. "Lots of blank DVDs and a DVD reader for some movies I want to upload free stuff."

"Agreed. Tell me what I need to know some other time." She stepped passed him, continuing to talk on her way to the garage door. "Tell your father I'll be home by mid-afternoon and don't forget I expect you to keep your word."

Climbing into the MX-5, she snorted. Somehow she simply couldn't feel sorry for him.

*

She drove to the beach, parked by the boardwalk and gazed out to sea trying to remember each detail of his carefree smile, the glint of his hazel eyes, his windswept hair and the touch of his hand against her cheek. What she saw was the sadness in his eyes when she left him, what she felt was the hurt brought on by his selfish deception, though Jack Caden had no idea about the judgement against him. He had intended no deception. He had hoped for quite the opposite and, in fact, was keeping his word.

The day was chilling with not a cloud in the sky, nor a snowflake in the forecast, yet he sat by the fire, waiting, not expecting she would come and thinking how Christmas had become one of many lonesome days. He no longer particularly liked the day, when once he had hurried to the tree to rip apart wrappings and adore the tearful sparkles of glee in her eyes. This year he opened a pizza box and at New Year's he ordered in Chinese, watched videos until the wee hours as he worked and woke Friday morning refreshed and resolute, determined to begin and live out the year like no other.

Jack ignored the French dip and finished his first glass of wine, pondering what a lonely and neglected woman would do at a ski resort with four friends. He should have held her back, not let her go. Yet she knew where to find him, if he hadn't misread the sorrow in her eyes or the warmth of her lips. He leaned closer to the flames, swirling the deep red wine. If she didn't come he would wait by the fire again in two weeks, praying each day she would not give herself to any other man, and the 16th, 23rd and 30th, until the day she would come to him and he believed to his core that she would. He wasn't wrong about her. She would one day love him and be his.

*

The theatre was empty, yet she sat in the top row aisle seat. Melissa and Timothy were leaving the nest, motivated by money well spent. The army would kill or cure Timothy and Melissa had more chance of plucking gold from a dead man's mouth than becoming an actress. Ted would no longer have an imposed reason to come home and she no longer had a reason to stay thanks to Timothy. The current semester would be her last, though she would wait until after Spring Break to announce her intent not to renew her contract for the coming school year. Any sooner and her resignation might filter through the grapevine to the kids and from Melissa to Ted, which she didn't want, and she would begin distributing her curriculum vitae throughout the private sector while considering the pros and cons of opening her own private practice. And if capricious dreams did come true, maybe she would share a condo with Michelle, two hot babes on the prowl and she chuckled at what a team they would make.

She didn't need the house. She wanted the thing she hated so much as recompense for years of thankless servitude and to spite him for never being a real husband or a father. She was adamant: He would not get the house if she had to burn it to the ground. Oops, she spilled the kerosene on purpose, she thought. Not good. The woods were too near. Or she could rent a bulldozer and collapse one beam at a time. She had the answer. She would hire a contractor and destroy the house from top to bottom, or do the job herself.

Kathy came home excited with travel information on Vegas and knocked on Timothy's door. He hadn't changed his mind. He would do his best and try not to let her down. In the hallway she called to Melissa, telling both of them to dress for dinner and went to her bedroom. She came down in tights, a short pleated skirt and raglan sweater. Passing the office she looked in, asking Ted whether he preferred changing for dinner or eating alone when he was finished working. He chose the latter. He was heading into a critical week, he explained offhandedly, and needed every moment to prepare. She agreed and closed the door.

The mood at the table was palpable. Melissa seemed anxious to eat and go to her room without the usual indignation or exaggerated fluster. Timothy, Kathy noticed, each time Melissa looked down to her plate, was openly ogling his sisters breasts and couldn't clear the table soon enough. He, too, wanted the privacy of his room and she thought no more about them as she went to the living room with her book and after-dinner drink. Once again she was dressed to please any man, most men, and she was alone on a Saturday night.

"Your loss," she whispered. "You should have been home when I called. You should have had a phone when I called…bastard."

Thirty-Six

She awoke Sunday morning in her bed, the last day of Christmas break. Ted was gone from the room and his bed was made-up. Good. He was beginning to understand and when she happened to glance at the clock she gasped a huge intake of air, not believing the time was 11:30. She scrambled from her bed, reached for the robe to her ensemble and galloped down the stairs, not intending to miss a single day of working out before Thursday.

Timothy was in the fridge, reluctantly pressed into service and she returned to her room to change and pack her sports bag. Once pulled and contorted into her leggings and hip-length belted tunic her coffee was waiting, Timothy's face was in the fridge and Melissa was sitting at the island.

"Mother! You can't be serious. Tell me you're not going out like that."

"Melissa, I am going out like that. And you know what?" The girl grimaced. "At the gym, with all those people around, I wear my thongs on the outside and my top looks exactly like a real push-up bra. Hello, like the models in my magazines, the old hags in their thirties. You should try it sometime. I've noticed you are looking a little...oh, I don't know, fuller." Kathy covered her mouth, feigning shock. "Melissa, darling, you're not..."

247

Melissa stormed from the room, past Timothy who hadn't moved. "What isn't she?"

"Nothing, I was making a joke and please close the door unless you plan to eat it." She downed her coffee. "Tell your father to expect me by mid-afternoon… and Timothy."

"I know, mom. I promise."

"Good boy."

"Hey, mom."

"Yes."

"It's sort of a cool look. You know, like the Robin Hood guy in the movies."

"Are you saying I look like a man?"

"No, no. I'm not. Just, you know."

"Yes, I do, and thank you." She paused at the garage door. "Fail not, young sir, in thy urgent quest to deliver my missive forthwith to Prince John, that I hath quit our humble hearth and shan't return till the amber sun hath set upon this eventide's hues of yon mountain's peak."

"Huh?"

*

Ted's reaction was never predictable to what Kathy might say or do. At times he was volatile, other times he was passive-aggressive or he simply shut the door. Sunday afternoon he went to his bedroom, pleased Kathy had gone out, pleased he had successfully eluded her superior and disparaging "I expected as much" stare.

At noon he called his home number from his cell, picked up and left the line open for several minutes before hurrying to his room. The taxi came for him at 1:00, waiting while Ted explained to Melissa exactly why he was leaving a day early: An emergency required his immediate input. The client couldn't wait a day longer and he left with a cold and practiced goodbye.

That evening he dined with Eileen and Kathy let the kids eat in their rooms. She didn't care that Ted had sneaked out. She didn't believe for a moment that he'd left to solve an emergency. Ted wasn't a problem solver. He was a conniver and not a very good one. His sole emergency was a two-week dry spell and the solution would presumably be over twenty-one. In any event, very soon, who would she be to talk? She would transmute to a cheating wife and with him gone she gained one extra night of peaceful fantasy. Her life was evolving into a three-month agenda, overflowing with the brightness of exuberance and rebirth to distil the daily and insidious darkness of turmoil and doubt, which didn't mean she was a bad mother. She wasn't, her one fear being that she might waver in her determination to break free, doing herself harm from which she would never recover. Her one hope was living for each tomorrow, leaving all but the memorable days to come in a heartless and forgotten past.

Melissa's departure had never been cause for mutual remorse: She was leaving and Kathy made no secret that she could not return to the easy life of her childhood after living the unchecked freedom of her university years, which was also her original objective for Timothy, her Achilles heel. Her offer to him was a good one, convinced in her heart he would never do better, and if she did nothing to distance the boy he would remain forever young and she would never be free. Sadly said, Timothy was burdensome luggage she need not carry.

*

Clint Evans was drunk with anticipation. He'd spent the last six days and nights studying every Burberry document from her parents' death certificates, his title deed to the house, to the updated and separate investment portfolios, making notes and a spreadsheet. From Burberry's perspective they were borderline middle class with a million-dollar home, his fifty-thousand in savings, no mortgage and no debt. From Kathy's perspective she was somewhat better off. Her

249

parents were very generous to her and, possibly the kids, not so nice to Ted, although he did have the house unless he walked out. She had an inheritance of two and a half million he didn't know about and thirty-thousand in savings after her recent expenses. Then, of course, Miss Midnight Rhapsody was a vital part of the equation with her quarter-million, by-passing dad and catching up quickly with mom. She had followed his cues like a pro and by Valentine's his influence over her would be even more entrenched. Whether he would meet with her or not was moot. She would follow his instructions and before Myrtle Beach, when he would meet her, he would know precisely how best to manage her career.

Curiously, he wasn't interested in porn, and certainly not gullible teenage girls, not that he considered gullibility a fault. The trait was actually requisite to his career. However she was determined to achieve stardom, she definitely had promise and he could guide her quite easily without detracting from his objectives. She had six weeks to perfect a routine erotic enough to keep her fans hungry for more until her promised debut in April, her coming out which she knew nothing about and neither did he.

Everything was set. He went to bed and slept like a baby.

Thirty-Seven

Winter's artic grasp would endure another nine weeks. Clint sat on the railing of the boardwalk sipping hot cocoa from his thermos, his hood pulled over his head, dark-tinted goggles protecting his eyes from the frigid and relenting sea breeze. The yellow and brown local bus groaned by and several minutes later the red MX-5 followed, slowing noticeably before speeding from sight. Kathy Burberry had stared directly at him and he didn't realize he'd stopped breathing. He remained as he was for long tormenting minutes, anxious to leave, afraid to stay.

He jumped down, certain she wasn't coming back to defy him and set out on his trek with snowshoes strapped to his backpack and steel spikes strapped to his boots. The meandering climb lasted thirty minutes. In summer he could easily jog the distance in five, though the deep snow forced him this way or that when his cleats digging into the icy road weren't slowing his pace. He talked his way up the hill, half-focused on the improvisation, half-cursing. He ignored the illogic, the irrationality of what he was doing. He was unthinking despite the endless hours he'd spent contemplating, planning and formulating. His purpose was closure. He would ring the doorbell and if Burberry answered he would ask for directions. If she came up behind him, he would say what was in his heart and walk away from her, from Rhapsody, from the whole damned family. He would. He promised.

251

At the summit he paused, self-satisfied. He wasn't breathless and took a moment to feel good about himself. Hooray for me, and he continued up the driveway. He rang the doorbell once, twice, a third time and sat on the steps of the porch. He peered into the garage, seeing the Lexus and he rang the doorbell once more, this time for sixty seconds before trudging his way to the back, inserting his key into the lock, disconnecting the wires and replacing the lock. At the front he rang the bell once more, waited, inserted his key and walked in.

He yelled out: "Darling, I'm home. Come to me, Teddy. Take me, big boy." No response. He laid out a woollen blanket, stepped onto it, dropped his backpack and snowshoes, stripped off his boots, outer gear and ran through the house with his goggles in place and ready to put down Ted. There was no need. Ted wasn't home and Clint breathed a sigh of relief, gathering his clothes into a duffle bag he'd pulled from his backpack, wiping the floor with the blanket, adding it to the duffle bag and climbing the stairs.

On a chair from the hallway he reached to the attic's access and slid the panel to one side, grabbing at the rope ladder. He stepped down, replaced the chair and climbed the ladder, making himself at home within a few minutes. His winter gear was stowed, his food for the week was laid out and he was once again in her second-floor bedroom not intending to use her shower until the following day. He was content simply being in her room, so close to her.

He had nothing else to learn from their rooms. What he wanted was to study them in their natural habitat without the veneer of civility applied each day or the artifice of costumes without the slightest idea of what he would do with the data. He was anxious for her to return, curious what he would see of Rhapsody and her brother before mom got home from the gym and he spent the day in her family room with his home-study book, a pen and copies of his and her handwriting in the various font sizes he had previously scanned. The week's agenda was planned. The house was his domain through to Thursday from whatever time she left until the local bus ground to an alarming halt several hours later each day, not discounting the second-floor panoramic view from the front bay window. Thursday through Sunday he would work nights, spend his days honing his forging skills and return each Monday.

*

Sitting with Michelle, Darlene, Sheila in the teachers' lounge, Kathy was consumed by a mood of absolute wickedness and she wondered whether they were imbued with the same stirred up emotions, or had the quarterly escapades become inherent to them. On the other hand, she felt like somewhat of a traitor. Her resignation would take effect the last day of final exams, and what of the girls? Would she continue being one of them, would they want her and, if not, how would she fill the void of their lost friendship, Vermont and Vegas in April? How could she ever again settle for the mundane existence she had finally escaped? They were her support. How could she simply venture into the private sector without them? Together they were mischievous and whimsical. Alone she would be an available target, unable and eventually unwilling to distinguish between a flighty weekend romance and reaching out pathetically for love. If he had lied to her, why wouldn't someone else, why wouldn't they all? And, if she had slept with him, what then? She would have been naked, her body vulnerable, providing a fleeting sensation and a convenient receptacle for his release. She wanted more. She wanted control. She wanted to be the one to walk away without regret.

Michelle placed a hand on her shoulder from behind, leaned forward and whispered. "Darling, you left us for a little while and we missed you. Everyone's gone to class."

"I'm sorry, I drifted."

"Thursday?" Michelle questioned.

"Yes, but not the way you might think."

"I cheated, darling. I tried on my gift in the bathroom and I look absolutely marvellous in red." She giggled. "And, between us girls, I was a little flushed and weak-kneed when I came out. ¿Comprendes, querida?"

"Michelle, you're absolutely evil."

"And hot darling. Don't forget hot, or that our next lunch is on me. Come on. We're late."

"Michelle," Kathy looked around, "mi amor…thank you."

"For what?"

"For being you. Don't ever change."

"I won't, Kathy, unless you forget to take me with you," and Michelle left the lounge giggling.
*

Melissa was in her fourth day of a short-lived normal life, notwithstanding her noontime trip to the mall where she met her accomplice and paid him for the liquor before purchasing garters, stockings, panties, a bustier and silk peignoir. When the 1:00 PM bell rang she was in class, the shopping bag safely stuffed into her locker and the litre bottle of vodka lay wrapped in her backpack. Attending any other school she would have feigned an illness, cramps, or anything else to go home, but her mother would be informed immediately.

Her excitement was electric. She was leaving her usual wardrobe of baby dolls and adult party costumes behind. No longer would she play the school girl in a tawdry little skirt with ruffled panties and pouting lips. Those days were gone forever. The reinvented Midnight Rhapsody would be refined and elegant, sensual and captivating and throughout the afternoon she was oblivious to the front of the class as she flipped through one of the lingerie brochures she had accumulated from a dozen or more boutiques. The women were glamorous and alluring, each one posing seductively, looking confidant and in control. Exactly the way she would with Clint's help.

*

At 3:45 the bus screeched to a halt. Clint stood away from the window, watched the kids trudge up the driveway and nonchalantly secreted himself in his garret. He was most interested in the "stay" code for the alarm system, one he couldn't afford to tamper with and he thanked Melissa with an appreciative nod.

Timothy went straight to the fridge. Melissa reached into a kitchen cupboard for a plastic garbage bag and went to her room where Clint was waiting for her. Closing and locking the door she moved methodically. She placed her shopping bags on her bed, her backpack on the floor and went to her closet. She dragged a suitcase into the middle of the room, pushed apart the row of hanging clothes for the bag of Christmas goodies and emptied both caches of costumes into the garbage bag, putting aside her crystals. She liked them. She liked the titillating sensation of the beads' constantly probing caresses. When she was done she carried the weightless sack to the kitchen and filled it with the previous day's refuse. Clint followed her into the garage and watched her drop the bag behind the others ready for Tuesday's pick-up.

In her room with the door locked, she placed her purchases on silk-covered hangers. The delicate items she placed in a small velour shoulder bag and when she was done she extricated the bottle from the bottom of her backpack and poured a drink without the benefit of a mix. She organized her desk with her books, checked the door handle and went to the closet. She couldn't wait.

Clint laid back, his glass filled with the same high-test

spirits. Her blouse came off first, her skirt second and despite the fact she seemed more like fifteen in her knee socks, panties and bra, he recognized the signature cut and rosette design. The kid had expensive taste. He would have to dig deep to outdo her, to impress her. Her bra came away, then her thong. He smiled, wondering how she would look in daylight, in February and March, wearing a film of glistening oil without the socks.

The perspective was intriguing and voyeuristic. He was peering down at her from a secret mezzanine and the sensation engulfing him spawned what he believed was a workable concept he would not ignore. If he was to become her manager they would have to learn to work together and her revenues would skyrocket. He sipped his drink, watching her at the closet in her socks, looking like a waif dipping into a box of treasures. She was no average teenager.

He leaned into the screen. She was sitting on the bed, tugging one foot free then the other. Standing, she dragged her chair in front of her mirror, where she stood struggling with the back hooks of the bustier. He chortled, watching Melissa contort herself into a frustrated state, losing her breath as much as her patience. Snapping a bra together was one thing, doing fifteen hooks was another. She seemed fascinated with the garters hanging from her waist. She pulled on her satin thong, stood to do a three-sixty and skipped to her bed for her stockings. She unrolled one length, feeding in her foot, extending her leg into the air and pulling the nylon past her calf to her knee and up to her thigh. She attached one clasp successfully, sat side-saddle to see the back of her thigh in the mirror and snapped that one closed. She did her other leg, slouching into her chair exhausted.

She would do alright. He was pleased and would tell her so another time. He also wanted to tell her she would never manage her basic necessities without significant discomfort if, in future, she continued to put her panties on under her garters. Meanwhile, he switched to the boy's room, zooming in and taking a full minute for the reality of what he was seeing to sink in.

Clint was seeing part of Midnight Rhapsody's performance from New Year's Eve in Kathy's bathroom, and not through the lens of her webcam. The lighting was different, the angles varied. Then Clint saw her in Kathy's closet, undressing, seated on the toilet and again in the closet reaching for another costume and wig. He watched over Timothy's shoulder for thirty minutes. The little bastard had filmed his sister performing and was creating separate files. The kid was one sick puppy and Clint's first imperative the next morning would be to search the sick little bugger's room. He switched to Melissa. Kathy would arrive home soon and she was one performance he did not want to miss.

The sight was comical. Her legs were bare. He'd missed that part because of her sick brother. Half the hooks were undone, her breasts were completely covered and her arms seemed on the verge of breaking. He hesitated, thinking he might discourage her, believing if she wanted to change her mind he'd be hard pressed to force her. Uppermost on his mind was what her brother had up his sleeve. He was a red flag if anything was. He dialled her number, seeing her almost fall to the floor from shock.

"This is Melissa."

"Hi Rhapsody, this is Clint calling."

"Clint, hi, I was thinking about you today. I haven't worked since I posted my message and I've rehearsed every day, like you asked me to, and I'm working on a really good routine."

"Are you rehearsing now? Did I interrupt you?"

"Yes and no. I bought some different outfits, Clint, and I'm sort of getting used to them."

"Like what?

"Really sexy French stuff, like garters and a peignoir. Tonight I'm working on a bustier."

"Are you wearing the bustier?"

"Not my stockings and pretty much half the bustier. I have a lot of work to do, but I'll be ready. You can count on me, Clint."

"They can be clumsy things, I know. Rhapsody, I should be with you, helping you, and I would be if I weren't out of country. Can you give me a one-on-one with your webcam?"

"No, not now. I don't have much time, but I can tonight, after eleven-thirty, or tomorrow afternoon at four o'clock.

"Tomorrow at four, ten PM my time and Rhapsody…"

"Yes?"

"I've been working hard for you. What you did for New Years was unreal, fantastic. But what I've planned for Valentine's will bring your fans to their knees adoring and worshiping you. I want to suggest we keep each other current. Let's speak once a week after tomorrow and let's do so by webcam which will allow me to follow your progress. Do we agree?"

"Yes, Clint. I can't wait to see you and I won't stop rehearsing. I won't disappoint you."

"I know and I'll see you tomorrow at four sharp. Enjoy your evening and your dreams, before they become a reality. Bye."

She pressed end, tossed her phone onto the bed and twisted free from the erotic straight jacket. Tuesday he would tell her to get rid of the bustier and buy a front-loading zipper model. Men had no preference regarding the mechanical intricacies of female armour. They wanted one thing: the unprotected female and that's what she would give them. He watched her push down her panties, pull on sweat pants, a hoodie and sweep her hair into a ponytail. She put away her lingerie, moved her chair to her desk and began studying. He was amazed. If she could switch so effortlessly from fiction to reality, he had every reason to believe they would work well together.

His one regret was Kathy. Had they met years earlier, they might have married. Melissa would be a beautiful, innocent girl and the boy a star basketball player. He would never have dreamt endless nights of hurting her, killing her, never allowing her to escape his nightmares, forcing her to lurk in the dark recesses of his mind until one day she would learn she had not been forgiven.
*

Kathy arrived home at 5:30 and he toggled her progress easily from the garage to her bedroom. This was the moment he'd been waiting for, the moment of truth, his finest hour when the bodies of Kim and Kathy would meld as one and he prayed he was not wrong. He reached for the bottle, poured without measuring and grabbed for the remote control. In the closet she turned away from him, nimbly unbuttoning her blouse, she unzipped her A-line skirt, stepped from the waist and Clint imagined himself in heaven. His senses hadn't misled him. She was Kim. In every minute way the woman he was watching was Kim, the woman he wanted to punish for doing him wrong.

Kim would always wait until in her panties and nylons to kick away her shoes. Kathy tossed her blouse into a bin, hung her skirt and walked into the bathroom, sitting on the toilet, standing, patting and walking to the sink adjacent to her vanity. She washed away her make-up, applied a cream, ruffled her hair, pulled her camisole over her head and Clint was alone to hold himself agonizingly in check.

She walked to the closet in tap pants, garters and the most erotic looking stockings and bare thighs he'd seen since Kim. She kicked away her pumps, raising one foot onto the ottoman to push the nylon from her thigh to her ankle and pull it away, raising her other foot and keeping him mesmerized. She unhooked her belt, dropped the garter and pushed her panties to the floor. He was fit to be tied, wanting to leap through to the second floor and run to her, grab her by the hips and hear her deep, guttural groans. She padded to her shower, danced for him in a slow, sensual rhythm, bending and stretching, her hands conducting a concert of quiet foam clashing with the exuberant and heated pelting streams of water. Only one other woman on earth was as beautiful.

She towelled herself, leaned into the mirror, cupped her breasts and smiled. "Kathy, girl, you're beautiful and one day very soon someone will love you unconditionally. You wait and see. Someone will love you and never want to let you go."

Clint's heart was palpitating, reluctant tears straining to form at the corners of his eyes. Why did she betray him, why did she after he'd treated her like the queen she was to him? He answered: "Someone does love you, Kathy. I do, and one day very soon I will tell you."

Kathy slipped into a simple satin teddy, covered herself with a knee-length kimono knotted at her waist and he practically passed out. She tied her kimono the way Kim always had and he wondered whether Kim might have died while Kathy's once lifeless body might have lain in search of a wandering soul. Her body was flawless, not the faintest scar or blemish because she had never been to death's door, to where she once delivered him, and he closed the screen before he began to hate her all the more.

Thirty-Eight

Tuesday he awoke in total darkness, the luminous face of his chronograph emitting an eerie and blinding shade of orange. The entire house was dark and Kathy lay in her bed. Melissa slept, he supposed possibly dreaming of her prince charming and the boy lay face down atop the sheets of his bed, the screen saver of his laptop concealing what Clint believed must be Melissa.

Clint threw aside his blankets, the attic was warm. He swung his legs over the side of his cot, planted his feet and reached blindly for the Coleman. He relieved himself into the empty jar and dressed in the previous day's clothes until he could shower and change. Until then he sat cross-legged and watched her sleep, remembering her breaths, her murmurs and the silkiness of her skin.

At 7:00 Kathy stirred. Trapped in her sheets, she kicked wildly, rocking from side to side to free her body. She was beautiful, an angel to be adored. He followed her into the bathroom, remembering when he would tease her each morning about not leaving the seat up for him as he would sit watching her, enthralled with her, in love with her. In her closet she tossed her teddy into the bin, selecting the day's wardrobe as he sat watching, a man possessed by his past. She eased against the wall, slipping into her thong. Her bra was push-up and her garter was one of the most delicate he'd ever seen. She sat, pulling on her stockings with measured ecstasy, not hurrying, closing the clasps with

261

fingertips as lissom as a surgeon's artistic touch. Her shirtdress was silk or satin, he couldn't tell, above her knees and she let the belt hang loosely from her waist.

He took a deep breath, following her to the kitchen where her dysfunctional brood ignored her. Not so much as a "hi, mom", "morning, mom" or "I love you, mom". He loved her. He could love her and wanted to love her. He felt her deep sorrow and saw the silent regret etched into her youthful face. Kathy Burberry was at the precipice of loneliness and she would willingly leap into his arms.

One digit on the panel separated coming from going. He no longer needed to tinker with wires and when she left he dropped the ladder and rushed to the window to watch her drive away, wrongly believing the day would be long and lonely. He began in Timothy's room after his shower, finding the DVDs in seconds and uploading the four hours of Rhapsody's New Year's performance by noon, jolting upright from his copy work at the sound of grinding brakes. His day was done. His time shared with Kathy would see him through endless evening hours, his time with Melissa and Rhapsody equally crucial.

He watched her come in, press the code, leave her brother as though he didn't exist and hurry to her room. She locked the door, placed her study books on her desk, poured a drink, undressed by the bed and went to the closet. She reached far to one side for her peignoir, her shoulder bag and selected the items she wanted with care. He watched her dress and at four o'clock...

"Hi, Clint."

"Hello, Melissa. First off, I wanted to keep your interest level high and have a big surprise for you. You're going off-campus for Valentine's, so to speak. Needless to say your wardrobe will match the venue and as you rehearse until then I want you to imagine yourself in a magnificent setting. You'll have one day to yourself, the thirteenth, for as long as you want, and on the fourteenth you'll go live to rock the world. I love your robe and, by the way, I want you to strip for me. Walk me through your routine."

"Promise you won't laugh?"

"Have you ever asked a fan that question?"

"No."

"Take off your clothes for me Melissa."

The peignoir fell to the floor. She stood tall, brought one foot to her chair, unhooked the butterfly clasp and guided the nylon along its silky path to her ankle. She grabbed the backrest of the chair, pulled away the stocking and raised her other foot, repeating the process. Then she pushed her billowy full panties to the floor and stood into the lens.

"Clint," she began, "like that?"

"If I weren't your manager, I would kill to be your lover. You're fantastic. I can't wait to meet you in person. Yes, exactly like that, with a few minor modifications. I agree with forgetting the bustier. You're not the type. Stick with the push-ups and point your toes into the seat, raise your knees and, most importantly, keep your stomach tight. Guys want tight stomachs, but don't squeeze your ass. It's a major turn-off and your pretty cheeks are tight enough. Also, slow down. Pace yourself. Remember, you're supposed to enjoy your work."

"I do. I don't want to do anything else."

"That should be obvious to everyone who's seen you. You're a natural."

"Thank you."

"Turn." She did. "Raise your arms and pirouette." She did. "Bend and put your hands on your ass." She did. "Melissa…"

"Yes, Clint."

"I have to go."

"So soon?"

"Yes, and before I do I have to say one thing. I'm so

glad we've come together and when we meet on the thirteenth we're going to have the most fantastic celebration. We'll deserve the best. The celebration's on me, the best champagne because we're going where no one has gone before and it's all because of you, your electric body and your charm. I love you, Melissa, and so will they."

She hesitated. "Clint...I want to be everything I can be for you."

"You already are Rhapsody. Let's connect live again in a week and don't stop rehearsing. Also, don't forget I'm your biggest fan and I love you."

"I won't, and thank you. Good-bye."

*

Kathy came home without the fanfare of a mother loved. She went to her room and undressed as she would for an invisible man, a discreet lover. She showered, pampered herself and dressed in a mini-skirt, tights and a wide-knit sweater to eat alone as Clint lay in his utilitarian cot observing her every move. In the kitchen she prepared supper mechanically, she allowed the indifferent duo to eat in their rooms and she sat in the living room after her solitary meal while the girl cleared her table and the boy washed the dishes.

When they were gone she poured a nightcap, traipsed to her room, undressed and lounged on her récamier cloaked in the warmth of a satin gown, her expression sadly dispassionate and at that moment he loved her as he had never loved her before. He wanted her and he would have her. When, he couldn't be sure and the where was equally perplexing. What he did know was the certainty.

The boy was now a person of interest because of his obvious perversion towards his sister, Melissa because of her potential and Burberry because, well, he wasn't sure. What he did know was that he couldn't let Kathy Burberry escape him, not ever again. As much as he wanted to kill her, he wanted to love her and worship her forever and ever and, in the morning, he loved her all the more. Kathy Burberry was in his grip.

Thirty-Nine

Wednesday he woke late. As he'd been watching Kathy sleeping on one screen, he watched the entire New Year's Eve production on the other, contemplating how little Timothy might have an accident one day. Whatever the kid was thinking wasn't good. His sister on the other hand was very good, or would be. She had guts doing her act and herself in her mother's bathroom and it wasn't rocket science to understand her brother wanted in, probably in more ways than one.

*

Wednesday night was déjà vu and Clint sat at his screen trying to figure out what kept Kathy coming home each day. Mother and daughter weren't so different, yet light years apart. The boy was deficient, which he attributed to Ted who, Clint believed, was not as big a man in Chicago Corporate as he put on.

At ten o'clock the phone rang and Kathy answered, a wide smile spreading across her face, happiness immediately washed away by horror. Her body language was animated, her voice forceful. She was shaking her head, insisting, a scolding forefinger stabbing the air and moments later Melissa grabbed for her robe and hurried to unlock her bedroom door. Kathy was leaving. Melissa was to activate the alarm when she was gone and neither she nor Timothy was to be seen or heard until morning. Kathy reiterated the command and left, going against Michelle's plea and dialling 9-1-1 before swerving onto Ocean View Road. By the time she arrived at the Cape Cod-styled cottage the police were leaving and Michelle's husband looked anything but heroic.

Kathy stepped in, identified herself as the caller to the cop in the living room and wrapped Michelle gently in her arms, joining with the lady cop to assure Michelle that pressing charges was her only option and the right thing to do. Being the first incident had no relevance. He would eventually strike out at her again and a weary, tearful Michelle let herself be photographed, squeezing Kathy weakly when the officer assured them the husband was being arrested and would be held until his court appearance on Monday at the earliest.

Michelle refused to go to the hospital. Nothing was broken, but she didn't argue when Kathy insisted they were leaving. At the house Melissa had left the lights on and the house was quiet as Clint followed the women from the garage to Kathy's bedroom.

"Don't be so argumentative. He won't be home until tomorrow and I'm sleeping on the sofa in the family room. I'll burn in hell before sleeping in his bed, with or without him, and I don't want to hear another word." Kathy walked to her closet and pulled a fleecy robe away from its hanger. "I'm running you a bath and when it's ready I want you out of those clothes and into your robe."

Michelle obeyed. She had no strength to argue. "Thank you, Kathy."

Kathy sat and hugged her, kissed her cheek and walked away wanting to scream or cry. Clint watched Michelle undress, grimacing as he watched her tug at her sweater and struggle from her jeans. He remembered her. She was one of the women with Kathy the first night in the restaurant. Who knew what went on in people's lives? Compared to the creep who beat her, he was a saint. He had never abused a

267

woman, not even a treacherous bitch who sent him to prison. He could see the agony scrawled across her face as she brought up each foot to pull away her socks, pushing down her panties required incremental steps to her thighs, knees and ankles and slipping into the robe was torture by the time Kathy called out that her bath was ready.

The water was deep and steaming and Kathy was sitting on the rounded edge. She dropped in pearls of scented oil, smiled and walked away, chancing to look into the mirror as Michelle dropped the robe onto a chair and stepped gingerly into the water. She was accustomed to seeing women at the health club, not all of them beautiful, but Michelle was very beautiful and seeing her body caused a foreign twinge. Although she forced herself not to stop, she did glance over her shoulder as she left the room telling Michelle she'd be up in a few minutes with soup.

She walked in wearing a fleecy robe of her own, passed Michelle the mug and without saying a word stepped in behind her friend. She perched herself on the rear porcelain lip, reached into the water with cupped hands and let scoopfuls of perfumed water cascade over Michelle's shoulders. Clint joined the party, taking a moment to fill his old-fashioned with vodka. Life didn't get any better than two women bathing and Kathy was reaching for the shower head. He took a long swallow, wincing as the gentle streams of water matted Michelle's thick red curls before they burst into a cowl of white foam spreading across her glistening shoulders.

"Kathy, thank you. I guess we can never tell how our days will end."

"Or how they'll begin. What happened, mi amor, and when?"

"Last night we argued over his obsession with porno. He's gone too far. The older he gets the younger he wants them and now he wants me to watch with him. I did at one time, years ago, for a turn-on, but what he's doing now isn't fun. It's sick and when I look at him I see a balding guy with a paunch and more pathetic each day. Then this morning we started again while I was packing. He saw my bikini in the suitcase and went ballistic when I told him we each had one. He's never liked me going with Darlene and Sheila, but he doesn't mind spending most weekends fishing or hunting with his so-called buds or going to strip bars and playing poker while I sit home alone."

"My God, this is my fault."

"No, darling, not your fault, his fault. He spends hours looking at naked bimbos on the web and his magazines are disgusting, yet he beats me because he can't bear the thought of not seeing the four of us dripping wet together. He's an absolute pig and I told him so. I told him our rooms would have spas and he didn't believe me."

"The rooms do have spas."

"I know. Good thing I didn't tell him we plan to use the one outdoors. Anyway, he got physical when I wouldn't give it to him. I pushed him away, he pushed me, I pushed him and he began punching and kicking."

Michelle tried to giggle, crying instead. Kathy leaned forward, kissed her shoulder and climbed from the tub. The bottom of her robe was drenched. She took a step back, shrugged the robe from her shoulders and reached for a bath towel, fashioning a sarong she knotted between her breasts. Stepping back in, she combed and wrapped Michelle's hair in a turban as Michelle finished her soup and leaned unabashedly into the wide "V" of Kathy's open legs.

Clint leaned into the screen when Kathy's hands went naturally to Michelle's shoulders, not certain how to react. Seeing any woman so up close and personal between her legs had never entered her mind, particularly a woman she worked with. She couldn't believe what she was seeing: Beautiful Michelle laying in steaming water, moaning

269

dreamily, her knees slightly raised, her hands clasped at her belly.

"I'm leaving him. You were right, Kathy. He should be arrested and I'm filing tomorrow for a divorce as well as an injunction to keep him away. He'll probably lose his job over this and he deserves to. The one good thing I can say he's ever done for me is shoot blanks. This will be a lot easier and faster without kids. Really, I should have left years ago. I should have listened to Darlene and Sheila instead of opting for quick fixes."

"I thought you looked forward to the weekends away and Girls' Night."

"I do, sometimes for validation and sometimes I like the guy I meet, but mostly I like being with Sheila and Darlene. I adore them, and now I have you."

"I'm leaving also, Michelle, very soon. I'm not renegotiating my contract after the finals and absolutely no one must know. I'm going alone, no baggage, and I don't want him hearing about it by some fluke…a blonde one to be precise."

Michelle tilted her head. "He's not getting back in the house. If you and the kids need a place…"

"The kids are half my problem. I'm taking care of them up front. They're not coming along for the ride."

"Can I? We could get condos in the same building, or share one and be like sisters. We could go on vacation and find a couple of handsome rich guys. "

"I'd say this is pretty sisterly, wouldn't you?" Her eyes travelled the length of Michelle's body "Honestly, I've thought about it, I mean sharing with you, not that rich guys don't sound good." "She cupped the sides of Michelle's turban, bringing their faces closer together. "Anyway, file your complaint on Monday. I'm going with you and what happened to you today doesn't change a thing. We're going to Vermont and, besides, perhaps we'll meet our rich guys at the lodge."

"No, darling, I can't."

"We're going if the three of us have you drag you. We'll pass by the house in the morning for your skis and Sunday you're staying here with me. We'll phone the police before going to your house on Monday."

"No guy's going to look twice at me. Kathy, my eye looks like a can of shoe polish and I think my nose will be something awful by morning."

She was wrong, Clint thought. In the dark no guy would care, not with her killer body.

"Yeah...I don't think you're wrong about that," Michelle turned her face into Kathy's bare thigh, groaning a protest, "but, you know what?"

She shook her fleece-covered head. "What."

"If some guy doesn't want you, I'll take you. Although I'm not quite sure what I'll do with you. Anyway, let's get you into bed before my legs fall asleep and I slide in behind you."

"Ooh, darling, don't tease me. I'm naked and I hurt too much to feel horny or laugh. I also have a very serious problem."

"What's that, mi amor?"

"How do I dry my back?"

Kathy shook her head, rolling her eyes. Michelle was a mischievous imp. She stepped from the tub, holding her friend firmly by the hips to steady her as Clint looked on wanting to scream at seeing Kathy help Michelle stand and softly working the towel from her shoulders to her ankles.

"How weird is this? I'm drying my girlfriend's butt."

"It's pretty weird, darling...and sort of sexy if you can get past the black eye and swollen nose."

"If you don't mind, I'll try not to think of sexy. I'm sort of sexy-deprived these days."

"You're very sexy and not only do I owe you a lunch, I

271

owe you a bath, a shampoo and a massage anytime you want, darling. And, by the way, I don't have a butt. I have a fantastic butt."

"I have no comment at this particular time." Kathy gave her a light smack, stood and thought what the hell, staying as Michelle dried her front, helping her into her robe not quite dispassionately. Black eye and bruises to her legs and back apart, she was hard not to look at. Who wouldn't want her, and who would ever want to hurt her? "I can't begin to imagine what Sheila and Darlene would think about this, mi amor."

"What else? They'd think you need a bigger tub for all of us, darling."

Forty

Thursday Clint woke to the persistent hum of his chronograph. He wasn't taking any chances. The previous evening was too unexpected and too compelling for him to consciously give up seeing them together again. Michelle was hot; she had a loser husband and would soon be in the market with or without Kathy. She'd be an excellent candidate. He had to discover more about her and the following Friday would be perfect timing. He also had to get out by 2:30 at the latest.

He knew Kathy didn't keep a diary. Her thoughts were private and so, apparently, was her mi amor. Mi amor, darling, tender moments in steaming bathwater and, when Kathy knelt to pat away the run-off at the Michelle's ankles, Clint gulped down what remained of the vodka in his glass, mesmerized. Kathy had eased away the turban, sat mi amor at her vanity, blow-dried and brushed out her hair in long, soothing strokes before leading her to bed by the hand.

He saw Michelle nod with a weak smile at Kathy's suggestion and moments later, with Michelle tucked in, Kathy was sitting cross-legged on the bed in a chemise and the two talked for an hour while the cognac and tequila took effect. When the conversation began to wane and eyelids droop, Michelle's fingers gave up the snifter easily and Kathy put out the light.

She was first to wake. In the kitchen she spoke with Melissa and Timothy, left them each an itinerary and saw them off, which meant locking the door behind them and waiting for the bus to disappear down the hill. She poured coffees and juice, laid them by her night table and woke Michelle with the weight of her body at the edge of the bed, the weightless touch of her palm and a whispered "good morning." When Michelle rolled over, a hand involuntarily clamped against Kathy's mouth.

"Kathy, it is you. I thought I was dreaming."

"More like a nightmare," she smiled, "except for the last part."

"What's wrong?" She touched her face, flinching. "What's wrong with my face?"

Kathy wrapped her arms around her. "Mi amor, I'm sorry. We'll have to spend a little time on your make-up."

"I'm not going."

"Then neither am I."

Michelle squeezed Kathy tighter the more her body trembled, letting her pent-up emotions take over. When she finished, Kathy's chemise was stained, Michelle's expression was disconsolate under a cloud of dishevelled red hair and her green eyes sparkled with wet sadness. "That feels much better." She nestled again into Kathy's shoulder, not letting go. "But I think another bath would really help."

"Then you would owe me two and we don't have time. Let's have our coffees, make you prettier than you are and get out of here. The ball and chain are gone."

They prepared breakfast, spoke endlessly as they sat at the vanity and dressed. The taxi came at 8:30 and they were at the airport thirty minutes later with both sets of skis. Kathy worked magic on Michelle's face and by the time Darlene and Sheila caught up with them she was again their whimsical mi amor, albeit less animated. The flight departed at 10:00, landing a hundred kilometres to the east of White Cliff Lodge at noon as the regional flight from

Cape City landed in Bayville with Ted and Eileen onboard and Clint sat in the family room with his lunch, his pen and note pad.

He was anxious to get home, wash his clothes, get to the gym, organize his week's work and plan his weekend. A change of venue was mandatory, he decided, despite adding over a couple of hours to his workday, which would serve his purpose until summer when he would return to increased tourism and a level of anonymity he felt was increasingly threatened.

He was pleased with the week's accomplishments, particularly at seeing Kathy lay out her clothes on the bed and dressing from one side while Michelle dressed from the other. Kathy was doing a little "I saw you, you can see me" thing, he was certain. He cleared his head, dispelling the disappointment that he wouldn't see the women Sunday night. He would be with someone else possessing the basic attributes of beautiful, slim, young and at least appearing affluent, although he was developing a keen sixth sense which seldom failed him. After all, he still had to earn a living and had no idea where his recent interest in calligraphy would lead in the meantime.

Each morning he worked on Burberry's handwriting, in the afternoon he copied Kathy's and at night, locked in his garret, he continued by the dim light of the Coleman when nothing was worthwhile observing. He was making definite progress, despite being uncertain towards what end beyond his resolve not to return to prison life with the stigma of being arrested for a few meagre thousands in bogus cheques.

At the sound of the motor he stood, peering out from behind the sun curtains, cursing. He should have had another ninety minutes and Burberry just cost him a few thousand dollars in tax-free revenue. He gathered up his papers methodically, put them into plastic files and turned in the doorway to verify. Under the access panel he held his

arms high, aimed and hurled the files into the darkness. In
the family room he scooped up his wrappings, swept a
sleeved arm across the coffee table and scrambled up the
ladder to close the panel as Ted believed he was disarming
the alarm with high-pitch beeps.

From his loft Clint followed him to the office and the
bedroom, giving him privacy when he disappeared into the
closet with his suitcase. When he reappeared he seemed
refreshed. He'd changed and went directly to his office
where he opened the drawer, poured two-fingers into his
glass and phoned Chicago. Clint heard each word clearly.
He may have gone to prison, Clint mused, but he never
sucked up and never backed down, not in business, not in
prison. And who the hell ever sucked up to a Lester?
Theodore Burberry.

He was on his cell explaining why he hadn't called in
earlier, when requested to do so by Lester. No, he would be
off the road until Monday and flying somewhere Clint
never heard of to replace a sales manager on vacation was
impossible. Eileen was having problems. No nothing
serious, a woman-thing and they had waited months for the
appointment scheduled for the next morning and she would
likely stay over to await the test results, hopefully negative.
Yes, of course he would keep Corporate posted. No, no.
Flowers wouldn't arrive in time. Anyway, Lester knew
Eileen and that his and everyone's well wishes would mean
more to her. Yes, he would keep Lester in the loop. He was
sorry to fail the team. The truth was: he had no choice. Any
other time. Lester did understand that, didn't he? Thank you,
Lester. Any other time, I feel terrible.

When Lester Lamarre ended the call Ted raised both
hands, one to digitally salute the gofer, the other to drain his
glass. Big man, Clint thought, easing over to his cot to undo
the backpack he had readied for his trip home, disgusted
with Burberry's squirming. He poured a generous shot of

his own, annoyed. He wasn't going anywhere until Friday, he would lose a night's work and Ted was indebted to him big time. Now Ted was on the phone with Eileen, suddenly quiet, nodding his head gloomily and when he hung up he took note paper from his desk, scribbled a note and went to the kitchen where he tacked it to the wall. Apparently, Eileen wasn't very pleased with being dropped off and forgotten.

In his office he remained standing, poured a shot for the road, locked the drawer and took up his attaché. Ted was leaving and so would Clint, as scheduled.

*

At the White Cliff Lodge the ladies congregated at the Instructor's Centre, resisting the temptation to dwell on Michelle's brutal attack, each one worried about her friend. Her ski goggles hurt her nose and the bruising around her eye, the rest was psychological until touched, jolted or until she laughed. Inexplicably the pain she felt was at once soothing, to finally feel free, and her penance for being so blind. She had never been beaten before and she didn't know how she should feel, persevering until her fourth or fifth tumble to inform her instructor she wasn't giving up, she simply needed a sauna and hot swirling water more than cold, hard snow.

Darlene and Sheila didn't notice, Kathy did and went with her, once again admonishing her argumentative friend. In the chalet, Kathy helped her with her boots and gloves. They climbed the polished log stairs from the great room one step at a time and in their suite Kathy gingerly helped Michelle from her thickly padded ski jacket. Sitting on her bed, she peeled away her layers of warmth and protection as Michelle purred quietly in peaceful slumber. Kathy unpacked the rest of her clothes, activated the spa, stepped into the bathroom and stepped out ready to relax and be pampered. Truth be told, she was also a little excited in that she was hoping for the right reaction as she stood huh-humming and testing the water.

"Wow! Kathy. You look fabulous." Kathy's backside was bare save for twin bands of sparkling gold appearing from slightly tanned and firm cheeks to her shoulders. "Let me see the front." Kathy turned. "Wow, we will be like sisters." The same narrow bands of gold scarcely covered her breasts and barely came together to form a miniscule and eye-catching "V" concealing what she had come to give away.

"I feel absolutely naked."

"Darling, you are naked. They're going to hate us when they come in."

"We won't tell them right away. Anyway, you go to sleep. I'm taking a spa, then a sauna and maybe I'll step out into the snow. I'll try not to disturb you when I leave, but I will wake you for dinner."

Michelle squirmed, trying to prop herself onto an elbow. "You get over here, right now, or I'm going home...after I tell them."

"You're not well."

"Kathy!"

"Tell me how you plan to crawl over the ledge, mi amor. You can hardly sit up."

"Get my bikini from my suitcase." She struggled to sit and Kathy stopped teasing. The girl was in pain.

She crawled onto the bed behind Michelle, embracing her full-circle, detaching the chrome buckles of her ski pants and folding over the front flap. She helped her to raise her arms, pulled Michelle's sweater over her head, undid her bra and sat back on her heels.

"The way I see it, and I've got a feeling I'm going to, we've got two choices: you put your little butt in the air and I push down or you put your legs in the air and I pull up. Either way, this thing's going on in the spa unless you plan on dating me."

"Legs in the air please."

Kathy waddled her way from the bed on her knees, walked around and eased Michelle backwards, taking a moment to plan her next move. She didn't want to hurt Michelle and they worked together, Michelle arching, Kathy tugging as smoothly as she could. Then came the leggings which stretched to triple the length before snapping free of her feet. Standing, Michelle inched her way to the spa, scrunching her face and instantly regretting the gesture.

"The plan's not working, mi amor. You're too sore to crawl over the side and I'm not strong enough to support you."

"Kathy I'm going in. I want them to see us at the same time or it won't be any fun." She pointed. "Bring over the chair, please."

"The chair?"

"Yes, darling, the ladder that looks like a chair."

Kathy shook her head and obeyed, unable to stop laughing once she began dragging the lounge seat across the plush carpet and saw her reflection in the mirror, dressed in gold stripes down her front and back. Michelle wanted to laugh, finding the effort too great. Instead she looked on, happy to have Kathy with her, happy they had become friends and when the seat was in place a big smile came to her face erasing the ugly bruise for an instant. One leg went over the arm with Kathy's help. She held onto the spa's edge, balanced herself and brought up her other foot, leaning over the edge to catch her breath centimetres from the water's surface with Kathy's open palms at the small of her back.

"Okay, it's official. We're dating."

"Alright! I hope you don't snore or beat up your women."

"That's not funny, mi amor." Kathy walked away.

"I'm sorry."

"You should be because I never snore. Now stay where you are and don't fall."

"We'll do this again when I don't hurt, darling."

Kathy stood at the lounge seat, thinking, "in for a penny, in for a pound" and "what the hell," especially after the previous night. "This is something I never thought I'd say mi amor…but, I'm taking off your panties." Michelle shrieked, wiggling her already bare bum, doing a shallow knee bend to assist. First one string, then the other and Kathy tossed aside the silky patch. "Okay, feet apart a little and raise your right foot", she did, "now raise the left one," she did, "and come down a little like you just did, mi amor."

Michelle managed to lower her body a few centimetres and Kathy leaned forward to adjust the bottom portion of the thong at the precise moment the adjoining door flung open. Both women jerked sideways instinctively. Michelle stumbled backward, grasping for the edge and missing. Kathy startled forward, crashing the side of her face into the soft flesh of Michelle's firm and curvaceous buttocks, wrapping her arms tightly around Michelle's thighs before sliding her cheek along the back of the nude body and her arms up to Michelle's belly to prevent them both from sprawling onto the floor.

Darlene and Sheila stood gaping, never to forget the sight of Michelle's naked body, her arms flailing, welded to Kathy in time as space. Darlene didn't waste a second, she hurried to Kathy's bed and Sheila followed a close second, rushing to throw herself across Michelle's, anxious for the show to continue. Regaining her composure Kathy straightened, Michelle hanging heavily in her arms, kicking awkwardly to free herself of the cushions and the strings trapping her legs. Kathy strained, not letting go until

Michelle's feet touched the carpet and she could lean forward to balance herself on the chair.

There was no point in rushing. Kathy stooped, pulled both sides of the slingshot to Michelle's shoulders, positioned the straps, adjusted the bottom "V" accordingly, gave her a playful spanking and dropped into the chair.

Darlene started. "Ladies, do we have anything to confess while we're on the subject, or the seat, the curvy one white one we saw stuck to your face, Kathy? Come on, fess up."

Michelle, still bent over, glanced over her shoulder with a familiar and superior look. Then she turned, careful not to trip herself, bracing her aching body on the arms of the chair and lowering herself onto Kathy who, surprising herself, wrapped her arms around Michelle's waist to hold her snugly in place. "We love each other. We're getting married before we go home."

"Mi amor, with you, nothing would surprise us." Sheila sprang to her knees. "Okay, where's the damn camera. I'm not leaving this room without a souvenir of this. Michelle where's your camera?"

Darlene continued. "So, what's happening here? Did we catch you guys practicing some sort of creative CPR? We know she's always had sort of a special thing for you, darling, but we never imagined this much."

Kathy craned her neck. "I bought Michelle a bikini like mine and, as you can see, she needed help getting into it. That's all."

"Why?" asked Darlene.

"Why what?"

"Why bother?"

Kathy helped Michelle reposition sideways and swing her legs over the padded arms of the chair. She draped an arm painfully around Kathy's neck, Kathy searching for a place to rest her hand that wasn't clamped to Michelle's far side, deciding on her belly and wishing she had a drink. The two exchanged wide, mischievous smiles.

"For later tonight when we're at the outside sauna and spa." Kathy said.

"We'll have to wear something." Michelle added. "We can't exactly go naked."

"You are naked," Sheila shrieked.

"So," Kathy went on, "don't wear yours." The intruders were quiet, uncertain. "They're by my pillow, ladies."

"And we hope they fit, don't we darling?" Michelle added, smugly.

"All I know is: you ladies are on your own. I've had all the filet mignon in my face and in my lap that I can digest for one day."

"Yeah, right, we see you pushing away your plate." Sheila laughed.

"Maybe she's waiting for dessert," Darlene added, pulling Sheila, assuring the couple they would knock before coming in.

They didn't. They flew from the room in a blur of multi-coloured nylon, leaving the door wide open, rushing back and into the spa in much smaller blurs of green and blue mixed with brunette, blonde and flawless white. The night was young, so were they and the White Cliff Lodge would never be the same.

Meanwhile Clint left the house as planned and decided not to chance working Thursday. His mindset wasn't focused enough, preoccupied with meeting Eileen Kimberly sometime over the weekend, convinced she was part of the complex Burberry puzzle and without her the puzzle would be incomplete.

Then there was Michelle somebody who worked at the college, Kathy's mi amor with the flawless glistening body he had wanted instantly to work with, the body which had heightened his every carnal impulse and desire. He would titillate and explore her with his fingertips, love her ardently and prove to her not all men were savages. He was certain Michelle would be unlike the other women he had worked with. She was completely at ease with Kathy, where most women would have cringed, covered themselves or made excuses. Michelle didn't make excuses, nor did she apologize. She was perfect, unashamed without being flagrant and cameras never lied. She was perfect for what she had awakened within him. The downside was Kathy Burberry. She was the single imperative, whereas Michelle would serve as his release after the closure he had waited years to achieve.

He went to bed. He deserved. He was exhausted after hours at the gym cursing Burberry for not thinking to install a workout room at home. He wouldn't work until Sunday unless Eileen decided to lay by the side of a real man who might not love her, yet make her feel loved.

Burberry wasn't real. He was pure fake without the sophistication of subterfuge. Clint laughed hysterically and rolled over, thinking himself a Good Samaritan, thinking he should get rid of Burberry and give Eileen and Kathy a better life free of deceit. One woman was his whore, wanting to be his wife, the other was a wife searching to be someone else's whore and Chicago Corporate was none the wiser. Clint wanted to sleep. He wanted all three women for what he could give and teach them, but most urgently he wanted temporary oblivion and drifted to sleep unaware his face had taken on a vicious smirk.

Forty-One

Friday morning was not a pleasant awakening for Ted. The previous evening with Eileen was needlessly stressful. She didn't understand. At dinner he didn't handle his wine well and in the casino he lost fifteen-hundred because he couldn't quit, while she won five-fold his loss. At home he went to his office out of habit, splashed a careless and unneeded hit into his favourite glass and went upstairs without caring to acknowledge the kids. Melissa's room was dark, so was Timothy's, absolving him of the need to bother with them and he wasn't saddened by the loss.

When he woke the kids were gone and the driver of the dark SUV had made several passes by the house hoping not to see fresh tire tracks. At 11:30 Clint drove past the driveway, paying no attention to the Lexus turning onto the gravel road, though he was a better driver and stayed behind Ted all the way into Bayville without being noticed. Neither was he noticed in the hotel, the restaurant or the museum, nor across from the many store façades as he waited for them to exit, Burberry's arms full while Eileen's swung freely.

They returned to the hotel, without visiting the seashore, neither one smiling, nor did they visit the harbour and Clint had to remind himself that she came from the seashore. So what? Lovers went to the seashore and his take was that Eileen Kimberly was royally pissed with Burberry. And who could blame her? She had probably looked forward to four days and three nights alone with him, not a lunch, dinner and a quickie that would leave her feeling like a cheap thrill or a whore while he went home to his family.

Burberry left her at midnight. She went to the bar outside the casino to sip Dom Pérignon poured from her private bottle. Clint Evans looked on, admiring, loving her as much as he could, imagining her naked, spread-eagle and sunning on the bow of his boat, drawing him closer with her charms and eagerly making love to him. He followed her into the elevator, pressing nine when she pressed fifteen. He bid her goodnight with a slight tilt of his head and an endearing smile. When the elevator returned to his floor he went directly to the counter to book whatever room was available.
*

Friday Kathy lay in bed watching Michelle who seemed so calm and peaceful. That she was leaving Ted was a given, if he wasn't man enough to divorce her first. Timothy and Melissa would be gone by the end of March when she would be free, unemployed and happy. Thursday was the happiest day of her past eighteen years and she wanted the weekend never to end.

Ted would turn apoplectic to hear she'd spent an hour in the outdoor spa with her girlfriends and four men, then thirty minutes in a sauna minus two of the men. The others having politely climbed from the spa when Michelle understood one of them wasn't interested in damaged goods and she stood to leave until Kathy pulled her onto her lap and kissed her, saying she wasn't ready to leave. She wanted Michelle in the sauna and, finally, when Sheila went with Darlene to change for an evening with their dates, she and Michelle lingered a while longer before going to their suite, Kathy commenting caustically that something was seriously wrong with any guy who wouldn't want Michelle. They spent the rest of the evening alone with the casual ease of life-long friends. Kathy's curtain of inhibition was completely drawn back and Michelle was unashamedly Michelle.

"Good morning, darling."

"Good morning. We slept in."

"Did Darlene and Sheila come back?"

"I don't think so."

"Thank you."

"What for this time?"

"For that unbelievable kiss in the spa," she paused, "and for not letting me climb out by myself in front of those guys. I hated the thought of giving them anything free, like seeing all of me."

"They were jerks."

"Did I mention the unbelievable kiss?"

"Yes."

"Wow!"

"Mi amor, you're a phenomenal kisser and I bet those pigs, if they're not gay, ran to their rooms for a bit of relief...but we both still like men, don't we?"

"I can't remember the last time I had as much fun with a man as I had with you yesterday. But yes, darling, we both still like men... thus far."

"We freaked out Darlene and Sheila. How do we explain the kiss? I wasn't counting, but I don't think I could hold my breath that long. My lips were numb till we went to bed."

"Tell me about it, and we have nothing to explain. I told them once at dinner that if I ever changed my religion to girls that you would be one sexy lover. I said I thought you were really hot and they've never stopped teasing me. So let's tease them back, for the weekend or until you find someone who's more fun. Agreed?"

Kathy flushed from the honesty. "You're all the fun I want this weekend, mi amor. I'll pair up with someone when you do, even if I have to wait until Vegas in April." She tucked her pillow under her chin. "You actually told them I was sexy and hot."

"Uh-huh, and I was right. No guy's ever kissed me the way you did, Kathy, which sort of makes me wonder. I might have to kiss you again, so I can be sure."

"You did kiss me, in the car. Was that a spur-of-the-moment thing? " Michelle didn't answer. She didn't have to. "Have you ever wanted to, you know, experiment without teasing."

"Yes, twice. And you?"

"I'm starting to feel good about myself and came here to ski and get laid only to discover at least six others are convinced I'm a lesbian and I'm thinking about a bigger bathtub in my upcoming condo, not to mention that a spa will be a definite must. So when were your two times?"

"Consciously, the second time was last night when we were alone in the sauna, but I know I wouldn't have pushed you away if you had slid behind me in your bathtub. The first was the night you drove me home and I wished we were at a drive-in or at the beach." She shrugged. "You did ask me, darling."

Kathy didn't trust herself to reply without first thinking. "This teasing thing…we do it until Sunday when Darlene and Sheila are around."

"And the jerks, darling."

"They'll be the most fun." She chortled. "God, I will be a lesbian by the time we get home."

"If you are, let me know. I believe I'll need another bath. Please."

Kathy turned towards the adjoining door, hearing Sheila and Darlene returning. Not only was she flustered, titillated and flushed, she had to admit she was a little aroused and curious. Michelle was gorgeous and there was nothing she didn't know about the girl's body. In fact their bodies were practically identical in size and shape. Nor could she deny a growing attraction towards Michelle and neither woman had hurried to leave the chair by the spa the day before.

She whispered. "I suppose you're naked under there."

"My undies," Michelle answered. "You should know, darling."

"Oh, God, you're right." Kathy sighed deeply, feigning disbelief when what she felt was intrigue for what she was thinking and sensual in a barely-there chiffon teddy. "Push over. Let's pretend we're sleeping and I'm the spoon until they crash through the door. Besides, when they're gone, I want to hear more about our condos."

Forty-Two

All day Friday Darlene and Sheila skied, while darling and mi amor spent the day talking, not realizing until dressing for dinner they were actually planning. At dinner they sat at a table for two, dressed to kill: Michelle wearing boots, tights, a mini-skirt and open-knit shawl sweater over a bra. Kathy wore a décolleté sheath, stockings and heels. Darlene and Sheila were in a banquette with their male trophies and sent over a bottle of wine.

The morning charade was a success, Darlene and Sheila refusing to leave until their sleepy-eyed friends told all. Michelle was the first to sit up, covering her breasts, not pretending to enjoy the soothing touch of Kathy's open palm on her bare back. Her pain was subsiding, though she wouldn't be skiing until the next day and Kathy decided if she was going to tease she would be convincing, crawling from under the sheets to sit behind Michelle with her legs and arms wrapped around her.

Sheila couldn't absorb what she was seeing and Darlene wanted answers. They'd come to meet men and, instead, the two girlfriends were doing each other. They ran from the room chattering. Kathy and Michelle agreed, asking each other twice, neither one very certain of the other, neither one very certain. Kathy lay back, swinging a leg over Michelle's head and laying by her side. They asked again, trying not to giggle as Kathy lay partly over Michelle, easing a hand under her waist as Michelle brought a hand to the nape of Kathy's neck in time for the double flashes to capture the torrid kiss.

The four ate breakfast and lunch together. Until noon Michelle and Kathy sat taking in the warmth of the sun. Until dinner they shopped and as the sun set they sat in the bar, holding hands when the jerks came in and continued the charade over après-ski cocktails with Darlene and Sheila. After dinner they undressed, went to the sauna wrapped in fleecy towels and robes and in their private chalet they dropped the towels before climbing into their private spa. Saturday they woke side by side, covered in thick, fleecy robes and holding hands.

"Darling, we're quickly becoming best friends."

"I never had a best friend. Hell, I never had a friend, period."

"They won't be coming in. I told them not to, darling, not to tease them. I'm feeling tired and want breakfast in bed today. I also want you to use your new skis. I'll join you later to take some pictures. This is one trip I want to always remember."

"Are you alright, mi amor?"

"I'm fine. I just want some time alone, not that I don't love you, darling. I do and I love those silly girls. But everything's starting to hit home and I have to sort things out. I have to be ready."

"Precisely the reason I'm staying with you. How do you expect me to concentrate on ski lessons when you're in here feeling horrible? Besides, I'd hurt myself and then you'd feel even worse. I hope. I'm staying. No arguments and I'll stay out of your way unless you want to talk."

Michelle buried her face into Kathy's robe and cried for what Kathy thought must have been an hour, happy mi amor told Darlene and Sheila not to come in. Yes, they would have a bit of explaining to do during the flight home. Yes, Darlene and Sheila would always have nagging doubts,

though, more importantly, she was with Michelle and she wasn't about to let her go or let anyone else hurt her.
*

Saturday Clint's day began early. He gave his bags to the concierge to hold until check-in, he asked the waiter for a table near the entrance and he ignored Eileen when she came in for breakfast. Burberry arrived near 10:00 and the couple left. When they returned late afternoon Clint was sitting in the lobby, seemingly pleased, and when she glanced his way he avoided eye contact. Shortly after Burberry arrived to meet her for dinner and by the time he left at midnight Clint was down another three-hundred in quarters and sitting at the slot machine by the entrance.
*

Eventually Michelle's tears dried, breakfast never happened and lunch for two was delivered to the suite. Kathy read her latest book, her head resting in Michelle's lap, enjoying the sensation of fingers running through her hair and by late afternoon the women were napping on the couch. At dinner only Darlene and Sheila were as well-dressed, still with their flings and this time Kathy had a bottle delivered to their table.

After dinner Michelle had a favour to ask. She wanted to walk with Kathy under the stars, sit in the snow in their thick snowsuits and pretend they were happy young girls. She didn't want the sauna or the outdoor spa. She wanted her friend to herself for the last night of the failed getaway and she didn't care what anyone thought. Kathy squeezed her hard, quickly rubbing the hurt away and they changed from stockings and dresses to skiwear and walked through the reception holding hands and laughing. They had one schnapps, sat in the snow face to face, huddled cheek to cheek with their legs entwined and said not a word. Later, they shared no pretence. They simply collapsed on one bed and cried together in thick, fleecy robes.

From Inside Her Bedroom

*

At the casino Clint wasn't enamoured of his losses. He was down another hundred. Worse: he was with the common losers, not the high stakes where he belonged. Burberry had just left and Eileen was walking towards the main doors of the casino as he stood and walked out.

"Hello, again."

"Hello, Mr…"

"Evans, Clint Evans, at your service. And, I must tell you, all the winners have left for the night"

"From the tables?" she asked.

"The tables and the slots." He took a deep breath. "So, miss, let me save you a fortune by offering you a drink at the bar. I have to admit, I've thought of you to the point of distraction since our elevator ride last night and you may well be the cause of my financial distress."

"I'm flattered, and sincerely apologize for the losses you incurred."

"Is that a yes?"

"Any other time, most certainly, however I'm connected."

"Is he joining you?" She hesitated. "Listen, I'm here alone, I'm single and I'm not looking for complications. What I would like, however, is a nightcap with an absolutely unforgettable woman. Please, don't disappoint me. One cocktail and I'll leave you to live my life without you, always to wonder what might have been. One drink and I shall leave you to wallow in my pathetic loneliness."

"How long did you spend practicing that spiel?"

"I must confess. I wrote quickly as I saw you approaching. That I would love you is my wildest dream, no less possible than to journey amongst the stars to the one most dazzling. I know. But that I might spend a few delightful and memorable moments with you is my heart's fondest desire, a beggar's heart exposed to a lady's gentle touch or piercing blow. "

"Barf. You can't be for real."

"Unfortunately I am, and I see that I'm alone for yet another evening. I enjoyed talking with you. Goodnight and I trust lady luck chooses to sit by your side at the tables."

He walked away, saddened.

"Mr. Evans, one moment please. That was inexcusably rude of me. I apologize. I made you the victim of my unhappy day. Perhaps one drink would not be untoward and loneliness is not yours exclusively this evening."

*

"I'm an electronics engineer. I own a small engineering firm in town which I'm currently in the process of selling to a larger corporation."

"What will you do then?"

"Take some time off. I'm thinking of hiring a captain and sailing in the Caribbean. It's something I've always wanted to do, yet somehow business always got in the way. Then I'll build a home by the ocean and offer my services as a consultant. I've had my fill of city life and I've decided I work better on my own. I don't particularly enjoy being a boss. If the deal goes through I'll be gainfully unemployed with my first suntan in years by May, although I won't know the outcome until the week after next when I meet with the top management in Cape City." Clint smiled, exuding an air of casual confidence. "Then I'll find a travel agent and an architect."

"Your meeting's in Cape City."

"Yes, on the twenty-second."

"My primary gallery is in Cape City."

"Then I'll have to drop in and ask your advice on decorating my home, which I want built somewhere along the coast by the fall. Are you familiar with Bayville at all?"

"No. This is my third visit. However I seldom go beyond the harbour area. I basically come to gamble. It's not my sole vice, though I must admit that I enjoy the atmosphere. I'm sure you'll discover that living by the ocean can sometimes be too quiet."

"You live by the sea?"

"Yes. I also sail. You're going to love your Caribbean adventure. However, be forewarned. Sailing gets into your blood pretty quickly."

"When do you go home, if I may ask?"

"Tomorrow afternoon."

"Bayville's loss as much as my own. I'm delighted to have met you and honoured that you joined me."

"And if I may ask, why are you staying at the hotel when you live here."

"As I mentioned, I haven't taken a vacation in years. My only real downtime is coming here once a season for a long weekend and leaving work where work belongs."

"How long will you be staying in Cape City?"

"I've booked a flight out on the Saturday, although I've found a reason to stay longer, if you don't mind me dropping by your gallery."

"Please do."

"I don't know anything about art, other than what I like. I seem to have a penchant for things abstract, albeit not too wild, and for the female form done with good taste."

"We can handle both. We can also mount the image and deliver by courier, unless you would rather have the work done locally."

"I can't imagine your work being anything but impeccable."

"Thank you. I'm proud of my reputation and, unless your timetable doesn't allow, you might want to put aside a few hours. Art is nothing one should rush."

"I'm told by those more knowledgeable that art is best discussed over dinner. Is there any truth to that?"

He was fascinated with her smile and her body, the way she carried herself and spoke.

"Yes, amongst many others."

"Then possibly I should visit your gallery mid-afternoon."

"Clint, my evenings are generally quite busy. Perhaps you should come by mid-morning. I do most of my entertaining at lunch." She glanced at her watch. "And talking about mornings, they tend to come all the earlier when I'm enjoying my evening the most. Thank you for the invitation, Clint. I've enjoyed meeting you and I look forward to seeing you in two weeks."

He stood. "The pleasure was entirely mine, Eileen. I suspect the coming weeks will be the longest I will have known for quite some time." He grinned, extending his open hand, wanting to feel her. "No, that wasn't a spiel and, if you'll pardon my rudeness, I would feel less improper by not escorting you to your floor. May I call the concierge to take my place?"

"Thank you for the thoughtfulness, I'll be fine. Good evening, Clint."

"Good evening, Eileen."

He remained standing until she disappeared into the lobby. Her skin was soft, her voice accented with a sensual huskiness and from the moment she sat she hadn't stopped grading him. What the hell she was doing with Burberry would remain an eternal mystery. In his room he went to his briefcase for his photo album, poured a drink and studied her every detail.

Eileen undressed, showered and crawled into bed, feeling a sense of nervousness. Had Clint suggested another drink, she would have stayed. He was attractive, charming and thoughtful, if not a little overly gallant. And what was wrong with that? He was flirting and she enjoyed the attention. She put out the light. Some girl, somewhere, would someday be very fortunate. He was attentive, a good dresser, successful and didn't go on about himself. He possibly wasn't without flaws, and certainly not without potential.

Forty-Three

Sunday the girls woke nose to nose, Kathy staring into green eyes, Michelle into hazel.

"Sitting in the snow was fun, Kathy. I'm sorry I spoiled your weekend."

"You call this a spoiled weekend? You made my weekend, silly. No one could ever have made me believe half the things I've done."

"So I guess I got my third kiss, or my thirtieth," Michelle snuggled a bit closer, "and a whole lot more. I'm not embarrassed, Kathy. I had a feeling something would happen between us."

"I had the same feeling when I leaned over you yesterday morning and I want copies of those photographs. Was that a turn-on or what? Anyway, we can blame last night on the wine and all that crying we did, something else I haven't done in ages."

"They'll never believe us."

"I know."

"Do you care?"

"No. I care about you. We had fun. Is what we did unbelievable and incredible? Yes. So what? How do you feel?"

"I've stopped hurting."

"And the bruising is fading, but you're still coming home with me. He won't be around until Friday or Saturday."

"If I wasn't coming home with you, I'd miss you." Michelle brought a warm hand to Kathy's cheek. "Will we be okay at school, Kathy? I don't want to lose you as a friend."

"I suppose that depends."

"On what?"

"Whether we can get off this bed with our robes on and without kissing. Besides, I'm leaving the school and I thought we were going to shop for condos together in the spring."

"Did we go too far?"

"I don't think we could have gone any farther. I'm no expert, but I believe we pretty well did everything. I suppose the real test will be waking up tomorrow morning. Personally, I think we'll be okay, but let's be honest with each other. Mi amor, we were both reaching out for the same reasons and I don't feel the least bit guilty. I feel liberated and, incidentally, I couldn't ask for a better lover."

"So I can still call you darling."

"I'll be hurt if you don't."

"Darling, before breakfast, why don't we put on our bikinis and soak in the spa?"

Both women shook with laughter, crying happy tears and pressed their lips together.
*

Clint sat waiting in his hotel room until he was certain Eileen left with Burberry for the airport. He had much to prepare for his upcoming week with Kathy and not much time. The unknowns were Michelle, how long she would stay and what time Kathy would drive her to the lawyer. He would be ready to leave his apartment the very moment the women left the house and if Michelle was coming with her, he would have much less time to organize himself.

He walked into his apartment at dinnertime, prepared his papers, food and clothes for the week and went out to his favourite restaurant. At home he poured a drink and opened his laptop. He wasn't interested in the boy or Melissa. She could wait until Tuesday. He wanted Michelle and Kathy. He wanted to see them both.

*

No sooner did Ted leave than Melissa walked to the living room window to watch him disappear and Timothy went to the fridge. As he sneaked up behind her, his mouth full, he ogled her. In his mind Melissa didn't exist, she never had. She had ignored him for so long and now he was closer to Midnight Rhapsody than anyone.

"You going out?"

"She swirled. "Like no, jerk-off."

"I'm not the jerk-off. He's the jerk-off. He just yelled "goodbye" while he was closing the door. He doesn't even use our names anymore. No wonder mom hates him."

"She hates him because he has a girlfriend on the side. He has for years and he's been with her all weekend. He does her, comes home because neither of them trusts us and then he leaves us to do her again. She lives in Cape City. She owns like an art gallery or something."

"No way."

"I can prove it. I've seen her. She must be like really rich. She's got a boat and everything."

"No way"

"Way... and I saw her like totally naked."

"When?"

"Over a year ago. He has an album of her in his drawer where he keeps his booze. He's even gone on vacation with her to something like an all-inclusive place while we get stuck going to Myrtle Beach. She's even gone there with him, golfing. "

"There's no way. The drawer's locked. I know."

"You're so stupid."

"You're lying."

She peered through the window. "I told you, I can prove it." She went to her room, called him from the hallway and walked into her father's office with her brother trailing behind. She knelt under the desk, jiggled the lock intently and pulled out the drawer reaching in for the bottle. "Want a drink. He won't know."

"Yeah."

She poured a large amount and passed the smudged glass to her brother who gulped his first mouthful, coughing what remained in his mouth across the desk. Melissa ignored him, reaching for the album and centring the thick collection of memories on the desk. She began flipping one page after the other, slowing, hesitating each time Eileen was nude at a beach, or in bed or partially dressed in lingerie.

"This is our father's whore. Her name's Eileen. She's the reason he's never home."

Timothy whistled. "She's like mom's age. Do you think mom looks like that...you know without her clothes? I think so."

"That's so sick, but Eileen's the reason she's gone like all crazy with her clothes and the personal trainer guy."

Timothy sat in his father's chair, drinking his father's scotch and flipping through the pages of the personal album. "Awesome, she's like totally naked."

"I told you. She's a whore."

"Every girl's a whore, Mel? I mean, look at the way you dress." He reclined, reaching out and pulling up the hem of her skirt, giggling when she slapped away his hand. "All the girls at school have done it, even you. All the guys talk about you, Mel. They say you're like real cold, but I think they're so totally wrong. I think you could make some serious cash, if you wanted."

"Shut up."

He laughed. "You're not even like wearing underwear under your leotards."

She grabbed for the album, startled when he ripped it from her hands and crashed backwards into the chair.

"No," he yelled, "I'm making copies."

"That's sick. She's like so old."

"Yeah, and she's naked. So like what's it to you?"

Melissa ordered him to stand and began wiping the desk, watching her brother select images he wanted face-down on his father's photocopier.

"You're sick, deadbrain. That's so totally sick."

He ignored her, tossing the album at her, turning off the machine and hurrying to his room. When he returned he poured the remaining scotch from his father's glass into his and dropped into the chair.

"We could bribe him."

"No, we can't. She already knows."

"Did you ever, you know, anything like this, let some guy take pictures of you?"

"Like, hello, what do you think, jerk-off?"

"You will one day. The guys, at school all have pictures of naked girls. I've seen them."

Melissa replaced the album, the bottle and glass and closed the drawer. "Get out, deadbrain. We're finished and don't ever come in here again."

"Mel, if you did, I wouldn't tell about that either."

"Get out. All I wanted was for you to see so you'd know what he's really like and you'd better hide those pictures because he'd like really kill you."

"Okay, but really, I wouldn't tell, Mel. Honestly."

She yelled at him to leave, staying at the desk until his bedroom door closed. When she was satisfied she had erased the intrusion she closed the door behind her.

*

"Ms. Lopez, what are you doing here?"

"Ms. Lopez is staying with us for the week, Melissa, until your father gets home. Her house was vandalized and

301

she's with us while repairs are being done. It's also a perfect opportunity to improve your Spanish."

"Hi, Melissa. I know, it's kind of freaky having one of your teachers as a houseguest and I won't say a word in Spanish unless you ask me. And, believe me; I know mothers can be so pushy sometimes."

Kathy's raised eyebrows and wide eyes conveyed her thoughts eloquently, garnering no reaction from Melissa and a giggle from Michelle. Timothy heard them, wisely remaining in his room and soon after Melissa went to her room while Kathy showered and changed. When she was done Michelle showered and changed and Clint leaned over his kitchen counter spellbound as the women made dinner, each one infused with the peculiar closeness of their special bond, comfortable with the silence or banal chatter, each one feeling they wanted to run away together and never come back. Each one believing the condos would become a reality and they had come into each other's life precisely on schedule.

The kid's ate in their room, Melissa, very out of character, serving her brother who didn't feel very well. After dinner Kathy and Michelle sat in the living room listening to music, Melissa took her 8:30 shower, Timothy never showed his face and at 11:00 all but the upstairs family room was dark. Over the years Kathy's ears had attuned to the stealthiest footstep creeping up the stairs. In fact the upper floor had become her domain, yet each woman had an open book on the coffee table ready to grab.

Michelle lay on her back, nestling her head in Kathy's lap. "Darlene and Sheila didn't believe us. They actually think we're lesbians," she whispered.

"Would you believe us?"

"I don't know. I think maybe."

"I never told you all weekend that you have such beautiful red hair."

"Oh, God, we are lesbians. Do you think we should we join a club or something?"

"Noooo. I'm very happy the way things are and we don't even know whether we'll wake up tomorrow and wonder what we've done. It's not as though we ever said anything foolish."

"I never talk with my mouth full, or I might have."

"You're terrible."

"You're delicious."

"I think you're right. We're definitely lesbians."

"Part-timers. Like we said, we still like men. Right?"

"I'll have a better answer for you when I find a real one, but yes." Jack Caden jumped into her thoughts. She had met a real one, one who proved too good to be true.

"Where have you gone to, darling?"

"To a bistro, a quaint little bistro with charm, elegance and warm flickering flames."

"Can I come?"

"I can picture you perfectly by the fire, mi amor."

"Thinking of the spa and sleeping with you, I'm going to be lonely tonight. Do you have a teddy bear or something for me?"

"Yes I do...me. After the last two nights, leaving you out here would be ridiculous, unless you'd rather not have a late-night bath filled with scented oils. I think we should wean ourselves. If we quit cold turkey we might always be afraid or too shy and I'm sort of curious about tomorrow when we wake up and either kiss or run and hide."

"That won't happen, but I'm sort of nervous about what will happen. I don't want you to ever hate me."

"Mi amor, I'm not. Whatever happens, we'll have memories only you and I can share."

Kathy eased Michelle away from her lap and went into the bathroom. By the time Michelle joined her, Kathy was in the tub and Clint coughed vodka from his mouth wondering what the hell had gone on at the White Cliff Lodge, despising them for flagrantly coming together to ridicule him.

Forty-Four

The next morning Kathy awoke early from an uneasy sleep. She made lunch for the kids, phoned the school for herself and Michelle and went to her bedroom with coffees. She roused Michelle with gentle caresses and a single, lingering kiss.

"We're alone, mi amor. Sit up and drink your coffee. We have a difficult day ahead of us. And why are you smiling like a mischievous little girl?"

"Darling, you didn't run and hide."

"I couldn't. I stayed up all night mopping the bathroom floor after I put you to bed." Michelle's eyes opened wide. "I'm joking, mi amor. But, wow, this thing we seem to have for each other is pretty strong."

"Darling, right now, I want this to last forever, but, in case we don't, this afternoon when we get back I want a hundred pictures of you."

"You don't need pictures, mi amor. Whether we're together anytime or all the time, you and I have found something pretty special." Kathy paused, inhaling deeply. "Ooo-kay let me go first and I can't believe I'm saying this. Listen, Michelle, after all we've been through...I can't imagine giving this up and settling for the way I was. Actually, that's not true. I feel sexy with you, erotic and completely insatiable. I mean, I don't want to give this up. I don't want to give you up is what I'm saying. Trying to

305

ignore what we've discovered about ourselves and each other would be tantamount admitting we've done something bad, and we haven't."

"Wow, darling, this is wild." Michelle sat up. "But let's not be stupid. We both have good jobs we want to leave, and loser husbands we are leaving. After that, who can tell? All I know is: I do want a condo close to yours. And, if no one good shows up for either one of us, why wouldn't we share a condo together? We'd be great roomies and, if miracle guys do show after the fact, for each of us, they'll have to understand or perhaps we won't tell them."

"You're evil. You're a little devil in a beautiful body."

"No, darling, I've finally found what makes me feel good and I don't want to let you go, at least not very far and not for long."
*

Clint woke an hour later in time to see Michelle on the phone and Kathy standing by her side. She seemed satisfied and whatever she said to Kathy brought simultaneous nods of agreement. A second phone call brought the same reaction and both women sat at the kitchen table talking and writing notes. They left at 1:00 PM and within the hour Clint phoned Kathy from the gravel road at the end of her driveway. When she didn't answer he went to the front door and walked in.
*

Lopez was being held until his court date on Thursday when he would be advised not to return home, which was the least of his problems. Michelle met with a lawyer Monday afternoon, filed for divorce and Lopez would also be required not to contest the sale of the house which would go on the market Thursday afternoon. She wanted out and she was getting out. Hearing that her husband had lost his job generated no reaction, nor did walking into her house with Kathy by her side who was adamant that Michelle would not stay by herself until completely healed and, if that meant staying over the weekend, Ted could sleep on the living room sofa. After the stern lecture neither woman spoke as they packed clothes for the week, throwing Lopez' wardrobe into his largest suitcase they would drop off at the police station.

They arrived home in time for dinner which Melissa helped prepare, not at all pleased that Ms. Lopez was in the house. She liked the discussion revolving around her final collegiate year even less and Timothy remained quiet. He didn't appreciate the invasion either. He felt awkward sitting between the women who were dressed as though they were going to a party.

After dinner Kathy and Michelle went to the family room to relax with digestives away from curious ears. They sat close together with complete ease, planning the week. They would return to work the next day, go to court on Thursday and each night they would research luxury condos, Vegas hotels and spend the weekend visiting high-rise properties.

Kathy had waited anxiously for weeks to cheat on her husband, excited by the thought of going to bed with a stranger, and in a matter of four days the dream dissolved. She spent her weekend intimately with a woman whom she brought home. She was planning more romantic weekends, a divorce, the sale of a house, and the purchase of a condo where Michelle would be a frequent visitor. Until her own divorce she would no longer need to waste her Friday evenings and Saturday nights waiting for someone she loathed.

She drifted away. Since her afternoon with Jack Caden she worried whether he would forgive her promiscuity until she discovered he didn't exist and, therefore, had nothing to forgive and she had no reason to worry. Nor did he have her to remember. Had he been honest she would have gone to him. She was definitely interested. She would have told him as invitingly as possible about the White Cliff Lodge. But that didn't happen and her honesty was moot.

She stroked Michelle's cheek, waking her. At 11:00 they showered, slipped into bed wearing silk teddies and woke feeling as though the seven hours had elapsed in minutes. Clint stood watching them, eating his breakfast fruit bar. The two definitely had a thing for each other transcending fleeting curiosity, which would make his time with each one all the more gratifying and when they left for school he set to work in the family room perfecting his copy skills.

*

When Kathy and Michelle strolled into the teachers' lounge together Sheila and Darlene were sipping coffees without revealing the slightest curiosity, waiting for the room to clear at the sound of the bell. Their students could wait a few moments longer. They'd spent hours talking on the phone Sunday and Monday night and had something to say. Girls' Night was too far off. The four had to have dinner together and neither Darlene nor Sheila was taking no for an answer. If Kathy and Michelle were joking, they were entirely convincing. If they weren't playing, both women agreed, neither would have missed being part of it for the world and that's all they had to say until dinner. Nothing had changed. They were a foursome and they were going to Vegas, which probably meant two happy men and one happy couple. They were good with Kathy and Michelle, just not curious enough to disappoint two men.

*

After school Melissa was expected to prepare supper. Her mother and Ms. Lopez would be late. They were dining with other teachers downtown and Melissa disguised her delight with a face devoid of expression. Clint would be calling her from Europe and not having her mother at home was a big plus. Deadbrain she could handle.

Kathy took Michelle to the health club, enrolled her, helped her select an outfit at the boutique and together they worked with the trainer whose day instantly improved two-fold. Post-workout was spent window shopping. Michelle decided the only truck moving her belongings from the house would be a garbage truck and she knew where she wanted to live. The place was a newly constructed terrestrial heaven and everything she and Lopez previously owned together could go to hell along with him. More importantly, not holding Kathy's hand was difficult, or wrapping an arm around her waist. She might have weeks earlier, the way girls do, but since White Cliff she wanted to and she was certain the difference would show on her face. After the school year that would all change and, new boyfriend or not, she would be herself.

No one ever questioned Darlene's choice of restaurant. The woman possessed an enviable palate for fine cuisine. Her wrapped gift was for Kathy; Sheila's was for Michelle, each one a photo album they flipped through together, seeing images of Michelle and Kathy kissing in bed, Kathy in a designer teddy kissing the camera, following a panty-clad Michelle to the spa and photos taken at breakfast, lunch and the girls' intimate dinners taken from Darlene's phone camera. Other photos showed the four in their slingshots, Kathy and Michelle nestled in the snow and several as the couple left the resort holding hands. The final photo, which Darlene's athletic date had willingly coerced from one of the jerks, was a souvenir of their defining kiss.

Darlene started. "First off, we have the same albums and you're not dykes. Sheila and I don't want dyke friends. Yeah, okay, this is blowing us away, but, really, we should have seen this coming Kathy. Michelle hasn't stopped talking about you since we began Girls' Night and the day you started with your new wardrobe Sheila and I thought we'd have to drag her to the gymnasium locker room for a shower. We should have known. So we're fine with everything whether you girls are in this for the long-haul or playing weekend touchy-touchy. Either way everything stays between the four of us."

Sheila asked. "Mi amor, is she good?"

Michelle nodded. "Honey, she's fantastic and I absolutely can't get enough of her."

Darlene cut in. "It's time you had something good in your life, mi amor, and Kath's the best." Sheila persisted. "Darling, I'm sorry, but I have to know or I won't sleep."

Kathy smiled wickedly. "You should already know…there's nothing sweeter than honey."

Sheila turned to Darlene. "Babe, I'm freaking here. We've got frigging lesbian friends."

"Ladies," Darlene raised her wineglass. "I'm not the least bit surprised. You deserve each other for as long as your love affair lasts. I guess we'll find out in Vegas. Here's to girls tall, short, fat and thin and neither of you fit those moulds. You're both gorgeous and sexy and, God, I need a man." She rested her wine on the table. "Now, tell us what happens. Should Sheila and I be planning a party, or what? And, something else: you girls were cool at school today, as far as everyone else was concerned, but we're worried about how you can maintain your sexy little secret."

Kathy and Michelle exchanged glances, Michelle nodding.

"Michelle's staying with me until the weekend. She's going to court on Thursday, I'll be a witness and over the weekend we'll be looking for a condo. Her house is up for sale."

"Darling, you're both looking for a condo?" Sheila asked.

"No. I'm helping her, honey. Although I am divorcing

my deadweight after the school year and, I should also tell you, Michelle and I are both resigning after the finals. We're going into the private sector and this, Sheila and Darlene, stays here. Don't test our friendship with a slip of the tongue and, by Friday, I will have made our reservations for Vegas. That Michelle and I won't be at college any longer doesn't mean we don't want you guys around us all the time. So to answer your question, babe, the party will be in Michelle's apartment as soon as she moves in. We can even make it a slumber party." Kathy turned to Michelle. "Mi amor, I'm sorry. We can, can't we?"

"Yes darling, of course we can." Michelle looked straight into Darlene's eyes and Sheila's. "But we're not freaks, Sheila. I love the album. I couldn't think of a more beautiful and special gift, but no more cameras. We're not freaks."

"Okay, okay, don't get all lesbo on me. Sure you shocked us, no shit. You guys were obviously and seriously into each other, but all we wanted was to share our weekend with you. We love you guys unconditionally and, yes, they're not quite the usual ski weekend photos." Sheila sipped her wine, her eyes warning the other three. "However, mi amor, I do have one more question."

"What?" Michelle's tone was somewhat tainted with frustration.

"If Kath hadn't come along when she did, if she hadn't joined us, would you, you know, have thought about me or Darlene?"

"You'll never know, honey, though I must admit you were both to die for in your slingshots. No wonder you both got laid."

"And we're taking them to Vegas."

"So are we, aren't we darling, with the smallest tube of sun cream because we'll be in our room most of the time."

"Babe, I'm freaking!"

311

Darlene drained her fluted glass and signalled over the waiter, rolling her eyes at Kathy. Neither woman quite certain which friend was worse, mi amor or honey.

Forty-Five

He waited until 8:45. Kathy wasn't home and the other kid was in his room rocking himself to sleep.

"Hi, Clint. Where are you?"

"I'm in England for another few days, Melissa, before travelling on to France, Germany and Spain and coming home with some very good news for you. I'm anxious to meet you in person. Have you been practicing for your Valentine's performance and audition?"

"Yes, the way you told me. I'm getting better"

"Excellent. I'm anxious to hear your concept for Valentine's."

"I want to do live costume changes, so each guy gets to see me strip off one costume and put on another that the next guy will see me take off. Pretty much like a merry-go-round."

"An excellent idea and I have something in mind that will complement the performances perfectly. Let me work on it. How long do you plan for each routine?"

"Ten minutes."

"Too long. You'll be exhausted halfway through. I would rather you do six five-minute slots each hour from noon till six. We'll make more and you'll be happier. Do you have something to show me tonight?"

"I can, but I'd like another week to improve. I want you to be proud of me. I'm wearing one of my costumes...new stuff I bought."

313

"New pieces, not stuff. You'll have to begin preparing for a more cultured life Melissa. You'll be meeting sophisticated directors, producers and debonair leading men you can't imagine. Stuff doesn't figure into their vocabularies. Exquisite, divine, charming and remember your wardrobe for the audition will be supplied to you. Now show me."

Melissa eased her gown slowly from one shoulder, then the other, stepping back to show Clint Evans a hopeful girl's young body in designer panties with garters and bra she wouldn't normally wear for another ten years. She turned twice with her arms in the air.

"Like this."

"Yeah, like that, although I want you to start rehearsing in stilettos. Start getting comfortable in them. I'm also working on a routine for your audition, something you'll like, something we can talk about the day before Valentine's."

"This is all happening so fast."

"It's all happening on time and if I had met you earlier you would already be driving something fast and European, in Europe, and you'd be wearing clothes you only get to see in magazines. You're beautiful. By the way, do you drink when you're not on camera?"

She hesitated. "Yeah, when I want to relax."

"Have one for both of us, Rhapsody. I can't relax, but I will when I see you and with a bottle of the finest champagne. You look great." He chuckled. "Once more before I go Rhapsody, turn for me."

Melissa faced away, posing, working her shoulders, hips and knees, praying she was doing well.

"Good. Real good, Rhapsody, and goodnight."

When she looked at her screen he was gone.

Clint continued monitoring her every move from the measured striptease in front of her mirror to the double-vodka she poured before dressing in flannel shorts, a matching jacket and bobby socks. She was a cute girl. She should have had boyfriends and date on weekends. Instead she was flaunting her body in real time for what she believed was big-time revenue. Where had her young life ever gone so wrong? He reclined, toasting her. She would be good. He had no doubt she'd be good, one of the best and one day she would die in lonely squalor.

She went to bed in her socks and flannels. He watched her breathe, he watched her fall asleep and transform from a lost and aimless porn star into an innocent and angelic waif. He finished his drink, poured another and sat watching her until the rumbling of a garage door opening pervaded the house.

*

Michelle showered as Kathy made lunches and reactivated the alarm system. Kathy showered while Michelle prepared a bed she wouldn't sleep in and made hot cocoa for the couple to enjoy while ending their first real day together talking about Darlene and Sheila, the week, the weekend and themselves. Each woman was certain one moment, uncertain the next, struggling quietly to understand while dispelling unwanted feelings of doubt and insecurity, neither wanting to hear or speak words of self-recrimination while camouflaging secret fears from the other.

They had shared an intimacy in front of friends and strangers neither would have dared in their separate pasts and neither the beautiful women with them nor the countless spectators had died as a result. In fact, for the first time each woman felt alive as Clint looked on from his dark loft mere metres above.

*

Wednesday as they woke the emotion was no less intense, the mystery of their attraction not yet resolved and noticeably less important for Michelle. Melissa and

Timothy left, the women left and Clint did his work. By Wednesday night Kathy hadn't spoken with her husband for the better part of two weeks and he hardly crossed her mind. Timothy lay in his room watching home videos, marvelling at his bravado, trying to concentrate on the principle of supply and demand he hadn't paid much attention to in class. He was certain he could make thousands after his birthday when he would have the tools with which to work. He'd be rich. He'd already made a hundred from the extra copies he ran off in his father's office of Eileen's most natural pose. He'd have to be smart, which he understood wasn't easy. The worst case scenario he imagined was going straight to the source herself, Midnight Rhapsody who was in the next room probably doing stuff.

He wasn't wrong. Melissa was in costume performing in front of the mirror. She was improving daily, proud of herself and anxious to meet her manager. School was a necessary evil made all the more so by her mother. In a matter of weeks she'd be free. She'd be with Clint and not in some jerkwater town. He would take her to Europe, teach her to be a lady and introduce her to producers, directors and real men. Real men, not the loser jocks at school who would end up like her father.

She didn't like old lady Lopez and what was the woman doing in her home all week? Her mother was like a total child and Lopez wasn't anything better, thinking they could be young again by dressing in mini-skirts, tights and sweaters and talking like they were girlfriends. They were old and married. Their lives were over, finished. They had their chances once and hadn't seen the big picture, not like her. Men were gullible pigs. She had quickly discovered men would pay to be pigs because they weren't happy at home, like her father, and not think twice about what they were. Her mother and Ms. Lopez weren't ugly. They had just totally ruined their lives, content with having nothing.

Together they were pathetic and a reminder of what she, Melissa, Rhapsody, would never be: a stupid woman, a wife or a mother.

Upstairs, beyond the hate and resentment, Kathy sat with Michelle.

"Are we ready for the big day?" Kathy asked.

"You don't have to testify, Kathy. The lady cop will be with me and I don't want you involved."

"Why?"

"This is my problem, Kathy. I don't want you involved."

"You're wrong. This is our problem and I am involved."

"What if they find out?"

"They won't and, if they do, I'll walk over and hold your hand. I told you, Michelle, I'm not embarrassed. I'm not certain what I am, but I'm not embarrassed." She paused. "Listen, mi amor, he beat you savagely. We have proof and he's not getting off. Tomorrow will be a good day for you, your liberation day," Kathy caught herself, her eyes sparkling, "your second liberation day and I'll be with you every moment."

"I know, Kathy. Thank you."

"I hope so and I want you to go home Friday after school, when we're certain you're safe. I think we should have some alone time to figure things out. We've been very close for an entire week, to put things mildly, and we might have gotten in over our heads. I'll be as close as my phone and, maybe by Monday after class, we'll look at each other and laugh."

"At what, Kathy? What's funny about exciting each other? So we're women, big deal. Even Darlene and Sheila think we're sexy together. You might laugh, I won't. I'll be very sad. I came to terms with myself last night, whether we occasionally get off on each other or become something more."

317

"I never want to make you sad."

Michelle shrugged. "However I will be going home. I've overdone my welcome and I don't want to be here when he comes home. Besides, I believe your daughter's about ready to poison my food and I've got things to do. So I'll leave you alone Friday, but Saturday we'll do lunch and see the apartment because you promised you would go with me. Then we won't see each other until Monday and if you feel like laughing I won't go to the gym with you."

Kathy touched Michelle's shoulder. "Mi amor…"

"I'm alright, Kathy, and you do have a point. We have been pretty addicted to each other and I suppose being alone for a while wouldn't hurt." Her lips curved into a thin smile. "Anyway, it's not as though I won't have a fantastic photo album to remind me."

"I guess I'm still a little scared. I'm trying to imagine having you as a lover with a man in my life? Remember what Sheila asked last night? She was being her usual self, yet as beautiful as they were in those thongs, you were the turn-on. I guess my point is, if I feel the way I do about you, and not them, how will I feel about men when the time comes?"

"Is there a man?"

"No. I thought there might have been until recently, until he disappeared."

"A lover?"

"No, not a lover, a dream, a quite a good-looking and charming dream."

"I'm sorry."

"Don't be. If he had come true, this week wouldn't have happened, whether I would have cheated on him or brought him. Then I would have cheated on the three of you, so I'm kind of glad he showed his true nature before charming me anymore than he did."

"Then I hope he's gone forever."

"He is; all the more reason for us to figure things out. He's not the only broken-hearted man out there and we should understand our feelings before he or they show up."

"You sound like a counsellor. What if they don't show up, Ms. Burberry?"

"That's all the more reason to understand our feelings, especially if we're going to have condos in the same building. You see, mi amor, last Wednesday was a no-brainer, girls being girls, so was Thursday. What I need to figure out is why the rest happened up to and including last night." Kathy smiled warmly. "Comprendo, chica?"

"Darling, your Spanish will have to improve if we're going to be lovers, pero sí, comprendo y te amo. If you're interested, I said I love you. Why? I don't know. It's enough for me to know I do. I suppose I should thank him tomorrow for beating me and I'm not going to spoil the time we've shared with a chart of pros and cons. So do what you have to do. I know I won't feel any differently. We were meant to be an item, for however long. And when we can no longer be with each other we'll deal with it, whether you laugh on Monday or we find someone either tall and handsome or petite and sexy. I guess we'll find out. And now, darling, all I want is to sleep. Not to escape you because I know you'll come to me in my dreams."

"Mi amor, you're a romantic. I agree. Let's go to bed. We're both tired."

"I don't feel romantic, Kathy. I want to sleep in here tonight and I'll have my shower in the morning." She kissed Kathy's cheek, crawled under the covers tucked herself into the sofa and closed her eyes.

Standing in the doorway, Kathy hated herself. She put out the light, went into her bathroom, showered and went to bed where she sat thinking, writing, crossing out scribbled words and writing more. When she awoke Thursday morning Michelle's arms were wrapped tightly around her, keeping her from falling from the sofa.

Michelle's eyes blinked open, filled with questioning.

"I don't need a weekend, mi amor, and I won't ever laugh. I said some stupid things last night. I'm sorry and I hate myself."

"I didn't help matters much."

She put a finger to Michelle's lips. "No one-upmanship. I was wrong and, please, clean up your face before you go downstairs. Your cheeks were wet when I joined you and I'm afraid I turned you into a pretty scary abstract with my lip gloss." Kathy eased herself onto the floor and stood, pulling back the covers. "And I hope this is the last time you sleep in your clothes."

"We're still friends." Michelle pushed out her lower lip and creased her brow.

Kathy knelt, whispering. "You're a terrible actress and, no, we aren't friends. We're lovers and best friends until one of us decides otherwise. Now go get undressed and cleaned up."

Kathy went to the kitchen for coffee as Melissa and Timothy were eating breakfast standing up, ignoring each other. After the customary "morning" they ignored her as well and went to their rooms. When they came out on schedule for the bus, they left without a word; she closed the door behind them and went upstairs. She and Michelle left at 10:00, met with the lawyer, the court case was at 1:00 PM sharp and at 2:30 Mr. Lopez was sentenced to an additional thirty days. He owned a prison record, he was compelled to authorize the sale of the house, the car and agree to whatever liquidation of the shared property the plaintiff saw fit to undertake. Michelle was free to begin her life and the For Sale sign was posted at 4:00.

Thursday night by 9:30 they were home from the restaurant, showered and dressed in long silk robes which Kathy insisted on buying to celebrate the day. She also bought champagne and by 11:00 they were light-headed, slightly more so by midnight after a second cognac and tequila. Clint had remained a day longer, knowing he wouldn't see Michelle again the way he had since Sunday and that he would miss seeing her as much as despising her closeness.

Friday morning the women woke together, frowning and hugging, knowing the week-long tryst was at an end until Michelle moved into her condo. Her house was off-limits, as was Kathy's. They would miss the intimacy and being together at school would be a horrible tease.

Clint watched them dress together for the last time, he saw them in the garage flipping through a book Kathy had taken from the trunk and laughing. He saw them drive away and he went downstairs to empty his jar and eat breakfast.

He left at 2:30, the kids arrived at 4:00 and Kathy walked through the door at 5:00. Ted arrived at ten o'clock and she left him undisturbed to work in his office.
*

Clint struggled with himself throughout the day, following them from the college to the health club and Michelle's home. Not working didn't make sense. Until he figured out what he was actually doing he'd lose tens of thousands and miss out on meeting and entertaining new clients, deciding he would restrict his workweek to Fridays and Saturdays. He couldn't afford carelessness. He was tired, having discovered the hard way that his self-appraised home-study was physically demanding and equally intellectually draining.

When Kathy left several minutes later, Michelle drove from her driveway and Clint followed, parking several spots behind her when she pulled into the grocery store parking lot. He waited outside, watching through the storefront windows, entering as she swung her cart into aisle four. He went quickly through produce filling his cart, tossing in a

321

two-four of bottled water and crashing aimlessly into her as she strolled daydreaming from aisle eight. She jerked back.

His concern was obvious. "Miss, I'm terribly sorry. Have I hurt you?"

"Uh… no, I'm fine. My head was somewhere else. It's my fault."

His concern became a wide smile. "My driving skills are usually far superior to this. I'm glad you're alright, or we'd have to exchange numbers." He tilted his head. "Please forgive my clumsiness and enjoy your evening."

In aisle twelve he saw her once again. She wasn't smiling. Neither was he, yet his expression was pleasant when she glanced his way. Then he went to the cash several aisles over, confident she was somewhere behind him. He spoke jovially with the packer and walked directly from the store to his vehicle, satisfied she could see him. He would miss her. He wouldn't see her again for two weeks when they would meet again.

*

Michelle watched him leave, forgetting him when she could no longer see him. At home she felt despondent and phoned Kathy. She couldn't wait for Saturday afternoon. She wanted to meet for breakfast, visit the apartment and have lunch. They spoke for an hour, making plans, repeating themselves and not wanting to hang up. Michelle would phone the developer, change the appointment to early morning and they would stop somewhere for a drink and review all the information. When she did hang up she felt enshrouded by loneliness.

Forty-Six

After nine days of warm scented skin, gentle caresses and soft urgent lips, waking Saturday morning with Ted in her room made Kathy feel sick to her stomach. Whatever she'd been thinking Wednesday night was flushed from her mind. She wanted Michelle. She crept from her bed, went to the kitchen, poured a coffee and called mi amor to check on her and confirm the appointment. No sooner had she put down the phone than her day went from lonely to miserable.

"Morning."

"I'm surprised you're here."

"The week went well. I did what I had to do. And, you'll be happy to know, I'm home until Monday morning. There's a project I have to work on for Chicago."

"What's your point? You'll be locked in your office all weekend as usual." Kathy chortled. "Anyway, I'll be gone most of the day. Don't expect me until after dinner. A friend needs me. She's going through a rough time."

"The one who's been here all week."

"Yes."

"And Sunday?"

"I'm cleaning the house. What do you think I'm doing, or are you taking me to dinner?"

"You know I won't have time, as much as I want to."

"Yes, I do." She grinned. "I'll take a rain cheque for whatever Saturday night you might be home before hell freezes over. And, while we're on the subject, let's not

323

make fools of ourselves on Valentine's. This marriage is enough of a joke."

"Glad to be home, Kath," he paused, "as usual."

"Yeah, the kids missed you. You remember whatsherface, daddy's favourite little girl and whatshisname, your pride and joy."

"I'll be in my office."

"And I'll be gone in thirty minutes."

Kathy went to her room, imagining how her life would change in a matter of a few short weeks, waking Saturday or Sunday mornings with Michelle in her condo with no one around to ignore her and how angry Ted would be. She locked the bathroom door, forgetting him. She showered, dressed and came out looking untouchable in her silk oriental dress with side slits and high collar. Ted hadn't seen the dress and slammed the door to his office after yelling that if she wanted to look like a slut she should go out and be one, find a street corner she liked more than her home, adding that she wouldn't be the only woman out there disgruntled with a perfect life.

Timothy knew to stay in his room. Melissa, on the other hand, needed to keep current but waited too long. Seeing her mother close the door to the garage she went to her room and planned a day at the mall, not entirely pleased with her Valentine's outfits and wanting to make a real impact the with Clint the following Tuesday. He was a very important a man and wouldn't waste his time with anyone who wasn't taking her future seriously.

Kathy decided against meeting Michelle. Instead she drove to her friend's house and they went for breakfast before continuing on to the luxurious downtown complex. Four units remained and the view from Michelle's favourite on the nineteenth floor was breathtaking. The spacious apartment boasted two equal bedrooms, a living room and dining room facing the harbour, two bathrooms, one equipped with a spa, a laundry room, a cinema room, a designer kitchen and a solarium. The outside terrace was private and would be ideal for sunning. The building offered a doorman, a health club, a rooftop pool and deck, an inside pool, spa and sauna and underground connections to shopping and entertainment. Well worth the six-hundred thousand which was well beyond a language teacher's budget and the property manager wasn't in the mood to make concessions.

Kathy sat into the plush sofa across from the man's desk. She patted the cushion beside her wanting a confused Michelle to sit. She lounged slightly, crossing her legs and asked the man for a moment alone. He obliged, after laying coffees on the table by their knees. Kathy saw no insurmountable impediment. Michelle's share from the sale of her mortgage-free house would account for half. She had a hundred K in the bank, she would soon be awarded half Lopez' financial assets in the divorce settlement and life was too short. They had each sacrificed enough. The time had come to start enjoying and what better proof did she have than Kathy who stood and went to the office door, deaf to Michelle's pleas. When she was seated, she crossed her legs, reached for her coffee and sat upright.

"Sir, the apartment is unquestionably gorgeous. Your price, however, is somewhat exorbitant. This is what we propose and we'll require an immediate response, although we understand you may prefer to confer with a partner. Five-seventy-five with two-hundred thousand down before we leave, another three hundred after the inspection and the balance held in trust for thirty days after we take possession. In addition, I would also want first refusal on the eighteenth-floor apartment at a similarly reduced price for which I will give you twenty-thousand this afternoon as a refundable goodwill gesture, should I change my mind within one month. I believe you'll agree your day has

325

turned out quite well."

"Ms. Burberry, you realize you're asking for fifty thousand dollars."

"Yes, I do, and I realize we're giving you substantially over a million, ninety percent of which will be in your bank before we move in."

The man stood. "May I leave you ladies alone for a moment? You were quite right, Ms. Burberry. I will have to confer."

He walked out and Kathy pressed an open palm between Michelle's breasts. Her heart was close to rupturing and Kathy had never seen her as pale.

"Kathy, I don't have the money. Let's get out of here."

"Mi amor, you fell in love with the place. Everything about this place is you."

Michelle wrung her hands, looking distraught. "I don't have the money, Kathy. What are you doing? We don't belong here."

"You do have the money, tied up in your house. Look at us. Of course we belong here: two professional women. Or have you forgotten?" She brought a slow smile to her face. "We just won't quit our jobs until we have something lined up."

"You're crazy."

"Just think of cozy winter mornings, your to-die-for terrace all summer au natural and the stunning roof deck."

The door handle clicked and a discreet moment later the man came in.

"Ms. Burberry, my associates concur. If neither of you ladies has had a change of heart my secretary is preparing the intent to purchase as we speak and I shall make arrangements to meet with my lawyer Monday evening. I trust you're both in agreement."

"We are." Kathy opened her chequebook and wrote a cheque for two-hundred-twenty thousand. "The money will be transferred to my chequing account first thing Monday morning."

"Thank you, Ms. Burberry, Ms. Lopez. You'll both be extremely happy living here."

"Yes, we will," Kathy answered.

When they left the office Michelle had lost her appetite for lunch. She was quiet, flustered and nervous. The past week was hitting home, which was where she wanted to go. Kathy understood, explaining as she drove that everything was fine. She had the money to help her friend and she trusted Michelle implicitly. Michelle's house would sell quickly, they would soon have lucrative careers, not frantic jobs and by summer their evenings and weekends would be spent on the terrace overlooking the harbour or on the rooftop deck making men horny and other women jealous. Then she walked Michelle to the door, despite knowing Lopez was still behind bars. What she wanted was to feel the warm softness of her girlfriend's lips.

Her day had changed abruptly; she was starved and didn't want to go home. The quaint bistro was on her left and she steered into the turning lane. What would she possibly do at the house? And most other restaurants would be crowded with fat, noisy kids and their lazy, loud parents dressed in sloppy jeans or sweatshirts. She wanted peace, and she wanted quiet. Most of all she wanted Michelle to celebrate with her and talk about their new homes.

The bistro owner was charming, his voice accented with European flavour which made her remember what Michelle had said about Spanish. She would learn Spanish and so much more. The owner seated her at a table by the window and left to fill her wine order.

"I believe madam will approve of my choice."

She looked up. "Jack!"

"Ah, I'm delighted the lady remembers the humble servant."

"Yes, I certainly do...the humble servant who doesn't exist."

His happy expression disappeared from his face. He placed her glass on the table by her hand and stepped from her comfort zone. "I do exist, Kathy. Except for last week, because you were vacationing with your girlfriends, I've spent my Saturdays here sitting by the fire, waiting for you to come. So you see I'm very real and when Alphonse told me you were here, I couldn't believe what he was saying. But I see I've upset you. I apologize. I'll leave you to your meal.

"I phoned you, or at least I tried, and guess what, no Jack Caden. I wanted to see you and not because I'm getting a divorce and need company. I thought you were a nice guy, something rare these days. So yeah, goodbye."

"Kathy, you couldn't find me because I don't have a landline. Why would I? I've recently arrived in town, I'm living in a temporary pied à terre and I meant what I said about finding a home by the ocean." Jack swivelled from his hip, signalling Alphonse. "Friend, please tell this beautiful and enchanting lady how I've waited for her each Saturday since our first flirtation and how I've left your fine bistro each night with a broken heart."

"He is speaking the truth, madame. Never have I seen such a desperately sad man."

"Thank you, Alphonse. I believe you." He left them alone. "I'm in the book."

"And don't think I wasn't tempted. In my defence I had no way of knowing whether you regretted our kiss and, by the way, you didn't look back which would have told me a lot."

"I wanted to, and I wanted you to call me." She looked around. "And why are you still standing. Sit down or go away."

He sat. "I missed you and I've thought about you every

day for hours."

"And I thought of you often, until I tried phoning. In fact you missed a very good weekend. I would have invited you."

"My loss."

"Yes."

He grinned, though not convincingly. "And someone else's gain."

"No, Jack. I'm not a slut. Actually, I spent the entire weekend nursing a sick friend. I barely got to wear my skis."

"You're still angry with me. I didn't mean to imply you were anything less than angelic, merely my envy of someone else's good fortune at the cost of my own."

"I'm far from angelic and I'm angry with myself."

"Because of me?" he ventured.

"Yes."

"Let me make it up to you. I want you for the afternoon. We can go to a movie, a museum, walk along the harbour, go shopping, make love," he beamed, his toothy smile picture-perfect and blinding white, "or stay here, which is problematic, or drive into the country and throw snowballs or make snow angles."

Kathy wasn't impressed. "Why is staying here problematic? Someone else called Kathy dropping by?"

"No. It's a problem because we're having lunch here and I'm taking you somewhere else for dinner."

"Are you for real?"

"Yes, Kathy. I'm for real and I have a real cell phone number, which I answer."

"Then a museum sounds good. It's been ages, though I'm not so sure about dinner."

"You must. An early dinner and I'll set you free. Besides, the first night we met, I barely got the chance to see you in your beautiful dress."

"You remembered my dress."

"Who wouldn't?"

She sipped her wine, not hiding the fact she was thinking, each one very aware he'd seen more than her dress that night. "An early dinner and we take both cars."
*

They agreed to meet at the museum an hour later. Jack's attire was too casual to complement Kathy's exotic dress. He settled the bill and left her. She stayed to finish her wine, not entirely convinced she would see him again until Alphonse assuaged her doubts and when he did arrive she was taken aback. He was wearing a dark tailored suit, Italian loafers and a white shirt that topped the brightness scale open at the collar.

They strolled side by side, talking easily, Kathy inwardly pleased she hadn't cheated on him in Vermont, her cheeks flushed with intrigue. He was refreshing and unpretentious, undeniably a man who knew what he liked. He didn't understand Impressionism, whispering that he considered the style somewhat childish and incomplete, not so the real masters whose names he could never remember. The human form, particularly the female nude, was intended to be well-presented, never abstract or made to appear imperfect. Life was sufficiently filled with imperfection, he believed, the fundamental purpose of any true artist being to balance misery with temporary joy and despair with renewed inspiration

She asked what inspired him. He answered: health, success and a beautiful woman to love. When he posed the same question, Kathy answered: close friends and true love. And when he asked of her the meaning of true love, she answered: The misery of being apart, the joy of being together and the despair of hurt feelings."

"You omitted inspiration, Kathy."

"No, Jack. I did not. Our inspiration is derived from the

one we love. Without love there is no inspiration, hence no joy, merely despair and misery."

"Kathy, please excuse me, forever. I think I'll find a window and jump out."

She chuckled. "You'd ruin your suit, Jack, and you did invite me to dinner. So stay where you are. Am I such a horrible companion that you want to jump from a window?"

"Your company is exquisite, although I should take your hand lest I be tempted to spoil our evening."

She held his. "Perhaps we should visit a less sombre salon."

"Yes, with a somewhat more inspirational theme."

She was fantastic. Not a couple passed who didn't ogle them and, the few times they sat, he barely managed not to glance toward the floor. As they spoke he visualized every detail of her legs and garters he had absorbed that first night. She was stunning, making him realize he had lived so long without the joy and inspiration of another's love.

An early darkness took over the day and once again Kathy insisted on driving separately. The dinner setting was romantic and elegant, candlelight bathing their faces in a warm glow. They danced and held hands at the table. He held himself in check, not speaking the words he felt, somehow believing Kathy knew. And she did know. He was considerate, soft-spoken, kind and attentive. He was handsome, strong and confident and she was cheating on Michelle.

"Kathy, the evening has been dreamlike. I knew one day you would come to the bistro. I felt it on your lips when you left me and I wasn't wrong to wait."

"My life is complicated right now, Jack. There's a lot going on. Truthfully, until April I'll be an absolute nut case. I'm headed for a divorce and I'm helping a friend through one. I'm moving into the city, my kids will be leaving, probably for good, and I'm leaving the public sector for a better in job in private practice. Yes, you've been on my mind, especially today, which doesn't mean I'm sleeping with you tonight. I need time to get my brain straight and having sex with you would complicate matters big time."

He smiled. "Thank you."

"For what."

"For wanting to make love with me. I can't deny I want to rip that dress from your beautiful body and never let you go. And while we're on the subject of going, I'm leaving town for a few weeks. Something I do once a year, visiting all the corporate offices in whirlwind tour. But here's the good news. We'll be together on the fourteenth, Valentine's, somewhere special with a special gift."

"A gift." She inhaled deeply. "I've seen you three times and you're buying me a Valentine's gift?"

"Yes, for a special lady. Your gift to me will be letting me unwrap you, love you and adore you."

"I just told you…"

"Kathy, one day is all I ask. Saying you won't sleep with me tonight means you would. One day, and if at dinner four weeks from tonight you want to walk away I won't stop you. You're divorcing a guy who bought you a briefcase for Christmas. Give it to him in the settlement and come to me."

She stared into his eyes and sipped her wine. "I'll phone you, Jack, and you'd better answer. I'm not in the mood for games."

"Then we're on for Valentine's?"

"Yes, when and if you answer."

"I'll answer and four weeks tonight I'll be the happiest man on earth."

"You said the fourteenth."

"Valentine's, yes, when I hope to wake up with you beside me. Bring a suitcase. I'll make reservations somewhere to fit the occasion where we can dine, dance and open your gift" He squeezed her hand. "I should order champagne."

She shook her head. "No. We should leave, though I've enjoyed myself immensely."

"Can we be together tomorrow, before I leave?"

"I'll phone you, Jack. That's when I'll know whether we'll see each other again, and how much of each other. Thank you for a wonderful evening."

In the vestibule he helped with her coat and at the entrance he kissed her lightly twice. The third kiss was passionate and neither one said a word until they embraced at her car. Sliding in behind the wheel, she drove off. At the ocean she pulled in by the boardwalk, looked up at her house and opened her phone, feeling her heart constrict. She pressed send instantly.
*

"Mi amor, what's wrong. I'm sorry. I wasn't at the house. I'm sitting in my car at the boardwalk."

"I didn't phone the house, darling."

"Why are you crying?"

"My house is sold, Kathy, for the asking price. The agent left an hour ago. I think she was a little drunk. They want to move in March 15th. Do you understand what this means?

"Michelle, I'm so happy. I told you. And, yes, I understand what you mean. We have a lot of shopping to do."

"Darling, can we be together for a few hours tonight?"

"Oh, mi amor," Kathy's heartache was real. "I can't. I'm expected at the...." She stopped abruptly. "Michelle, mi amor, I love you so much. I'm putting you on hold. Don't hang up on me." Her heartache turned to self-hate. The phone rang twice. "Ted, it's me. Go upstairs, if you can walk, and look out the window."

"What?"

"Go to the bedroom and look out." She waited impatient seconds. "Just do it, goddamnit."

He did, not at all quickly. "I'm here. So do I wave or what?"

"Do you see the light lights flicking on and off at the boardwalk?"

"Yeah, I do."

"That's me. I was with a friend today and as I was coming home she called to tell me she needs me again. I can't say what time I'll be at the house. I might stay over and, if I do, I won't call. I'll be there when I get there, possibly tomorrow."

"We'll miss you, and give him my regards."

"Up yours, jerk," and she disconnected. "Mi amor, I'm coming right away."

"Kathy, you're going to hate me."

"I'll never hate you. I thought we got over all that."

"I booked a room for us at the Delta. I don't want you here." She cried. "I don't want to be here anymore."

"Stay where you are. We're going to the Delta and I'm driving. Pack lingerie for me and one of your dresses. I love you. You know that, don't you?"

Michelle burst into tears and Kathy hated disconnecting. When she arrived Michelle's face was a kaleidoscope of emotions. She had spent the half-hour packing for two, her suitcase was by the door, they kissed with ardour and left.

"Darling…"

Kathy shushed her with a slap on the bum and marched her into the shower. "Wash your hair. We'll get you all dry and comfy and then we're going downstairs to celebrate."

"What if someone sees?"

"Everyone will see. And who cares? Do you?"

"No."

"So let's go celebrate. You've got a condo and I have something to share with you. Nothing bad, but I want you to know."

"You'd never hurt me. Go get dressed. I want the red one and then you can do my hair for me."

Kathy came into the bathroom in her stockings and heels. Michelle sat in the chair huddled in a thick, fleecy robe.

"You're not dressed."

"I don't want to be. I have something to say and thought this would be more convincing."

Michelle peered into the mirror. "You're scaring me, darling." Kathy kissed her head and began brushing out the long, red curls. "Kathy, let me go first. Okay?"

"Yes."

"Yesterday, after you left me, I went for groceries and met this guy. We collided in the aisle and I had a funny feeling about him. I think I could have liked him if he had stuck around, but he left thinking I was a complete loser, Michelle the absolute loser."

Kathy shook her. "So you think I sleep with a loser. You think I dream of a loser and miss her every moment? I don't. And I certainly wouldn't be seen in one of the best hotels holding hands with a loser. So let's get real." Kathy filled her lungs with air to where she thought she'd faint. "That guy I told you about, the creep at the bistro, well I saw him again today and he's not a creep. He's a nice man and I had dinner with him. I like him, mi amor, which changes nothing. We're moving you very soon, me a few weeks later and nothing changes. I need you to believe me."

"Did you sleep with him?"

"No, I did not sleep with him. We had dinner and we left separately."

"I'm okay with it, really."

"And I'll be okay with your guy, whoever he is. One guy bounced into your cart, probably not by accident, because you're to die for gorgeous and someone else will."

"What if you're wrong?"

"Then, mi amor, on my heart, you will never come second in my life." She kissed Michelle's neck. "Now, do we go downstairs and knock their socks off or do we stay here and cry all night for no reason, high-class condo owner?"

Michelle's face brightened. "This is all so unexpected. I want you, I'm not sure about men, you want me, we want each other, I'm a little jealous and I want you to be jealous when I find someone."

Kathy stroked the hot air through Michelle's hair. "Mi amor, I already am jealous and when push comes to shove, I'll shove him away for you. In any case, if you haven't noticed, I'm delicious, I'm backless and I'm ready for a late-night snack. Let's go tease and have fun. We'll have lots of time to think about this guy thing after tonight. Tonight is our private Girls' Night and we have a whole lot to celebrate."

Forty-Seven

Sunday afternoon Clint awoke invigorated, counting his Saturday as a great success. She was one of his youngest, a professional student who hadn't worked a day in her life and didn't have a care in the world, not as long as daddy kept the monthly allowance cheques coming. She was into good times, a party girl, and he partied with her until the early hours when she collapsed face-down onto the bed covers.

He stood staring at her, thinking no one had ever taught her a lesson. Everything about her screamed "spoiled" from her designer shoes to her designer wallet in her designer purse that was filled with gold and titanium and not one but three bank cards. Daddy wouldn't be pleased, nor would mommy, if there was one, when the girl would inevitably call to ask him or her to bring clothes and underwear. Greeting daddy at the door in a bath towel would be one lesson, likely already taught by the time Clint swung his legs from his bed and stretched, the other would likely have come very shortly after as daddy and daughter discovered together the loss of eighteen thousand dollars in cash advances and withdrawals.

He grinned into the bathroom mirror. The mini-dress, coat, panties and boots would make some homeless squeegee girl very happy. Each item in the hotel laundry bag had European names with matching price tags and the jewellery she'd tossed aside like cheap trinkets would bring

337

him an extra few thousand from the pawn shop. And his Friday client, after his run-in with Michelle, despite being much less lucrative, was equally athletic in and out of bed. The woman was incredibly turned-on hearing him describe his lovemaking with Kathy and Michelle and fell asleep promising to join his threesome the following week. Of course the foursome wouldn't happen, nor would she be so quick anytime soon to spend three thousand for a night of titillating sex with a charming stranger.

He considered three thousand a fair price for dinner and phenomenal lovemaking in a beautiful hotel room the woman would never forget. What was three thousand over a lifetime? In her case: fourteen cents a day and possibly a quarter for Saturday's girl, certainly affordable, particularly since he assumed the cost of doing business which made the entire experience all the more reasonable.

He wondered how much he would see of Kathy over the coming week, certain nothing would compare with the previous week. And he wondered how easily Michelle would fall in love with him. To think Michelle was beautiful was to think nothing. She was beyond beautiful and wasting her life teaching future drop-outs and office clerks an equally beautiful language was hideous to contemplate.

She wouldn't be an easy catch, but catch her he would as surely as Kathy would one day fall into his open arms. "Kathy, sweet Kathy," he murmured, "one day very soon, my sweet Kathy Burberry, my darling, mi amor, my lesbian at large and caregiver to the frail you will purr in concert to my gentle caresses and not feel the sting of my gentle touch. And then, my insatiable and exotic Kim, I will leave you forever."

His flight to Cape City was scheduled to leave Thursday evening. He was anxious to meet with Eileen Kimberly, take her to dinner and leave her with an eagerness to taste true love.

*

"Darling, thank you."

"Okay, enough of this 'thank you' business. I'm darling, you're mi amor, and that should be enough." Kathy kissed her. "Did you see those two guys drooling last night? That was so cool to see."

"Pigs," Michelle answered.

"Mi amor, you're the little piglet. If my dress was any shorter I would have needed a chastity belt and yours was no better."

"I can't see enough of you," she took a long breath, "and you don't mind about the guy in the grocery store?"

"No, I don't. And you shouldn't mind about Jack because if he doesn't like you he's history."

"I don't like him. I want you to myself. I hate him."

"You will like him, mi amor. You will. And now we're going to have breakfast in bed, enjoy the morning and miss each other terribly until tomorrow. At least you're going to a nice, empty home. I'm leaving a spectacular woman for a cesspool of hate and contempt." Tears welled in Kathy's eyes. "And, mi amor, I have no idea why. I never loved him, but I did love them at first." Her body convulsed and Michelle brought her in close, hugging her to the point of suffocation, "Now I want them out of my life forever. All I want is you. I will always want you, no matter what."

"Darling, thank you," Michelle clamped a small opened palm across Kathy's lips, "for letting me to take care of you for once. This weekend is my treat. You're not going home until late this evening. I won't let you."

Michelle called the desk to extend their stay and Kathy arrived at the house moments before midnight wearing another of Michelle's dresses. Ted left before dawn Monday, ignoring her on the sofa, and Michelle woke Monday morning resisting the urge to scream. Her life, she was certain, would always revolve around Kathy. She would never leave Kathy and she would die if Kathy ever left her. Yet the man in the supermarket continued to ricochet from one corner of her mind to the other and that made her afraid while Clint leaned nonchalantly against his backpack drinking hot cocoa by the ocean.

Forty-Eight

Clint drove from the Cape City airport to the Regency entirely engrossed by his passenger and feeling confident Melissa was in his grasp. One nagging question was what the boy would eventually do with his videos besides going to bed happy each night. With the exception of her nightly showers and morning wardrobe, he'd scarcely seen Kathy all week, more intent on her handwriting style which he was coming close to perfecting.

As captivating as Kathy was to him, the week without Michelle seemed monotonous. He loathed one woman as much as the other and would never see them together again, which didn't mean he would ever forget their sweet words, their lithe bodies moving in concert and their undisguised disdain for him. He understood clearly listening to Kathy's phone conversations that neither woman wanted their love affair tainted by what they were leaving behind. The condos were his biggest shock of the week and he'd stayed awake through to Tuesday morning pondering whether the unexpected development was a setback or a positive thing. Either way, Burberry was being put out with the trash and the kids were going with him.

The weekend was the first break he'd given himself in four months and he looked forward to relaxing, somewhat disappointed he hadn't met the thirty-year-old flight attendant in a place better suited to his needs. She worked First Class for a reason and after she left him Friday morning he rescheduled his return flight on Sunday to avoid possible complications, being of the opinion that wild sex inevitably led to more wild sex, eventual expectations or hate. In any event, she'd never be lonely.

After breakfast he toured the streets, surprised at how much more temperate the region was than Bayville, a place where he could definitely live, a place where he could start over with ample business opportunities. He would see Eileen Saturday morning, curious about the outcome and equally anxious for his return flight and coincidental meeting with Michelle who occupied his thoughts as frequently as Kathy.

He ate lunch by the ocean, amazed by the lack of snow and cold and after dinner he selected his date for the evening from the hotel lounge and went clubbing with her until he took her home. He left empty-handed, being that he was on a sabbatical and had promised to see her later that night. She was acquainted with the best places, was never refused at the door and his time with her was money well-spent. He saw the potential and was eager to see more of her and the city.

Las Cuatras Galerías was walking distance from the Regency and he arrived with a bouquet of flowers and a box of Belgium chocolates. She was magnificent, slender, dressed in black, her dark eyes set in a finely sculpted face and flawless skin.

"Mr. Evans, I trust your meeting concluded satisfactorily."

"I'm happy to report very satisfactorily." He held out his arms. "I thought a diamond ring might be somewhat obvious."

"Thank you, they're delightful. And I love chocolate." She passed the flowers to an assistant. "I did mention, did I not, that I'm attached."

"Yes, I believe you also made reference to a fence of

342

some sort."

She chuckled. "Yes, I did."

"I can but hope he's fallen off?"

"Coming close to being pushed off."

"He's either stupid or blind. What I see before me is the finest work of art in your gallery."

"He may also be a little speech impaired. I haven't heard such a gallant compliment in a very long time."

"You should be complimented every day, every hour."

"Mr. Evans…"

"Clint."

Her smile was disarming. "That's right. We did leave on a first name basis, didn't we?"

"Yes, and I've come to learn something about art and invite a breathtaking lady to lunch. Mind you, nothing romantic. I'm having enough trouble at the moment not proposing and carrying you to my castle."

"That would be your castle by the ocean?"

"Naturally, and which I'm seriously considering building right here in Cape City. I had free time yesterday and did some sightseeing, so don't go marrying anyone before you have the chance to reject me."

"Then you'd better hurry. However, in the meantime, why don't we select a piece of art for you? I believe you mentioned we would do the mounting."

"Yes, indeed. And I'll be returning to the city in a month's time."

"Continuing business obligations?" she asked.

"To meet with an architect and hopefully dine with a beautiful woman."

"You're serious."

"Perhaps you can recommend a firm…and a restaurant."

"Let me take your coat, Clint."

She passed his coat to another assistant and began her work. She spoke in-depth about each piece without the slightest hesitation, all the while remembering her flirtation and that she would have stayed longer that night in the bar, had he asked. She enjoyed the attention then and she was enjoying him now, not oblivious to the side-glances and the fact the women in the gallery were well aware she was wearing an outfit reserved for special occasions. At the casino hotel she hadn't believed he would visit the gallery, yet she left home excited about her day after taking extra time to do her hair and dress and he was returning in a few weeks and couldn't possibly be serious about building a home. They left the gallery mid-afternoon after Clint signed a cheque for six thousand dollars. His manners were impeccable, his sense of fashion au courant and he was a practiced conversationalist.

"I am serious. I want the thing built by August, with a dock for my sailboat."

"You don't sail."

"You'll teach me."

She chuckled. "I'm practically married, Clint."

You are married, and you sleep with a loser. He grinned. "Or practically single, depending on one's point of view." He looked at his watch. "I suppose dinner's out of the question."

"Yes, I'm sorry."

"I share your lament." He paused. "Eileen, may I ask a favour of you?"

"Certainly."

"Keep my artwork until my home is built. I don't see the need for unnecessary shipping, if you agree"

"That's very trusting of you, and I do agree."

"Not really." The pages of Burberry's album flashed across his mind. "This way I won't have to invent reasons to see you."

Lunch was at an end. Staying longer would lead to dinner and dinner to what made Eileen question herself the most. About to leave the restaurant he didn't hesitate. He cupped her face in his hands, pressed his lips to hers and told her he'd never imagined a woman so easy to love.

*

Saturday evening he was talking with the barman in the hotel lounge when his date from the night before arrived. He took her to dinner and let her guide him through an evening of sophisticated clubbing that went on till midnight when he drove her home. Cape City would soon be his city to adopt and explore. The opportunities were endless and he stayed with her until noon when he drove to the hotel en route to the airport.

Despite arriving at his apartment unusually late and exhausted he prepared for the week ahead, deciding he would do his laundry at Kathy's. As full as his agenda was with three women, a wannabe porno queen, Burberry, the house, calligraphy and his weekend schedule in another city, each component was critical to the end result: creating a better life in Cape City with Eileen and punishing Kim Moon.

Eileen came to him unexpectedly. She was his destiny and he wouldn't let her go. Kathy would find solace in Michelle. She was leaving Burberry and disowning the girl who, along with Michelle, came to him as equally unexpected windfalls when all he ever wanted was to love Kathy Burberry for as long as he needed to hurt her, particularly since her despicable treachery: At first she had invited him to join them in their erotic lovemaking, taunting him, soon after ridiculing him by excluding him, no better than Kim. The boy was strictly a nuisance.

Over the past five weeks his garret was his second home by night, the family room his workspace by day. Nothing remained to discover, he had no further reason to delve into their lives. The family was now simply part of his daily agenda. He needed the assurance of seeing mother and daughter progress, becoming more confident each day as they worked toward different destinies.

Timing was critical. He had decided on February 01st as the day to initiate the disruption of their lives or the end of his, which would leave seven weeks to accomplish the impossible before Burberry would bring his brood home from Myrtle Beach to learn of his pending divorce. Or seven weeks of freedom before being returned to prison to feel seething hate for one woman and never love the other.

Monday night Kathy bathed in deep, steaming water and her daughter practiced in front of the mirror. Tuesday was no different and his conversation with Rhapsody was brief. The hour in Germany was 3:00 AM and he was tired. He liked her idea of changing outfits, with a twist. She would change from dresses and skirts with sweaters and blouses into her lingerie. She was to buy six outfits, one for each hour, undressing for one client and dressing for the other. The shoot location was spacious, luxurious and she should begin showing the world she was a vibrant woman. Above all she was to practice moving with ease, confident with her body and sensuality. He would talk with her again the following week.

Wednesday his hand cramped several times throughout the day, satisfied with his achievement though not willing to relax his stringent daily schedule for the sake of a few days. The following Monday was D-Day. After her shower he watched Kathy select her ensemble for Girls' Night and Thursday after gym class he watched jealously as she dressed for Michelle. He spent the evening with Melissa approving the first of her six outfits. With his guidance her clients wouldn't be disappointed and Friday he left mid-morning after drying himself with Kathy's towel.
*

Michelle stopped at the end of the aisle, reaching for a box of crackers while trying to hide her face with her raised arm and when he walked by she breathed a sigh of relief. Into the next aisle she peeked around the corner and proceeded, wanting to abandon her cart and hurry out. In aisle eight he came alongside her cart from behind.

"Hello again."

"Pardon?"

"I'm the poor driver from two weeks ago, remember, when I crashed into you. I hope your injuries weren't too extensive."

"I remember. And, yes, I healed well."

"I think I'll make eight my lucky number."

"Why?"

He pointed upward, then glanced at her cart. "Certainly not enough to feed a family and I don't see any male-oriented junk food. So you're either shopping for an elderly grandparent or you're getting ready to decline joining me for a coffee."

"With insight like that you don't need a lucky number."

"I should have braced myself against the crushing blow."

"Really."

"Now I have to deal with the terrible shame of rejection until I'm gone from sight."

"I'll close my eyes. You know what they say."

He laughed heartily, throwing back his head. "And I see your mind is quick. But it's Friday night, you're an absolute vision, alone, and I don't see a ring. My name is Clyde Van and I'll be a perfect gentleman."

"That's an oxymoron. And the coffee shop here is terrible."

"Then a glass of wine. There's a place across the street that's quiet, the lights are bright and it's not the least bit romantic or suspicious."

"Look, Clyde, that's very nice but I'm not in the market for company these days." He extended a forefinger, tilted

347

his head and frowned. She glanced in both directions. "Okay, one glass, no phone numbers, no addresses and no "I have to see you again."

"Agreed, as long as we can sit at the same table."

"And no sarcasm. I know the place. I'll meet you in thirty minutes."

"Uh-oh, we've got a runner in aisle eight."

"I wouldn't know. All I see is you still standing here."

"Who shall I tell the waiter to look out for, if not the most dazzling redhead he'll ever cast his eyes upon?"

"Michelle."

"Michelle…?"

"That's right."

*

Michelle didn't know what to think of him. He was mid-thirties a successful political strategist, though what guy wasn't successful when he was with someone for the first time. He did leave his phone number, did not ask for hers and did mention he preferred grocery shopping Saturday mornings as soon as the store opened. He had an easy manner, didn't press her to enjoy a second glass and didn't ask to see her again. Though she believed he wouldn't be the type of man who would want his girlfriend spending a long weekend in Vegas with her friends. Her feelings for Kathy would be an absolute blow to the ego, which would be his problem. She was not about to ruin the April trip she and the girls had spent most of the previous Girls' Night planning.

Arriving home she phoned Kathy who understood, her voice tinged with a hint of jealousy. Michelle was moving Monday, March 01st, giving her home over early and Kathy promised to spend each of the coming Saturdays and Sundays shopping to decorate and furnish the condo. She would help on the Monday, take the day off work and help each night until Michelle's first weekend when Sheila and

Darlene would come over to party and Ted Burberry would be home that last Friday night of the month and remain at the house through Monday morning.

Forty-Nine

Month Two

Ted Burberry met with the real-estate agent February 01st to interview her. She was young, a novice and a little naïve, yet she was enthusiastic and had sold three properties over the winter months, which was rare. They agreed to work together and signed the contract. The asking price: one-point-two million, priced for a fast sale.

He was moving from the area with his wife to do missionary work in Africa. She was a nurse, and he'd worked as a land developer until their boy and girl perished together a year earlier in a tragic accident while returning home from Trinity College. Since then the grieving couple found peace and comfort in prayer. They also discovered a true calling, wanting to devote themselves to combating poverty and disease. They wanted to make a difference and keep the memory of their departed children alive by helping those less fortunate

They had much to be thankful for and passed their weekends together in prayer and quiet reflection, remembering the children. The agent would screen appointments a day in advance. No open listing would be allowed, no open house and no signage with strictly serious enquiries through the agency and potential buyers would be welcomed between 10:00 and 2:00 on weekdays in order to properly appreciate the ocean and lake views.

The agent arrived at precisely at 10:00 on the 02nd. She photographed the house, took measurements and made notations. Mrs. Burberry introduced herself, offered the woman coffee and returned to her sitting room. The agent left an hour later, when Mr. Burberry went up the stairs to his wife, undressed her matter-of-factly and enjoyed the full value of the five-hundred dollars until two o'clock when she also left and he climbed into his attic.

The woman was on call and hoped he would call her often over the coming weeks. He came across her Friday night after Michelle had gone. She'd been out looking for love and was ready to barter her body for a meal. He went one step better. He took the deal, drove her home, stayed the night and offered her a job. She fit the bill perfectly. She was nondescript, about his height, unemployed, cleaner than a hooker, less expensive than an escort and he hoped he wouldn't need her more than twice a week through the month.

Best of all, she understood his predicament: He was going through a wretched divorce, the house was in his name, the wife had wiped out his savings and was coming after the house which he wanted sold by month's end and occupied by the middle of March to avoid losing his job and ending up on the street. His home was all he had left. Otherwise he would have to walk away and see a lifetime of hard work reduced to living on a park bench…and risk losing Eileen. Mrs. Burberry also understood how he must hate pretending and didn't mind at all that he'd gone back to his premature grey hair and glasses which, she thought, gave him an air of sophistication. What she didn't notice were the grey contacts behind those glasses.

Clint Evans phoned Melissa closer to midnight, 5:00 AM in Madrid, Spain and patiently sat through her costume changes.

"You're ready, Rhapsody. Everything you did this

evening was superb."

"I want to save my dresses for next Tuesday, Clint. They're really expensive and feminine."

"Melissa, my car's waiting for me. I'm expected at a shoot in an hour. On the thirteenth, let's meet at ten and get to know each other over a late breakfast. Then I'll leave you alone for the day to relax in lavish comfort and get used to your surroundings. Sunday I'll be the cameraman for your performance. I'm thinking that way you won't have to worry about where to stand. I'll be able to follow you anywhere, get great angles and blow the minds of your fans, if you think that's okay. I don't want to frighten you. Above all, I want you to be comfortable, especially with me. There's no pressure. I want you totally relaxed. I'm not like the pros you'll be working with, but I've been around long enough to know what they want and it'll be good practice for your audition in March."

"I trust whatever you do, Clint, and you're right. Following me will be great for angles and give me practice working with people."

"Good, get to sleep. I'm super excited. I can't believe I've come across you. And Melissa..."

"Yes, Clint?"

"Have you ever been on a private jet?

"No."

"It's something else we'll talk about on the thirteenth. The fourteenth, however, will be all work and very gruelling. You're big time now. Got to go. Get some rest." He disconnected and watched Melissa hang her clothes, finish her vodka and go to bed excited.
*

Wednesday evening Kathy was home for dinner with Timothy, secretly pleased he didn't want to go out. He was seventeen, thrilled with his DVD reader and ignored his mother through most of the meal and birthday cake. Kathy

352

was equally pleased with the distraction and didn't mind Melissa eating in her room and refusing a wedge of cake.

"Is it the model you wanted, Timothy?"

"Yeah, it's the best mom. Thanks."

"Happy Birthday, and have you thought about my proposal?"

"I don't want to go to university. I'll try the army first, this weekend, and if that doesn't work out maybe barber school or something."

"Good. I'll expect to hear something by the weekend."

"But, really, I think I'll be good at photography or something and with the money you're giving me I can get all sorts of stuff."

"Stick with the army. We're talking about your life here, not a hobby. Your teachers have agreed to write letters on your behalf. Believe me, in a few short years you'll be a different person with money in the bank."

"I'll think about it. Can I go to my room?"

"Yes."

They said goodnight and Kathy did the dishes as an exception. When she was done she went to her récamier, read until her shower, called Michelle to wish her goodnight and fell asleep dreaming of her condo and how much more fun her life would become in a month, sleeping over instead of sleeping alone.

Fifty

Thursday the woman was once again playing the dutiful Mrs. Burberry. The tour of the house lasted twenty minutes and the agent left with the couple undecided. Mr. Burberry escorted them to the door, said goodbye and took his wife to Melissa's bed before sending her home with another five hundred dollars. If nothing else, he thought, by month's end she'd be a few thousand richer and a better lover, which could well turn her life around.

*

Thursday night Kathy came home late after shopping and dinner with Michelle. The house was quiet as she prepared lazily for the next day and lounged in her bed with a nightcap. She hadn't seen him in almost three weeks and he hadn't phoned, yet he was expecting to see her in nine days and sleep with her. She wondered where he was, who he was with and how much of a mistake she was making. She and Michelle had agreed. Unless they did, they would never know for sure. It wasn't as though Michelle hadn't taken several long weekends with Darlene and Sheila. So she did like men and Kathy had eagerly anticipated her weekend at the White Cliff Lodge until that fateful night. So why not test the uncertainty with Jack and, if something eventually did happen with Clyde Van, so be it, but the "it" would have to be seismic. Michelle would accept nothing less. Either way, they each had something too special to walk away from.

"Hello."

"Jack."

"Yes, this is Jack."

"This is Kathy."

"Kathy, my sweet Valentine."

"It's late. Am I interrupting you?"

"No.

"You answered."

"Of course I answered."

"I was lying here, curious…about Valentine's, about what you said."

"I'll be happy with dinner, if that's what you mean."

"And if I do bring a suitcase?"

"Then I'll do my best to be the man of your dreams and make you part of my life."

"I'm a little nervous."

"I'm not. I'm delirious."

"I'll phone you again before the thirteenth. I have to be certain. It's a big move and I don't need mistakes I might have to explain to someone else later."

"I understand."

"Goodnight, Jack."

"Goodnight, Kathy. Sleep tight."

She pressed end, threw aside the duvet and padded downstairs for another splash of tequila.

She felt terrible, as though she had slapped or spoken cruel words to Michelle. She was anxious for the end of the week, for gym class, dinner and shopping.

*

Being around Kathy was like having the winning number and hearing the banks had closed temporarily for restructuring. Her condo was three weeks away and the shopping wasn't half done, quite intentionally, and the women had agreed to meet at noon. At the grocery store Clyde Van offered no pretence. He was standing at the

355

entrance with a tray of coffee and doughnuts.

"This could be considered stalking."

"Not really. I was here first." He paused. "Or, perhaps it is stalking. Good point."

"I was out shopping with a friend last night and ran out of time. Prices here are always more expensive on Saturdays."

"I had no idea whether you preferred cream or milk, brown sugar or white. And can you believe I had to put a deposit on the tray?"

She took one of the cardboard cups. "Thank you for the thought. I take mine black and the doughnuts were a nice gesture, but one minute of pleasure becomes an hour of grief at the gym. I've got enough grief at the moment."

He handed the tray to a passing teenager. "I found a fantastic restaurant for dinner, if you're interested."

"I can't tonight. I'm busy with my girlfriend."

"Hmmm. Well, how about breakfast and maybe we can agree on a day when your girlfriend will be busy, like next Friday."

She sipped her coffee and scanned the parking lot, thinking. "Breakfast sounds okay; however we'll put Friday on hold. I'm not rushing into something I have to rush out of and I have no intention of finding another grocery store for at least another month."

"The place we met last week serves breakfast."

"I'll meet you there and, please, let's not do anything predictable like collide in aisle eight." In fact he had previously bought his supplies for the coming week and sat in his SUV until he saw her at the cashier, when he stepped out and crossed the street.

*

Melissa was happy her mother went out early to drop off deadbrain wherever and her father called to say his flight was delayed due to bad weather in the south that was affecting most air traffic east of the Mississippi. She poured a double-vodka and went to the kitchen for soda. She hadn't searched through her brother's room in the months since his grounding and she had the entire morning.

She checked all the pockets of his pants, between each shirt on the shelves of his closet, in his drawers and under his bed. She looked into his suitcases and his backpack. She flipped through his schoolbooks and notebooks, opened his computer and searched through his files, then his library of CDs and DVDs. Those with titles were banal and childish and many had no titles. She checked under his mattress, his pillow and stood to think in the middle of his room with her glass in-hand. Then she knelt by his bureau and put her head to the floor.

She reached into the cramped space and slid out one envelope, then a second and his DVD reader. She sat on his bed and sipped her drink, anxious, a wide grin spreading across her face. She opened the first envelope and saw the photos of Eileen, half a dozen copies of each pose done this time on glossy photo-grade paper. The little bastard was selling pictures at school of his father's whore. She gulped her drink, setting down the glass and reaching into the second manila envelope and, at first, she didn't understand. Then a sensation of unimaginable cold shot through her veins to her heart.

She was seeing hard copies, all glossy, of a midnight performance taken from under her bed. The resolution was dark, but clear. She was horrified. He'd been hiding under her bed taking pictures of her working. Then she saw the last blow-up and shrieked. She ran to her room, filled her glass with straight liquor and hurried back. She was frantic. The time was 9:30. Her father would be home at 2:00 and her brother any time after that. She ran to the office and shredded both sets of photos, keeping one each of Eileen as proof. She emptied the bin into the garbage in the garage and mixed in trash from the kitchen.

Back in his room with envelopes of blank paper she tugged the bureau away from the wall, probing underneath with no success. She pulled out each of the drawers, checking the side and bottom panels and found nothing. Then she gulped her drink, gasped for air and fell onto the bed too horrified to cry, her mind a maelstrom of fear and hate. She reached for the reader, the tray was empty and she reached for the stack of DVDs.

Nothing, nothing and nothing, then she turned it over, fanned them across the bed and played the last one, her body catatonic, her mind frozen and her head throbbing as wildly as her heart, watching her striptease in front of her webcam, posing and bathing in her mother's bath. She fast forwarded, pressing play to see herself in her mother's walk-in closet and, again to the end of the two-hours, to see herself sitting on her mother's toilet between performances. She was losing her mind. She inserted the second disk, reflexively gulping air into a dry throat and wailing. Her performance had lasted four hours, the runtime ending with her in the bath, her face a mask of intense emotion. She put in a third and burst into convulsive tears. Her brother saw her on the floor, twisting, gyrating without her glasses or wig. He saw her kneeling over the tub, removing all traces and gathering her costumes. He saw her on the toilet. Her brother knew who she was.

The minute hand ticked past 10:30 as she sat looking at her performances, slowly understanding how much her brother had seen, how intimately he knew her, remembering all the sly grins over the past several weeks and the way she would often catch him ogling her. She wanted to vomit. She pushed the bureau against the wall, slid the envelopes to where she found them and ran to her room. Her Rhapsody computer was safe. She inserted one of the three disks, imported partial data and failed twice to successfully delete the disk. She didn't try again. She continued importing, loading a second disk into her school computer and ran to her father's office with the carrousel. By 12:45 all but one disk was shredded, the reader replaced under the bureau and the shredded debris disposed of in the garage. Her head was spinning, swallowing what was left in her glass and resisting the urge to pour another.

She hurried to the bathroom, guided by the walls, ran a shower, locked the door and stood under the frigid water shampooing her hair for as long as she could. Towelled and dry she looked down at herself, wanting to die. Anyone but deadbrain, she thought, anyone. She checked the time, ran to the kitchen, dropped her bundle of clothes by the door with a fresh towel and ran naked into the yard.

A light snow was falling. She fell to her knees, bathing herself in freezing white crystals, hurling her body forward, face-down and making a snow angel. She rolled over once, twice, three and four times and lay on her back, swinging her arms, crying, groaning and laughing. She sprang to her feet, covered with snow and ran past the far end of the house where she stood shaking and staring at the road. Then she ran to the other end by the garage, seized by the temptation to run all the way round.

She skipped to the front corner, peeking around, her body trembling, running as fast as she could toward the far side, slowing, not caring, falling into the snow and laughing. She sat up, her entire body tingling with the strangest cold heat. Then she crawled to her feet, her body blanketed with snow. She completed the front of the house, the side and stopped at the kitchen, her heart about to explode.

She towelled herself dry, her body never feeling so alive, nor her heart ever racing as much. Once wasn't enough. Inside she peered at the clock and scurried to the front door for her knee-high boots, slipping and falling as she hurried to pull them on. At the kitchen she took a deep breath, rubbed what little warmth she could into her icy body and ran to the rear corner of the garage, walking to the front where she lingered in full view of the road before scampering past the entrance in knee-deep snow, leaving a zigzag trail to the far end where she stopped to throw snow into the air, snowballs at the house and gaze at the road.

She swirled in circles, squealing with delight. She jumped up and down, stood with her hands by her side and felt alive. She looked beyond the wall of fir trees ending at the road and towards the curve at the opposite end, listening, smiling, her body shuddering. She threw her arms into the air in a "V," squealed, and ran along the front of the house following her jagged trail. From the garage she walked to the kitchen caressing herself without glancing over her shoulder and wondering why never before.

Once inside the kitchen she dressed in warm drawstring pants, soft velveteen boots, a hoodie and made a double serving of hot soup to warm her body that refused to stop quivering. Her father arrived home sixty minutes later and she greeted him from her open door, explaining that she wasn't up to helping with supper. When he enquired as to why, she answered "you know," which was all he did need to know.

She was exhilarated, her body still burning with cold. She had never felt so free or daring and she thought of the dunes at the seashore, feeling an instant twinge of excitement. So what if her brother saw and heard her. She snorted, thinking of all the guys from school who downloaded videos and never had a clue because she was good. Rhapsody wasn't Melissa. She didn't "like, duh or whatever." She never had because she always knew one day someone like Clint would come into her life and he wouldn't want a dumb blonde.

Timothy came home at 4:00 and quickly went to his father to ask if he was in trouble again. Ted asked him why he would be and he didn't know. He was checking because the house was too quiet. Timothy went to the door for the pizza at 6:00, took a few slices to his father's office and knocked at his sister's door with his foot. When she saw him she flushed and stepped aside when he pushed his way in.

"Nice room, Rhapsody," he filled his mouth, sitting in her chair, "and like a super-hot chair." He took another bite. "I know what you look like totally naked, Mel." He took in her body. "There too. I watch the stuff every night in bed. It's sort of sick, I know."

"You're a pig."

"I'm a guy. You're a whore, like I told you."

"I am not. I'm a businesswoman with a body men will pay to see."

"You're a whore."

"I'm the same as the girls at school, only way smarter. I don't send pictures of myself naked to asshole guys for free who show them around."

"I have copies, you know. Here and in my locker."

"I don't believe you."

"I do. That's why I wanted the reader. I can show little bits at a time and make a fortune off each ten minutes." He pushed the rest of the triangle into his mouth, "and the last thing you did to yourself on the floor will bring in at least three, four hundred: Midnight Rhapsody without her wigs and stuff on, getting herself off for real. I thought you hurt yourself or something, like when the guy told you what to do in the chair, like you were totally doing some guy or something. You did everything he wanted. I heard you. So I figure a hundred for a straight ten minutes and two hundred for the in-between stuff like you on the toilet. Who wouldn't pay to see snotty Melissa Burberry pissing naked, let alone Midnight Rhapsody?" When he stopped laughing he filled his mouth with soda and took another bite. "Hey,

361

you know what? From now on you won't have to close the bathroom door when the two of them aren't home."

"You're totally sick. Really, you are." She was surprisingly calm. She ignored the plate he passed to her; her stomach was too knotted to eat. Instead she went to her backpack, took out the bottle and poured a double shot. "You don't know who you're like dealing with, deadbrain. I'm professional. I have a manager. He's a very important man and won't be scared by a little shit like you. I'll be speaking with him very soon and telling him what you did. If I were you, I'd keep staying home. It's the only place you'll be safe if you don't give me the copies. And this," she held up the glass, "go tell him. I dare you, like he'll care. Besides, I have the copies you took from his album. He'll like totally freak when he finds out you're selling nude pictures of his girlfriend."

"No one'll find me. I'll be gone as soon as school's over and the videos are my ticket out. Why should I work if you don't?"

"You'll never work this hard. And your big idea won't happen. Some guy will buy a copy and burn his own. Then you'll be screwed and that'll keep happening until you go broke because you don't have a single brain cell."

"Then I'll sell them on the web."

"And he'll kill you. My manager's going to make me the best actress ever. We have big plans that don't include you getting in our way. So get out of here and give me what I want on Monday at school."

"You don't have a manager."

"Okay, I don't. Just keep your cell open and don't run in here when he calls to say he's going to break your legs or something. His name's Clint." Timothy stopped eating, his face paled. Melissa sipped her drink. "That's right deadbrain, the guy you heard. He was testing me. He liked what he saw and I'm the one leaving. Tell them if you want.

I'll be eighteen in four weeks and I already make more money than he ever will. Now leave me alone."

He shrugged and stood. "I still know what I know: ooh, ooh, aah." He giggled and walked out leaving the door open.

*

Michelle went home anxious for Sunday. When Kathy got to her house she knocked on Ted's office door, offered a polite acknowledgement of his being there and went to Timothy's room. He wasn't accepted by the army, he confessed. He couldn't do nineteen push-ups or sit-ups and the thirty-five kilo bar fell from his hands. A sixty-year-old man would have been well-rested waiting for him at the end of a two-point-four km run and a sixty-year-old woman could have effortlessly exceeded his single chin-up. He was required to perform six and the soldier walked away telling him to try again in a year, or go over to the enemy. Timothy handed his mother the score card, hanging his head.

He had decided on trade school. He was dropping out and becoming a barber. He had the application papers requiring one parent's signature and the courses began April.01st He figured with the ten grand he could open a salon or something in September and start making money right away. Kathy signed the form. She knew he was all about the ten grand, which was her expectation as well as her motivation. She told him she would drive him to the institute Monday morning with the tuition cheque and that she would deposit the ten thousand dollars into his bank account the Friday before Myrtle Beach, adding that after Spring Break he would work part-time, pay room and board until he found a place to live and not get another dime from her. She patted his head and walked out feeling nothing.
*

Kathy couldn't sleep. She went to the family room and began composing an updated CV, Michelle and Jack each vying for space in her thoughts. Melissa lay in her bed feeling rejuvenated, no longer bothered that her brother had seen her and was probably in his room watching her. She was anxious for Tuesday, to speak with Clint, to tell him of the videos and how she had frolicked so freely in the open air. She hadn't practiced all day and wouldn't the next day, excited by thoughts of walking to the dunes dressed in her snowsuit with a blanket, her camera and sandwich in her backpack. The revelation of her brother's invasion made her realize that soon everyone would know. She was at her point of no return, and why would she want to return to a life she was working so hard to escape? She wanted freedom, the same kind of freedom she'd found in the snow.

Timothy fell asleep with his reader closed by his side, his last conscious thought being of his mother's cheque and the videos. Her threat didn't matter. By month's end he'd be allowed out and would buy more DVDs at the mall. He would have two weeks to burn new copies and one week in Spring Break heaven to launch his career and not go home.

Ted stayed in his office as long as he could, his head lolling heavily this way and that from fatigue. Climbing the stairs he saw the light, cursed under his breath, said goodnight and went to bed. Kathy feel asleep on the sofa after pressing save, wanting Michelle and thinking of her upcoming weekend with Jack and what she would wear.

Clint Evans was about to go home, not looking forward to driving in the worsening snow. She was dead to the world. At first she'd wanted him insatiably, in lieu of sweets for an alcoholic, he thought. Then she sobbed, wanting to go home, but she'd waited too long. She was at home and the man inside her wasn't her husband who lay immobile and tormented in his room, listening to her cries of joy and regret.

Clint dressed. He studied her bankbook, noted her PIN and took the gold and ATM cards from her purse. He strolled to the kitchen, opened a beer and walked through the house looking into the other rooms along the hall, clenching the bottle at the door to one room when he saw the unblinking eyes staring at him from behind a blank and sallow mask wetted with streaks of glistening tears.

He nodded his head, scanning the dimly lit and austere room, the wheelchair, the railing and the pan.

"I'm sorry," he offered, "I didn't know." The man's smile was lifeless. "Believe me, sir, I treated your wife with respect and will not see her again," and with that the man closed his weary eyes, leaving Clint without the slightest idea whether he had died or wanted to.

In the other bedroom the woman lay breathing quietly. He returned what he had taken from her purse, put his beer on the side table and left.

Fifty-One

Sunday Jack Caden gazed towards a harbour he couldn't see, drinking his first morning coffee, deciding where to sleep with Kathy in six days and what to say to her as she woke in his arms. He knew how she would feel, how she would move. He remembered her legs, her smooth lips and her scent. He studied the photo of her striding away from him on the boardwalk, imagining what was left for him to discover. She would call him Wednesday or Thursday, wanting to appear casual when all the while her excitement was mounting, titillated by the thought of being with another man after so many years. He refilled his cup. Time would tell.

*

Clint was angry with himself. He had mistaken the Saturday woman's quiet manner for shyness and uncertainty, not infidelity, when no one would love her more than the tearful and frail man lying so near yet so far from her bed.

His expenses were growing of late and neither generosity nor precious time wasted was high on his list. He put her from his mind. What was done was done. He called downtown Luxor Hotel to make reservations for the coming weekend. His Midnight Rhapsody deserved the best and her sizes were not an issue: he'd previously researched her drawers and closet. In the afternoon he would shop for her outfits, buy yet another camera, vodka and champagne, anxious to speak with her and further cement their

relationship. But first he called Kathy's stand-in to confirm she hadn't lost interest or found a job. She hadn't.
*

At the real Burberrys Kathy made breakfast, insisting everyone eat in the dining room, allowing robes. Ted spoke with her about banal non-issues, ignoring the kids and Melissa stared piercingly at Timothy throughout the twenty minutes, unaffected by his silly grin. When she was finished eating she cleared the table, excused herself and went into his room to wait while he washed the dishes. Hearing his slothful footsteps, she stood behind the door.

"I want the videos." He jolted. "Now."

"You scared the shit out of me."

"Because that's what you are. Give me the DVDs"

He grinned. "No. I haven't finished looking at them. There's too much to see," he shoved his hands into his pockets, hunching his shoulders, "unless you want to trade the disks I have here for a live show, right now."

"No one sees me for free."

"I have." He guffawed. "I was watching them all last night. Then I had like a vision or something."

"Like what?"

"Like Myrtle Beach. I'll make a killing."

She tightened the belt on her robe. "Are you staying in your room for a while?"

"Yeah. What about it?"

She looked into his eyes, concentrating, distracting him with her intensity and smashed her folded fist solidly into his jaw, flailing him onto the bed.

"You can't get a girlfriend to screw you so you fantasize about me. Look at them all you want, freak. You're frigging sick. It's a body. I do what I do for me as much as for the money, not for them and never for pimple-faced shitheads like you." She put her hand to the doorknob. "You don't have much time."

367

"I'll tell everyone at school."

Melissa laughed mockingly. "Like, yeah, you do that. You tell everyone at school before you burn copies and show them on your little TV." She put a finger to her lips, musing. "You'd be giving me thousands more a week...idiot, thousands, and you'd get nothing. Why would anyone pay a little creep like you when they can dial-in and like actually speak with me, ask me things and hear me using their names? So I'm squatting on the can, big deal. Like how long would that last?" She chuckled. "Until they see me better than ever, freak, unless you're stupid enough to try selling to an undercover cop. Enjoy the show tonight, deadbrain, and your little boy thing."

She walked out and spent the morning in her room until Kathy left for the mall and Ted fell asleep on the living room sofa. She made a sandwich, filled a thermos with hot soup, took a bottle of soda from the fridge and emptied half into the sink to make room for vodka. Snow was falling more heavily than Saturday and she could feel herself tingling. In her room she took a deep breath, dropped her chemise to the floor, eased off her panties and pulled on thick winter socks and her snowsuit. The feeling was immediately sensual. She pulled on a fur-lined Cossack hat, took up her gloves, her backpack and left.

Each step of the downhill trek was erotic, her belly constricting with nervous anticipation, her bare skin interacting with the fleece lining. Crossing Ocean View Road she could see no one was parked at the beach and at the boardwalk she looked in both directions. Visibility was reduced by half and she walked from one end to the other. Returning to the midway point she followed another boarded path towards the sea, stopped halfway and jumped the rail onto the dunes, walking until she came to a dip between snow-covered knolls which would conceal her from the boardwalk and the beach, unless she stood.

She unzipped her backpack, took out the bottle, drank a mouthful and laid out her woollen blanket. She sat to pull off her boots, crawling onto her knees to bare her torso, standing to push down and kick away the insulated one-piece suit from her ankles. She laid the suit front down, protected from the falling snow. She pulled away her hat and socks and stood facing the ocean to scan the beach and for as far as her eyes could see through the snow she was alone. She stooped for her bottle, swallowing a few mouthfuls as she looked out to sea, snowflakes coating her hair, shoulders and breasts. She sat to eat her sandwich, saving her soup for later and when she was finished she stood, relaxed and unworried, not knowing for sure whether she was alone. She pulled on her socks and boots, folded over her blanket and strolled through the meandering knolls to the snow-covered sand, looking both ways and sauntering to the water's edge.

She was euphoric. Not once in her young life had she felt such wild abandon. She wanted to run along the water, pausing a moment to think. Losing sight of her clothing in the snow would be too easy, too disastrous. Instead she skipped a hundred steps, back a hundred and strolled to her blanket gaily swinging her arms. She reached for her bottle and camera, sipping as she made her way to the boardwalk where she clambered over and searched both ways. She set the camera on the railing cleared by her body, set the timer and scurried to sit on the opposite railing and pose for the flashing red light.

She leaped down to reset the camera for a second series, this time mounting the railing as she would a horse, slowly, each click commanding a different and provocative pose, her body arching backward, forward, standing and dismounting. She left the camera, marking her location by sweeping the snow from the wooden slats in case the camera fell, and jogged one way counting a hundred paces before running back, passing her mark, adding a hundred more steps and strolling as she would wearing a bikini on a hot summer's day. At the camera she positioned the lens to follow her path to the blanket, catapulted over, set the timer and walked away, twirling around when she'd counted to fifteen. She shivered once and hurried to her blanket where she drank her soup as quickly as she could in-between excited breaths, addicted and wanting more. She loved the exhilaration of the danger.

She scanned in both directions and ran to the boardwalk, climbing the rail for a better vantage, satisfied. She ran back, swept up her backpack, her suit, put on her hat, grabbed the blanket and pranced to the water's edge where she reorganized her possessions. She wanted to run by the ocean, as fast as she could into the falling snow. She touched herself where heat should have flowed, yet there was none and she finished her soup. She jogged one way, until glancing behind her she could no longer see the blanket. She slowed to a stop, taking a moment to lean onto her knees to catch her breath and walked briskly back, stopping to quench her dry throat.

She was intoxicated with adrenalin, light-headed with liquor and she dashed carefree once more into the thickening snow, losing count, slowing, stopping and straining her eyes to see the shadow appearing in the distance, disappearing as quickly into the curtain of snow. She squatted, putting her open palms to the icy water, patting her face and shielding her eyes with an open hand. The shape was no longer an obscure shadow. The person was real.

Melissa stood tentatively, pausing a moment, calming herself, part of her wanting to run, part of her wanting to stay. She watched the person come steadily closer, not hurrying. She could see the unveiled curiosity clearly. Then, without thinking, she filled her lungs with cold winter air and scampered in and out of the thinly ice-coated surf to her blanket in a crooked line, playfully, elated, without the fear any another girl might feel. She was laughing. Another girl wouldn't dare. Anyway, distance was on her side, her body strangely warm, and she turned to see what distance she had gained, shocked at how close the person was. She could see the woman clearly, her features, the dog straining at its leash to catch up with the playful young girl who wanted to run and Melissa decided not to panic. Instead she would perform.

She lowered herself onto her woollen blanket, focused, reclined and kicked away her boots. Reaching for her suit she huddled into her knees, slid in both feet and tugged the suit to her thighs, trying her hardest to appear unhurried and casual despite her throbbing pulses. She raised her feet into the air, sliding into her fleece-lined boots and stood confidently with surprising demureness, bringing to mind all her rehearsals. She could no longer ignore the woman who was mere steps away. She smiled and faced the sea, pulling the suit to her waist as though she were alone, feeling a sexuality she'd never experienced before, her mind filled with Clint, her director, producer and the woman. She manoeuvred her damp and crystal-covered torso into the jacket and zippered in the warmth. Adjusting her hat she slipped her hands into cold gloves and patted the Golden.

"Good morning, young lady."

"Hi."

"My husband didn't feel like walking our dog this morning. He'll never believe me, even if I was inclined to tell him, though I do suppose telling him would get him off the couch."

"I'm sorry. I thought I was alone. I hope I didn't embarrass you."

"You didn't, and don't apologize. You're very pretty. I enjoyed seeing you run, aesthetically speaking. You seemed so carefree. I wish I had nerve enough to run naked and free. I might have twenty years ago, although I believe even then I would have preferred a warmer beach."

"I'm glad I did it. The feeling's incredible." Melissa placed the woman in her forties. Ruffling the dog's fur, she looked both ways. "Why don't you? Go ahead. I'll hold your dog and you can use my blanket."

"Good heavens, no. With my luck I'd trip and break an ankle or my unmentionables would blow away and he'd think I'm having an affair. But, thank you."

"I won't let anything blow away…and no one's around." The woman's cheeks blossomed into to wider smile, shaking her head. "Can I share a secret with you, something really special?"

"Yes, of course."

"Yesterday I ran around the outside of my home without my clothes, completely naked. I rolled in the snow and made angels. I don't know why, but I'm glad I did. That's why I came here today. You could do that, couldn't you?"

"I suppose I could. We're very private at home. What's your name?"

"Melissa."

"Thank you, Melissa. I might just do as you suggest. Although next time, if you intend a next time, you might not outrun the person who happens by. You're so very pretty and I'd hate to read something horrible about you in the papers."

"Yes, ma'am, but I saw you weren't a guy. I would have run a lot faster."

"Dorothy, please." She touched Melissa's cheek, inhaling deeply. "I'm very happy I ran into you, so to speak. Your love for life has brightened my day, Melissa. However I believe you should be going home. I didn't see another car, so I assume you live nearby and I don't believe your suit will warm you as much as a nice bath. May I drive you?"

"No ma'am. Thanks anyway. I'll be okay." Melissa rolled her blanket and stuffed her pack. "Dorothy?"

"Yes, Melissa."

"I can stay awhile longer. I was scared at first, until I undressed and then I felt totally free, like it was the most natural thing in the world, not dirty."

"From what I saw," she grinned, the glint in eyes shining through her sunglasses, "and I don't believe there's anything I didn't see, you are the most natural thing in the world, so beautiful, but I think I'll start in the backyard. In fact, I might yank the old fart from the couch and make him join me. Thank you for bringing a ray of sunshine to my day. This is certainly one stroll I'll always remember."

"Dorothy," Melissa let the dog lick her, "do you have a daughter?"

"No, Melissa, I don't. It never worked out for me."

"Are you happy?"

"Yes, very…most days."

"Then…maybe it did work out for you."

Melissa stood and embraced Dorothy the way she would a mother she loved and walked towards the dunes. At the entrance to the arm leading to the main boardwalk she waved, Dorothy waved, and Melissa disappeared from sight. She was hooked. She couldn't believe what she'd done, or for how long and that Dorothy had seen her naked, performing, a woman and not the least bit disgusted. Clint would be proud of her for being so spontaneous, so creative and she couldn't wait to win his praise. And why would she spend a day alone in a hotel room when she could learn about her manager, her career and enhance her portfolio in winter white, something never done before.

At home she showered with steaming water, drank warm soup, poured a single shot of vodka and went to bed with her buzzer set for five o'clock. When she woke her mother was home, insisting that she dress, her father was in the dining room enjoying a cocktail and her brother was in his room waiting for the last call. Her mother was wearing tights, pumps and a thick cable sweater that came to her mid-thighs and Melissa competed with tights, stilettos and a cowl neck sweater cinched at the waist and not covering much more, expecting an outcry. In lieu of which her father raised his glass, her mother told her she was beautiful, just not old enough to wear the outfit outside and her brother ogled her every move. She went to her room furious.

Fifty-Two

Monday Kathy drove Melissa to school and met with the administrators of the trade school. Melissa sat in class scanning the photos she had uploaded to her phone, each one without the slightest blur, hoping Clint would be enthusiastic about her idea. At home Mr. Burberry sat quietly in the living room, thankful for his wife who was alone in her sitting room, seemingly woeful. The visiting couple adored the view. The agent had previously told them the tearful story and they felt guilty about disturbing the boy's and girl's room with their curiosity. The man and woman loved the house, the tranquility and the proximity to Surfers' Beach and the lake. They were definitely interested, as was Clint, in getting the wife away from the house before 2:30 and he wasted no time calling for a taxi while she cleansed herself of her wifely duty. He wanted time alone to look through Melissa's room.

He no longer observed them at dinner. He was pleased his plan was coming together, however a trained notary was a far cry from a naïve, novice real-estate agent and he demanded perfection of himself. What he did enjoy was listening to Kathy speaking with Michelle, wishing he could hear both women and crashed a fist into an open palm. He could, which would bring him that much closer to putting Michelle into a suitable bed. He switched screens. Melissa was sitting in her chair by her desk in a knee-length dress, practicing crossing and uncrossing her legs, lounging without slouching, showing the right amount of leg to titillate, holding her head at the proper angle, not too high, not too low, avoiding shadows, standing and sitting.

He switched to Kathy patting herself dry at the shower, thinking he'd seen her naked more in the past several weeks than Burberry had in several years. She selected her clothes for the next day, dressed in a long slip for bed and put out the lights. When at last she stopped tossing, he closed the screen and lay on his cot.

*

Tuesday he left at 10:00 and drove the Lexus to an electronics firm he hadn't previously worked with in town. He paid cash and returned directly to the house. An hour later he had full access to Kathy's bedroom phone and the one in Ted's office. At 8:30 in the evening Melissa went to the bathroom, coming out in her robe fifteen minutes later. He watched her change into lingerie and a dress to begin her nightly rehearsal. Whatever he might think, the kid didn't lack guts and determination. He was anxious to speak with her, equally impatient to hear Michelle's sweet voice as he kept on with his calligraphy exercise by the dim light of the Coleman lamp.

"Hello, darling."

"Mi amor, I miss you after so few hours. Are we doing the right thing?"

"Yes, I believe we are. How else will we know? Are you phoning him tonight?"

"No. I'll call tomorrow."

"Do you know where?"

"Not the Delta." The line was silent. "We're not doing the right thing, mi amor. And why am I staying in this lousy house for a lousy million dollars I might not even get and a couple of hateful brats?"

"We don't have long to wait. March isn't very far away."

"What about you, have you decided?"

"I suppose I'll let him take me to dinner on Friday. I don't want to get trapped into any of this Valentine's crap, except with you. I have something for you, darling, and we're having dinner on Sunday."

"And I have a gift for you."

"That should tell us something."

"Yeah, if we move in together, we'll bankrupt each other with love."

"Darling, if I'm going to be busy on Friday and you, Saturday, perhaps we should wait until dinner on Sunday to," Michelle giggled, "debrief as it were."

*

Clint's phone buzzed. "Hello."

"Mr. Burberry, this is Janice from the realtor."

"Hello, Janice."

"The couple are very interested. They want to visit again on Friday, so they can discuss your property over the weekend."

"That won't do, Janice. I've told you why. Tell them Monday at 10:30 and also tell them they'll have first refusal. I'll consider the visit as an unofficial offer and give them until the eighteenth to decide, at which time I'll agree to a Friday visit in order to sign the papers."

"I'll do my best and call you tomorrow. Thank you. Goodnight, Mr. Burberry."

*

"He thinks I'm screwing around, but I'm going to use you as an excuse, mi amor. Maybe I should tell him the truth and get it over with, tell him I'm in love with a woman. Please don't hate me for using you."

"I don't darling, because I'm going to use you if things don't go well with Clyde and I know you won't leave me."

"Not a chance." Kathy paused. "What did you buy me, mi amor?"

377

"You're right. Not a chance. Goodnight my darling. I'll see you tomorrow and hope I dream of you until then."

Kathy hung up the phone, swung her legs from the récamier and went to her bathroom. Clint closed the screen. He waited until Melissa finished her rehearsal and dialled-in to her.

*

"Clint, hi there."

"Hi, Melissa. We're getting closer. I have your wardrobe for the March audition, your hotel reservation for Valentine's and a bottle of champagne. What's Valentine's without champagne?"

"That's so cool. Where are you?"

"Germany…leaving tomorrow. Are you ready?"

"Yes."

"Then surprise me on Saturday, nothing tonight. I want you to rest until then, no more rehearsing."

"Clint, about Saturday, I have an idea."

"I'm listening." He leaned into the screen.

"Don't be angry, but Saturday, when I was alone, I ran around the entire house, outside, without my clothes. I felt so good I did it twice, in the middle of the day."

"Did anyone see you?"

"No, and Sunday I went to the beach when the snowfall was pretty heavy and did the same thing. I was right outside for over half an hour, right at the water, completely naked and no one saw me. Well, this woman did, but she didn't mind. She said she liked seeing me. She liked seeing me, Clint. I was actually performing for her, thinking about you and all the things you've said. She really liked seeing me and said I was a ray of sunshine. So I was wondering about this Saturday. If it's snowing and no one's around, could we meet at the beach instead of the hotel?"

"You could have been hurt, or worse. You must understand that I worry about you."

378

"I do. That's what she said. Please don't be angry and I was thinking, if it's snowing, you could take some great audition shots, or a video. I even took some pictures of myself at the boardwalk. I think they're really good, Clint. Imagine what you could do."

Clint mentally flipped through the pages of his agenda. "That wouldn't leave much time to set up. Let's do this. Let's stay with the programme and, if you're heart's set on doing this outdoorsy thing, we'll fit it in sometime before Myrtle Beach. How's that?"

"Yeah, I like that. Thanks, Clint. Can I e-mail them to you anyway?"

"No, Melissa. Burn a CD, make hard copies on good quality photo paper and bring them to me on Saturday."

"I will." She hesitated. "Clint…"

"What's wrong?"

"There's something else, something I never told you." She took a deep breath. "I live at home. I'm legal, Clint, and I am leaving in a few weeks. I just wanted you to know before I tell you."

"Tell me what?" She wasn't talking. "Listen, Melissa, you can tell me anything. Go ahead."

"New Year's Eve, the four-hours…"

"I'm listening."

"I did that in my parents' bathroom. My brother, he's seventeen, he was in the dark videoing the whole thing, even the costume changes…and he has footage of me on the toilet and…"

"And what?"

"When I was finished I was cleaning up and he videoed all that. Then I felt so turned-on, especially after talking with you, that I couldn't help myself."

"He has a video of all that?"

"Everything and he's threatening to sell copies and even go on the web."

"That would ruin you. What's his name?"

"Timothy."

"How do you feel about him, besides what he did?"

"I've never liked him. He called me a whore." She chortled. "I punched him so hard he fell onto his bed. He's more of a pussy than I am."

"We need those videos, Melissa."

"I know."

"Have you told him about me?"

"I told him I had a manager. At first he didn't believe me, until I told him your name and he remembered you from January."

"I'd hate to forget about you, Rhapsody. I have such great plans, including Paris in April. The deal's ready to sign as soon as the producer sees the March audition and from Paris we travel to somewhere very special."

"Where Clint?"

His self-satisfied grin leered into her screen, "somewhere very, very exotic."

"He has one set in his room and another in his locker at school."

"What's his cell number?" She told him. "Don't worry. I'll get them, Melissa. Nothing's coming between us. You're headed for stardom and no kid is going to get in our way. Besides," he chuckled into the screen, "you're quite right. The producers would love to see footage of you frolicking naked in a snowfall by the ocean. You're brilliant. I'll call you tomorrow, on your cell. Goodnight, and don't think I don't miss seeing your act."

The screen went black and Clint stood to stretch. The little bastard was about to screw up his entire plan. He dialled the cell number.

"Yeah."

"Tim, how's it going?"

"Who's this?"

"Good question, squirt. The name's Clint, I'm your sister's manager and we need to talk."

"What about?"

"The videos, your sick little mind and the fact I know where you go to school and where you live. Listen, kid, you don't even rank as an amateur. So don't get hurt for nothing. Give her the videos, the ones you have in your room, and we can talk. Be smart about the whole thing. Give her the ones in your locker and then, who knows, we can use a kid with smarts. Be stupid about it and I'll get it from your locker myself and send your mother a sympathy card. I'm calling your sister in fifteen minutes, don't disappoint us. I'll call her again tomorrow and if you've been smart, like I think you will be, I'll call you and we can talk about your future. My company starts off guys like you as messengers and escorts for my stars at about one thousand a week. It's a good deal, kid. So get past your petty differences and go knock on her door." He paused. "Actually, wait fifteen minutes. Let me call her. She'll give you five hundred tonight for the first set and five hundred tomorrow for the second."

"No way."

"Yes, she will, right now. We'll just deduct the grand from your first paycheque. She'll be expecting you in fifteen minutes. Oh, one more thing. Call her a whore once more and one day I'll come from behind and snap your neck. It's painless, apparently, and very permanent."

Clint pressed end and watched as he opened the other screen to Melissa's room, pressing speed-dial.

"Hello."

"Rhapsody, it's me, Clint. Put something on if you're not dressed."

"I'm wearing a chemise."

"The kid's coming to your room after we're finished talking, with the videos. Give him five-hundred cash or a

381

cheque…"

"What?"

"I'll reimburse you, and tomorrow give him another five for the locker version. I'll take care of you on Saturday. I won't let anything happen to my little girl. You do know that's how I feel about you, that I want to protect you and nurture you?"

"Yes, Clint, I do."

"I've also offered him a job, so just go along with it and I'll explain everything to you on Saturday. I've got a plan, with you in mind. You're my sole concern and I wish I could see you; however your cell was more expedient. Just go along with whatever he says and, the snow thing, that's very exciting. I like originality, so will your producer and don't let the little bastard see more of you than he has. And, before I forget again, Friday get your hair cut short, something cute but sophisticated and buy all new wigs to match your real look. The days of bobby socks and showing your bare bum are a thing of the past. You're a woman, be proud, especially after the woman at the beach. I'll reimburse you. From here on you don't pay for a thing. Bye for now."

He pressed end, watching the kid move sluggishly around his room and Melissa throwing on a robe. Timothy left his room, knocking the door she opened right away.

"Get in and like shut your mouth, deadbrain. I told you, didn't I. Clint won't take shit from anyone." She took the DVDs, burying them in her backpack and retrieving her designer wallet. "Clint said I should give you five-hundred and the rest tomorrow."

"He's giving me a job or something."

"Shut up. I don't need to hear you."

"You're different when you're Rhapsody, Mel, like really sexy. You're not like the same at all."

"Because I'm an actress, idiot. You're the one who

treated me like slut and called me a whore and don't think I'll ever forgive you. I won't." She gave him ten bills. "Get out, and I want the others before she gets home tomorrow."

Timothy sulked from his sister's room. Once in his, he danced and jumped up and down, hiding the money in his wallet and went to bed.

Fifty-Three

Wednesday Clint searched Timothy's room from top to bottom for more DVDs; in the afternoon he watched Melissa in her father's office printing a few dozen photos of her at the beach, and after dinner he made certain the boy obeyed his instructions. He spoke with Melissa to demonstrate his concern, reiterating his desire to see her with a different look, a womanly and sophisticated look and told her what to wear to the hotel on Saturday.

He called Timothy to thank him for honouring his commitment, adding they would soon meet and that he was to treat his sister with respect. He was to go to her room as soon as they finished speaking and sincerely apologize to her or the job deal was off because she had real power over him. Clint watched the supplication in progress, chuckling to the point of hysteria as Melissa entirely emasculated her brother, turning stone-cold when his phone buzzed.

"Hello."

"Clyde, this is Michelle, the girl you invited to breakfast."

He laughed. "Michelle, the most beautiful nymph in the entire world and I wallow at her feet."

"Good start. However for the time being I'll keep my feet to myself. How are you?"

"You ask that of a lowly man so desperately in love with a woman beyond his grasp? How cruel the meekest sex."

"Spare me, lover-boy, and I mean that euphemistically."

"You slash an already weakened heart."

"Good, which means you won't be alive to take me to dinner on Friday. Goodnight, Sir Bleedalot."

"Wait, wait. Don't hang up. Okay, I over did it. I'm sorry. Let's start over. You asked how I am. I'm fine, lonely as hell since meeting you, despite feeling on top of the world knowing you want me to take you to dinner."

"I don't want you to. You invited me last Saturday. What I'm saying is that I'll join you if you still feel the need for company."

He surrendered. "I do and knowing that I'll be with you makes me sad."

Michelle blew air from her mouth. "I'm listening."

"I can't imagine how my poor heart will manage to beat through so many lonesome hours until then. Forgive me if I die." He heard another sigh. "Friday it is, at eight. I'll survive, only to see you and I'll send a taxi to..."

"To your house. I'll get to wherever on my own. Leave me a message when you've made the reservation."

He coughed discreetly. "Eduardo's, Michelle, however you may have to help me with the menu. My Spanish is somewhat nonexistent."

"Eduardo's at eight. See you then."

"That's it?"

"Clyde, if I stay on the phone with you we'll end up talking cutesy. None of it would be real. We'll spoil Friday and, please, wear a suit. Goodnight."

"Goodnight, Michelle." He hung up. "Bitch."

Kathy was in her family room, reading, sipping her after dinner drink and he could tell she wasn't seeing the words. She went downstairs. He met her in the dining room where she poured another shot of tequila and he waited to see her in her bedroom where she paced the room, the closet and her bathroom, finally bouncing onto her bed and reaching for her cell phone.

"Hello."

"Jack, this is Kathy."

"Kathy, hi."

"I have a question."

"Sure, go ahead."

"Should I pack casual or informal?"

"You're serious?"

"Understand something, Jack. I'm in a bad situation, which doesn't mean you're an escape or that we'll walk down the aisle. The only aisle I want at the moment is on an aircraft or in a theatre. Understand? This weekend means I like you, possibly a lot. I don't know, but I'm hoping I do by Sunday and if you're using me, well, I'll live with the rejection after I wake up don't see you."

"You'll see me. Of course you'll see me. How else will I serve you breakfast in bed?"

"Don't expect me to say anything stupid, like I love you."

"I won't"

"And don't expect to hear darling or honey or sweetheart. You're Jack."

"Got it."

"So, what do I pack?"

"I booked a package for two at a spa an hour's drive from town. The men's schedule is different from the women's so you'll have time without me and, for the evening, they prefer casual elegance. Check-out is ten the next morning. You'll be home by noon to hate me or miss me. I wanted another night but didn't want to crowd you. I also have an early flight on Monday."

"Wow. That's a pretty special weekend for a first date, not to mention a little presumptuous."

"Wait till you see what I've got planned for our second date. And, I have to tell you, you might just hear that I love you."

"Where should we meet?"

"I suggest the casino. You can leave your car and we'll drive together."

"You know, Jack, I'd prefer driving alone, just in case. Why don't you meet me at Surfers' Beach and I'll follow you?"

"You're afraid."

"You're damned right I'm afraid."

"I suppose you do have a point. Why don't we meet at, let's say, noon?"

"Noon at the beach and casual elegance. See you then. Goodnight, Jack."

"Goodnight, Kathy."

Kathy pressed end, reaching for the table phone. She dialled the number in a haze.

"Is one of them dead?"

"No, Ted, you still have a reason to come home, just not this weekend. I've decided to go to a spa with Michelle Lopez from noon on Saturday to midday Sunday. They've got a special for forgotten and ignored wives. Got the picture?"

"So I'm stuck with the kids, again."

"No, you're not. Melissa's a few weeks away from being a woman and let's forget for once that Timothy can't find the front door. He'll have to one day so I'm giving them the run of the house for the weekend. What I'm saying is: the choice is yours. Come or stay. Either way, I'll be with Michelle for as long as you're here."

"In that case, I'll stay. Thanks for the FYI."

"I thought you might."

"You've been spending a lot of time with this Michelle."

"Yes, I have. Actually we're lovers. Does that do anything for you?"

"It would have once, if it were true."

Kathy chortled into the phone. "I'll be home Sunday at noon, looking beautiful for the mirror. Our pride and joy will be fine until then. Don't bother phoning. I'll do the spot-checking."

"I'll see you next Friday. I'll be home mid-afternoon."

"You're never home, Ted. You haven't been home for years, if ever." Kathy sipped her tequila, knowing he wouldn't speak. "Ted, tell me something, when you're with her, with any of them, do you ever think of me?"

"No, I don't. Thinking of you would ruin the moment."

"You hate me that much."

"I don't hate you, Kath. What I hate is my life."

"With me, naturally."

"No, with all of you."

"You know what's funny?"

"Nothing I can think of at the moment."

"That you do hate me, or despise me, yet someone else loves me so much and someone else wants to. How can that be when I've always been your wife?"

"I'm not into riddles, Kath. Are you cheating or not?"

"How could I possibly cheat on a cheat?" She snorted. "No, I've never cheated on you."

"I wouldn't blame you if you did, yet someone loves you and someone else wants to."

"You almost sound sorry I never cheated."

"Listen, Kath, this is going nowhere. You want me to say something you're not going to hear. Cheat if you want. We're not different from a million other couples, including some of our righteous neighbours. We made decisions when we were the least prepared and we were expected to live with them for the rest of our lives, for whatever reason: money, security, family or social criticisms, whatever. Listen, I'm glad you've turned around, that you're working out. You look great, you do. It just doesn't do anything for me. You're an attractive woman, but to me you're Kath, the mother of my children who think I'm shit on a stick."

"Ted..."

"Yes."

"You are shit." She burst into tears. "I'll see you next Friday, maybe. Give her my regards."

Kathy crashed the receiver into the cradle. She phoned Michelle and cried with her while downstairs Timothy was calculating, Melissa was preparing her wardrobe for her upcoming Valentine's performance and, above Kathy's bathroom, Clint Evans sat quietly content.

Fifty-Four

Thursday Clint called for the taxi and left after a lunch which he ate in Melissa's room, studying each of her self-portraits. As much as Melissa had practiced since New Year's for Sunday, he had rehearsed a hundred times in his mind how to approach her, how to deal with her in the hotel room, how to reassure her. The girl was a natural. Who else would think of prancing nude along the seashore in the dead of winter? The last thing he wanted was to frighten her and neither one could predict how she would react to him following her every move as she entertained her fans.

He was anxious for Friday to see how easily Michelle would forget her darling Kathy or dismiss Clyde Van as a happily failed experiment, mildly disappointed he wouldn't be privy to her late evening follow-up with Kathy, or Kathy's report to her after screwing Jack Caden. He didn't want Michelle's money. He wanted her body and her mind, that which was most precious to Kathy, which would bring her the most grief and him the most gratification. And Monday would hopefully be the quantum leap he'd been working toward, the coup de grâce which would bring Eileen to him and purge his mind of Kim Moon.

*

Friday evening Michelle went out of her way to avoid dressing seductively. She wasn't on a date, she told herself. She was more interested in how she would feel about him in the morning. The restaurant was elegant and Clyde Van

looked remarkably different out of his jeans and leather
bomber jacket. He focused on her eyes, undressing her was
too tempting and women inherently knew when men
thought of dinner as foreplay to the evening ahead. He'd
seen her naked and carnal so often at Kathy's that he
already thought of her as a lover and, had he known her
intention was to dress down, he would have laughed. Her
cashmere dress hugged every curve, a wide belt
accentuating perfect hips. She looked divine.

They spoke endlessly, not once touching on either career.
She was going through a divorce and moving to a condo.
He never married, although he had lost at love, his heart
ripped out and Michelle was the first woman he'd even
thought of dating in ages. She had three close friends, all
girls. He had no friend, which didn't particularly concern
him. He was accustomed to being alone, not once sounding
forlorn or pathetic. She loved to travel, so did he. They both
enjoyed fine dining and the arts. She was somewhat of an
aficionado while he simply liked what he liked. Would she
ever marry again, he asked? She didn't know. Michelle
asked whether he would and he placed his cell on the table
prepared to reserve two seats on the Red Eye to Vegas at
midnight and he would never stop loving her.

"That's what the last guy said. Then he stopped a lot of
things. In fact, he's getting out this weekend."

"I would never hurt you." He beamed. "Now, loving
you, that's an entirely different matter."

"I've enjoyed the evening, Clyde. The meal was
exquisite and the company charming."

"Charming enough to share your delightful company
next Saturday for dinner and a show?" She brought her
napkin to her mouth, patting the corners. He reached into
his jacket for an envelope. "The best Latin troupe to come
out of Mexico, a table for two, lots of people, very safe and
I won't offer to drive you home."

"I'll call you."

He smiled. "Or you can tell me tomorrow in aisle eight."

"I did my groceries this afternoon, Clyde, in case this evening didn't work out."

"And did it?"

"Yes."

"Call me." He signalled the waiter for the bill. "And, Michelle...I wasn't joking about Vegas."

*

Kathy listened closely to Michelle's recap. He was a nice guy, the evening was comfortable, but sparks didn't fly. The kiss on her cheek was friendly, noncommittal, and she probably would join him for dinner the following Saturday. When she hung up she went to bed where she gave him no space in her dreams, though Clint couldn't get her out his mind, certain she would call. Sleep evaded him. The entire weekend would be sleepless and hopefully the following weekend with Eileen would be no less stimulating and equally promising.

Melissa was thrilled by her mother's unexpected gesture of confidence, albeit increasingly nervous about meeting her manager and hearing about her future. She decided to take her selection of lingerie and wear one dress on Saturday, believing Clint would want a preview. The rest she would carry on Sunday with her accessories. She wanted to please him. Since her show at New Years, and all she had done to prepare for the next two days, her bedroom performances would no longer be fulfilling. She needed more.

Fifty-Five

Saturday Clint woke, showered and left his apartment. He checked into The Luxor, let the bellhop carry his luggage to the suite, checked out the five-hundred-dollar-a-night investment and went for breakfast.

Melissa was up at 6:00, dressed and too agitated to eat, not much different from her mother who joined her at 8:00, giving her final instructions, making her promise to be home in time to prepare dinner and showing real surprise at her daughter's new hairdo. Melissa left for the local bus at 8:30, headed for the mall where she met her alcoholic friend, paid him in his preferred currency and went out to hail a cab. She arrived at The Luxor precisely at 10:00, changed into her shoes and went to the courtesy phones following Clint's instructions. Once connected, he asked whether she was hungry. She wasn't and took the elevator to the twentieth floor.

"Come in, Melissa. I'm Clint. The big day is finally here." He took her shoulder bag. "I wouldn't have recognized you. You look amazing. Please, give me your coat and boots." She did, her wide eyes absorbing the luxury.

"I brought you the pictures, Clint, and everything except five dresses I'll bring tomorrow. I thought you might want to see some of my act today."

"Sure I do. I also want to see your photos. Hey, listen, it's a little early, but how about a cocktail to make us both a

393

little more comfortable. I can appreciate how this is all a little overwhelming for you."

"I'd like that. I still can't believe I have a manager."

Clint opened his portable bar. "Help yourself whenever you want, Melissa. Just don't leave here drunk. I don't want you waking up with a hangover and tomorrow you're drinking ginger ale until you're finished the final performance. Understood?"

"Yes."

"Good. Now why don't you unpack? I want you to feel at home before I leave. I won't be staying long and let's see those fabulous photos."

He examined every piece of lingerie, nodding approvingly and took the envelope from her. "That was pretty gutsy, doing what you did at the beach."

"It was unreal."

"Let's sit on the couch." He placed his drink on the table. "How many sex partners have you had?"

"One."

"Did he ever photograph you?"

"No, Clint."

He took his time with each glossy. "These pictures are unbelievable. You were right. We will go to the beach. I'm in Europe next weekend, so why don't we pencil in the twenty-seventh? I can't believe I'm seeing you naked on a boardwalk in the middle of snowstorm." He downed his drink and stood, taking her glass. "I'll get us a refill and give you a tour. I'm sure you'll be very comfortable here. Try to relax and enjoy the day. I took the liberty of filling the spa. I didn't think you're a flower girl so I added pear-scented oil."

Melissa stood. "Thank you, Clint, for everything. I won't let you down."

He passed her the glass, tossed a small envelope beside her lingerie and took her hand. "The thousand I owe you for your brother and another two-hundred for taxis and lunch. Do not order wine."

He walked her from the sitting room into the bedroom, her mouth agape, and into the bathroom lined with marble and decorated with bronze fixtures which was twice the size of her mother's.

"Clint...wow!"

"I figure we'll start with you at the front door, perhaps removing your coat and hat, no winter clothes. You'll find them in the closet, then as you're speaking with your fans spend a few minutes in the living room, make your way to the bedroom, undress and climb onto the bed. I'll leave the rest up to you. Remember, be natural, not over rehearsed."

She looked around. Clint reclined on the king-size bed.

"I can't believe this."

"And Myrtle will be that much better, also more demanding, which is why I think the beach is a good idea in a couple of weeks. The Europeans want sophistication. You'll be working with a leading man, if and when you decide you like him. Nor will you do any explicit scenes until you're entirely comfortable."

"I am, really. It's like a dream."

"Come here." She walked over and he sat straight to clink their glasses. "To our mutual success, Melissa." He emptied his glass, smiling warmly. She did the same, putting her glass on the bedside table. "Are you sure you're ready? Are you certain you want to take your career to the next level?" She nodded. "Good, then undress for me."

She unbuttoned and shrugged away her dress with practiced ease, slowly, looking into his eyes. She brought her steady hands to the rosette clasp of her bra, smoothly sliding off one side then the other and placing it neatly on the bed. She sat on the bed beside him, crossed one leg over the other, bringing up her foot, unbuckling the strap and pulling away the stiletto. Then she did the other. She unclasped the garter at the front of one thigh, falling back, raising her leg into the air, undoing the clasp at the back of her leg and, with her leg still straight in the air; she guided the stocking to her ankle and pulled it away.

Sitting, she unhooked the other front clasp, leaned onto her side and asked Clint to help her. He did and, with the clasp undone, she raised her leg into the air and groaned as Clint's hands encircled her thigh and moved slowly towards her toes. Sitting, her hands worked deftly behind her, freeing the lacy belt. She didn't look at him as she stood, stepped in front of him, facing away and teasingly pushed her thong to her knees and back, turning before pushing them to her ankles and onto the plush carpet. She stood before him, vulnerable, her arms by her side.

"You're sensational. I think it's time for your soak."

She hesitated. "I guess you're coming in with me."

"No. I'm not. Doing a show in front of a webcam in one thing, having a make-up artist, hairstylist and a crew is way different. I had to know you wouldn't be intimidated."

"Do I look different in person, you know, better?"

"Yes, and in the future I'm the only non-crew who sees you this way unless you're working, not even you trainer. Understood?"

"Yes."

"Come here, baby girl." She did instinctively and sat on his knee. Her heart was about to burst. She could feel her cheeks burning as one firm hand rubbed warmth into the small of her back while the other travelled across her thighs to rest against the curve of her hip. "Before I leave I'll give you my private number. Not many people have access to me this way and I want you to call me whenever you feel you need me."

"I will."

"Good. Now go relax." Helping her stand, he spanked her lightly several times. "Scoot, and promise me you'll be every bit as good tomorrow."

Clint left Melissa to finish luxuriating in the scented foam, feeling like a woman for the first time in her life and wanting tomorrow to come quickly. She was ready. Seeing a man actually react to her body had aroused her, seduced her. Clint was right. Real acting wasn't the same.

*

Jack Caden sat in his vehicle running the motor, letting his mind wander. They would arrive in time for a late lunch, Kathy would have an afternoon of spa treatments while he trained in the gym, enjoyed a sauna before sprawling in the snow and later he would join her for a thirty-minute massage. He had decided the evening of dinner and dancing would be the appropriate prelude to their lovemaking and that he would give her space.

At the house Kathy told Timothy he was no longer restricted, however in lieu of retuning his credit card she gave him one-fifty to cover the coming four weeks and cut him off. He carried her bag to the MX-5, standing aside dumbly as she thanked him and asked that he not burn down the house until Melissa got home. She backed into the driveway and drove off without waving.

At Surfers' Beach Jack stepped from his vehicle, opened her door, helped her out and kissed her. He asked once whether she had changed her mind about driving and she said no. He agreed and they arrived an hour later, giving the luggage over to the bellhop to avoid at least one awkward moment. At lunch they discussed the afternoon. She would see Jack again at 5:00.Until then she'd be pampered, steamed and float in a sensory deprivation tank, and when the meal was finished he suggested she might want time alone to change. When he knocked on the door she answered in a robe.

"When don't you look beautiful?"

"Most mornings."

397

"I don't believe you." He took her hands, holding them away from her body. "Are you...?"

"Yes, I am. And so will you be. Don't embarrass me by coming for the massage in boxer shorts. Please."

"Sorry, micro-fibre imported from Italy."

She shook her head. "I believe a towel under your robe will do."

"See how much we already know about each other. I can't imagine by dinnertime." He pinched her chin. "How are you feeling?"

"Not as nervous as I thought I'd be. Lunch helped."

"You know, I brought pyjamas...as a precaution."

"Great. My first affair is with a boy scout, and not quite the precaution I had in mind."

He reached for her knotted belt, grinning mischievously. "So, I'll see you at five."

"I expect you'll see quite a bit. I hope you're not disappointed."

They kissed on cue and Kathy strolled down the corridor, glancing once over her shoulder. Inside the room, Jack hung his clothes, changed, went to the gym, used the pool, the spa and rushed out onto the patio to try a brisk rub with handfuls of snow. He wasn't impressed and spent the next half-hour lounging in the heated, swirling water. At 5:00 he made his way to the massage studio dressed appropriately. Kathy was lying face-down on a table, glistening with oil, draped with bath towel from the rise of her buttocks to her feet.

"I knew I'd like the view."

"You're not supposed to talk."

Jack's masseuse patted his table without telling him to jump up, making another silent gesture which told him to lay face-down and she discreetly whipped away his towel to cover his lower half. Within moments Kathy was purring while Jack was grunting in concert to the more aggressive treatment of the knots in his back.

Kathy's towel was pulled gently to her shoulders, barely reaching the bottom curves of her perfectly round cheeks, her purring sounds unbroken. Jack, on the other hand, focused on her blissful expression until her attendant brought the towel to her hips, patted her bum and told her to turn. Jack's breathing all but stopped, twisting onto his back. He was mesmerized seeing the masseuse's hands manipulating the tight skin from Kathy's shoulders to her belly, caressing her breasts more than kneading and Kathy's expression never changing. Meanwhile Jack required all his concentration to contain his pleasure, made all the more intense by hers, waiting to see how much of her legs would be uncovered.

When the treatment ended Kathy was covered from her breasts to the very apex of her thighs, Jack lay covered from his waist, each resisting the urge to sleep through the requisite facial. When the attendants left them, Kathy lay with her eyes closed.

"I feel heavenly."

"The view is certainly heavenly. Any chance we can skip dinner? I can't wait to touch you."

"When you invite a girl for dinner, you give her dinner." The lighting gradually became brighter. She took a deep breath and forced herself to sit, holding the towel to her chest and wishing she hadn't been so relaxed. When she opened her eyes: "I hope you're ogling me because you're pleased."

"I can recall the exact moment I last saw such a beautiful body." He paused. "The very first moment I laid eyes on you." He winked.

"You have me at a disadvantage. You're dressed, I'm not."

He held up her robe. "Jump down and turn. I won't peek."

"I don't believe you. Give me the robe and you turn."
He shook his head. "Jack."

"You'll have to trust me. You can't sit clinging all night to a towel which isn't doing much at all to hide you."

She pursed her lips, slid from the table, stepped closer to the robe, spun around and dropped her towel, sliding her arms into the sleeves. "You're looking, aren't you?"

"And I hate myself for lying to you, but I'm also standing here paying for my sin with my life. You're killing me."

Not holding hands as they meandered to their room was out of character, however Kathy did insist upon dressing for dinner right away and in private. In the bathroom she held a damp cloth to her face, flustered, thinking of what was to come. When she walked out he stood, his eyes devouring her, thankful she had given him sufficient time to finish dressing, the look in her eyes telling him he should have booked a second night.

To Jack's way of thinking dinner was an extravagant, delicious impediment, whereas to Kathy the unique culinary dishes were measured lead-ins to a night of sexual release which she realized was actually a comparative study of her options. She couldn't make love to him because she didn't love him. She loved Michelle. He would have to prove himself overtime, though what remained of the evening was the premiere test of endurance and the bar was set high.

Neither one wanted more to drink and left after their last dance; he, anxious for discovery; she, afraid of disappointment. They kissed inside the door, waiting longer would have been ridiculous. They were a novelty to one another, the sole raison d'être at the moment to have sex, to explore, probe, overexcite and titillate, or satisfy, sleep and leave early the next morning.

Hotel Services had prepared the bed for sleep and Jack put out the light. They kicked off their shoes and inched their way into the middle of the room lit by the filtered radiance of the moon. He threw his jacket aside, lifted her into her arms as easily as she would a child and laid her in the middle of the bed as gently as a feather.

"With each kiss a more daring and lingering touch, my passion, until you want my kisses and my heart to stop."

He put an open palm to her breasts.

"That's pretty daring. And you didn't kiss me first."

The heat of their lips melded to a single source. Jack eased himself to his knees, not wanting to break apart, bringing her with him as they kissed, hooking his thumbs under the hem of her simple sheath dress and pushing it past her breasts. Their lips parted, Kathy helped him and threw her dress to the floor before tearing away his turtleneck. They pressed their lips together again, this time more ardently, Jack easing her to the mattress, a single hand slowly travelling the length of her slender back to release her breasts.

She nudged one way, then the other, letting him toss away the delicate fabric, groaning the instant the warmth of his hand cupped one breast and the moistness of his lips the other. Her hands went to his waist, unbuckling his belt, unhooking the tab and tugging at the zipper. They kissed, at first tentatively, giving way to abandon. He pulled her over, her nipples tracing soft lines into his chest. He pulled her higher, sitting her on his chest and sat upright so that she was under him with her legs in the air, each one against a sinewy shoulder. He leaned forward, kissing her hard, searching as she searched. He unclasped one garter, pushed her leg forward and undid the other, sliding her stocking up past her toes. He moved to her other leg, undid the clasps and fought not to hurry. He leaned forward, her arms clinging to the nape of his neck, forcing him closer, tears welling in her eyes. He pulled her up, rocking her, hugging her close, feeling her arms squeeze him tightly as he plucked away her garter belt. He set her down, pressing his mouth to hers and sat straight to see her bathed in the dim light. His hands reached out to cup her breasts, squeezing gently, his fingers delicately pinching her aroused nipples.

He tucked his thumbs into the ribbons of her panties. "My passion, tell me to stop and I will."

She breathed deeply. He could smell her urgency mounting. "This better not be an anticlimax, Jack Caden. Dinner was superb, but not that good. So rip off these expensive panties and get down here."

He tore away her panties from one side, then the other, bringing them to his nose, inhaling deeply, letting them drag lazily across Kathy's face before shoving them into a pocket, retrieving a foil and raising himself onto his knees to push down his pants. He wasted no time. He went into her easily, their kisses muffling their groans, their pleasure and ecstasy. They rolled onto their sides, kicking away his pants, Kathy refusing to have sex with any man wearing socks. He agreed, counting to three before he pulled out. She tore at the socks and by the count of five Kathy Burberry's screams were being muffled by a firm yet tender grasp.

When she woke the next morning her lips were numb. Raising the sheet she saw her labia were swollen, a deeper shade of pink and tingling. And she was naked. She had nowhere to hide, no towel to cover her body and no make-up that wasn't smeared. She looked over to Jack. She went to kiss him, curious how she would feel and smelled her own pungent scent, remembering everything. Ted had never kissed her there. He'd never been romantic with her, virile or daring. In fact, Michelle had taught her the feeling.

"Good morning, passion. That is what I called you, unless I'm in the wrong dream."

"Good morning, and how weird is this? I'm naked in bed with a man who laid me like a floor and I've only seen you three times."

"Four," he corrected. "Last night was number four"

"So, this is number five?"

"My mouth hurts."

"My whole body aches."

"I'm sorry."

"Don't be. No pain, no gain. Right?"

"Now that you mention it, I think I'll stay away from hot water for a while." Jack paused. "Passion…"

"Kathy."

"No. You're passion to me and I can't let you go. I don't mean this morning. I mean, I can't let you go."

"Jack, you can't judge a book by its cover."

He smirked. "I can from what I'm feeling under this cover, as painful as it is."

"Part of me is starting to like you a lot. The other part is hoping you're not a prick. No pun intended, because oh-boy! I thought I was having a tonsillectomy last night, but I'm not naïve. Not everything is as it seems, not you, not me."

"What are you saying?"

"First off, the drive-through is closed. What are we talking here, three or four dips?"

"You insult me. I counted five."

"Five. Shit. I've never done myself five times. Anyway, I'm closed for repairs and will shower alone because I don't want you to think I'm easy or that you have to stop working at impressing me." She put a finger to his lips. "You're off to a good start. That's all I'm going to say. I don't love you, although I think I might want to and you won't hear the words until I do. Then I want to remember last night as amateur night and for you to show me what you've really got."

He reached behind to the night table. "Passion, last night at dinner was not the right timing because we didn't know. Now the moment is proper. You've stirred emotions in me which I thought were gone forever." Jack draped the diamond pendant over Kathy's neck, letting the jewel rest in his palm, kissing her lips with ardent desire, guiding the gem between her breasts.

"Jack, it's lovely. I don't know what to say. I wasn't expecting anything like this and it's a little extravagant. Chocolates would have been fine. Besides, Valentine's never entered my mind."

"Your gift to me is a hundred times more precious. However I suggest you have your shower and get dressed before I regret my selfish desire. Because, passion, I want you and waiting isn't uppermost on my mind."

She kissed him, threw aside the covers and leapt over him. "Yes, and it's your fault, Jack. Number five could have come before a shower. Next time, please don't be so greedy all at once."

"Don't blame me. I didn't stop because I was tired. I stopped because you got too slippery to hold."

She gathered her overnight bag, her fresh clothing and padded into the bathroom, coming out in cords and a thick cable sweater. In his robe, his clothes hanging from his forearms, he looked out of place and hurried to correct the comical imbalance. At breakfast they held hands, in the room they kissed and again by the cars before Kathy followed his lead to Surfers' Beach.

"Passion, let's walk a short distance."

"Don't you have a flight to catch?"

"I haven't missed one yet and our time together has come to an end too quickly. I want more."

They strolled along the boardwalk hand in hand as lovers into a flurry of snowflakes.

"Thank you for my lovely necklace."

"Thank you, for you. I'm cursing myself for always booking trips so far ahead and, Kathy, on that note, over the summer I want you to travel with me."

"Let me digest this weekend first, Jack. It's probably a good thing you're leaving town for a while. Last night was pretty intense. I don't want anything to cloud my judgement, like the fact you have my panties in your pocket." She held out her hand. "Thank you."

"You can't fault me for wanting a souvenir of the best night of my life. I expect you to call me, and I'll call you."

"Yes."

*

Kathy drove up the hill to her house in a daze, trying to piece together the past twenty-four hours. She felt a surge of tremendous guilt and she knew the reason, thankful she hadn't asked Jack to join her in Myrtle Beach. Yet she was consumed with an overwhelming sense of having found herself. She understood Michelle, Sheila and Darlene as she never had before. Jack wasn't wrong. Moments before she collapsed onto his chest, falling into a deep slumber, he must have summoned all his strength to hold her sweat-coated body in place. And, in the morning, seeing herself in the bathroom mirror, she was horrified by her blackened eyes, her smeared lips and matted dark auburn hair stuck to her forehead in thick strands. He was also right about something else: the jets of water streaming from the showerhead stung terribly as the steaming rivulets flowed from the chiselled contours of her belly to her thighs.

She despised herself for what she had missed in life and for what she had done to Michelle, her lover, the one person who ever truly loved her and whom she truly loved. At first she believed Ted's lack of attention and endless affairs drove her to Michelle when, in fact, he had driven her to long for a weekend of cheating in Vermont. Nothing drove her to Michelle out of desperation. She and Michelle simply discovered real love for each other which transcended being girlfriends and Kathy doubted she could truly exist without her. Michelle would always come first in her life.

405

*

Jack Caden drove to his apartment to change and eat a light lunch, still marvelling at her body, her litheness and her urgency. She was a woman neglected; a woman searching for love, a word which she made quite clear was verboten yet she called out "my love" a dozen times or more. He watched her as she lay sleeping. He knelt by her side, trailing kisses from her lips to her toes, absorbing her, tasting her, inhaling her bittersweet scent, his temptation quickly becoming irresistible. When she woke he told her five, not six, and when he was satiated he remained awake to watch over her until she stirred and he lowered himself stealthily against her side.

He promised to call her, and he would, from wherever he might be. She was too special; she always was and wasn't at all disheartened to discover their schedules might not align for a month or so. What he counted on was the necklace, a constant reminder when memories of his prowess might fade. He closed his door and focused on the weeks ahead, confident Kathy would not forget or dismiss hm.

*

Clint Evans arrived at The Luxor at 11:45 and he was all business.

"Are we set?"

"I am, Clint. Do you like how I look?"

"Yes, as much as I did the first time. What I'm anxious for are your latest purchases. How was yesterday for you?"

"I lounged around. I ordered lunch without wine, rehearsed a little and left at six. I really hated to leave. I got here about three hours ago. We're all set."

"Get used to this, baby girl." He paused, seeming to think. "I'm sorry. I didn't think to ask whether I can call you that." He shrugged. "I feel good calling you by that name."

"So do I. It's pretty special."

"Good…and what I meant by "get used to it" is this: Very soon you'll be on private jets, private beaches and at private parties with beautiful girls and good looking guys."

"Once I pass my audition, right?"

"Don't worry about the audition. These guys will love you. Now, let's have a drink to loosen up, no more. Between takes I'll take care of the set, you take care of yourself with a different outfit each hour. Try to stay away from the spa unless you can keep your wigs dry."

"Yes, Clint."

"Melissa, can I ask you something?"

"Yes, Clint."

"I was married once. We had a child, a girl. She'd be close to your age today. Anyway, there was an accident, a terrible car accident and she was killed. I wasn't to blame. Some guy ran a red and slammed into the rear side. Anyway," he sighed, "my wife couldn't bear to look at me, she hated me so much, but, the worst part, I never got to hear my little baby girl call me daddy." Clint sipped his vodka. "Melissa, would you call me daddy when we're alone?" He wiped his eyes. "It would mean so much."

Melissa stared at him, her mouth wide open, thinking how strong he must be to expose himself so tenderly. "Yes, daddy, I will. Now we both have someone to make us feel better."

"Yes we do and your anxious fans await. Let's roll."

Rhapsody tapped into her computer, recognized the face and Clint's lens took over. "Peter! I don't believe it's you. I was hoping you'd be my first Valentine."

"Rhapsody, I've been going nuts without you."

"Well here I am, as promised, new and improved."

"Holy crap, your hair, your outfit, you're like ten years older. In a good way," he added quickly, "in a super good way, like runway good."

"Thanks Peter. We haven't seen each other for a while and we won't again for a few more weeks. So I hope you leave me wanting more of me. This is my temporary studio. How do you like it?" Clint adjusted to wide angle as Rhapsody removed her hat.

"I love the place."

"You helped me get here." She eased off her coat and went to the bar. The champagne was ginger ale. "Come into my bedroom, Peter. You might have noticed I have a cameraman. Doing everything alone was becoming overly demanding and not fair to you. I was too limited."

"I hope you're not paying him, Rhapsody. Everyone dialling-in would work with you for free."

"You're sweet. How's your wife?"

"She's upstairs, with her sister."

"Have you told her about us?"

"No."

"Why don't you?" In the bedroom Rhapsody unzipped her skirt, letting it fall to the floor and looked straight into the lens. "Can you see me better, Peter?"

"Five on five."

"So why don't you get your wife involved. Women are so much fun." She undid her blouse one button at a time, shrugging it away and walked into the bathroom. "Don't tell me she wouldn't like to see me in my lingerie, getting ready for bed or my bath. I might even give you a free password. It's not like you don't deserve something, but I only want her."

She and Clint could hear Peter's breath blowing through the mike. "I'll frigging do it, this afternoon."

She unhooked her bra, tossed it to the edge of the spa and pushed down her panties facing away from the lens. She looked down, frowning.

"Peter," she giggled, "I'm so excited about my bath that I forgot my shoes."

She raised one foot to the Romanesque framework, undid the strap, faced away and unhooked the other, kicking into the air. She was wearing stay-ups without garters and leaned into the tub to test the water which would remain at the ideal temperature for the next six hours. She pushed away one stocking, swinging her leg into the water. Clint moved in, adjusting the angle. She pulled away her other stocking, tossing that one into the air before easing backward, swinging her leg in a high arc and bringing her feet together in knee deep water. She crept into the middle of the spa, squatted until the water reached her shoulders and stood.

"Peter, I want to see you again this afternoon. I want your wife to see me like this, or in bed. Goodbye and thanks for always coming to me."

Clint closed his lens, the screen went black in the living room and Melissa stepped from the spa.

"Get dry and dressed. You've got five minutes and you've got that guy wrapped around your little finger. Think he'll bring his wife along?"

"I hope so. Lots of women buy my videos, but I've never been with one live, except for Dorothy at the ocean. I suppose it'll happen one day."

Clint followed her into the bedroom. "You'll notice a huge difference in a few weeks. The shoots will take a couple of months, not hours and you'll have as much time as you want for wardrobe changes. You'll be the boss."

"Not you?" she asked.

"Only when something happens you don't like. That's when I'll get involved, apart from your contract."

The afternoon went as planned, except for Peter who didn't keep his promise to her and she didn't look the least bit tired. At 6:05 Melissa was soaking in a steamier spa, relaxing with a double-vodka and Clint was sitting on the edge.

"You've never done better work, baby girl."

"Thank you, daddy. I've never felt so much like a real woman. I hate having to wait until March for my audition."

"Actually, baby girl, a lot of the footage I shot this afternoon will be edited as part of the audition. Your work was excellent and deserves to be included and, if the winter beach thing works out, we'll make sure the producer sees that footage." He refilled the glasses. "I've thrown your wigs into the garbage. You won't need them any longer. No more performances until your audition and from then on it's the real thing: Melissa Burberry starring as Midnight Rhapsody. By the way, today's revenues are entirely yours. My commission begins the day we leave for Europe. Now get out before you shrivel."

He held out the towel, enfolding her and patting her dry. He watched her dress, unable to disguise the smirk on his face. The next four weeks would be interesting between a cheating mother and an insatiable teenage porn star and he would be with them to bear witness. He and Melissa would talk more frequently. She would restrict her rehearsals to Mondays through Thursdays and she would meet him on the twenty-seventh for a picnic at the beach, weather permitting.

When she left he ordered room service and spent the night acclimating himself to luxury.

*

Kathy was at dinner with Michelle when Melissa arrived home.

"You know how much I love you, mi amor."

"I do, darling, and I know how strange we each feel saying those words to a woman. It's not the natural order of things, until it happens. This guy, Clyde Van, comes second and he'll have to blow my diaphragm into orbit to make points. Even then, how do I give you up? The good thing is we're girls. We have more latitude."

"I'd be jealous."

"So would I. I didn't sleep a wink last night. I thought about you every minute. So, how was Jack Caden?" Kathy hesitated. "Tell me the truth, darling."

"He was you, mi amor, with a penis."

"That good?" Michelle questioned. "Alright! Then maybe we should share him or double-date if Clyde works out. Wouldn't that be ironic: men wanting to be the lovers of women who are lovers?"

"I'm not sure what he'll think of us."

"Don't tell him. Has he told you who he's laid over the last year?"

"No."

"We worry about these two guys too much. We just met them and don't owe either one a thing."

Kathy pulled the diamond pendent from under her dress. "This is his Valentine's gift to me." She looked forlorn. "I didn't have time to refuse."

"It's a lovely diamond, darling. However in my book diamonds are hugely overpriced with male genitalia in mind. We women seldom buy our own because," she giggled, "we know when we're getting screwed. Emeralds and rubies are the way to go, in your case emeralds. To my Valentine, darling."

Michelle placed the tiny green velveteen box by Kathy's linen serviette. Inside was the darkest and clearest emerald she had ever seen.

"Mi amor, I can't. You're a teacher and you've just bought a condo."

"Don't spoil my day. This is one reason I couldn't sleep. Read the inscription.

"Don't go without me," Kathy read.

"I think, darling, those are the most romantic words I've ever spoken to you."

Kathy slid the ring onto her finger, tears trickling to the

corners of her mouth. "I cheated on you."

"No, darling, you didn't. We agreed, and I might well do the same if this Clyde Van doesn't turn into a weasel or isn't on the ten most wanted. We agreed"

"Michelle, it's gorgeous."

"Yes, because you're wearing it. Without you it's a worthless bauble."

Kathy reached into her purse. "I should hate you for showing me up like this, mi amor. My gift to you is embarrassing compared to mine."

Michelle grabbed for the box. "I want my gift." She tore at the wrapping, opened the lid and gasped. "Darling!"

"You're a child."

"I know." Michelle ran her fingers across the silver bracelet, linked together with ruby and red jade teardrops. "Darling, help me." She held out her wrist.

"The affect is stunning."

"And you think we don't love each other." Michelle stood, leaning across Kathy, cupping the nape of her neck and kissing her mouth. "If you don't...they all do."

"Oh, God, do I have your lipstick on my mouth?"

"Yes, darling, you do, and a radiant glow on your face."

"Will you ever grow up?"

"I hope not."

Kathy took Michelle's hand. "I would never say we don't love each other and you're more precious than any emerald or ruby."

"Kathy, how did Melissa work out at home by herself with Timothy last night?"

"I haven't seen her to know. I spoke with her once during the evening and everything sounded alright. Why are you asking?"

"Because it's Valentine's, a day for lovers and I booked us a room. I also brought you a change of clothes for tomorrow, outfits I've never worn." Michelle lowered her head, pouting. "I'm sorry. I guess I wanted equal time with you."

"You're still a terrible actress." Kathy pushed herself away from the table without explanation. Five minutes later the attentive waiter was pulling out her chair. "We're on for tonight, mi amor. I'm sure the house is safe but, quite frankly, I don't care. And, Michelle, don't ever change. I love you exactly the way you are and I don't care who knows or sees."

Fifty-Six

Clint's wake-up call came at 7:00, followed by a room service breakfast at 7:30. He checked-out at 8:00, went to his apartment and arrived at the house in time to set himself up for the week, welcome Mrs. Burberry and make a fresh pot of coffee for the agent and prospective buyers.

After a thorough walk-through of the house he let the couple speak privately with the agent before they thanked him and left. The young woman's face was flushed with excitement. The asking price was accepted subject to a favourable inspection report and the earliest possible move-in date. Mr. Burberry excused himself to consult with his wife, returning a few moments later with his open agenda and shook her hand. Subject to the inspector arriving within the week, an agreed upon move-in date of March 14th and a final meeting with the notary on Thursday, the eleventh, he and his wife would move out on the Friday in order to avoid confusion.

When the agent left Mr. Burberry went upstairs, undressed his wife and took her into Kathy's shower before giving her the envelope and calling a taxi. She was becoming a better wife, despite being upset about the sale of the house until he assured her more work remained for her to do. Later in the afternoon Clint took the call from the realtor in his garret. The inspector would arrive the following day.

That evening the house was strangely quiet. Melissa lay

on her bed dreaming of what he thought must be her success on Sunday, or her surrogate daddy and Kathy walked around aimlessly. Clint lay on his cot, his chin resting on his crossed forearms. Mother and daughter weren't so different, he believed. Both were lonely and desperate to begin new lives. Timothy was like his father: distant and waiting for the punch, rather than ducking or being the aggressor. How he would have enjoyed seeing the real Theodore Burberry in action, not actually needing to. He'd seen so many Burberrys in another life: the ones at his trial whose eyes ridiculed him. Now who was laughing?

He reached for the phone.

"This is Eileen."

"Good evening, Eileen, this is Clint Evans. You might remember…"

"Clint, coyness doesn't become you and, yes, your artwork is very safe."

"I'm certain. However that's not why I'm calling. I've sold my home, Eileen. The deal's ninety-nine percent done."

"Congratulations, Clint."

"Thank you. I'm wondering, Eileen, if you might have the name of the architect who built your beach house readily at hand. I'm flying in Sunday morning and staying through Tuesday. I'd like to meet with him. I figure if you're happy with him, I'll be ecstatic." Eileen gave him the information from memory. "Eileen, did I mention I'm arriving on Sunday?"

"I believe you did. Yes, you did."

"Sunday's a depressing day, don't you think?"

"No. It's one of my busiest?"

"Will you be in Cape City or one of the other galleries?"

"Clint?"

"Yes?"

"Do you want to take me to dinner, or not?"

"Yes…and breakfast, lunch, the Caribbean and the moon."

"I'll settle for dinner."

"Can I hope in my wildest dreams that you're a free and spectacular agent of the universe?"

"No, however I will help you to decorate your new home at, "Eileen hummed, "twenty off the going rate. So you're really serious, Clint."

"Yes. First the architect, this week, and when I have his preliminary sketches I'll ask your advice on location. I'm hoping somewhere not too far from the most enchanting woman in Cape City."

"Should I make reservations to ensure a table?"

"Please do. I'm thinking French, elegant and dancing."

"And I'm thinking Italian, relaxed and a view of the ocean."

"I love Italian, and looking into the eyes of a beautiful woman by the ocean. We could have Italian for lunch, see a bit of the town and later we could have French with candlelight and dancing."

"I haven't seen the sun set at the harbour for months. Why don't we say my gallery at two? Then we can drive along the coast and see some potential properties on our way to the marina."

"I'm counting the moments." Clint paused. "Did I mention I'm not leaving until Tuesday?"

"I believe you did, and did I mention I'm attached?"

"Ouch, yes. I seem to remember that, but, I'm not letting go."

Clint disconnected a few moments later feeling one step closer.

*

Tuesday Mrs. Burberry arrived on time, the inspector gave the house a passing grade and Clint knew precisely when his phone would hum with Michelle on the other end. He

416

would meet her at the casino for the dinner show, eager to be with her, to love her, to play her game by his rules. Anyone listening to the phone conversations between her and Kathy would clearly understand Clyde Van and Jack Caden were pawns in a game of validation.

He called Melissa to reinforce his opinion of her, unable to speak at length because air traffic control had just given his pilot clearance. Melissa had taken his advice to heart. Despite what he'd begun calling her, she was no longer a little girl and had replaced six of her school outfits with the dresses and skirts worn on Sunday. He approved and promised to call her the following week, content to have the rest of the week to himself, anxious to return to work on Friday if only for one night.

What remained for him to accomplish was no longer wishful thinking. The pages of his agenda were filled through the end of March with a chronology he expected would lead him to Eileen Kimberly as a wealthier man no longer haunted by hatred. Fate brought him together with Kathy Burberry as cruelly as the first night he laid eyes on a naked Kim Moon, the night she loved him to the point of exhaustion, the night she began spinning his life into a downward spiral. Kathy Burberry was a name. Her body and mind belonged to Kim Moon. Each night, as he watched her undress and bathe, he saw mahogany hair and black eyes. He knew every curve of her body, every thought in her mind which would suffer no greater torment than to realize she had brought misery and shame to Michelle Lopez on whose body he would leave his indelible imprint, whose mind would never expunge him.

She called him Wednesday after speaking with Kathy. Thursday Clint left the house and Friday he called the Cape City architect. Friday night he drove an hour to work and Saturday he left his traditional breakfast spot knowing somewhere in the downtown core a woman was sitting at the edge of despair. Beware the tallest wave, he thought, for behind it lays the deepest trough. He snorted, thinking he would save that one for Eileen.

At the apartment he tossed the bundle of fifties beside her jewellery and the bills he'd taken from her purse. He slept through the afternoon and dressed for his date with Michelle, smirking into the mirror at the thought of her expression if she were ever to discover the number of times he'd seen the women's gentle caresses surge toward unadulterated and insatiable cravings for one another. At the casino he watched her from a distance as she crossed the hotel lobby.

She was a total woman and he had no idea what she was doing meeting him, going out with a man to confirm or deny what she already knew.

"I don't see a suitcase, so I guess we're not flying to Vegas."

"Good evening, Clyde." She shook her head. "No, we're not flying to Vegas."

"If you were any lovelier I'd feel the need to hide you. I must admit I'm jealous of your friend Kathy spending next weekend with you."

"We're very close." Clint caught himself. "Kathy's been there for me through some rough times." And on top of you, he thought, in the shower, the bath, her bed, the sofa and Vermont. "We spend a lot of time together. In fact we were together all day buying the final pieces for my condo."

He held out his arm. "Shall we?"

"Yes."

"I'd like to meet her, and I can see I'll have to make a good impression or I'll be going to Vegas by myself."

"We're like sisters."

Not quite, mi amor. "Perhaps we can double-date."

"First, let's see how much I enjoy the show tonight."

The restaurant was full to capacity and by dessert he

was making appreciable progress.

"I can't understand anyone falling out of love with you, Michelle. I love everything about you, not to mention how I feel to see everyone admiring you. I'm a lucky man. Even the other women were eyeing you."

"It's the red hair."

"You mean gorgeous red hair and the greenest eyes I've ever seen. You captivate people, Michelle. The same way you captivated me the instant you crashed into my cart."

Michelle tilted her head, arching her eyebrows. "Tell me you're joking."

"I'm joking." He sighed deeply.

"Am I boring you?"

"Not for a nanosecond. I was simply thinking how happier a man I'd be if I had met you years ago."

"I wasn't the same person years ago, so you have no real basis for that particular and peculiar thought."

That's right. You've only been a lesbian slut for seven weeks. "May I see you the week after your big move?"

"I'm having some friends over."

"I'm a friend."

"Once a month we have a No Men night, girls only."

He smiled. "Are these ladies anywhere near as lovely as you?"

"Actually, I'm the ugly sister."

"That's not possible."

"I'm afraid so." Michelle sipped her wine, extending a pensive moment by twirling her bracelet.

"You have exquisite taste in jewellery."

Michelle extended her arm. "Kathy's Valentine's gift to me."

Yeah, I watched her wrapping it like a giddy teenager. "That's some friend." And, by the way, she loves her ring. She kisses it every night. "You're fortunate. Men and women love you. I hope she likes me."

"I wouldn't count on it, not at first. She's very protective of me."

"Not at first. Is that a yes for two weeks from tonight?"

"Yes…and the evening will be my treat. That way, if I have to call this friendship off, I won't feel badly."

Bitch. The only thing you want to feel is Kathy's naked body. He looked at her strangely. "You wouldn't feel badly about killing a man, ripping out his heart and shredding his soul?"

Michelle peered into his eyes. "No."

He believed her. "I'll bring the wine."

"That won't happen for a while. Sorry. Bring yourself, but give me a few days to think of something. Call me after the move."

She jotted down her number as the curtain went up.

Fifty-Seven

The regional jet touched down in Cape City at 10:02 and Clint arrived at the gallery holding a box wrapped in pink foil and a yellow ribbon.

"How could I come empty-handed to such a breathtaking enchantress? You've stolen my heart, Eileen, and my most ardent wish is that you never return it to an empty shell."

Eileen Kimberly shook the box. "Clint, please tell me I won't be embarrassed when I open this." He remained silent, the women working at the gallery refusing to move as she unfolded the paper. "Clint, really…"

"The first moment I laid eyes on you, I felt my heart stop. Strangely, now it beats only when I'm with you. You do see my extraordinary predicament." Her face graduated from white to pink to red to crimson. "I have embarrassed you. I'm sorry. It's a friendship bracelet. I didn't think an inscription was appropriate at this time. If it were, I would have required a much larger piece."

"It's lovely, and very inappropriate."

"Wear it for me today and this evening, if never again."

She shooed the women away. "They've been unbearable to work with for the past month."

"I've missed you." He raised his hands in defence. "There, I've said it. I want as much time with you until Tuesday as I can beg, borrow or steal. Eileen Kimberly, I have never known a woman as intriguing or as compelling as you. Though you may break my heart, and deservedly so, I will fight to win yours."

Eileen slid the bracelet over her wrist. "Clint…"

"I have exceeded the norms of propriety, and I apologize. So let's get out of here, grab a burger and breathe some salt air. I want you all to myself for the rest of the day," he paused, "and for a little part of tomorrow."

They drove along the sandy coastline in Eileen's vintage Aston Martin.

"You're quiet, Clint."

"I've suddenly discovered I'm a pauper chasing a princess. This is some ride."

"Do you think so? That's so like a man. No man is a pauper who loves, though, I do agree, all women are princesses and," she slowed to a stop, "this place is for sale. The asking price is one-point-five."

"How close is the most beautiful neighbour?"

"A ten-minute walk."

"I want something closer."

"Ten minutes is pretty close" She looked straight ahead, trying to decide. Then she did an abrupt U-turn and screeched to a stop before he could catch his breath. "This is my property. That one, over there, is old. It's being demolished and about bloody time. The asking price for the property alone is one-point-seven-five. The owners will assume the demolition and the rickety dock is swimming distance from mine."

"Sold."

"You're serious about this."

"Very serious."

"I'll call them to set up a meeting."

"Thank you. Just don't tell them I'll be paying one-point-six, or that I'm falling in love with you. Let's meet them Tuesday, early in the AM."

Eileen went to bed that night to endure sleepless hours

of introspection and self-doubt. She didn't love old Kimberly, she never did. Ted was a part of her life she could no longer define and now a stranger had come into her life from nowhere to turn her quiet existence into a maelstrom. She had offered Ted a job, a million dollars, and still he was indecisive, afraid of losing a job he no longer wanted and staying with a woman he didn't love. Clint Evans wasn't like that. She believed intuitively he was a man who knew what he wanted from life: Life. Yet, she felt deeply for Ted Burberry for whatever reason, accepting that, possibly, history was meant to be rewritten.

She would be with Ted in March, golfing with another woman's husband, their longest time together since Valentine's which had come as a complete shock to her because, according to Ted, Kathy had a fling going on. Meanwhile Clint Evans, who had kissed her so passionately hours earlier, would soon be her neighbour and, she suspected, her lover. She cried herself to sleep thinking of Clint at the marina, not Ted sitting in his armchair looking out onto the ocean and the neighbour's back half.

*

Monday Eileen called in sick to her managing assistant who chided her with loving frankness. There was nothing wrong with getting on with life, she insisted. Eileen deserved a real man and Eileen agreed in a weak effort to placate the woman. An hour later she arrived at the gallery as Clint was meeting with the architect at his office.

They spoke for the better part of the morning, drove to the property adjoining Eileen's, met with the aged couple and agreed to meet with the realty agent later in the day when he signed a cheque for twenty-five thousand to be held in trust. He wrote another for the architect. Then he phoned Eileen. When she came to the phone, he thanked her.

"For what?"

"For being my neighbour."

"No."

"Yes. They'll tear the place down in March, start building in April and I'll move in sometime during August. In the meantime, perhaps I'll live on the boat you're going to help me pick out."

"Clint, last night, the kiss, it was very nice, but this neighbour situation, I don't know."

"I do. Listen. The kiss last night was from heaven, you're from heaven and your angelic touch has twice saved me from the loneliness of hell. If the guy you're with falls on your side of the fence, one day I'll invite you to my wedding, to a woman I'll never love as much as you. If he falls on my side, all I ask is a chance to love you more than anyone ever could. Eileen, I love you pure and simple." He took a breath. "Are we on for dinner?"

"No, Clint, we're not."

The pause was long and uncomfortable."

"Eileen…"

"Clint, I need room to breathe. You're suffocating me, and I don't know whether that's good or bad. I did enjoy the day with you. I simply need time."

"Time to toss a coin you've tossed countless times before."

"That's cruel of you."

"There is no cruelty to a man in love. I adore you."

"I scarcely know you. You came into my life from nowhere."

"Where does anyone come from when they're lost, but from nowhere? I love you." Clint stopped, the second hand of his chronograph ticking from ten to fifteen. "I'm meeting with the architect and contractors in early April. Until then I won't stop thinking and dreaming of you. Goodnight, Eileen."

"Goodnight, Clint."

*

Monday night Clint enriched himself by three thousand. Tuesday he boarded a noon flight to Bayville, forgetting Eileen. Wednesday and Thursday he stayed in his apartment hating the swirling snow keeping him from seeing his protégé and Kathy. Friday he called Melissa from his apartment to encourage her. He hadn't seen her for two weeks and he missed her. He wanted to see her. He called Michelle to wish her well in her new home and Eileen so she wouldn't forget him. Life was good and he went to bed a happy man.

Fifty-Eight

Saturday Jack Caden phoned Kathy. His business trip concluded successfully a day early and he was inviting her to lunch at the bistro, disheartened to hear Michelle was waiting for her. The movers were expected shortly, to empty Michelle's house of any and all things moveable and transport the load to the mission.

Jack roared with laughter, doubling over when Kathy added how Michelle gave away her soon to be ex-husband's car. In the afternoon her new furnishings would be delivered to the condo and the evening would be a Girls' Night sleep over. She had one more bit of news which she didn't share with him. She would soon give the developer a cheque for two hundred thousand to secure her eighteenth-floor condo and would initiate divorce proceedings immediately after Spring Break. Ted had no place between Michelle and Jack, nor did the kids and the house no longer mattered.

They spoke a while longer. He was eager to see her, touch her and smell her. He thought of her every waking moment and slept with her in his dreams, his words rekindling within her the heat of unrestrained and torrid arousal. He would call her during the week and hope not to die before once again feeling the softness of her lips and the warmth of her sweet breath.

*

Winter's demise was three weeks off as the most difficult

and darkest season struggled to survive. The falling snow was wet and heavy, the sea air mild and damp. Clint Evans stood where she had told him and moments after he arrived Melissa pranced along the boardwalk.

"Hi, Melissa."

"Hi, Clint. The day's perfect. I brought lunch and your favourite vodka. That is okay, isn't it?"

"Yes. We're here to enjoy and take some fun pictures that will show the Europeans another side of you." He looked around. "Are you sure you'll be alright? The day's pretty damp."

"I'll tell you when I'm getting cold. This time I brought an extra blanket."

"Then let's do it."

Melissa clambered over the rail, reached for her bag and ran into the dunes, leaving Clint to follow and by the time he caught up she had laid out the blanket. She passed him a shot glass, filling his and hers before taking his hand and walking him to the ridge of snow-covered sand.

"From here I can walk to the water in about a minute, thirty seconds if I run."

"I can barely see the ocean."

"I know, and without my clothes you'll barely see me."

"So to speak," he added.

She giggled. "What would you like me to do?"

"Let's have another drink while we're getting you ready. Then we can walk to the water, take a few stills, some footage and come back for a lunch."

He could see the excitement in her face. Melissa ran to the blanket, stooped for the bottle and filled their glasses. Clint sat, wondering how long he could manage in the cold. Melissa downed her drink and kicked off her boots. She pushed her suit to her knees in one fluid motion and leaned onto Clint's shoulders as she freed her legs. She tugged on her boots and stood with her Cossack tied under her chin.

"I'm ready."

Clint grabbed up his cameras, took her hand and they walked to the ocean. "This is bizarre, even for me. I'm walking with a beautiful and very naked girl on a deserted beach in the middle of a snowstorm."

"It's fantastic."

"Run for me."

She bolted, Clint's SLR freezing every step in time. At the water she ran in one direction, until she disappeared, his high-pitched whistle piercing the heavy air. She raced back, passing him, her footprints zigzagging in the snow until she once again heard his warning. She skipped to him, her eyes sparkling, her cheeks rosy red and she led him towards a hot lunch where he laid his equipment on the blanket, brought her into his arms and rubbed warmth into her body.

"You should try it, Clint. It's so fantastic."

"For a beautiful woman's body perhaps, not so much for a man's." She giggled and began serving her sandwiches and soup. "You tell me when you're cold."

"I will." Melissa stood and strolled to the boardwalk with her soup, returning without a care in the world. She sat cross-legged on the blanket and bit into her sandwich. "Will we do this down south in March?"

"Not quite like this. What I have in mind is a dinner setting on the veranda with candles and gorgeous outfits. You'll be a young, sophisticated woman with a lover who adores you. He's older and I think you should call him daddy, in a cute way, the way you call me. However the camera won't see him. It'll be as though he's photographing you. And you get to keep the costumes, which are actually designer pieces."

"Wow. Do I have a script?"

"Not this time. We want to see how you ad lib. It's not much different from what you've done in the past."

"I'll practice every night."

"Restrict yourself to Monday through Thursday. I want you well rested. I'll meet you Monday, the 15th at 1:00 PM. Please don't arrive late." He reached into his jacket. "This is the address. Call me from the lobby." She shivered. "You're cold."

"No, I'm happy."

He poured double shots of vodka.

"Run for me, to the water. Come back right away, collapse onto the blanket and let's see how you can ad lib. Do your thing, Melissa."

She filled her mouth, felt the instant heat, stood and ran away without looking to see who might be near, confident Clint would protect her. Within seconds she disappeared as he kept the camera running, a minute later she grew clearer, her knees buckled and she dropped onto the blanket in front of him, panting.

"Oh, daddy, I love running. The water's so cold and I feel so alive when we're like this by ourselves. I love you and I can't wait for our vacation, our special time alone." Clint breathed hard into mike, aiming the lens downward. Melissa smiled coquettishly, bringing her hands along the inside of her thighs until they met. "That's so naughty. But, daddy, can't we have one special afternoon together at home? I hate being at school and I almost never get to see you?"

Clint practically passed out. He put the camcorder aside.

"You're unbelievable. I wish I could have videoed your New Year's Eve special instead of your brother. What a production that would have been, not that you weren't superb. You were delicious. But, Melissa, were you serious, or acting? I would love to film you in your home environment. It would lend such an air of realism."

"Clint, I live on the hill, behind where you drove in." She pointed.

"But that's your personal life, baby girl. This is

business."

"I don't feel bad being like this. It's who I am and if bringing you home can help my career, why shouldn't I? No one else cares about me as much as you do. Can I call you?"

He hesitated. "That's pretty risky, Melissa."

"No, it's not. I'll stay home one day this week. I'll tell her I'm getting my period and that I ache all over. My mother never gets home before five or six and deadbrain never before three-thirty."

He combed a hand across his wet hair. "You're sure?"

"Yes, I'm sure. And I need to practice in real time. The mirror thing is getting pretty boring."

"Call me any day this week except Friday. Let's do this thing. You're right. Real time is much better and I'll bring a surprise."

"What?"

"Your itinerary for Europe." She sprang into the air, landing on him, forcing him backward. He eased her away. "And now I think we should go. You're turning blue."

"I don't want to."

"And I don't want you sick before your audition."

He stood, held out his hand to her, rubbed warmth into her and helped her to dress. He walked her to his SUV, drove her up the hill and let her off by her driveway, honestly taken aback when she leaned over and kissed his cheek, wondering when she last kissed Burberry.

*

The eighteen-wheeler drove away from Michelle's past life fully loaded, thousands of dollars headed toward those in need as the women headed downtown towards luxury and a fresh beginning. Sheila and Darlene met them, Sheila insisting on a tour of all the facilities before the dozens of deliveries began arriving, complaining to Darlene that teaching left a lot to be desired: like a luxury condo.

By late evening the apartment was complete, including the guest room and the four women sat around an empty pizza box discussing Vegas, the condos and Kathy's as yet unannounced divorce. Kathy and Michelle had decided Jack Caden and Clyde Van were not topics of interest, particularly for Sheila who, despite being exhausted, wanted to know what lesbians actually did before falling asleep.

Kathy responded "I kiss her the way I did in the spa for those jerks in Vermont, then we do the same thing you and Darlene will do because the spare bed is a double."

Michelle took Kathy's hand. "I can't wait for warm summer evenings and hot afternoons on the terrace. Oh, baby, yes. Yes," she screamed.

Darlene rollicked. "And I didn't bring anything to sleep in," she took Sheila's hand in hers, "on purpose."

Sheila shrieked "I'm freaking out here. I'm starting to need a man really bad."

The four hurried to their rooms, changed into bikinis and robes and headed for the elevators. The spa area was empty, the pool was lukewarm and the sauna was desert-hot with dry heat. They did laps and splashed in the pool, waiting for the privacy of the sauna to strip off their bikinis and wrap themselves in fleecy towels. Once in the apartment they talked incessantly until Michelle sank into Kathy's lap and Sheila curled into Darlene's.

"So, Ms. Burberry, what are your intentions towards one of my three best friends?"

"I love her, Darlene. We're going through a question period right now, which doesn't mean we don't adore each other. And who would have thought before her horrible night that this would happen between us? Not me, not in my wildest dreams."

"Or do you mean in your wildest prayers. I'm not surprised, Kathy. Michelle's always liked you. This little one and I told you that. Personally, I believe she's always

431

had the hots for you and never realized." Darlene looked down at Michelle purring. "They don't come more beautiful than Michelle and, since you, she's even more radiant. Don't you see that?"

Kathy stroked Michelle's hair. "The hardest part until she moved was not being with her or, worse, seeing her each day at school and not being able to touch her."

"The two of you are doing a great acting job. Sheila and I don't know how you do it."

Kathy glanced down at Sheila as the sleeping beauty curled instinctively closely into Darlene, wrapping her arms more tightly around her friend and confidante.

"Honestly, Darlene, doesn't that feel good?"

"Of course it does. I love the silly thing...most days."

"I know. You haven't stopped stroking her hair since she fell asleep. So would I if she were in my lap. Now just imagine if she were awake right now, apart from her freaking out again. That's how I feel with Michelle every moment."

"Then why the so-called question period?"

"We want to be sure, for you guys as much as for ourselves. We want to be certain we're not each other's crutch in uncertain times."

"And you think you can stop just like that, date guys, screw around in Vegas and maybe get married again?"

"That's what we don't know. It's what we have to find out."

"Kathy, darling, don't do it. Don't play games. One or both of you will get hurt. Tell the girl she's got you for life and cancel your condo. It's ridiculous, the two of you feeling the way you do and living one floor apart when you'll be in each other's bed at night. If you don't know, we do. We see you. I remember hearing about this prophet who died years ago, before I began reading his books. He was passing a man one day on the street, a stranger, and went up

432

to him. He said: "Sir, go this very instant to your home, to your wife and your children. Do not delay." I remember his words Kathy and, when the stranger asked why, the prophet responded: "because, sir, this afternoon you will die." Kathy, the prophet's words so scared the man that he went home to spend time with his family. He died later that afternoon."

"A fable Darlene, whose moral is lost on me."

"No, not a fable. The prophet saw the man as the man could not see himself. He saw death and the man died with his family because of the chance meeting. Honey and I see you and Michelle. We see the joy of love, not the pallor of death. You and Michelle should be together, not leave each other because you're both afraid and unsure. That's why Sheila and I are here for you." Sheila stirred. "Kathy, I'm totally into men, the pricks that they are, but I have to admit she is sexy."

"And she's going to ache like hell in the morning, this one too if we don't get them up. How do we put them to bed?"

Darlene's face came to life with the widest smile. "We don't. We put ourselves to bed and leave them here on the carpet." The glint in her eyes was unmistakable. "It'll be my first time with a lesbian. They'll both freak out, especially this one."

Kathy chortled, covering Michelle's ears. "I'm the hottest lover you'll ever have, babe."

Darlene's smile subsided. "Kathy, darling, I'm quite certain I meant sleeping, like really sleeping, and freaking them out, not me."

"Okay, I'll behave. Believe me, Darlene; one woman in my life is quite enough. Let's do it."

The next morning Darlene woke first, rolling over to see Kathy's face nestled in her pillow, not quite certain how to wake her until she thought to pinch her nostrils together. One eye opened, then the other.

"What time is it, babe?"

Darlene didn't answer. She stayed on her elbow looking down, leaned forward and kissed Kathy's cheek. "It's time for you to wake up and not do anything foolish. The girl loves you and you love her. Don't be stupid about it."

"Thank you."

"Now, let's go get the vacuum and clean the living room carpet."

"Let's."

The two threw aside the duvet, bounded from the bed and came to an abrupt halt in a living room devoid of slumbering bodies. The kitchen was empty, as were the powder and laundry rooms. The next room they peeked into was the guest room where Sheila and Michelle were in bed, wrapped in a tight embrace, their slip-clad bodies squirming in unison. The intruders stood in the doorway exchanging glances, covering their mouths, nodding silently and walking to the loveseat where they sat to watch and wait patiently for the closing scene.

Moments later Sheila sprang up from under her honey-coloured hair for air. "Okay, okay, this was her idea!"

"But, honey, you're so, I don't know, different," Michelle's voice implored. "Come to me."

"That's not funny, Michelle."

Michelle pulled her closer. "But I want you."

"Kathy! Come get your girlfriend off me, right now, or, I swear, I'll kick her in the balls."

"Honey, Michelle doesn't have balls. She has something so much sweeter. Darlene and I assumed you would know that, especially since, you know, Michelle's indoctrinated you. Mi amor, you did," Kathy continued, "didn't you? Or should we show honey how it's done?"

Michelle bounced onto all fours. "Oh, yes. Oh, yes, my darling. Come to me now. Take me. Ravage me the way only you can."

Sheila leapt from under the sheets. "Okay, I'm out of here. I'm taking a shower and I'm locking the frigging door." She scurried from the room, started the shower and ran back in. "Okay, ha-ha. The three of you are totally sick." She hugged each one and ran out.

Darlene and Sheila left after a day of unpacking more boxes, a swim, a sauna and dinner created by Michelle and her three sous-chefs in a kitchen any real chef would envy, and not before Darlene took Kathy aside.

"We love you, Kathy, and we love the girl who's head over heels in love with you. In Vermont we thought you might be experimenting. Who doesn't like vaginas? Half the world has them and three-quarters want them, but the two of you are not an experiment and very important to me and Sheila. So do not screw up."

"I won't, Darlene. I promise." The two friends hugged tightly. "Thanks. It seems I needed you this weekend as much as I wanted Michelle."

"You keep thinking that way. She's absolutely to die for. She's a gem and put your condo on hold."

They went to the door teary-eyed. Later, when Michelle asked what the matter was, Kathy smiled and kissed her. That night they slept in their bed and drove to work Monday in Michelle's bright yellow MX-5. During the pre-class coffee in the lounge Kathy managed a simple yet eloquent exchange with Darlene, her mouth forming two words, her eyes speaking volumes.

Fifty-Nine

The Final Month

Monday, March 01ˢᵗ, Ted Burberry left the house infuriated as much by waiting for the taxi as by the wife's absence throughout his entire thirty-six hours alone in hell, conceding inwardly that her absence likely made his hell a more tolerable place. Something wasn't right. The wife was spending less time at home and Eileen over the past month had become distracted in bed, if not unwilling, resisting his probes, preferring what he recognized as mundane marital sex.

Something was wrong. More importantly, his flight was on time and he'd be in Miami in four hours fully prepared to unseat his strongest rival.
*

At school Melissa didn't feel well. She went to Kathy's office for taxi money and left. Once at the house she opened the door to Clint Evans whose footprints in the snow from earlier in the day had filled in.

"I wasn't expecting your call so soon, Melissa. Can I have the grand tour?"

Melissa led him room by room around her home. "This is my room, where I began my career."

"Here's what I'm thinking. I like this daddy idea and not because you make me feel good, remembering my own little girl. The producers will love the realism. Why don't we do this? I don't think we need any clothes, just come up to mom's bedroom when you're ready and we'll shoot."

He left her and went to Kathy's bathroom to set up. When she joined him moments later she was dressed in a robe. She reached in, turning the water to its hottest level and tossed her robe into a corner.

"I'm ready, Clint."

"Good. You're with an older man, someone about my age and he comes in to surprise you. He likes you calling him daddy, like you did at the beach, and we go from there. Don't be nervous. Whatever we don't like, we'll edit."

Clint stepped into the hall, Melissa stepped into the shower and he filmed her for as long as he thought believable, breathing heavily into the mike as he walked closer.

"Oh, daddy, you're always sneaking up on me." She absorbed her body, giggling. "I look like a snowgirl, all white and fluffy. Don't I, daddy?" He breathed into the mike as Melissa's body rinsed clean. "Daddy, I have vodka in my bedroom. Would you mind, while I dry off?"

She stepped out. Clint went downstairs with his camcorder, calling her when he was ready and Melissa came bouncing down the stairs into his lens completely naked and carefree to enjoy a few drinks in the living room and pose irreverently while talking about the audition. Then Clint had an artistic thought and took Melissa to her father's bed. He photographed her running up the stairs, jumping onto the bed and glancing at him over her shoulder.

"Come, daddy." She was giggling. "I love this part most of all."

He had to admit he was tempted. Instead he directed her. She moved this way and that, obeying his every word until his free hand was perfectly focused, gliding over the youthful smoothness from her thighs to the small of back. Then he changed the angle to a head and shoulder shot and told her to be herself.

"Thank you, baby girl. That was spectacular and I have some important news for you."

Melissa sat on her father's bed like an innocent teenager. "What, daddy?"

"You're flying into an exciting career the day after you get back here from Spring Break. The production crew can't wait to work with you."

She flung herself at him. "Really?"

"Yeah, really," he added. "A private jet, the whole nine yards." He held her at arm's length. "There is, however, one itsy-bitsy thing you won't like."

She frowned. "What?"

"Your brother, deadbrain, I want him to come with us."

"What?" Melissa's body stiffened. "No way, the guy's a freak."

Clint pulled Melissa into his arms. "Listen to me. Yeah, he's a bit unusual. I agree. But I'd rather have him close, where I can keep an eye on him. He won't see any of your acting. He's seen enough of you already. In fact, after we arrive you won't see him at all. He'll have a separate hotel room. We'll spend one night in Paris and fly out the next morning on a private jet to your future. Believe me. You won't give him a second thought. You'll be too busy and when we fly home, you and I will spend a few days in Paris by ourselves."

"Where Clint? Tell me where."

"To the most exotic place in the world, a place with crystal clear water, white beaches, erotic nightlife that will revolve around you and where you'll have bodyguards to protect you and answer to your every whim."

Melissa fell back onto her father's bed. "Clint..."

"Yes, baby girl."

"I wish you were my real father."

He sighed. "Melissa you are the girl my daughter would

have become. She would have looked very much like you."

"Clint, I'm ready."

He cupped her breasts, squeezing gently. She was ready.

"Not that ready. Now let me get out of here before the cavalry comes."

Sixty

Monday night Clint went to a downtown restaurant, not intending to work until he saw the woman eating alone. He waited until her meal was finished and invited her to join him for dessert. The evening was too young for an attractive woman to spend alone in an empty hotel room and the nightclub across the street catered to a less trendy crowd, people who wanted to dance and hear each other talk at the same time. He also found her fascinating, delighted she came to town twice a month on business. He'd been living there since the fall and hadn't met anyone who didn't want a free meal, a weekend on his boat or marriage. He did want to marry eventually, for love, not a half-share in his business.

They danced all night. Her first kiss the most costly, her last the least remembered. By dawn he'd finished breakfast, alone as always, paid for with his recent revenue, thinking he hadn't taken more than what she would pay for a two-week vacation cruise. He was at the house at noon, the woman forgotten as quickly as the clothes he'd thrown into the hamper. Uppermost on his mind was Melissa. The girl was coming on to him and puppy love had no place in porn. She would have to learn that lesson and she would very soon.

In twenty days she would launch a career she never imagined after an audition which was now gratuitous, part of his original plan which he had promised her and could

440

not undo. He had not the slightest reservation that she would be the best, the most sought after, equally concerned the girl needed to feel loved, to understand he cared for her, that she was his baby girl and that's what the audition was all about. He phoned her and told her to connect with the internet.

"Melissa, you look different."

"I've started wearing my Valentine outfits. I don't feel good wearing girl stuff anymore."

"Girl what?" he questioned.

"Sorry. I meant teenage fashion."

"I didn't want to hurt your feelings yesterday. I thought you were getting a little caught up in the moment, you know, acting."

"I wasn't. I feel special when I'm with you."

"You are special. Listen, we'll make Myrtle Beach very special. I'll give you more time and don't forget Paris when we fly home."

"Do you want to watch me rehearse for the audition?"

"No. I have to concentrate on my work and you're too distracting."

"But I am your work."

"And a whole lot more. Oh, one more thing. Happy Birthday, albeit a day early." She gasped. "And I hope this is the last time you're dishonest with me."

"Clint..."

"I saw your student card in your backpack yesterday when I went for the booze. There's a big difference between seventeen and eighteen when you're sprawled out naked on a bed, or acting."

"I'm really sorry. After everything you told me, I couldn't let you think I wasn't ready. I've worked so hard to get here."

"The important thing is that in a few hours you will be a woman, officially. This could have messed up the entire plan."

"Don't hate me."

"How could I ever hate my baby girl? Goodnight."

"Goodnight, daddy."

He watched her close her laptop, clasp her hands to her face and walk in circles muttering. She should have been a pretty girl with a boyfriend, going to parties. Instead she had taken two years to drink herself into believing she had to show men her body to find happiness and escape. He plucked his cell from his belt.

"Hello."

"Clyde, this is Michelle."

"My favourite lady in the entire world."

"Tell me, do you enjoy ballet?"

"I'm not taking classes, if that's what you mean."

"Do you enjoy ballet?"

"I've never seen a production, but I'm willing to try."

"Then I'm taking you to an early dinner this Saturday. I'll let you pick me up at my condo on Harbour Front Drive at six."

"Ritzy. I should have gone into teaching." Or have a lesbian girlfriend with tonnes of money in the bank.

"It's the premiere. I'll be wearing a knee-length formal gown."

"And…"

"And a lock."

"Touché"

"No. That's the purpose of the lock."

"You know…I'm beginning to love you."

"It's the red hair."

"And your mesmerizing green eyes. Oh, and just to let you know, we're dating on the thirteenth. I'm thinking a spring sleigh ride, maple syrup in the snow, a cozy fire, dinner by candlelight and dancing into the wee hours."

"That's all you'll be dancing into, Clyde."

"I'm not running anywhere unless you push a lot harder than you are."

"So, we're on for the ballet"

"Yes, we are. Are we on for a sleigh ride and a cozy fire?"

"That's a little more romantic than I feel these days."

Yeah, right. Unless your groping and kissing your darling Kathy. "We'll be sitting under a horse blanket looking into a swishing tail and a horse's unpredictable ass. How romantic can that be? And at dinner I'll douse the candle if you feel yourself losing control."

"Can you cancel once you reserve?"

"Yes."

"Then go ahead. I'll see you at six on Saturday. Goodnight."

"Yes you will. Goodnight."

He watched Melissa performing without the same enthusiasm as Monday in her parents' house or at the beach on Saturday. She needed an audience. She needed to hear the words. He scrolled to the number and pressed send.

"Yeah."

"Tim-boy, this is Clint."

"What?"

"Wake up. Try to sound interested. A few things: Tomorrow's your sister's birthday. Make sure you buy her something nice."

"Like what?"

"A gold bracelet with an inscription and don't spend under a few hundred. I'll reimburse you. The inscription should read: I'm sorry.

"Sorry for what?"

"For being a little shithead. Secondly, I want you around when Melissa signs her contract. She'll need family with her. I'll have more details in a few days and, lastly, I want to meet you in Myrtle Beach. If you're going to work for me you're going to look professional. I'll give you a grand to get your wardrobe started and give you a few months to reimburse me. All my employees wear suits, so don't go getting lost on the beach and keep your phone open."

Timothy sat straight. "Yeah, sure."

"And don't forget your sister. She's the one who stopped me from snapping your neck. You owe her big time and we don't need anyone knowing you've spent that much on a sister you hate."

"I'm not that stupid. I'll get her the bracelet and keep my mouth shut."

"See that you do."

*

Wednesday Melissa awoke to another blah winter day. Her mother was in the kitchen making the lunches and her brother looked as confused as ever. There was nothing out of the ordinary. She'd been right not to expect gifts.

Kathy waited until Timothy went for his books. "Happy birthday, Melissa. Your father and I had no idea what to get you so we thought you'd prefer cash this year, for a spring outfit. I've noticed your style has changed recently."

She held out the cheque, proffered and taken without emotion.

"Thank you, mother."

"Would you rather order in tonight or dine out?"

"Order in Chinese."

"Do you want some friends over?"

"No."

Kathy nodded and went to her bedroom. When Melissa and Timothy left for the bus she phoned Ted and left a message to remind him that phoning his daughter after school might be a good idea and that he owed her two hundred and fifty dollars. After school Melissa was finding her studies increasingly difficult, unable to concentrate longer than a few moments at a time before dreaming of her audition and Clint Evans. The knock on her door shook her. Timothy was asking to come in. He had something nice for her.

"That Clint guy phoned me. He said to buy you something because you stopped him from killing me or something."

"He will kill you because he loves me and he doesn't like what you did to me."

Timothy held out the box. "Happy birthday. It's a bracelet." She opened the box, honestly surprised. "Inside it says "I'm sorry." I shouldn't have spied on you, Mel. It was pretty stupid."

"How could you, your own sister?"

"I know. Anyway, he says I'm going with you to sign your contract or something. He's getting me some clothes or whatever in Myrtle Beach for my job."

"Don't say a word of this to anyone. I am not going to university, no way, and Clint will kill you if he finds out you're in the way."

"I won't be."

"He wants to take care of us. He's going to make me rich and famous."

Timothy shrugged and Clint watched him walk out. He had no one to phone. The timing wasn't right for Eileen, Michelle would feel stalked and speaking with Melissa would only serve to delude her all the more, finding it more impossible each day to deny he didn't feel something for the girl. She was young, sexy and as beautiful as her mother's mirrored image, a young woman whose name might have been Melissa Moon in a perfect world. But the world was imperfect, their times together intentionally provocative and his temptation was overwhelming.

He phoned the occasional Mrs. Burberry as Melissa slipped in and out of her dresses, requesting the woman's services for the evening of the eleventh. He would take her to dinner to celebrate after the meeting with the notary and he felt he wanted to do something memorable for her, to thank her and he wanted her to dress the part. She was to buy a wardrobe for the occasion, go to the salon and he would compensate her apart from the usual five hundred. She was delighted. She hadn't bought a dress in months and, for the longest time, a visit to the hairdresser was an unaffordable luxury. She thanked him, her voice breaking, and she would meet him downtown at 7:00 on Thursday.

*

Thursday he left the house early. He had no reason to stay. He went to a haberdasher for evening wear and bought shoes. Friday he was six days away from the most crucial meeting of his life, looking forward to Saturday with Michelle and the following Saturday for the sleigh ride, dinner and literally penetrating her world. He chuckled, projecting his thoughts to the weeks following Spring Break, partly regretting he would never be privy to the full extent of the outcome.

Sixty-One

Saturday Jack Caden sat in his apartment, frustrated, wanting to call Kathy, wondering why she hadn't called.

"Hi."

"Can you talk?"

"Yes. He's not home yet."

"I want to see you at the bistro tomorrow. After what we've shared I'm not giving you up. I want you in my life Kathy and your friend Michelle will just have to get used to me."

"Wear protective coating the first time you meet her. She can be a hellcat."

"No sweat. How tough can she be?"

"Very, where I'm concerned." She paused. "I will meet you at the bistro tomorrow for a glass of wine, Jack, but no loving. You did a real job on me."

"I must be good. We're talking three weeks ago."

"You were good, are good. Let's say about three tomorrow for a late lunch."

"And the loving part?"

She wasn't prepared for that conversation on the phone. "I have to go. We can talk about loving tomorrow."

"Okay, just one thing."

"Which is…?"

"That I do love you, passion, my future Kathy Caden. See you tomorrow."

*

Saturday evening Clyde Van met Michelle at the entrance to her condo building. The doorman called her to announce the gentleman, dialling an intercom code unrelated to her apartment number. In the lobby the doorman helped her with her coat after both men found the appropriate words which brought a demure smile to her lips.

At dinner he couldn't take his eyes from her, or stop remembering her every curve and at the theatre he endured the two-hour libretto with surprising alertness, compelling a vivid imagination to commandeer the stage: the backdrop a glowing fire, the solitary prop a dishevelled bed, his leading lady Michelle Lopez lying naked beneath him, glistening from the fire's heat and her frantic release. As the curtain fell she slid her hand from his.

"Where were you, Mr. Van, if I may ask?"

"Mr. Van… hmmm, that sounds like a setback. When do you mean, exactly?"

"The last two hours, you weren't with me."

He grinned. "I realized immediately that ballet is a woman thing. No man wants to sit for hours watching other men springing into the air with painted-on tights or fluttering around on tippy-toes. And since it's a woman thing, and I'm accompanied by the most beautiful woman in the theatre, I thought you deserved my attention more than the dancers."

"Ballerinas."

"I didn't leave you, Michelle, not for a moment. I took you with me to next weekend, to candlelight and soft words."

"Clyde, I'm not ready for soft words." The hell you're not. "That's going to take a while."

The theatre emptied. He exhaled a deep breath, took her face in his hands and kissed her. "God, I've been waiting to do that. Listen, Michelle, I feel something happening, at least on my side of the barbed-wire."

Her face came alive with disgust. "That's so horrible of you."

He hesitated. "Yes, you're right, and I'm sorry. I suppose I wanted to beat you to the punch this time. Listen, we're on for next week until I hear from you that we're not going, there or anywhere." He touched her cheek. "Will I ever be able to make you smile and laugh?"

"I don't know." She reached into her clutch and passed him the ticket stub for her coat. "Let's have a drink and talk about it." She paused. "One drink, Clyde. A second will make you history."

He took her hand and she let him, wanting to hate herself. Any Clyde Van wasn't supposed to happen. She was deliriously happy. Her sad moments had become her times spent without Kathy. After so many quarterly excursions with no expectations other than the immediate, Kathy had come into her life like a quiet wave whose undertow she didn't want to escape. With Clyde Van and Jack Caden in the picture she and Kathy would drift apart, their love would grow faint and, with either man demanding time and attention, her time with Kathy would inevitably become contrived and seem dirty.
*

Sunday Kathy went into Ted's office with cool aloofness, speaking as she would with a stranger, an interloper and not her husband of eighteen years. Four days remained before their departure and the thought of sleeping in a hotel room with him was repugnant, completely impossible.

"Melissa's too old to sleep in a room with Timothy, or the inverse. It's not right. So he'll be in your room and I'll stay with her."

"You think I'm spending ten nights with a teenager in my room? Get real."

"Unless you want to pay for a third room, if that's even possible. Then you'll be responsible for the in-room movie charges and putting a lock on the mini-bar."

Ted weighed the problem. "Kath, you know what? I've got a bonus coming. The deal in Miami is virtually guaranteed, which is where I'll be again this week, if you're interested."

"I'm not."

"I'll get a third room." He leaned forward onto folded arms. "Why the hell are we even going?"

"Because, Ted, while you're off golfing, I'm finding a quiet spot and wearing those bikinis I showed you. We also booked six months ago with a non-refundable deposit." Kathy crossed her arms. "Moot point. Get your room and this is the last year. Daddy's little girl won't be around anytime soon after she leaves for university and when Einstein leaves he'll need a GPS device to find his way home."

"I'm serious about the room."

"I'm serious about my suntan. I'll also be registering under my maiden name, in case you feel the need for one last dip in the pool after a few too many scotches."

"I'll do my swimming in the ocean."

"Sure you will." She twirled. "I'll be home late. Melissa's in charge of dinner and make certain you're home Wednesday early enough to do more than sit in your office. The flight departs at three."

She closed the door quietly and Ted poured his first drink of the day as he watched her disappear down the driveway. She turned onto the gravel road before he reached for his cell. When he pressed end he poured his second drink and wondered why Eileen wasn't ecstatic. The worst case scenario would be the occasional dinner with the brood, scarcely interrupting a week with the woman he loved, golf and romantic sunrise breakfasts.

*

"Hi. You're late. I've been waiting here alone for what

seems like forever."

"Poor you, you don't even have our wine."

"Alfonso's slow today. Sit. No, don't. I want to see you undress for me."

"Jack, that's not becoming."

He ogled her. "Passion, you are the most incredibly gorgeous woman in the world. Turn for me, I beg you. Let my heart touch what my hands cannot." Kathy rolled her eyes and scanned the half-empty bistro, dropped her jacket onto the sofa and did a double pirouette. Her velour top came to her belted waist, her stretch tights aiding and abetting his imagination. "You are divine. Kathy, in my mind I see every millimetre of your perfect skin, your undulating and warm flesh."

"That was pretty fantastic three weeks ago."

"Superb." Alfonse brought the wine and menu. "I see that being married to you will require extra insurance."

"Okay, you're joking, and that's cute, except my life isn't cute right now, Jack. So I need you to either leave me alone or understand."

"I'll understand, passion. You know I will."

Kathy sat. "I'm leaving him in a few weeks, and before you ask, because it's convenient. I'm not implying he has privileges. Understood? In fact, he's never home. I mean, really, he's never home."

"I understand."

"What I want from you is more time. The sex we had was hot, but if you don't have time on your side that's good too. I'm giving you the choice and, having said that, we all have secrets, Jack."

"Meaning what exactly?"

"Meaning, recently, my life got complicated."

"So, you're telling me I'm in second place."

"No, Jack. You're tied in second place," Kathy's eyes welled with sorrowful tears; Jack reached forward to put a

451

glass of wine in her hands, "with a very special person."

"Are we talking about Michelle?"

"Yes, Michelle."

He leaned into the sofa. "I do have to admit that revelation is a little unexpected. How serious is the complication?"

"We don't know."

Jack swirled his wine. "Listen, Kathy, I'm not naïve. I don't imagine you and Michelle are exceptional in that regard and I do understand. You were both reaching out for comfort and compassion from someone you trust to get you through your difficult times. Not a thing is wrong with that in my view. I wasn't enough for you at the time. In fact, I can appreciate that I'm one of the problems. Listen, she's a beautiful girl and a great friend from what I've heard. All I ask is that you don't let temporary affection, as sincere as she is, keep you from me. I love you. There, I've said the dirty words." His laughter was forced. "How could I not after the injuries you left me to suffer in agony?"

Kathy curled into Jack's open arms. "How can anyone want to love two people at once?"

"Kathy, don't you know? It's not a question of how much we love, rather how little we hate. We seek love to dissolve or camouflage our hate, for whatever the reason or need. You both have someone to hate, from which has emerged your love for one another and my love for you." He kissed her heated cheek. "I do know Michelle will one day come to like me, I hope, and we'll get through this together. I'm not stealing you from her. I promise you and I love you." He clamped a hand gently over her mouth. "I do love you. I always have and I'm here for you as I always was."

When Alfonse happened by he didn't linger. The moment was for uncertain lovers.

Sixty-Two

"I don't want you to go home, Kathy. I want you to stay the night with me. I have another outfit you can wear. I don't feel like being alone and I won't see you for such a long time. Besides, we're already cozy and you'll hate going out into the cold."

"Mi amor, how can I stay away from my family, my loving husband and my adoring children for you?"

"That is not funny."

"Okay, bad joke. Then how can I stay away from you, someone who does love and adore me?" Michelle didn't answer. "I see I have to take the highroad here. You're right. Two weeks is a long time and I'll miss you. You know, mi amor, this could be the real litmus for us. I won't see Jack until I get back and it's pretty obvious your guy wants something I'm feeling very jealous about."

"I want you to be, because I was jealous when you went with him."

"Jack."

"Him, and I can't believe you told him."

"Why wouldn't I? He didn't seem overly disturbed, a little surprised maybe. At least he knows and can't say I lied to him. Anyway, if I had to choose between you, he'd lose and I believe you're on the verge of the same discovery, which you can't do if I'm hanging around telling you I love you, or if we do a recap in our lingerie after each date." Kathy reached for the phone. "Melissa, I won't be home

453

tonight. I've had a few glasses of wine and don't trust myself to drive. Tell your father and make supper. That's right, Ms. Lopez. I'll see you and Timothy tomorrow at school. Goodnight." She returned the receiver to the cradle. "It's the first time in weeks I've wished her goodnight, and she's probably skipping into his office to tell him I'm drunk on the floor, which he'll probably believe."

"What he believes doesn't matter. We matter." Michelle padded from the room, began pouring a bath and moments later leaned into the doorjamb wearing a towel. "Your bath's ready, darling." She waited until Kathy was by her side to open her arms. "And, Kathy…"

"Yes, mi amor."

"I promise you, not in our bed."

*

The next morning two sports cars left the building. In the afternoon Clint set up for his final week at the house, sad in a way that he was leaving. Yet his time had come to move on, to reinvent himself and open himself to untapped and unlimited potential. He'd been part of the family for ten weeks, closer to mother and daughter than they were to each other. Each night he listened to their most private thoughts, read their solitary expressions. He witnessed their vulnerable and intimate moments, he watched them dream and when they were gone he learned more about the father, the mother, the boy and the girl until their past and present melded to devise his future.

He experienced first-hand the final chapter of a family's history, co-written by Ted Burberry, a man on the verge of self-destruction; Kathy, disgruntled and uncertain, who once let her father determine her destiny; Melissa, a girl so driven to escape her bonds she would commend her mind and body to an absolute stranger; and, Timothy, whose mother rightly believed should never have been born.

After Myrtle Beach he would never see Kathy or

Burberry again, their fate quite clear in his mind for he had authored and choreographed the closing scene into which he wrote Michelle Lopez and Eileen Kimberly. Melissa's memories of him would diminish with time as her career would soon demand more of her.

At first he hadn't known what to do with her. Letting her infatuation with him flourish would be a simple matter, with or without Midnight Rhapsody. His dilemmas were explaining her, what he had done and not knowing how long the fixation would endure? Better that she continue with her career, focusing on becoming the best and the most sought after, that she would one day forget her whimsical romps on a snowy beach, her upcoming audition and her love for him. She would have so many others. And, he believed, she would likely forget her darkest moment: the instant she decided to become Midnight Rhapsody.

Timothy was inconsequential, destined to spend his life forgotten in the deepest crevices of everyone's mind.
*

Monday night he ate an early dinner of a meal replacement bar and diet soda. For dessert he had a double-vodka and drifted into a badly needed sleep. Tuesday and Wednesday he probed meticulously through each room of the house, including the kitchen, logging specific information alongside times as part of his agenda. He took panties from Kathy's clothes hamper which he would return and each day he climbed into his loft at the sound of screeching brakes.

He hadn't seen much of Burberry over the ten weeks, and not until Wednesday evening did he understand the extent of Kathy's disgust. Ted called at 10:00 to say he'd be arriving at 11:30, he hoped. Kathy took her shower early to avoid him and Clint devoured every twist, bend and stretch, thankful he had wired the family room where she went to sleep before Burberry arrived. When Ted did arrive, at midnight, he went to his office, opened the drawer and emptied the first glass before sitting to stare at the phone. He'd be calling only one person at such a late hour with his blood-alcohol steadily climbing. He poured a second glass and Clint reached for his headset.

"Eileen, it's me."

"I'm anxious for tomorrow night."

"So am I." He gulped his drink. "The Miami deal fell through."

"Their loss, and don't forget you were called in at the last moment."

"The gofer's already on my ass. When he hears about this...I don't know."

"Tell him tomorrow. I don't want this spoiling our vacation and, if he won't shut up about it, quit. What about Kathy?"

"I'm telling her next Wednesday at dinner, after the kids have gone."

"Is that a commitment?"

"Yes. I'm realizing how long I've waited and how unfairly I've treated you."

"Sweetheart, I will have one million dollars transferred into your account at the start of business next Thursday. Don't disappoint me. Don't renege on me and I don't want you in that house after tonight. Do you understand me?"

"I'm not a child."

"Precisely the point," Eileen retorted. "We're both touching forty and the games must stop."

"Don't forget you've played your own games over the years. We've each had our reasons." "Yes, I know. Although Kathy hasn't made you a millionaire, Randolph has many times over and, while we're on the subject, I don't expect you to let Lamarre walk all over you. The only million he'll ever see is on his life insurance. Get him off your back once and for all. Tell him you want a one-on-one to set things straight, your way, and invite him onto our twenty-metre yacht for an evening cruise after his dinner in our oceanfront beach house."

"Eileen, I have to keep my job. You know I need the independence. I can't be a lover and an employee at the same time."

"Where's the independence when you're continually worried about corporate sneaks and cheats? Tell them to get lost. Okay, so you're not interested in art. Do your own thing. A million still goes a long way."

"Yeah, I know." Clint agreed: a long way to cutting off your balls. "Listen, I will call him tomorrow. And I'll see you for a late in-room dinner. How's that sound?"

"It sounds like you'd better mean what you say."

"I do and, the gofer, I'll get him off my ass." He sighed. "It's late and I haven't had the best day."

"I'll see you tomorrow."

"Goodnight."

Burberry dropped the receiver into the cradle and poured another drink, his haggard face despondent, a man emasculated in his own house…well, not his house any longer, Clint mused. The beautiful and exotic Eileen was giving him a million dollars, yet he was sitting in his chair looking as though a high-rise window would suit his needs. The man had no self-esteem. He was soon to become financially secure and yet he feared the reaction of his squirrelly boss over a single business transaction. Clint closed his eyes, recalling the sweet taste of Eileen's lips and their reciprocating pressure. He would not allow Burberry to get in his way, feeling contempt for the man as Burberry sat in his office until plugging his bottle with its cork became a contest.

In the morning Clint maintained visual contact with the office, of greater consequence to him than Melissa whom he would see and touch again, although Kathy was the most important. These were his final and precious moments with her, the last time he would see the sculptured and animated nude of Kim Moon. Never again would she hold him spellbound in the morning and at night, snapping the clasps of her garters against the firm flesh of her thighs, posing in front of the mirror while her hands caressed and verified the perfection of each contour, transmitting sensual approval to her eyes. From the moment she woke until her departure, he traced her every move, not allowing her a moment to herself. Not his finest moment, merely his time to remember passion's heat.

By noon Clint had Burberry pegged. He hadn't called Chicago Corporate. What Clint couldn't understand was Eileen's willingness to invest a million dollars in a lost cause as he bid Kathy farewell. He kissed his fingertips and pressed them to the screen as she walked into the cool warmth of winter's final days. He hurried to the family room, watched her slide into the first taxi the way she did into the police cruiser two thousand nights past when his eyes crossed with hers and she didn't see him. At 3:00 he phoned the airline, verified the departure and began his systematic work.

In Kathy's room he boxed her jewellery, ornaments of value and personal items from her desk along with what little Burberry had to offer in the form of high end cufflinks and clips. From Melissa's room he took the two computers, her stash of vodka and her jewellery, which he discovered was from far from costume and, from the boy's, his computer and DVD reader. In the office he emptied the safe, changed the code to zero and emptied the desk completely. Lastly, he removed any and every trace of his sojourn from the loft, briefly lamenting the part of his life he was leaving behind. Everything went into the Lexus and from there to his apartment. From his apartment he drove the Lexus to the worst part of town, left the doors unlocked with the keys in the ignition, hailed a cab and went to dinner anxious to meet with his wife.

At the notary's office the transaction was completed with ease, though no one could hear his pounding heart, including Mrs. Burberry. When the meeting concluded he gave her a thousand in hundreds, kissed her and asked if he could see her again, for a romantic dinner in a fashionable part of town. She accepted. He would call her over the coming week and wanted her to wear exactly what she was wearing at the moment. She was beautiful in a way he had never seen her, though what she might wear underneath he would leave up to her. She was always beautiful, which is why he had approached her in the first place and over the past few weeks he had come to think of her differently. Seeing her so redefined a lot of emotions were coursing through his mind: Where he had gone wrong in life and why? Why were two lonely people who deserved better and, obviously had a comfort zone, not acting on it? He didn't know, but could she give him a chance? Yes, she would, and he kissed her in a way she'd never been kissed before.

Upon his return to the house he denuded the walls of paintings and photographs. He cleared the kitchen of dishware and glassware, cutlery and small appliances making everything ready for the next morning's refuse collection to which he added all sundry and personal items from the bathrooms and laundry.
*

Friday morning before Kathy woke to see Melissa in the bed beside her, Ted woke to see Eileen facing away from him and Clint was at the house, his SUV taking the place of the Lexus. By breakfast he transferred Melissa's quarter-million to his off-shore account, which was the easy part and Timothy's paltry ten-thousand was child's play. Clint's real work took the rest of the day, by which time the funds for the house were deposited, Ted Burberry was penniless and Kathy had sufficient funds remaining to pay for her new condo. He couldn't do to her what Kim had done to him, though his banking would not be complete for another seven days. Not counting his personal portfolio, which had diminished greatly over the past few weeks primarily due to Melissa, his current net worth had risen to three-point-three million dollars.

Sixty-Three

Friday night he cancelled the phone, the electric service and cable supplier, requesting the cell phone service not be interrupted until the following Friday. Then he swept through the house filling the calculated number of bags with clothes and linen with the exception of Kathy's wardrobe.

He loaded his SUV with little space to spare and made deposits into several of the city's mission boxes. Later he placed Kathy's wardrobe into the MX-5 and drove the sports car to the airport wearing a long coat, wide-brimmed hat and gloves At Arrivals he stepped into a cab and went to the casino hotel where he enjoyed a delicious meal, perusing the pages of Kathy's secret memento of Vermont and, when he finished, he travelled by cab to another hotel where he disposed of his hat and coat and took a third taxi to the house.

Saturday morning nothing was left but the furniture, appliances and big ticket items which the homeless society had gratefully accepted several days earlier and eagerly awaited. He did one last tour of the premises. He checked the attic, removed his ladder and sat in the empty garage with his final glass of vodka. He'd done it. He'd succeeded and was gone by noon. Not a single hair remained in the house and Sunday morning the new family arrived with key in hand as Clint lay troubled in his bed, staring at his account information. If not for Kim Moon he would not be wealthy beyond his dreams and had given thanks with the bottle of Dom Pérignon brought to his table the night before to share with Michelle, the ultimate bitch, the one woman he'd wanted to conquer above all others, the one woman who walked away without the slightest regret.

*

Sunday afternoon Kathy sat as far away as she could from the crowd with a tiny bit of beach to herself, her thumb hesitantly pressing send.

"Hello, darling."

"Hi, mi amor, just calling to see if you still love me after your wild night on the town."

"I do, darling. I always will and I miss you."

"Is he with you now?"

"Kathy, I promised you…not in our bed. No, he is not here."

"But you did."

"Yes, I did."

"How was he? Are you alright?"

"As a man I suppose he did better than most, though he could never replace you and, yes, I'm fine. So are we, you and me."

"Will you see him again?"

"I might, if he recovers. I'm not certain and he's not my biggest concern."

"You told him about us?"

"In a manner of speaking, pretty much when I blurted out "Kathy!" as I was, you know, right there. The look on his face was priceless. Anyway, yes, I did as I was leaving. I walked out on him."

Kathy coughed out a laugh. "You walked out?"

"I was thinking of you…obviously, and you were courageous enough to admit how we feel to Jack. I couldn't do any less. I love you, darling, and this proves that I do." Kathy began crying. "Darling, I don't need your tears, I need you. These guys won't come between us. Te aseguro,

462

mi querida."

"What?"

"Oh, God, you're so white. You see, that's something we have to discuss. When we make love and I'm speaking with you, you have no idea what I'm saying. You really must get with the sexiest idioma in the world, darling."

"What are you saying?"

"Chica, I'm telling you to wipe your eyes. You're coming home to me. At least that's what I want."

Michelle waited for Kathy's emotion to ebb. "So, what happened, mi amor?"

*

His dinner conversation with Michelle revolved around the sleigh ride and taffy pull until Michelle explained clearly that she was nervous. She conceded that he had planned a marvellous day, a delightful evening and there was no better time to discover where they were going. In the darkened room he watched her undress, she watched him and as they came together he asked why tears were streaking her cheeks. She shook her head in response and lay on her side awaiting his first hesitant and intimate touch.

He was gentle, his hands gliding across her body with long, seamless caresses. His first kiss was fleeting, his second more pressing and his third imploring. He swept her beneath his ready body with no effort, waiting, searching her eyes for approval. Finally, forcing himself not to plunge his way into her innermost warmth, he groaned contentedly and wiped away her tears.

When he was done he reposed on an elbow, caressing her nakedness, fondling her breasts, kissing her lips and her eyes. He loved her again, more ardently, until he abruptly pulled free of her in shock, causing her to gasp. The expression on his face spoke volumes and she slid from the bed unrepentantly, cloaked in darkness, explaining why as she dressed and left him to go home and miss her darling

Kathy.
*

Kathy began her days in the hotel gym and running the beach, remaining true to her trainer. She ended them strolling along the breaking waves, relishing the appreciative glances as recognition that her hard work had paid off. Her midday hours were spent lounging by the pool of the hotel which didn't cater to the typical Spring Break crowd, attracting as much attention as her daughter. She insisted Melissa and Timothy join her for a late dinner each evening, ostensibly as family time, the true purpose being supervision, after which they were given more time alone until mandatory roll call. Her evenings were spent shopping for bikinis and summer fashions with both dark auburn and deep red in mind, preferring a quiet nightcap in the lobby bar to sitting in a room with a resentful teenager.

Late Sunday Clint boarded a plane, trying to imagine the conversation he knew took place between the two women. He landed in Myrtle Beach four hours later and went directly to his hotel, not the least bit tempted to go in search of Eileen. He would see her in the morning.
*

And she was on time, dressed in a satin cover-up and low-heeled sandals which she removed at the hotel gate leading to the beach. Halfway to the ocean she removed her cover-up, Clint's mind instinctively flipping through the photographs in Burberry's album which were now in Clint's hotel room. The Rio was intended to conceal very little, albeit nowhere as tiny as Kathy's strings and she walked for the better part of an hour with him trailing close behind, concealed by oversized sunglasses, a billowy beach shirt and a baseball cap.

Burberry was a fool to let her out alone. The woman was a knockout. He followed her along most of the beach, remembering her kiss, bewildered by her decision to give a

464

million dollars to a man with so little to offer in return. When she turned to retrace her steps to her hotel he was gone, sitting midway between the ocean and Kathy's hotel. When Kathy sauntered onto the beach she didn't bother with a cover-up, simply a thong under the shorts she pulled off, a sports top and through his lens she was as close as he wanted her.

At 10:00 he was in his room when the phone rang. Moments later Melissa stood by his chair on the balcony.

"What have you been up to?" he asked, showing his disapproval.

"I've been sitting around the pool, sunning."

"Since Friday?"

"Yes, Clint. Why are you so upset with me?"

"Come here." She went closer, standing in front of him, not flinching when he pushed her top up past her breasts. "Now turn and show me your ass." His voice was stern. She faced away, leaned forward and pushed her jean skirt and panties to her knees. "This is why I'm upset. Look at you. I was expecting to shoot this afternoon at the studio, but how can we with these tan lines? What were you thinking? You won't get rid of them at least until midweek which screws up my entire schedule."

"Clint I'm sorry." Her mind raced. "Take me to a nude beach."

He chortled, disdainfully. "This is South Carolina in March. The entire place is a nude beach. Why didn't you wear a thong? At least then the lines would be appealing, these are just," he paused, "unattractive." She went to say something and he stopped her. "Give me a moment to think. This isn't good...after all our plans."

He stood and went to the fridge in his room. When he came out Melissa's clothes were piled neatly in the corner atop her running shoes and she was laying face-down on the chaise-longue.

"I can do it, Clint. Please don't be angry with me. I'm really sorry."

He gulped a mouthful of beer. "No, baby girl. I'm the one who's sorry, but you do have to get rid of those lines. I'll be back by five and I want you gone by then. Tomorrow I want you here at ten and gone at five as well. We'll do the shoot here on Wednesday between two and four. I would have preferred the seaside studio, but it's too late to change the reservation." He knelt beside her, drawing thick lines of suntan lotion from her shoulders to her ankles. "You know, with your make-up artist, your personal trainer and fashion coordinator who will absolutely adore you, not to mention your leading man, you'll have to get used to people fussing over you, touching you, Melissa." He massaged in the lotion slowly with both hands." When you're hungry order room service and pay cash. No booze. I'll leave money on the bed. Put on a robe and when the guy is gone I want you on this balcony working on this beautiful body. Do you understand? You have complete privacy, a view of the ocean and no one will see you. Feel free to use the spa before you go."

"Will you be here tomorrow?"

"Yes, for a little while. Now, flip over." He drew one line from her neck, across one breast to her toes, and from her other foot in a parallel line over her other breast. He massaged one leg to her waist, then the other before making widening circles across her belly and moisturizing her breasts in unison. "Remember what I said. Be gone by five."

She sat up, wrapping her arms around him. "I can stay later, Clint, if you want me to."

"No, you can't. I don't trust myself. I don't want you falling in love with me and, whatever you do, do not burn."

He eased her down and left. When he was in the lobby he scrolled to Timothy's phone and pressed send.

"Yeah."

"Where are you?"

"At the pool where we're staying."

"Where's your mom?"

"I don't know. She's at the beach or something. I think it's because she's wearing a thong or something. She doesn't come here except for lunch. It's like totally freaky, even though she's wearing some sort of a thing or something."

"There's nothing wrong with a cute ass, kid. I would think you'd know that after what you did. Anyone ever call you stupid?"

"Yeah."

"Okay stupid, get cleaned up. Put on a clean shirt, proper pants and wear street shoes. We're going shopping. Meet me outside your hotel, which means in the front, in thirty minutes. Do not make me wait."

He pressed end and went to the bar hoping to see Kathy, which he would manage several times over the next few days. By late afternoon Timothy had two suits and accessories for each which he was instructed not to wear. Rather, when packing to go home he was to take his new outfits and leave behind whatever he wasn't wearing.

At 4:30 Clint returned to his hotel room to see Melissa napping on the chaise-longue. He poured double-vodkas on the rocks and they stood gazing out over the ocean until he told her to put on her clothes and leave. He ate dinner alone, went for a late-night jog, asked the concierge to recommend a suitable bar and returned to his room with sufficient funds to enjoy the week and repay himself for Timothy's wardrobe. In any event, he was free to roam. Neither girl would remember him or likely leave their room for days, though he dared not sleep.
*

He was at the beach at an early hour, watching Eileen stroll

467

into her own world. He was tempted to phone her, go to her, but he wouldn't. She would come to him, when he would be better able to give her his full devotion. He let her fade into the distance, walked back a kilometre and sat in the sand waiting for Kathy who jogged by twenty-minutes later in her sports top and thong and, when she glanced over her shoulder the auto-focus kicked in and he waved with a smile from behind his camouflage and a zinc-coated nose. The woman was enjoying her freedom.

At 10:00 Melissa walked into his room, laid her clothes on the bed and joined him on the balcony.

"Hi, daddy."

"That's good, baby girl. Play the part until you become the part. Listen, since we're not working today, why don't we have a beer? The mercury must be hundred out here."

He squeezed past her in the doorway. When he came out she was standing, leaning against the rail.

"I suppose you're leaving."

"I have things to do."

"I thought this would be more fun."

"I wanted to enjoy our time as much as you, until you decided you'd rather have a white bum," he twirled her, "which isn't as white as yesterday. Thank you."

"Thank you, daddy. I won't disappoint you again. I didn't bring a thong because of my mother." Melissa took the beer. "Now she's wearing one everywhere. Even the young guys are looking at her like she's fantastic."

"I'll buy you one, Melissa, to wear when you're with her at the pool for lunch on Thursday."

"No way!"

He shrugged. "If she can wear one at the pool, you can. I want you to. Imagine her expression when she sees you with no lines."

"She's my mother."

"And you're a woman. Let her know that you are. In any

468

event, I want a series of shots of you at the beach early Thursday morning before my flight."

She squealed. "I'll do my absolute best for you at the beach. You'll be so proud. And, okay, I'll do what you want."

"Tell you what. I'll take one of you beside her, from a distance of course."

"That'll be too wild."

"You haven't protected yourself." He passed her the bottle. "Put some on and give me a few minutes. You're right. Lying here alone all day can't be fun. Thing is, I didn't bring a bathing suit. I was expecting to work." Several minutes later he came out wrapped in a towel and holding fresh beers. He gave her one and eased into his chair. "This will have to do."

"You have a nice body, Clint."

"Thanks, baby girl." He stretched out, smiling. "You're not so bad yourself. I think I'll be very jealous watching you act with other men."

She looked down at her body. "It'll be work, not like today."

"It's your career. Work is something we don't like." He sipped his beer. "Tomorrow's a special day and, talking of special days, I'm curious about something baby girl."

"What, daddy?"

"I'm curious about how you got into this great business." Melissa's frown spread across her face. She paled and he reached out to take her bottle, placing it with his on the balcony and guiding her onto his knee. "What's wrong, baby girl? Tell me everything. That's the rule. We have no secrets."

"When I was almost sixteen I went to this crazy party. One of the guys was my boyfriend. We never did anything much until then, but we did that night because I thought he loved me. Like I told you before, daddy, it was one time.

We were drinking and found a really dark storage room. We drank a lot more and I gave myself to him. When he finished he went out to get more drinks. When he got back he told me to take off all my clothes and we did it again because I loved him. Then he left again. He said he wouldn't be long and the next thing I knew he was all over me. He couldn't stop and when he finished he got up and turned on the lights." Melissa's voice sounded distant, almost phantasmal. "There were three of them, daddy, three of them laughing at me, saying they'd finally screwed the hottest whore in the school." She tried to laugh. "They were right. I was and I am the hottest girl in school. And I knew I could never trust another man, except you, Clint. They made me feel like a slut and soon everybody was talking about me. They made me feel dirty, but I wasn't. I thought he loved me. Then later I realized how they looked at me and how I actually liked them seeing me, so I started checking the web and learned how easy it was to make lots of money by doing the very same thing."

"No one will ever laugh at you again." Clint shifted. He brought his arms under her, picked her up and laid her onto the chaise-longue. "Melissa, I think you need me to stay a while longer today. I want you to tan your backside and rest. I'll get you a real drink to help you relax. I'll wake you before I leave. "

"Thank you, daddy."

He went into the room, coming out soon after with the double-vodkas she expected. They downed them together, she rested her head on the canvas pillow and he returned to the room for his camcorder. He spent the rest of the morning working on his tan, beating the heat with a few beers, recording her body from different angles and generally enjoying himself. At noon he ordered lunch with wine, woke her, ate with her and watched her lounging under the sun before he left to stroll along the ocean with no

470

idea of what he would say to Michelle after dinner.

*

"Hello."

"It's Clyde. Listen, before you jump all over me, I thought I was doing pretty well on Saturday until you changed gears and blew my socks off, not that they weren't already off. I want a second chance. We've been dating while you've been seeing a woman, which means you must feel something. Or am I missing something here?"

"I left you because I didn't want my vagina to become a depository for your male fantasy runoff."

"You didn't give me time to react. I mean, holy crap, I'm doing my best to get you off and you yell out a woman's name. Then you dress in front of me like a goddess. What the hell, Michelle? My head hasn't stopped aching. Okay, I know you don't love me yet, but do you feel something. Can we at least have dinner on Saturday and talk about all this?"

There was a long pause. "Clyde, I don't know."

"Kathy must be one special woman, but doesn't she have a friend?"

"Yes, she does."

"Does he know about this?"

"Yes, he does."

"I'm lost. He knows, I know, the two of you know. Who doesn't know? Michelle, please have dinner with me. I would prefer you scorn me to my face, not hang up to laugh behind my back."

"I never laughed at you. I cried."

"Then cry with me. Let me hold you when you cry. Don't throw me away."

"Call me Friday evening. I need time to think. So much has happened too quickly."

"Do you mean I'm still in the running?"

"I mean I haven't entirely discounted you. If you can

live with that, call me Friday."

"I will. Count on it. PS: I love you. I'm not giving up on us and, quite frankly, after all the women I've seen giving you the once-over, I'm not surprised Kathy would love you. Goodnight, Michelle."

Clint dropped his phone into his beach bag and ran into the first crashing wave.

Sixty-Four

Wednesday morning Clint sat in the sand waiting for Eileen as Kathy jogged by, jumping to his feet when the reality hit him. She and Eileen were going to cross paths. Kathy's morning runs lasted an hour, Eileen always ambled along and the moment he saw her could virtually pinpoint ground zero. The first photograph of the women waving was priceless, the one of Eileen spinning around seconds later and admiring the scarcely clad Kathy was once in a lifetime.

He assumed Melissa was in his room, anxious for her big day and he was in no particular hurry to see her. The week was working out better than planned. He was going home with thousands of dollars he hadn't anticipated; he'd discovered the true nature of Spring Break and Melissa's affinity towards him surpassed all expectations. He went for an early lunch and shopped for a bottle of champagne and the smallest bikinis he could find, feeling inspired. He was on a high and didn't want to touch terra firma anytime soon. Melissa was sunning when he arrived. He added the gift boxes to the others he'd hidden in his closet, laid them on the bed and called her in.

Melissa was speechless. She stared at the dozen colourful boxes wrapped with ribbons, then at him, her mouth open wide. She began with the smallest, wasting no time to tie herself into the thong and fit her breasts into the tiny triangles. The second one she placed on the spare bed and, by the time she was done, one elegant pant suit, a dress,

473

imported lingerie, stockings, garters and shoes lay on the bed with bracelets and necklaces. He poured a shot of vodka for himself, letting her ooh and aah over the wardrobe.

"This is how we'll do the audition, baby girl. Choose the dress you like best. We'll put the rest out of sight. We won't have time for a change. First I want you to dress in your shorts and tee-shirt, come in from the hallway, ad lib, undress and climb into bed, maybe prop yourself on pillow and I'll pour you a fake drink. Then I want you to have a spa while I set up and get changed. We'll shoot you coming from the spa, doing your make-up, dressing, exactly as you've practiced and we'll finish out on the veranda where I'll offer you champagne, not ginger ale this time. We need realism and we'll finish off with you stepping into the hallway. That should pretty well complete the first shoot."

"You said we won't have time for a second."

"Because of the lighting, so this is what I want you to do. I want you to wear these shorts and tee-shirt to dinner and come here when you're done. Put on your wardrobe and we'll do a night scene where you decide you can't stand the heat and you undress for your lover."

"Will my lover undress?"

He grinned. "I don't believe so. Although we never know, do we? Then I want you in one of these thongs and we'll go down to the pool for a dip. I bought a bathing suit."

She beamed. "Are you serious, Clint?"

He nodded. "Yes, I am, and tomorrow after a few poses on the beach we'll go for a long walk and play in the ocean for a while to top off your tan."

She was ecstatic. She stripped away the bikini pulled on her shorts and top and started putting away the spare outfit while Clint filled the spa. The session ended with very few retakes and as she dressed to leave Clint eased into the spa for a well-deserved soak, evoking a furrowed brow as she passed the door. When he heard the deadbolt sliding into

place he chuckled, toasting his self-discipline.
*

As usual Ted's call came late in the day. He would join Kathy for dinner at her hotel by 7:00, unexpected news which was equally unwanted. Eating dinner with mute teenagers was uninteresting enough, trying to ignore or make light of his absence over the week was impossible and Ted was no less eager to leave.

"Hey, guys. Give us some space for a few minutes. Your mother and I have something to discuss."

No further discussion was necessary. Melissa said she would eat something by the pool, Timothy took a fistful of breadsticks to eat on his way to the arcade and Clint caught everything on tape from the mezzanine deck.

"Good of you to tear yourself away from your bimbo, Ted. How's the golf? Getting many holes in one?"

"I'm divorcing you, Kath. I'll be seeing a lawyer on Monday."

Kathy's grin caught him off-guard. "You'll lose the house. You do realize you're handing me a million dollars or more."

"It's not an issue. I should have left you years ago."

"You never should have knocked me up."

"As I recall, your pants were the first to come off. Don't open the door if you don't want company."

"You're disgusting."

"Always the prude. Anyway, I won't be moving back in. My things will be moved out by the end of next week. I'm sure you won't take long to find someone."

She chortled. "Don't worry about it. It's under control and I'll meet with a lawyer as well on Monday."

"The girl's taken care of; the boy's your concern. That's the condition. You'll get a hundred percent of the profit from the house, and the kid. He's not coming with me. He wouldn't fit in and I'm actually moving to another city."

"Promotion?"

"In a manner of speaking." He looked her over. "Too bad you didn't start taking care of yourself like that twelve years ago, Kath. I might have stayed home."

Kathy's subdued mannerisms signalled the alert. Clint grabbed for the camera, Kathy reached for her glass of ice tea and Ted's disbelief was recorded forever. Kathy stood and sauntered away, telling the waiter the man at her table would settle the bill. Melissa was nowhere in sight at the pool and Kathy prayed she wouldn't be in the room. She wasn't and Kathy ordered dinner with a bottle of wine from room service before phoning Michelle to give her the good news, which included going on a vacation together before looking for new jobs.

*

"You're ravishing, baby girl. Now I want you to stand on the small x. It's very important. Whatever you do, when I'm part of the shoot, stay on the x."

"Yes, daddy."

Clint made a final adjustment to the camera, said "you're on," and began filming.

"Daddy, get me champagne. It's so hot."

She let the gentle breeze caress her, ignoring the camera while letting the lens capture more of her. Standing alone she undid the single button of her linen jacket, shrugging it from her shoulders and dropping it onto the chaise-longue. She cupped her breasts, inhaling deeply, unclasping the front of her bra. She raised one shoulder slightly, then the other, letting the bra fall to her elbows and onto the floor. She leaned against the stuccoed wall, her body bathed in moonlight and backlit by the ambient light of the room. She stretched seductively, combing her fingers through her damp hair, tracing them over her breasts and burying her hands into her pockets.

When Clint came out he walked to her beyond the lens'

476

field. He passed her a fluted glass, whispering, "Melissa, your breasts are delightful and perfect." He dipped a finger into his wine, letting a single droplet splash onto one nipple, then her other and he stepped into the shadows to see the glimmering affect.

"Daddy, I'll miss you when you leave. You always make me so happy, and then you leave me, like you did after our picnic in the snow and when we made love." Clint couldn't have asked for better. "Daddy, make love to me now." Melissa held out her hand, letting him take the glass. She brought her hands to the high waist of her flared slacks, unhooking the snap, undid her zipper and let them cascade to her ankles. Stepping from the crumpled linen she bent from her waist and handed them to Clint. She undid the right snap of her panties, pressing a hand into the apex of her thighs, then the left. "Daddy, please help me."

Clint pushed away from the wall, drained his glass and went to the camera to confirm the angle. He zoomed in for a close-up, showing her from her waist to her stilettos, perfection he knew would make most men hunger for more while driving others to the brink of insanity. He went to her, indicating she should face the sea. He put a hand to her back, while his other cupped her cheeks playfully before tugging away the flimsy material trapped between the soft mounds.

His voice was low, his breathing hard. "Let's go to bed, baby girl. I can't resist you a moment longer."

Melissa twirled. "Oh daddy, I've waited all day."

He stepped back, flipping the quick-release, putting the camera in his hands. He signalled Melissa into the room where she went to the bed, threw aside the covers, and lay in the middle wearing her stockings and shoes. Clint was breathing hard, not strictly for the camera, very aware Melissa was no longer acting.

"That's a wrap."

"I was sexy, wasn't I Clint?"

"Melissa, bring those beautiful knees together, unless you want me to die of a stroke. You're killing me. Come on. Take off your stockings and shoes. We'll have a few drinks and go to the pool."

She swung her feet from the bed, undoing her stilettos and pulling away her stockings. "You want me, Clint. I know you do. You're not like the other guys."

"No, Melissa. I'm a whole lot worse."

"I don't believe you and if you don't do me here, I'll make you love me in Paris."

She tied herself into the strings of her bikini. Clint changed in the bathroom. At the pool they were alone, save for another couple who weren't much different and he did have to concede that simply standing in the water talking seemed pretty foolish. At that she climbed onto his back and made him walk. She'd never felt so feminine and she somehow made her way around to his front, giggling at his expression when she draped his shoulders with the tangled strings no longer tied to her body.

An hour later he hoisted himself onto the deck, following her to the shallow end with a towel, meeting her halfway up the steps to cover her. The girl had no inhibition. The one element holding him in check was Eileen Kimberly. Melissa was sexy and alluring. She was his for the taking and if she were anyone else she'd be waking up in a few hours poorer and smarter. She simply wasn't worth the risk, yet he couldn't deny that her teasing for an hour in the heated pool had aroused him.

He watched her dress, refusing to join her and walked her to the elevator, telling her where to meet him in the morning. In his room he worked until well past midnight, clearing his mind with a walk along the strip and into the first lounge he thought would suit his needs. The late-hour selection was surprisingly good, her willingness even better and by dawn the girl who might have been Melissa's older sister had satiated both needs.

Sixty-Five

By the time Clint finished his room-service breakfast he'd completed the Myrtle Beach portfolio comprising a letter, a CD of select photos he'd taken over the past weeks and a DVD of exceptional quality. He walked the package to the courier who guaranteed next day delivery and went to the beach for his final glimpse of Kathy and Eileen. When both had come and gone he went to meet Melissa.

"How do you feel being virtually nude in public for the first time?" he taunted. "All told, one of my hands would cover more of you."

"I feel like I did last night in the pool."

"That was very bad of you."

"You didn't stop me. And you could have spanked me for being bad."

"And we both know what would have happened." He put an arm around her shoulder, partly for the benefit of passers-by who clearly envied him. "Listen, Melissa, I'm leaving in an hour. I want you at the airport with your brother no later than ten o'clock on Monday. The flight departs for Paris at noon. Make certain you have all your documents and don't bring all your outfits. You won't need anything else. We'll do some shopping in Bangkok before the meeting."

Melissa broke free and swung in front of him, jumping up and wrapping her legs and arms around him. "Daddy, are you serious?"

"I did tell you somewhere exotic." He squeezed her gently, enjoying the pressure of her legs and the feel of her youthful skin. "Melissa, over the last week I've come to see you as an enticing woman in every way. This daddy-baby girl thing we've enjoyed should stop. I'll find another nickname for you and, yes, I'm serious. We'll stay for three days, romp the best beaches in the world and return via Paris. We'll find a way to ditch your brother somewhere he won't get lost."

He set her down.

"Wow! Bangkok."

"Keep it to yourself until we're in Paris. Deadbrain has enough in his head to think about."

She was skipping, pulling him. "I'm going to be an actress," she yelled.

"You are already. Now, there's one more thing I want you to do for me. I want you to find yourself, establish who you are."

"What do you mean, Clint?"

"I want you to join your mother at the pool for lunch." He chuckled. "I want you to drop your cover-up beside her and jump in for a dip. When you're done, climb out using a ladder and lay beside her."

"She'll freak."

"She'll be as bare as you and you'll be asserting yourself, telling her you're no longer a child. Just be sure to cover up before deadbrain comes around spewing testosterone." He hugged her. "Time to go, Melissa. You be good until I see you and, if anything happens in the meantime, you phone me at this number. Can I trust you to trust me?"

"Yes, Clint. Why wouldn't I trust the man I'm in love with?"

He watched her skip away and went in the other direction. He had a drink at the bar, changed his clothes and strolled to her hotel not waiting long before seeing mother

481

and daughter come together. Kathy showed no surprise, as though she expected her daughter to show up the aging mother in some overt way, and returned to her book. Not to be snubbed and true to form, Melissa dived in, swam to the concrete steps, climbed out and strutted around the entire pool on her way to the beach, certain Clint was photographing her, not knowing he'd returned to his hotel to sleep away the afternoon on the veranda.

*

Thursday night he went out on the town. Friday morning he counted his proceeds, paid the hotel bill with cash, converted much of what was left to larger denominations and climbed into a cab. He was in his Bayville apartment by early-afternoon feeling decidedly disconnected. He dropped his bags onto the floor and focused on a single priority. He opened Ted's computer, logged in, completed the transaction within minutes and danced around his living room a million dollars richer, somewhat less frustrated that for the coming forty-eight hours he would be unable to monitor critical and sequential events, the consequences and his ultimate success.

He stared at the phone asking himself why, what the eleventh hour conquest would give him. The answer was satisfaction for him and lasting memories for her. He wanted her body one last time; he wanted her never to forget. He wanted her memory of him to be synonymous with Kathy Burberry. He wanted his loathing of her to be mutual for what she'd done to him, usurping him, stealing his love for Kathy the way she had so long ago, loving her and mocking him so many times.

"Hi, I'm calling to speak with Michelle Lopez, the beautiful and charismatic Michelle Lopez."

"Good evening, Clyde."

"Ah," he corrected, "the relentless and determined Clyde, who must admit he's been pacing the floor for the past little while."

"Oh, you must be exhausted. You should stay home this weekend and rest."

"I can't. I'm taking you away for the weekend."

"Sorry, I'm committed for Sunday."

"Then we'll carry on where we left off."

"Translation: Skip dinner and get straight into banging the lesbian."

"Did you rehearse these come-backs all week? That's not fair. Sure, of course, I want to make love with you. Who wouldn't, besides a million other guys?" His laugh failed. "And certainly not on an empty stomach."

"You can take me to dinner tomorrow at Gregorio's. Pick me up at eight. If I think there's a synergy happening between us by the time dessert's served, considering how you acted last week, I might be inclined to stay over for breakfast...in a hotel, Clyde, a five-star and don't bother packing a bag. For where we are at this point that would be a bit too comfy."

"Do I have this right? You're blaming me for last week, you want the best restaurant in the city, a five-star hotel and maybe you'll like me enough to make love with me and not scream out your girlfriend's name?"

"Yes, except for the screaming part. If your brain hadn't been lodged in your penis you might have thought of my little blooper as a compliment."

"A five-star..."

"Think of it as a lottery."

"I'm not flipping a coin for you. You've got your five-star and breakfast in bed. I won't be seen wearing the same suit twice in twelve hours and you're not going home before breakfast."

"Then, I'll see you tomorrow."

"Yes, you will, and Sunday morning. Goodnight, Ms. Lopez."

Michelle hung up and called Kathy, hearing the recorded message that service had been disconnected. She tried again with the same result. Clint tossed his phone into his suitcase and went to work in his apartment hoping and praying his portfolio had been delivered into the proper hands.

*

Ted and Eileen were at the nineteenth hole. She had honoured her part of the bargain and he would move to Cape City the following Tuesday after removing his most personal possessions from the house and Chicago Corporate would never be the wiser. They toasted an uncomplicated life. He was hers for the next day and a half without talk of divorce or the house, when he would leave her for the last time to maintain a lie.

*

In Chicago the CEO of Corporate raged into his intercom, ordering his secretary to get Lester Lamarre into boardroom PDQ.

"Where's Burberry?" he wanted to know.

"Sir, I believe he's in Myrtle Beach with Eileen."

"Is that a goddamn fact? Sit your ass down and don't say a damn word until this sick and perverted show is finished."

The gofer swivelled in his seat to face the wall-mounted plasma screen. Fifteen minutes later he had witnessed a slideshow of Eileen relaxing in the nude on her yacht and dancing amidst the turquoise waters and splashing waves of an island resort. He saw another woman jogging along a beach in the skimpiest bathing suit possible, smiling and waving at Eileen and more close-ups of that woman naked in bed with yet a third woman before he witnessed them kissing in a resort spa. He saw a young girl posing naked in a snowstorm and lying unabashedly on a deck chair, clearly in Myrtle Beach. Hundreds of photos meant to tell a sordid tale.

The gofer gulped. "Sir…"

"We're not finished."

The first scenes on the DVD showed the same young girl bouncing naked, fitfully on a chair in a bathroom, running in falling snow, crashing onto a blanket and speaking with her father. They saw her taking a shower and running to his bed. They watched her dress and undress several times in a hotel room by the ocean, they saw her leaving and reappearing, leaving once again as though she wanted to cry and they witnessed the heated argument between the second woman and Burberry. The closing scene was the most compelling, neither the CEO nor the gofer exchanged glances as Burberry's young daughter undressed for him in the moonlight and went to his bed yet again without the slightest shame.

Then the CEO flung the letter across his desk into the gofer's lap. "Read it, and try not to puke."

Lamarre took the folded paper and read: "Gentlemen, the woman onboard the yacht is Eileen Kimberly, not Ted Burberry's wife. She lives in Cape City, not Bayville, his mistress of twelve years. I am his wife, Kathy Burberry, the woman who passed Eileen on the beach, the woman in the restaurant throwing tea into his face when he told me he wanted to see me with Eileen the way he has with other women. He wanted me to sleep with his mistress. The girl lying nude on his chaise-longue is our daughter, Melissa. She's eighteen and he's treated her this way for years. What kind of man would do that to his daughter, photographing her in the nude, taking her to his bed, bathing with her and making her undress in a snowstorm? I've had enough. I can't take his abuse of me or her anymore. My daughter and I need your help or I will have to take this public."

The note was signed: Kathy Burberry.

"Lamarre, you get Burberry's sorry ass in here

tomorrow on the first flight. I don't give a good shit about Saturday, Sunday or that beach. You get him here and, whatever you do, do not mention a word of this."

The gofer left, struggling to control his breathing. He'd never so much as visited a gentlemen's club, let alone seeing such explicit photographs, videos and women kissing.

*

Ted Burberry's phone buzzed midway through the meal. Eileen's primary social dictum being no cell phones while dining. He returned the call after signing the restaurant chit, the one-sided conversation telling Eileen everything. The gofer was summoning him to Chicago and he didn't have the courage or think to argue for the sake of forty-eight hours. He left early Saturday after a ruined evening and quiet night. Eileen never argued and never raised her voice. She considered such behaviour beneath her and possessed a facile ability to transform the warmth of her flesh to the coolness of a marble figurine and her deep, dark eyes to searing coals.

Returning from her morning walk she cancelled her tee off time at the club, reserved a table for dinner alone in the dining room and went with him to the lobby where she left him with scarcely a simple "adieu" to spend her day by the pool. Her phone chimed quietly not long after. Her staff was well-trained, well-paid and aware not to call her unless all four galleries were burning to the ground with loss of life and old Kimberly never called. He had nothing to say. The response was curt.

"What?"

"Eileen, this is Clint Evans. I apologize. I should have called you at the gallery. I wanted to tell you I'll be in Cape City the week after next to meet with the architect and I want to see you."

"Clint, my manners seem to have abandoned me. Pardon

my rudeness. You know you can come by the gallery anytime."

"That's not what I meant."

"Clint…"

"I was thinking of flying in on the Friday, having a quiet lunch and I'd also like a second opinion at the architect's office. We will be neighbours, after all." She didn't answer. "I've caught you at a bad time."

"Actually I'm in Myrtle Beach enjoying a cocktail uncharacteristically early."

"I apologize. I'm interrupting your vacation."

"No, you're not."

"Eileen, truthfully, the architect needs another week. I want to see you. I was hoping lunch on Friday might lead to dinner on Saturday after visiting a few marinas, assuming you can manage some free time. Don't forget I'll need something suitable for my dock."

"You've forgotten one tidbit of information."

"Are you alone at the beach?"

"Clint, that's hardly your…"

"That sounds like a yes."

"Things happen."

"Yes, they do, like warm lips pressed together and eyes that don't lie. Our eyes said more during one fleeting moment than we did all day." He paused, "You can't have forgotten."

Eileen sighed. "No, I haven't, which doesn't mean I was right. You caught me at bad time. I wasn't myself, my defences were lowered."

"I don't believe you. We drop our defences when surrender is the best option."

"Clint, I'd love to see you at the gallery anytime. However, seeing you again outside of business wouldn't be appropriate."

Clint followed the second hand of his chronograph from

zero to ten. "Then I'll settle for the memory of a perfect kiss and the thought of soon having a beautiful neighbour. You have my number, Eileen, if you decide to mend my broken heart, which doesn't mean what we shared was wrong."

"Goodbye, Clint."

*

Ted Burberry exited O'Hare at 3:00, signed-in at Chicago Corporate an hour later and was escorted to the boardroom by security.

"Good afternoon, sir." He acknowledged Lamarre. "Sir, I suppose this is about Miami. I should have told you. I was wrong not to bring my failure to succeed immediately to your attention."

"We know about Miami and that's the least of your problems."

"I don't understand."

"You're not entirely alone in that regard. Sit down. I don't expect this meeting to last long and you'll be on your way home to the Mrs." Ted sat. "And how is Eileen?"

"She's fine, sir, although I left her at the beach. Thank you for asking. She told me to make sure I tell you how much she's looking forward to the tourney."

"Good, which prompts the question: Who is the Mrs.? I mean, who's the real Mrs. Burberry?"

Ted coughed a laugh. "Sir, I don't understand. She's the beautiful woman who came to the Christmas party."

"This one?" The CEO flipped over a photo of Eileen lounging on the deck of the yacht. "What is that, fifty, sixty feet?"

"Sir, how did you get this?"

"From this woman, Burberry," he turned over a photo of Ted joining Kathy and his kids for dinner, "the one with the boy and girl who bear a striking resemblance to you? She wrote to us."

"Sir, those are my nephew and niece, Melissa and

488

Timothy. The woman is their stepmother.

My brother's wife died ten or twelve years ago and this one's never liked me or them."

"Your niece?"

"Yes sir."

The old man breathed a visible sigh of relief. "Ted, I am glad to hear the young lady's your niece. Since last night I've been troubled by the distinct impression that you take photographs and videos of your daughter in the nude and force yourself on what is obviously a disturbed young girl…and apparently not for the first time."

Ted lurched forward. "What?"

"Burberry, we have something to show you and I don't want you out of this room until the filth is over, otherwise you'll be arrested forthwith. Security has orders to restrain you, should you attempt to leave without my permission. They're stationed outside the door."

The CEO initiated the slide show and left with the gofer at his heels. Ted came out from the darkened room thirty minutes later, pale-faced, his tan obliterated.

"Sir, that isn't me."

"And I suppose that's not Eileen either, or your wife's signature. You're depraved and a liar. The woman in the tub is your real wife and I can only hope not for much longer. Molesting your young daughter and forcing your wife onto other women is horrendous and scandalous Burberry. Your blatant stupidity about the entire affair is quite another matter. You're fired. Your career is over, here and anywhere else. You'll get your two weeks in the mail and not a cent more. Argue the decision and this information goes to the police." The CEO threw a manila envelope at him, adding "from your wife Kathy. Now get out and, when you get to wherever you do live, load up your vehicle with company property and call Lamarre. We'll do the rest. We will also contact Social Services on Monday to see that your daughter gets the help she needs."

Ted Burberry was issued from the company unceremoniously to hail a cab on the street and find a hotel. He checked-in, too sick to eat and went to bed too drunk to remember why.

Sixty-Six

Hundreds of kilometres away a man Ted Burberry never met, the man who brought his life to an instant standstill, sat on the edge of a bed feeling satiated, admiring Michelle Lopez' nude silhouette. He stood, framed a single memento with his cell phone, put her panties into his pocket and walked to the closest ATM feeling victorious.

When Michelle woke she rubbed the sleep from her eyes, scanned the room calling his name and phoned the front desk. Her next thought was to run to her purse, her second was to call Kathy only to hear Friday's mechanical message repeated. She dropped the phone into her purse, murmuring, tears streaming from the corners of shimmering eyes, telling herself Kathy would understand. Then she phoned the bank's hotline and, not long after, housekeeping interrupted Ted Burberry's drunken stupor in downtown Chicago.

He had no job. He couldn't go to where he wasn't wanted and he couldn't go home to Eileen to say what, that Corporate executives had seen her naked, that someone had photographed her with Kathy at the beach. Images of Melissa were running repeatedly through his mind, calling him daddy, stripping and acting like a common slut: images no father wanted to see, yet the young woman he watched was not his daughter and he hated himself for what he was thinking. He booked another day, ordered a bottle of scotch and wanted to kill his daughter to expunge her, to eradicate his thoughts of her.

*

Late Sunday morning Clint Evans packed his worldly goods into his SUV along with Rhapsody's laptop, Ted's, Kathy's and Timothy's DVD recorder. Then he drove to the furnished upscale condo he'd rented for a month. He went shopping for food and liquor, made the place look lived in and phoned the convincing Mrs. Burberry who'd spent the day in an excitable state as she waited for his call.

*

Kathy arrived home with Melissa and Timothy late in the day, anxious to speak with Michelle, to spend a few hours with her after dinner, until the taxi had no sooner driven off and the trio froze where they stood on the porch as the wary stranger opened the front door.

The exchange was incoherent to both the man and Kathy. The man's wife came to stand by his side, bewildered by the fuss as Kathy yelled frantically for them to leave. Her phone was out of service, as were the other two and the man refused her entry into her own home. She told Melissa not to move, Timothy to stay with her and she ran down the pebbled driveway to a neighbour where she called the police who came with sirens blaring and lights flashing, not knowing what to expect. Still the man refused the hysterical woman entry into his home. She ran to the garage windows and saw vehicles she didn't recognize. She called Ted from one of the officer's phones. He didn't answer. She left him Michelle's number and called Michelle who promised she loved Kathy with all her heart and would arrive as quickly as possible.

Michelle arrived within minutes. The women embraced, Michelle wiping away Kathy's tears and finally the man and his wife allowed them access with the understanding the police would evict her at his request and without hesitation or question. None of the furniture was hers. She asked to see the entire house and the man agreed, one officer staying with the children and Michelle.

No, she answered, she was not religious. Her boy and girl were alive, with her as proof and she had never owned a bible in her life, let alone dedicating her weekends to prayer. She asked to see the safe and the man agreed, not surprised when the combination failed. When the police asked permission to see inside, he refused, demanding a warrant, although he did produce the duly notarized deed signed by Theodore Burberry and Kathy tried Ted's cell again, cursing him. There was too much to understand amidst the confusion and the only one who spoke calmly was Melissa, politely asking to see her room.

The officers looked at the new owners who acquiesced. The room was no longer hers, nor was the closet. When she came out she smiled, thanked them and asked if she might use their phone. She called for a taxi, explaining to her mother and stunned onlookers without expression how she hated Kathy; how she wished she'd never been born. She was eighteen and legal, she reminded her mother, and free to do whatever she wanted. She was an adult. To which Kathy replied with caustic indifference that she wouldn't be an adult until she truly did leave home, not simply run off to the mall in a taxi. Adults didn't stay with their parents. They didn't go on paid vacations or to college with stuffed dolls swinging from schoolbags. And, she added, they didn't use their parents' credit cards. They moved out to face reality and get on with life. Kathy snapped her fingers and held out her hand.

The bank card sliced through the air, landing at Kathy's feet. Melissa walked to the door, calling her brother who ran after her. At the entrance she spun around more dramatically than she intended, her defiant expression fading, her throat constricting at seeing Michelle's arm wrapped tightly around Kathy's shoulders, the same cold and unyielding glare as her mother's challenging her. She

493

wasn't seeing her Spanish teacher. She was staring into the eyes of someone who would not think twice. The moment had come. She would stay in a hotel with her brother until they could find an apartment, she seethed. She had a job. She wasn't returning to school and they walked out leaving the driver to handle the luggage as the cops stood by like cartoon characters doing nothing. There was nothing for them to do until the detectives arrived, which wouldn't happen until Monday morning because no apparent crime had been committed. The man had possession of the house and proof of ownership. Kathy had frayed nerves, a passport, driver's licence and not much else.

Twisting in their seats at the bottom of the driveway Melissa and Timothy saw the familiar house for the last time. The door hadn't opened behind them and their mother wasn't running after them. Melissa was dazed. Finally she had the freedom she always wanted and suddenly needed Clint to tell her she would be alright. Timothy didn't care. He knew his sister. She was bluffing, being an actress. They would both be home within a week.

As soon as they arrived at the condo Michelle put Kathy into a steaming bath and gave her a mug of warm soup with a sedative, both women too disoriented and numb to cry or think rationally. Confessing to Kathy how Clyde Van had manipulated her, how he had stolen three thousand dollars, would serve no immediate purpose, she thought, until the chilling possibility leapt into her mind and she ran for her phone and Kathy's purse. Whoever had taken her house would have access to her banking information. This time Ted did answer the phone.

"I'm glad you called, Kath."

"You're drunk."

"Oh, yeah. Hey, listen, the woman in that bed with you, the hot redhead whose mouth you're trying to suck from her face in the spa, is she the famous Michelle?"

"What?"

"Why'd you do it, Kath? You're getting the house. Why'd you do it? Is that why you weren't with the kids last week? Was your dyke friend taking pictures of you flaunting your naked body up and down the beach? And talking about bitches, where's that little bitch Melissa?"

"You're talking crazy."

"They fired me. That's why they wanted me in Chicago. They fired me because they saw pictures of Eileen. Yeah, Eileen, my Eileen, the woman I love. How long have you known, Kath? You should have been honest. They saw her on our yacht... yeah, our yacht. She was naked, like you and your girlfriend. All this time I didn't think you were serious, but I saw it all Kath. I know, including Melissa humping a chair buck naked in our bathroom, running all over Surfers' Beach during a snowstorm without any clothes, calling some guy daddy, the same guy who did her in my frigging bed. I saw more of her in half an hour than I've seen of you since day one and you damn well know that wasn't me in the videos. Why did you do it, Kath? Put her on the goddamn phone."

"What are you talking about?" Kathy screamed. "She's not here. I'm at Michelle's."

"Why am I not surprised about that one?"

"Ted, you're rambling. I'm here because the house is gone, sold with your signature on the deed. So do something intelligent for once in your miserable life. Get back here. The cops want to interview you. I don't care about your girlfriend. I care about my mine and the fact someone who can sign your name sold my house the Thursday we left, the one detail saving your ass at the moment."

"I told you, I don't want the damn house. I don't need it and for your information I don't need the job."

"You're not listening, you never have. Strangers are

495

living in my house. They moved in while we were gone and there's serious money missing from my account."

"I don't need your money."

"Well, someone does, almost two million dollars, like maybe somebody who owns a yacht. I'm curious, Ted. How does an underachiever like you possibly come to own a yacht? Don't think I won't mention that one to the cops. So, yeah, smart guy, the cops want to talk with you."

His hysterical laughter turned to coughing. "Two million…and you think I'm talking crazy."

"My parents made provisions for me and you were never to know. So, you see, Ted. I never did need you."

"I didn't take your money and I can't come home right now." He tried to stand, stumbling onto the bed.

"I know. You're too drunk to fly and too drunk to listen. There is no home, not that we've ever had one, and Melissa's gone somewhere with Timothy. God knows where and, quite frankly, I'd prefer she stay away forever."

"You let her get away with too much. All those clothes, letting some guy do her in our house, in my frigging bed. It's your fault. I'll kill them both."

"Ted, just get here. The house was sold by Mr. Theodore Burberry….you, and the police don't seem to care that the description doesn't fit. They want you here tomorrow. They didn't care much about the house at first, but since hearing about the money they've had a change of heart. They want to know why you weren't with us all last week, why you're not here with us now and how someone could sign your name so perfectly."

"What the hell is happening? Is this Melissa getting back at you?"

"Ted you're an idiot and they should have fired you years ago. Oh, and while we're on the subject, you might be interested to know your precious Lexus was also stolen along with all our papers and computers."

Kathy crashed the phone into the cradle, finished a snifter of tequila and fell asleep in her lover's lap without feeling Michelle's teardrops splash onto her cheek.
*

Melissa waited until she exited the first taxi to call Clint, following his instructions to meet him at The Luxor and from there they took a third taxi to his condo.

"Calm down, make yourself at home and tell me what happened."

"Clint, we got home and these people were living in our house."

"Did your mom phone the police?"

"Yeah, and when they came I couldn't take all the yelling and crying. That's when I did like you said and brought him with me." Melissa began crying. "And, Clint, they took Rhapsody's computer. Whoever they are, they know all about me, my account information, everything."

"Not necessarily and the worst thing you can do is panic. Listen, we have to be calm about this. There's nothing we can do until tomorrow and this evening I have a dinner engagement. I wasn't expecting this and I'm meeting with an investor I cannot disappoint. He's this close to investing millions with us."

"Clint, I had almost a quarter of a million." Timothy's eyes bulged. "It can't be gone, not after all my hard work."

"And probably isn't. On the other hand, if it is, the money was tax-free Melissa. We can't exactly go to the authorities." He paced the floor, deep in thought. He passed her a vodka, told her brother to get a soft drink from the fridge and explained what he thought was a workable solution. "Listen, Melissa," he reached into his jacket for his chequebook and pen. "Here's a hundred thousand. Cash it after we return from Paris and I'll insist on an additional one-fifty when we sign in Bangkok. You're worth every penny. You should have been with me to see their reaction

497

to your work." He downed his drink. "Listen, by the time we get back the thing with the house will be straightened out and you won't be a dime out of pocket. By the end of the year you'll think of a quarter-million as chump change."

She took the cheque. "Clint, I can't."

He chuckled. "Thanks for the morals. Yes, you can. You've earned every cent and tonight you're both staying here. The kid can have the guestroom, that way I don't have to see him when I come home. You take my bed. I'll crash on the sofa and try not to disturb you. In the meantime, there's a spa in the master bedroom. Go relax while I keep deadbrain occupied."

Half an hour later Melissa came out dressed in Clint's bath robe. He went to change and before he left he gave Melissa a tour of the kitchen, telling her not to drink until after she finished cooking. He didn't want to lose his star actress to a needless accident and he kissed her the way any woman would want to be kissed by the man she loved.

And not long after he kissed the woman he had come to love, the woman who portrayed the grieving Mrs. Burberry throughout the final days of the nerve-wrecking ordeal, with as much passion and urgency as he could muster before she'd barely opened her door. They went to dinner and after the extravagant meal he bathed with her in her bath and laid her upon her bed, awakening her innermost latent desires.

He spoke to her of the weekend to come, when he would take her for a sleigh ride, drip hot sap into the snow, lick the hardened taffy and run towards the heat of a raging fire to warm their quaking bodies. They would dine by candlelight, hold hands and stare into each other's eyes knowing the moment had come when they could no longer deny the truth. Alone, shadowed by darkness and accented by the moon's faint glow, he would see her, all of her, sweep her into the air and love her as insatiably as Michelle Lopez, Kathy's lesbian bitch he had made his own.

True love had come to her. She called him tender names and loved him unequivocally. She purred in harmony with his every intimate probe, her body jerking and twisting involuntarily in a final crescendo. She sank limply onto her mattress, her body beaded with sweat, his hovering over her, his eyes closed, kissing her one last time as she drifted into a place of calmness and pleasant dreams from which she would at long last awaken beside a man who loved her in a way she had always wanted to be loved: with caring and devotion.

Clint would no longer visit his favourite restaurant for breakfast. After reimbursing himself for the cost of the evening and the money he'd paid her in salary over the past few weeks, he wiped her cards clean, dropped them into a sewer and returned to his condo where he was genuinely shocked to see Melissa sitting in the living room dressed in the pant suit she wore for the photo shoot in Myrtle Beach, the button undone and holding out a glass of wine.

"Melissa, it's six AM. You should be sleeping, sweet thing. "

"I know. I slept until one. Then I had a bath and waited for you." She put up a hand. "Clint, I'm eighteen. At least until I start working professionally, let me be yours. They say a girl always remembers her first. It's true, and now I want to forget what happened to me. I want something nice to remember. I've reheated the spa every hour and haven't had a sip to drink since you left. I know what I'm doing. I know what I want. And I know what you want. I can see it in your eyes."

"Melissa, I'm exhausted." He reached for the wine, pulling away her jacket with his free hand. "Thank you. A good soak sounds like a perfect ending to my evening. The investor committed to financing your first five films based solely on your audition, something that will make your producer extremely pleased. You've done it, Melissa. You reached for the stars and have become one, but our lovemaking should wait until Paris, the City of Lights or, for us, the City of Love. You need to rest."

"And I need you. We can make anywhere our City of Love."

He filled her glass and walked with her through the bedroom, where they undressed, and into spa. They stayed until 8:00, climbing out with no time left to sleep. Melissa was euphoric; she'd never experienced such tenderness and Clint felt satiated. The cabdriver called up at 9:30, they arrived at the airport at 10:00 and the flight departed at noon. Clint sat in the aisle seat, Melissa in the centre and Timothy by the window where they could watch him. The flight would land in Paris at midnight local time and once the cabin lights were dimmed Melissa held his hand and leaned into his shoulder, not quite certain how she could ever pretend to love another man.

At the hotel Clint gave Timothy a key for the room he was to share with his sister, until the boy stepped in first and she closed the door behind him, standing defiantly in the hall. Clint shrugged, held out the key to his room and walked in behind her. Seven hours later they were seated in the private lounge of the executive jet service.

Sixty-Seven

Monday morning Michelle called in sick and Kathy called in to give advance notice of the resignation she would tender later in the week, explaining to the dean how Melissa had made a decision to pursue an acting career and Timothy had dropped out with parental consent. Within the hour Sheila and Darlene were on the phone to them and when the conversation ended with an invitation from Michelle to join them that evening, they listened to the message from the police suggesting a time to meet at the house with the occupants, the notary and the real-estate agent who witnessed the transfer. Much to the relief of the new owners, the two invitees concurred formally that they had not previously seen that particular Mrs. Kathleen Burberry. The transfer of the house was legal, finalized with the authentic signature of the sole previous owner and, whether she was the real Mrs. Burberry or not, the house was not hers in either case. No documentation to the contrary existed. And where was the supposedly real Mr. Burberry?

The detectives asked about the children. Kathy answered that one was an adult and had left with her brother calmly and without provocation. She looked directly at the uniformed cops, grinning at the humourless irony, adding that before witnesses Melissa had become Timothy's legal guardian. They asked whether Kathy had photos of them. She didn't. Why would she? Nor did she have her bank account or car.

The cops were stoic. Whoever planned the scheme had spent several days or weeks in the house, particularly with access to all four computers between Thursday and Sunday when the money went missing. They inquired as to the contents of the safe, she enumerated each item and the man of the house allowed the detectives to view the actual contents which were entirely different. Not only did the perpetrator infiltrate her home, he knew everything about her.

They canvassed the neighbours who corroborated every word Kathy had spoken. A bank fraud unit would be in touch with her, they advised, cautioning her to expect the worst and understand that most vehicles stolen generally ended up in Russia. When they inquired as to what time they might expect Ted Burberry, she said never and advised them of the yacht, volunteering information about Chicago Corporate. When one of the detectives contacted Lester Lamarre the gofer recounted the sordid story with relish, offering to forward a copy of the CDs and DVDs. The cop agreed and thanked him. When he returned he asked Michelle politely whether they might continue the conversation at her condo Tuesday or Wednesday evening, adding when she didn't answer, or at the precinct.

*

Ted's wake-up call came early. He called down for the healthiest breakfast on the menu. He stood in the shower for as long he could tolerate the ice-cold water, terrified, and dressed in freshly laundered clothes before he left for O'Hare.

The one remaining seat available on the earliest flight to Cape City was in First-Class, departing an hour before he could speak personally with his financial account manager. Vivid images of Kathy kissing Michelle so unabashedly and of Melissa refused to leave him. What he could remember of his conversation with Kathy was impossible, what he'd seen on the boardroom screen and hotel television was impossible. But if everything she said was true, his million would also be gone. Eileen would despise him and never forgive him. He fought the temptation to use the in-flight phone. What he needed to know was personal in the extreme and the wrong answer would drive him insane, a perceived threat to other passengers and he pictured himself being shackled to his seat and dragged away in handcuffs.

He was the first passenger through the Jetway and into the concourse. He hurried to the member's lounge and made the call, holding his breath, listening absently to fingers tapping on a keyboard. When the tapping stopped he sank into his seat. Eileen's million had vanished and his reaction sincerely surprised him. He began laughing, first quietly, then more loudly, pretending he was engaged in conversation until the ruse began to wane and he went into the men's room to escape the side glances, sitting in a stall unable to stifle his tearful moans as he pressed send.

"Good morning, Ted. Let me tell you before you say anything cute or stupid that I'm furious with you and you will never put me in second place again. Where are you?"

"I'm in deep shit, Eileen. I'm in shit up to my neck. They fired me. The bastards fired me."

"What's your point? And where are you?"

"I'm at CC International, on the can getting pissed. They fired me. They think I'm a sex maniac. They showed me the filthiest pictures and videos of my daughter and of Kathy with another woman. They even had some showing you with her at the ocean and the ones I took of you on the boat."

"What?"

"It doesn't matter, nothing matters. They know about Kathy and the kids and they're reporting me to Social Services."

"You sound pathetic."

"The police want to see me in Bayville. The house was sold while we were gone last week. Kathy says everything's gone: the cars, the papers," he gulped, "everything."

"And you're telling me this sitting on a public toilet in the airport instead of coming to me like a man and talking it through rationally."

"I didn't know what to do."

"People don't lose their homes unless their targeted and someone knows what he's doing. Why would anyone target you?"

"I don't know."

"But you assume sitting on a public toilet will help you get it back. And how's Kathy coping? Is she alright?"

"How's Kathy?" He chuckled. "Kathy, my prudish Kathy turned sex bomb is a card-carrying lesbian. She's shacked up with someone called Michelle."

"Good for her, if she's found somebody she loves. As I recall, you didn't seem to mind meeting the dozen or so I've introduced you to at the galleries. I also recall you didn't want to stop talking about them the first few times."

"Before I saw my wife mocking me in public and my daughter prancing around outside in the nude for some sick bastard with a camera."

"She's a young woman, probably enjoying herself with a special friend before she dives into a rut like the rest of us. Or she's impressionable. Either way, I'm more interested in "my prudish wife" and, "mocking me." How can she mock you if you supposedly love me?"

"You know what I mean."

"Actually, I don't."

"I do love you. I never would have married her if I'd seen you first." He swallowed the few remaining drops in his old-fashioned, expelling a wet cough. "Eileen, the million, it's gone."

Eileen remained poised and silent. She hadn't

misunderstood, quite the contrary. She finally did understand everything very clearly: She'd been a fool, and more the fool to think she had ever loved one. "The million I gave you for the house is gone and you're telling me this from a toilet?"

"Yes, and I think Kathy said they took two million from her."

"Excuse me. You're saying Kathy had two million dollars to lose?"

"I never knew. I thought she had something like a few hundred thousand from her parents that she was keeping for the kids. She never told me."

"I don't blame her, and Ted..."

"What?"

"My vacations are sacrosanct. I value my alone time and speak with virtually no one."

"I know."

"I can think of one woman I paid attention to on the beach during the entire week. Does Kathy have auburn hair cut short, and in the photographs is she wearing a string bikini?"

"Yeah, they saw you standing there, gawking at her. Why would you do that?"

"Don't be absurd. I admit I looked twice. I remember thinking how great she looked and how proud she must be of her body. And, if you must know, I was envious of her joie de vivre attitude. What would Kathy think of that, Ted, me being jealous of her? Imagine the irony. I understand completely how anyone would want to love her. She's looks great. What I don't understand is why she would ever have married you. More importantly, why did I ever think I could marry you? The million was a gift, a frivolous gift I can afford. What I can't afford is you, Ted. The beach house will be put on the market with the boat. Whenever you can, send me a single e-mail with your next address. As the transactions are finalized I'll send you half the profits minus my initial investments and I'll absorb any loss. Do not call the galleries or show your face at the beach house or I'll report you for harassment and take out an injunction against you. I'll be staying at the mansion with Randolph this evening."

"Eileen..."

The line went dead and Ted's old-fashioned crashed unheard onto the floor.

*

Redialling would be futile and humiliating, which would make her despise him all the more. Eileen regarded weak men with the greatest contempt. He shuffled away the broken glass, went to his lounge seat, ordered another double-scotch and soon after requested a courtesy cart which carried him to Departures. Outside he gave the limo driver directions and slumped into the plush rear seat thinking it was a wonderful day to die. The winds were furious, the sky was dark with ominous clouds and a vicious rain was assailing its victims from every direction.

Awakened by the chauffeur's discreet coughs, Ted struggled to open his eyes. He clambered from the limousine, refusing the man's help, paid with a single hundred-dollar bill, punched in the code and staggered through the slowly swinging wrought iron gates dragging his carry-on around the far side of the beach house to the dock where he mindlessly let go of the handle.

He was drenched, shivering from the swirling cold. Once onboard he stripped away his wet clothes and changed clumsily into the warmth of cords, a thick sweater and foul weather gear. He went to the bar, checked the watch she had given him and tossed it onto the floor, laughing. He poured a scotch, one double, then another, taking the bottle with him to the canvas-covered pilot station where he brought the engine to life, the GPS and radar screens already blurred.

He stumbled onto the deck, crashing to his knees, half crawling, half lurching from cleat to cleat to cut the lines free. The weather was a proper bugger, his aging neighbour would have remarked, though to Ted the stormy skies and violent seas were an invitation. The ocean was taunting him, calling upon him to prove his worth as a man, beckoning him to pit his prowess against all odds beyond the relative calm of the private bay and channel leading to the surging breakwater. He raised the storm jib and mainsail, trimming both to endure a course into heavy weather and high seas, not waiting long to assist the difficult steerageway with autopilot. No other craft was visible on radar. He alone ruled the sea. He was the king of the sea.

He made his way hand-over-hand to the companionway, stepping onto the ladder, losing his footing and crumpling unceremoniously onto the cabin floor. He tossed away the empty bottle, crawled to his knees and grabbed for another. He'd been in open water for thirty minutes and the vessel had pushed its way through five nautical miles. He clawed his way into the cockpit on his knees, stayed on all fours and stared up at the following seas. Pulling himself to the helm he eased the throttle forward, the howling wind silencing the purr of the responsive engine, thick white walls of seawater relentlessly washing over the bow and deck.

Eileen would see the empty dock the next day, he jeered. She was so damned proud of her boat. Not once did she let him bring the thing safely to dock. He was a laughingstock at the club. Now who was laughing? He was. Ha-ha. He threw his glass overboard and brought the bottleneck to his mouth, guzzling, spilling more than he put into his throat and bloodstream. And when would Kathy hear, or his slut daughter with all her daddy this and daddy that? And who was her daddy in her videos. He wanted to kill them all.

They were all deceitful whores. His precious daughter, doing what she did while pretending superior innocence; his wife, acting so pure, all the while fornicating with another woman; and, Eileen, who had scarcely spoken to him all week, married to an old man and thinking more of her money than a man who loved her. He wanted to kill them all.

He coughed scotch through his nose. He'd been at sea for an hour, sailing twelve nautical miles south by east. By daybreak the autopilot, the wind and current would carry the yacht a few hundred miles offshore and another hundred by the time any search would begin. He lurched violently sideways. The wind was increasing and the yacht began yawing more aggressively. He took a long swallow of scotch, lowered the mainsail, maintained the jib and overrode the autopilot until the vessel stabilized, screaming into the wind at Eileen that he didn't need her for everything. He didn't need her for anything. He'd never felt so exhilarated. He was conquering a raging sea. He screamed until his throat burned and his head ached. He was doing what no one at the club would dare. He was invincible. He gulped more scotch, screaming this time at himself, asking why he had waited so long, why he'd wasted his life with one woman who didn't love him and another who loved her money more.

He stared at the bow rising into a dark sky, the yacht teetering atop a foaming crest, torrential rain slashing at the windshield as he plummeted into yet another black abyss. He corked the bottle, buried it into a pocket and crept from the cockpit. In such turbulent seas freeboard didn't exist. Water was swirling wildly across the deck in all directions and he was mere centimetres from an ominous sea reaching out to claim him, ridiculing him. He clung to the railings, inching his way forward. He grimaced from the stinging in his eyes. Seeing beyond his hands was impossible and his head throbbed from the strain. At the bow, he lay flat as the vessel rose into the air, yelling at the sea that he would never lose again, that he was the king and, as the vessel began its rapid decent he leapt forward, grabbing for the narrow rail at the bowsprit and wrapping his legs around the port and starboard vertical members.

The seawater washing over him was incredibly cold, the rainwater beating at his face incredibly fierce. He reached for the bottle and gulped what he could before the bow plunged into another menacing black trough. The bottle flew from his hand and he cursed. He swore at the sea and the rain, at Kathy for destroying him and Eileen for deserting him. He swore at his daughter who had shown the world how deeply she loathed him.

Frigid seawater swirled around his legs and waist, penetrating his rubber gear and numbing him. He tried to look aft, unable to. His end was at hand. The yacht's pitching was worsening and suddenly, of all those he hated, he hated himself the most for discovering moments before his death that he was a coward. He let go of the rail with one hand, gripping the anchor chain. He was sobbing invisible tears, not for those he was leaving behind but for himself, regretting he'd left the gun in the cabin. He would not lose consciousness until the thirty-kilo anchor carried him halfway down the two hundred metres in seconds. He would not have time to struggle for breath; his eyes squeezed shut to block out the terror, his fingers grasping at his throat. He would crash to the sandy bottom already dead from severe cold and pressure, his body twisted and disfigured, insignificant and meaningless, to sway to and fro like a mariner's ghoulish inverted pendulum.

He reached behind quickly, pulling chain frantically from the hawsepipe, wrapping himself as he went as much for stability as for his final purpose. Not once in his life was he as focused, working with frozen hands, babbling, ignoring the spittle flying from his lips, the dribble from his nose and blinding tears, determined not to drop the shackle tied to the anchor line. Then he was done, the last half-metre of chain looped snugly around his neck, the end link connected to one at his chest. He lay flat, freeing the anchor, holding the shank in place with what little strength he had left, waiting, anxious to escape the vicious maelstrom swirling around him. Ted Burberry made ready, bracing one foot against the hawsepipe as the vessel hovered high in the air, obeying the sea, preparing to drop. He knew when and cried aloud one last time, heaving the anchor forward, propelling himself downward through the railing and over the roller to scream his last precious breath into oblivion.

Sixty-Eight

Tuesday Melissa and Clint went for breakfast alone and arrived at Roissy-Charles de Gaulle Airport at 6:45 AM with Timothy in tow. The security didn't care who they were and the executive jet service had them listed as Mr. Clint Evans and Family. The flight to Dubai lasted six and a half hours, touching down at 5:15 local time.

Melissa kept her nose pressed to the porthole throughout the entire trip, when she wasn't talking business with her manager or being pampered by the in-flight attendant. Timothy was plugged into the entertainment system. Once settled into the hotel they took a taxi along the Dubai Creek to the downtown shopping area where Clint gave Melissa carte blanche to shop for a few outfits. They dined under the stars in Old Dubai and Melissa both felt like a worldly lady and looked like one. However 4:00AM would come early. The jet would be one of the first in line for take-off and Clint didn't want delays.

As Melissa lay sleeping in his bed, he stood on the balcony overlooking the city. The girl's dream was hours from being realized. She loved her body, strived for adoration and arousal and he questioned whether he would miss her, think of her being with other men who would enjoy her as much. He thought not. Business was business. She wasn't in love with him, thanking him the best way she knew how: with her body, with what she valued above all other things. To Melissa that was true love.

511

He stayed awake throughout the night. Flying did nothing for him, he would sleep onboard. He pulled away her thin cover and sat capturing each angle and curve so that he would never forget his greatest achievement. He woke her at 3:30 with gentle kisses, tender caresses and what might be their final moment of rapture before he would lose her to others. At 6:00 AM the sleek jet soared from the runway. Timothy was asleep and Melissa was nestled into her man's side.

*

Michelle and Kathy stirred from their sleep together at home, the gloomy weather well-suited to their mood.

"Mi amor, what's wrong. All you're doing is fussing over me and you haven't said a word."

"Kathy, I didn't want to make things worse with everything that's happened to you. My god, you lost everything, including your job."

"No, you're wrong. I quit. Remember? Now be honest with me."

"I've held something back from you, darling. It's about Clyde Van."

Kathy forced a smile. "So I have lost everything."

"No darling. No. It's not what you think." She took Kathy's hand. "I wanted to be sure, like you want to be certain about Jack. When you were gone I went to dinner with him. The deal was, if I felt comfortable I would stay for breakfast and you would meet him. The reality was, we had sex, I felt comfortable enough to stay over and when I woke up I was out three grand and two bank cards. Van was gone."

"Michelle," Kathy swept her friend into her arms, "you should have told me. Do the police know?"

"That I'm an idiot. Yes, they do. So does my bank manager. They also think I'm a whore. I know they do."

"Well, mi amor, if you are, you're mine. And don't ever

use that word near me again. I love you too much."

"So you forgive me.?"

"I have nothing to forgive."

"How are you…and tell me the truth?"

"I'm fine. The money was a bit of a shock, I must admit, so much for a rainy day. Frankly, it's more frightening to realize someone was in my house for such a long time. In that way, I'll never be the same. What I don't understand is why they left four hundred thousand in my account. They took everything else."

"Six hundred," Michelle corrected. "I owe you two. Remember? And I'm so glad you told me mañana, mi querida." She sat up. "What about Ted? What do you think?"

"Down deep he's a coward. We won't see him again. I can't believe the horrible things he said about Melissa. He was ranting."

"So Melissa's still a concern?" Michelle asked.

"No. She's gone and I don't feel sorry for her. She was hateful and I never understood why. As for Timothy, somehow I believe I'll never see him either. And I'm fine with that. He'll never make it in the real world."

"And Jack?" Michelle questioned. "You haven't mentioned him once since all this happened."

"No guy wants to walk into a mess like this. I'm surprised you haven't run away."

"Darling, you have a definite way of expressing yourself at times which is not amusing. Should I call Sheila and Darlene and tell them what a hurtful thing you just said?"

"No, mi amor, phone them and tell them I'm stupid."

"I'm staying home with you today. We'll work through this together, minute by minute, day by day and if the cops call they know where we live. One way or another we will figure out who did this to you."

*

513

Eileen crawled from the bed in her private boudoir feeling nauseous. She had lost a million dollars and the man she was supposed to marry in June. She called the gallery, excused herself and fell against her pillows, writing notes into her agenda. After breakfast she would call a realtor, get rid of the beach house and, in the afternoon she would meet with the marina to figure out what to do with the yacht. She was furious with herself, in no mood for work or idle chatter with her husband and she took time to calm herself and dress before going to him in the solarium.

"Randolph, dear, I would like a moment with you, if I may."

"Come in, Eileen." He smiled warmly. "You haven't called me dear in such a long time. Might I be correct in supposing this is the day?"

"I don't understand."

"You want to ask me for the divorce."

She sat by his side and took his hand. "Yes, I do, and I will not hold you to our agreement. Nor will I forget you. We will continue as friends. I also expect you to attend each of my exhibitions and buy my artwork."

"Will you be happier?"

"I will, although not because I'm leaving you."

He smiled. "Burberry?"

Eileen showed no surprise. "I should have known. No. Not him, not anyone. I simply feel the need to redefine myself."

"I won't contest and our agreement stands. I've known about him for quite some time, choosing never to broach the subject due to pure cowardice. I didn't want to lose what little part of you was mine, though I never thought we would last this long. I hope I haven't imposed excessively on your life to the point of ruination."

"You helped make me who I am. I thank you for that and you won't lose me."

He nodded. "Go now. I daresay closure will come very quickly, within a few weeks. Favours are always ripe to be plucked from an ever-blossoming tree. I won't keep you dangling."

"Thank you, dear," she put her hand over his, "dear friend."

At noon Eileen met the agent at the beach house and midway through the tour she notified the Coast Guard who immediately computed the tonnage of the missing yacht, the available power, the current, wind and waves recorded over the past twenty hours. The Sea Babe was located a few hours later drifting not quite two hundred nautical miles offshore without power, the storm jib torn away from its mast and the anchor missing along with the captain. The salvage company of Eileen's choice was dispatched to meet them, took charge of the vessel and Eileen would be available later in the day to meet the Coast Guard and Police. There was no doubt and no hope. Ted Burberry gave himself to the sea by choice or by negligence and would never be found, which, in Eileen's mind, was fortunate. She had come across his carry-on and had found the CDs and DVDs, storing them in a safe place. He took the easy way out, rather than facing adversity and proving his innocence.

The Coast Guard was satisfied and walked away offering practiced condolences. The police were equally respectful and sympathetic; particularly the Captain of Major Crimes who was married to one of Eileen's preferred clients and left with information relating to Chicago Corporate and Kathy Burberry. That's all she knew. He killed himself for the simple reason that someone had gone out of their way to destroy him. She had watched the videos, photos and read the letter. She would over and over again, trying to make sense of what happened. She called the gallery to advise she would take the week off and the next day a For Sale sign was posted at the beach house.

Sixty-Nine

The three weary passengers slept through most of the seven-hour flight to Bangkok, landing at 2:30 local time. In the taxi, Clint sat in the middle separating them. Melissa's deep feeling of resentment towards her brother for what he did to her in January hadn't diminished. She scarcely acknowledged him throughout the thirty-six hours since their departure from Bayville. Hearing that Timothy would join them for a dinner cruise was too much for her and, as much as she loved Clint, she insisted dinner cruises were romantic, for lovers, not pimple-faced kids. She was right, of course, and Clint ordered separate tables for a moonlit evening on the Chao Phraya River Rama.

First though, he had a business meeting to attend. He left Melissa in charge of her brother. They could use the hotel facilities, particularly the pool to combat the 30° C humid weather and they were not to drink alcohol. Clint flagged a cab, asked a simple question and peered through his side window to see what he could of the clustered and congested city. Upon arriving he told the driver to wait and climbed out. The same scenario happened three times before he waved two hundred-dollar US bills into the rear-view mirror and told the driver to get serious. He wanted quality, not disease, and that's when he met Mr. Lim.

Clint could never retrace the route, unable to see the walls of passing buildings for the people. He expected to see something dirty, something smoky and dingy and smelling of sweat. Not so. The building's façade had the appearance of a boutique hotel and an elegant woman greeted him at the reception as she would any other guest checking-in.

"No, thank you. I don't want a lady. Thank you. I want your boss. I want to do business with your boss, Mr. Lim."

"I'm sorry. I do not understand."

"I have a girl, a very special girl with beautiful blonde hair, white skin and she's untouched." Clint smiled. "The girl wants to work for Mr. Lim. If you don't help me, someone else will and I believe you will be in serious trouble when Mr. Lim discovers your lack of vision on his behalf." Clint positioned the DVD reader towards her, showing the woman excerpts of Midnight Rhapsody and Melissa. "Please tell Mr. Lim I am anxious to meet him. He will not regret our meeting."

The woman was taking too long to consider the consequences of disturbing her boss and he walked away.

"No! Wait. I will ask if he wishes to see you."

She returned moments later, bowing discreetly. Lim's office was modern, the décor Western and the man imposed a no-smoking policy. The niceties were formal and brief, Clint concentrating not to feel out of his element.

"Why do you think I will be interested in your girl? We have many pretty Western girls in Bangkok."

"With respect, what you have are young girls screwing old men against their will. This one is eighteen and lives to be seen, touched and praised. Believe me. She is addicted to the type of pleasure you offer your clientele. Your best clients, the ones with sufficient money to pay for quality will pay for her and reserve her. She will be one of your best."

"Where does she come from?"

"From far away and she doesn't want to return. She wants to escape her past and enjoy her work. Her name is

Melissa. Her working name is Midnight Rhapsody. Midnight dot Rhapsody to be more precise. You may have heard of her."

Lim shook his head. "More importantly, is she truly untouched?"

"Yes, except by me. I did not want to bring you damaged goods, nor did I want to bring you an untried baby. She is good, very good."

"My girl says you have proof." Clint opened the reader. The DVD ran for ten minutes. "How much are you asking?"

"Twenty thousand cash, in US dollars."

"Too much."

"Too much, my ass." Clint stood, closing the reader. "You would have begun making a return on your investment in a month, with something very different for yourself on the side. I would also have thrown in her brother as a goodwill gesture, something for your clientele with more acquired appetites. Goodnight, sir."

Clint made it as far as the door.

"Fifteen thousand US."

"Thanks. I think I'll work at finding Melissa a better home."

"This is the best home, with the best clients."

"Twenty thousand and I throw in the boy. He's seventeen and stupid, yet somehow I believe you'll straighten him out." Lim hesitated, rubbing his chin. "So, Mr. Lim, do we have a deal?"

"Yes we do, Mr…"

"That would be Mr. Twenty Grand, in large denominations. I'll take ten now, ten later this evening when I bring them to you. I'm taking her to dinner on the Chao Phraya. Expect her about eleven."

"Mr. Twenty Grand," Lim smirked, "you will leave with your ten grand…and one of my girls who will accompany you to dinner. She is one of my best girls in many ways. I would suggest that you do not give her reason to doubt your integrity."

Clint's face broke into a wide grin. "I agree. Keep your friends close and your enemies closer. Or, in this case, those you don't know or trust. The boy will be a perfect dinner companion for your lady, as long as they're not seated at my table and as a precaution I would suggest you advise her not to discuss our agreement with the kid."

Lim nodded. The men shook hands and Clint returned to his hotel with the girl whom he put directly into Timothy's room before going to Melissa."

"The deal's done, Melissa. They want you. I even brought deadbrain a treat, a dinner companion. He's getting laid big time as we speak."

"Deadbrain has a live woman in his room? They're screwing?"

"As we speak and, unfortunately, you and I won't have time until later. You have to dress and look special for me. The producer's name is Mr. Lim. He'll love you as much as I do. We're meeting him after our romantic dinner and I want you to look your best for him."

"I will, Clint."

He watched her dress one last time, thinking she had come a long way since New Year's Eve. The dinner was a great success. They danced, kissed under the moonlight and he wiped away her tears. She loved him, he loved her and destiny had brought them together.

He helped her from the taxi, assuaging her fears. Mr. Lim would love her, they all would, and together they looked at a cheerful Timothy and his smiling companion. He had never looked so content as the foursome walked into the building. They acknowledged the receptionist, climbed one flight of stairs, then another and went into a room where a bundle of American bills lay on the table. Their Thai escort bowed to Clint and left them. The evening was young and she had more work to do.

Clint took the money, faced Melissa and slid her purse from her shoulder. "Melissa, I want to show you something."

Melissa saw the photo and gasped. "Clint, that's my mother."

"No kid. This woman is my ex-wife and history's worst bitch. Her name is Kim."

"Clint, I don't believe this. They could be twins."

"That's right. They very well could be, which is what drew me to your mother in the first place and, subsequently, to Midnight Rhapsody which was completely unexpected. So, you see, as I told you that day on your father's bed, you are the girl my daughter would have become. She would have looked very much like you, Melissa...had she ever been born. Good luck, kid. You're dreams have come true. Lim agrees with me. You will be the best he has, if you don't screw up and get yourself hurt. We might even see each other again someday, if I recognize you. The Orient changes people. One's thing's for sure: I will be able to afford you."

Clint turned to walk away, halting abruptly when Timothy grabbed his arm. "You're not leaving us here by ourselves."

"Kid, I haven't liked you from day one and if you hadn't been born with such a sick mind you'd be learning how to cut hair next week instead of watching some old guy's head bobbing up and down in your crotch." He smashed his fist into Timothy's face, crashing the boy into a wall.

"Clint, you're scaring me!" Melissa was trembling, blue-green tears streaming down her cheeks.

"Goodbye, kid."

"Mommy!"

Clint faced her, wearing a curious expression. "Mommy," he chortled. "Don't expect your mommy chasing after you the way you've treated her, disrespected her. She's not coming for you. Your mommy is in love with Michelle Lopez. That's right; your Spanish teacher is your mommy's lover. They're incredible together and they don't want you getting in the way. They have a life together all planned out. The same way you had yours planned out. I told you: We get what we deserve in life, what we work towards. The good thing is you're talented. You'll have the best clients. You decide right now, before he comes for you, that you'll be his best and he will take good care of you."

Melissa was sobbing. "This isn't happening. I love you, Clint. I want you to take care of me. You love me. I know you do."

"Yeah, it is happening. Kid, you're the one person who can send me back to prison and that's not going to happen. Think of yourself as a beautiful blonde geisha and you'll do fine. You'll even enjoy it, like you always have."

"Clint, please don't do this. I don't want to go home either. I'll go anywhere with you."

"We wouldn't work out. I don't think my new wife would appreciate me doing her ex-lover's daughter on the side." He knelt beside Timothy, glaring, rolling the boy onto his side and reaching into his pants for his wallet. "You should have been happy with a few pictures of her, Tim-boy. Midnight Rhapsody was way out of your league and still is. She'll leave you behind."

As Clint Evans opened the door they had come through, Lim came through another. The men exchanged nods and both doors closed. Clint stood on the other side for a moment, listening, skipping down the stairs once the girl's whimpering was brought to an abrupt end with the sharp thwack of a stinging slap. At the hotel he went through their suitcases removing any evidence of who the brother and sister were. He destroyed the passports, bank cards and photo IDs, snorting at seeing the nude photo of Melissa in her brother's wallet and thinking the kid had also found what he wanted most in life. Unfortunately, now he couldn't afford her.

He went for a midnight swim, enjoyed a few drinks by the pool, checked-out and the executive flight was en route to Dubai at 6:00 AM. The pilot assured Clint that with a twelve-hour stopover they would land in Paris by 1:00AM Friday, well ahead of the 5:00AM departure to Bayville where he would arrive at 7:00AM to sleep away his weekend in preparation for his trip to Cape City.

*

On the other side of the world as Clint was sitting at the pool and Melissa, torn from her brother, was learning respect, her mother and Michelle were finishing lunch, waiting for the police to arrive and hoping for any good news.

"Ms. Burberry, Ms. Lopez. I'll begin with the worst news. In fact, I have nothing good to report. Your husband, Theodore Burberry, is presumed dead, lost at sea as it were." Michelle grabbed Kathy's hand. "Apparently, a sailor best described as a fair weather enthusiast, he left dock during a severe storm well beyond his capabilities. They assume he was intoxicated. The lines were severed, the anchor was missing and two liquor bottles were removed from the bar: one empty, one not found. I'm truly sorry."

"Don't be, Detective Johnson. He was drunk when I called him on Sunday. He'd just been fired. He was talking irrationally, talking about our daughter, a woman called Eileen and the two of us. Nothing he said made sense."

"We've spoken with the Cape City Police, which is where he died. The boat was found two hundred miles from shore. Apparently Ms. Eileen Kimberly was his friend for many years. She has, on your behalf, called the company to set the matter straight. I'm told you should expect a call from the HR department. Your husband was well insured. I believe the amount mentioned is two million."

"Detective Johnson," Michelle began, "won't this Eileen have a legal claim?"

"The detective in charge of the case knows her personally. She neither wants the money nor does she need it. She was the registered owner of the sixty-foot boat. She paid cash for the thing and owns several well-known art galleries."

Kathy went to stand. "I need a drink."

Michelle stopped her and stood. "Detectives, anything, coffee…water?"

"No, thank you, not that I won't tilt a few when I get home" Fielding answered. "We'll wait for you, Ms. Lopez."

When Michelle was seated the senior cop continued. "We have also spoken with Chicago Corporate, before we knew of the accident, to a man called Lester Lamarre."

Kathy shrugged. "I don't know anyone at the company except by name. He's the gofer. I was never privy to that part of Ted's life. Now I know why. I always thought he didn't want me in the way, you know, flirting, having affairs."

"Sometimes, Ms. Burberry, our job is awkward, despite what we see most days. Mr. Lamarre sent us information and, in fact, after speaking with him our office was contacted by Social Services."

"Whatever for?"

"There was a letter, apparently sent by you." Johnson handed Kathy a copy. "Is that your signature, Ms. Burberry?"

"No, it is not." She was adamant. "Any time before Sunday I would have said yes, but I never sent his office a letter."

"Please read what someone had to say." Kathy and

Michelle read the letter together, not disguising horrified expressions. "Ms. Burberry, we've brought copies of the videos and photos which we believe are a partial collection. My partner and I are truly sorry. To put it delicately the imagery supports the letter, displaying your daughter in a very promiscuous light, if not with her father being abused. There are also images of you and Ms. Lopez together."

"What photos?" Michelle asked.

"Intimate photos of you and Ms. Burberry in bed and an outdoor spa, kissing. I should add that we're more concerned about finding your daughter, as your son has not been mentioned in any of this and we have no interest in what adults do consensually."

Both women paled. Kathy was the first to speak. "Detectives, Michelle's divorcing. Her husband abused her badly."

"We're familiar with the specifics of the case. There's no need to explain."

"Yes, there is. I was also abused…by my husband's neglect and my children's loathing of me. I lived alone in that house for as long as I can remember. Those pictures you're talking about were taken during a girls' weekend, and not the way you might think. We were four friends wanting to get away. The first night there were a couple of jerks in the spa and I kissed Michelle to send them a message." Her laugh was weak. "Unfortunately, I also surprised our two friends. The next morning, and I assume those are the photos you're talking about, we kissed as our friends came through the door for innocent shock value, knowing they were coming in. The funny thing is: Michelle and I were the most shocked. We found each other."

Michelle broke in. "We're not dykes."

"Ms. Lopez, my wife and I have two wonderful friends sharing a similar relationship. My partner and I are not judging you and our copies of these visuals are under lock and key. They will not be seen by others and will be returned to you when all this is settled. These copies are for you to study and, after you've stopped being sick, tell us if you discover anything you believe might assist us, whether regarding your late husband or whomever. There is no timeframe."

"Thank you." Kathy sipped her drink. "And where do I stand with Social Services?"

"Mr. Burberry is dead, your daughter's reached the age of majority and, unless you specifically request action, nothing will be done to locate your son."

"Timothy won't come home, and if you bring him home he'll leave, as will Melissa, and I blame their father. He was never around for either of them."

"I'll inform Social Services this afternoon. However we do want to speak with your daughter. She's a person of interest, particularly since there seems to be no love lost between you. It's possible she might want to embarrass you and your late husband. If not your husband, someone was holding the camcorder. We believe your daughter either has a friend, Ms. Burberry, or an accomplice."

"Detective Johnson, she was a loner. She never went out and never accepted dates. She stopped seeing her friends over two years ago."

The cop clutched his hands together. "Ms. Burberry, how close is she to your son?"

"They despise each other. They absolutely never speak." Kathy's eyes opened wide. "No! What you're suggesting is preposterous."

"Yet, they left together and the first-response officers have told us your daughter made quite a theatrical exit...with your son in tow."

"Personally, I was floored by Timothy, though I don't believe Melissa's little performance, and she was performing, came out of the blue. Not only is she very good at histrionics and playing sides, she's calculating. She's probably rehearsed that scene a hundred times. The fact is: Timothy doesn't have the smarts or initiative. I think he'd faint if he ever saw naked girl, let alone photographing his sister." She paused, looking at Michelle. "Detective, the photographs of Michelle and me were part of an album which I put in my car, where no one would see them because my daughter has a curious nature. Whoever did steal my house also stole my car and very precious memories. They also had sufficient time to decode the safe, study personal documents and learn to copy our signatures. The question is why. Apart from the money, what would anyone gain by ruining his career and probably driving him to commit such a horrible suicide?"

"We hope to find out, Ms. Burberry. However at this point we have no idea, which is why we need to speak with your daughter. Please call us as soon as you hear from her." The two cops stood. "I don't envy what you must do this evening or tomorrow, but watching these CDs may help us."

Seventy

Thursday Eileen sat alone in her beach house, at first hating Ted for what he had done; slowly discovering she actually hated herself for not realizing her mistake years earlier. A stranger's kiss had filled her with self-doubt, yet she gave him a million dollars with a single wish in mind: to marry him. Ted, she thought, chose a propitious time to kill himself. What was worse, she didn't miss him.

"Hello."

"Clint, how's the unemployed electronics engineer? Am I calling at a bad time?"

"No, Eileen. Bad times are when you don't call."

"Where are you?"

"Bayville for the time being, where else?"

"I was wondering, when you're here next week, perhaps we could have lunch or dinner."

"I'm scheduled to arrive next Friday, I think midmorning." He heard her sigh and counted down. "Eileen, nothing's keeping me here. I can change my flight to this weekend and arrive Saturday."

"I think I might like that. Things have happened. The man I was seeing was killed in an accident, which isn't why I'm calling. I believe I would have called anyway."

"Eileen, I'm so sorry. May I ask how?"

"He drowned. Officially a boating accident, unofficially we don't know."

"You weren't with him at the time?"

"No. The conditions were horrible. He should have known better, unless…"

"We never know what's in another's mind. Bad things happen. There's never a good time."

"Clint I am talking about lunch or dinner, not a search for comfort."

"I'm your friend, first and foremost, as much as I want more to happen between us when the timing is right."

"So I'll see you Saturday, and possibly visit a few marinas."

"I'm cancelling my flight the moment we hang up. I won't need a jet. I'll be floating to you over the next two days on cloud nine. I'll call you from the hotel as soon as I arrive."

"I'm looking forward to seeing you."

"I guess this is where we say goodbye."

"Or, au revoir."

"That sounds much more appropriate. Au revoir."

Clint pressed end and boarded his flight to Paris.

*

Michelle and Kathy were numb; neither woman slept through the night. What they witnessed on the CDs and DVDs was devastating, to think someone hated her that much that he or she would engineer Ted's death and humiliate her. Who knew them so intimately, and why did they want to know her in the first place? Who influenced Melissa to where she would act so unabashedly and lewdly, who followed them to Myrtle Beach after selling her house with such ease? How could anyone gain entry to her home, her safe and computers without help and where was Melissa? Then an HR clerk from Chicago Corporate called at the beginning of business to confirm Kathy would receive the two million in death benefits after the processing of requisite documents, ending the call without condolences.

"You should call him, darling, to be fair."

"I didn't want to hurt you. We've had enough hurt."

"Darling, I resigned this morning. You see, we already have secrets," Michelle kissed her, "or surprises. I was too nervous or excited to tell you before I was certain. I've been to several interviews at the Mexican Embassy, without telling you. I'm the new head of their translation services and my teaching substitute's taking over from today. Being stuck with me is the downside, at least half the time. I'm alright with it, darling. Go ahead. Call him." Michelle scrolled the directory and pressed dial.

"I'm seeing Michelle's name, so I'm guessing you're calling to say goodbye."

"No, I'm not. I'm calling because Michelle made me. She's sitting right here."

"And listening to my every despondent word."

"No. I wouldn't do that. I'm not a teenager, Jack. She wants me to give you a chance."

"Then tell her I love her already. I thought you had your phone disconnected because of me. I must have called you a dozen times."

"Jack," Kathy's pause became speechlessness.

"What is it, passion? What's wrong?"

"Jack, my husband was killed this week...in a boating accident."

"A boating accident," Jack's tone revealed sincere shock, "at this time of year? How is that possible?"

"I don't know."

Kathy, I have no words. When did it happen?"

"He drowned Monday somewhere off Cape City. Precisely where is impossible to determine. He was lost at sea. The boat was recovered. He's just...gone."

"He died at sea, at this time of year?"

"Yes. Anyway, I wanted to tell you."

"Listen, I'm in California. I'll fly out tonight. Can I see you tomorrow? Can we meet at the bistro?" He hesitated.

"I'm sorry, that was improper. Can I come by Michelle's? I want to meet her. I want her to meet me. I want her to know me and like me."

"Jack, the bistro would be more appropriate for the time being. I'll meet you at seven. I'm not ready for you to meet Michelle. So much has happened that I don't want to discuss on the phone. And then you can decide."

"Decide what, passion?"

"Simply put, whether you want an unemployed bisexual widow on your hands. I won't give up Michelle, not for anyone. She's too special to me."

He took a deep breath, exhaling slowly. "You mean a woman who no longer has a husband she hasn't loved for a very long time, and a close friend who's by her side to comfort her. I seem to remember explaining that I wasn't naïve and your heart, Kathy, is big enough for us to share. I'll see you tomorrow, but let's meet at four. The bistro will be practically empty and I want you to myself. In the meantime, give my regards to Michelle. She will like me, I know she will."

Seventy-One

Clint Evans walked into his pied-à-terre Friday morning, still reeling from the news of Ted Burberry's death. Although not totally unexpected, he hated not knowing and was anxious to hear the details, curious whether Burberry had leapt from the tallest wave, slid into the deepest trough or had just fallen overboard.

Ideally, he would have preferred some R and R before flying south to Cape City, until Eileen Kimberly's phone call catapulted him from the uncertainty of a would-be lover to within easy reach of her life and her bed. Nor would Burberry's departure require drastic modifications to his original plan. He would maintain his condo a few months longer and travel to Cape City on the weekends for meetings with the contractors. He would build his beach house and buy a yacht, possibly with Eileen and possibly not in Cape City, certain she wouldn't want him in a home once shared with Burberry or aboard a yacht replete with constantly haunting memories. Both would be sold.

Working that night was out of the question, as was waking at 4:00 AM to catch the seven o'clock flight. So he booked for later in the afternoon and went to bed.
*

Jack Caden went to the bistro for a late lunch hours ahead of Kathy to speak with Alfonso who would personally attend to his wishes. He wanted Kathy to know exactly how he felt, what was in his heart and he took great pains not to

531

overlook the smallest detail.

*

Kathy arrived early, Alfonso seating her by the fireplace and not at a table. He brought her a tequila splashed with soda, telling her that he would be a few moments. When he returned he explained that Mr. Caden had dropped by earlier in the day and would not be joining her. An urgent matter required his immediate attention and, regrettably, he hadn't noted Miss Michelle's number. The gentleman apologized profusely, Alfonso affirmed, certain she would understand once she read the note he'd written. The owner of the bar smiled sympathetically, placing the gift-wrapped box and letter by her side and stepping away to let Kathy read in private.

My sweet, exotic Kathy, believe me when I say how much I might have loved you had you not come to me in the exact image of another whom I once loved and whose treachery is expunged forever from my mind. I am finally free of her and I owe my freedom to you. I regret that I deceived you and leave you with these parting gifts which will explain everything.

Go to her, Kathy. She wants you more than I ever could. Go to her now. My gifts are to her as much as they are to you, as is a letter I have written to both of you. Goodbye.

Kathy walked from the bistro in shock. She drove Michelle's car home in a daze, trying to remember Jack Caden, the first time they met, the boardwalk and his touch the day he gently raised her naked body from the bed. The note made no sense whatsoever. What treachery?

In the condo she and Michelle sat with the box between them. Under the layers of wrapping they saw the letter and read in utter disbelief.

Mi amor and darling, I am truly happy for both of you, now that I am finished with you and able to regard you differently.

Kathy, I loved you at once that first night in the hotel bar, despite calling you by a different name in my mind. I knew then I must have you, that you would be my one hope of salvation and the first night I saw you bathe so lovingly with Michelle I knew I must have her also, that through her I could hurt you the most. How I enjoyed watching you throughout your first week together, touching, exploring, learning of your true natures. My vivid memories of you together made our lovemaking at the spa all the more pleasurable. Your panties taken from your hamper I return to you with the greatest reluctance, the lingering scent arousing me as I write this letter.

Kathy, your MX-5 is at the airport in spot L18. In the trunk are your memories of Vermont, your papers from the safe, your new wardrobe which I so enjoyed watching you select each morning and your jewellery. How I suffered for you each night in my little loft above your bed, witnessing the sadness etched in your face, hearing you whisper tender words to your lover, to our Michelle. The rest is gone, including the Lexus and I'm sure you understand the reason I could not return any of the computers. I'm sorry about Ted. I suppose some men never have what it takes, however once the confusion with Eileen Kimberly is understood by Chicago Corporate you should once again be financially secure. I also believe he would have wanted you to have his private photo album, which I leave to you on his behalf.

And what of little Melissa? In the first DVD you'll certainly recognize the venue she chose for her New Year's Eve party of one. Timothy, or deadbrain, was the videographer. He did a pretty good job for a sick kid. However I had the distinct pleasure of filming her in the second and third DVDs in the snow at Surfers' Beach and in your home. I'm particularly proud of my work on Valentine's and at Myrtle Beach, although you might be interested in one day viewing a popular site known as Midnight dot Rhapsody. Melissa, your prissy daughter, also did quite good work on her own.

And Michelle, or should I say mi amor, you were refreshing if not an outright bitch. The first time I saw your body I knew I must have you. Through you I would inflict the most harm, though I can't deny the ecstasy surging through me, so to speak, the instant your body shuddered and you cried out Kathy's name. One night was not enough. I needed you once more and I would have you. I will forever treasure the image of your nude silhouette as you lay sleeping in our bed. The three thousand was to cover my costs, not to do so would have been unfair to my other nocturnal clients. However, enclosed you will find your bank cards and panties, no less difficult to part with than darling's, no less pungent, a testament to what we might have shared.

Am I wrong to imagine both of you crying, consoling one another in a tight and loving embrace?

Best regards to both of you, Jack Caden and/or Clyde Van.

*

He wasn't wrong and not until their tears evaporated did they flip through the pages of one album, not hating Eileen for what she had done and amazed at the yacht that had carried Ted to his death. Closing the album, Michelle threw it into the garbage. The second album brought more tears and Michelle laid that one on their bed, refusing to let Clyde Van or anyone else cast a shadow over cherished memories.

They sat through New Year's devastated, too shocked to look away, Michelle barely able to remove and shred the DVD. Kathy trembled throughout the second video, seeing how willingly Melissa took part, seeing how happy she looked with Caden. The second disc was also destroyed, Michelle arguing in vain against viewing the third. Kathy was adamant. She would see them all, not expecting the flood of unstoppable tears wetting her face as she saw the smiling and visibly relaxed nude girl on the chaise-longue, imagining Caden standing so near. Then she saw herself with Ted on the terrace and, when she witnessed Melissa undressing, urging her daddy to help her with her panties, Kathy leapt from sofa and ran to the powder room. By the time she returned Michelle had destroyed the final DVD and nothing remained but the letter, memories of White Cliff Lodge and the disturbing need to know. Michelle reluctantly went for her computer and dialled into Midnight dot Rhapsody. When they had seen enough, Michelle held Kathy tight, rocking her gently and not letting her go until dawn.

Saturday morning they called the detectives. Reading the letter, the men's compassion for the humiliated women was sincere, accepting at face value that Michelle had destroyed the DVDs and both albums, somewhat taken aback when she explained the website and allowed the cops the use of her laptop.

They were speechless, and when Kathy broke the silence, asking how long her daughter might have been in porn, Fielding took a few moments tapping several keys and making a few calculations before replying "just over two years at approximately two or three thousand a week." He asked Kathy whether she had changed her thinking about finding her daughter and son. Kathy shook head and walked away saying she was a couple of years too late and in the meantime they seem to have found themselves. The detectives silently agreed. Midnight Rhapsody was better off not being found.

The cops returned mid-afternoon after going to the house on the hill, leaving the occupants visibly shaken to know someone had lived for so many weeks in the attic and had wired many of the rooms, the wires still remaining. There was no Jack Caden, nor Clyde Van. The hotel and spa records showed cash payments. They would send over a police artist, both men of the opinion that any such description would serve no purpose. Anyone who could successfully engineer and perpetrate the destruction of an entire family, their home and a man's career while feigning love for two women, abusing one in order to hurt another for no understandable reason would not do so without an extreme degree of certainty he would never be recognized. He had, in effect, committed his crime in broad daylight using the legal system as his primary accomplice.

He had stolen a house, the contents of the house and a car. The rest was speculation and would likely remain so.

Seventy-Two

Thursday, July 01st

Clint Evans lay on the bow of his motor yacht which he had no idea how to pilot, propped up on one elbow and staring at the back of the woman he was going to marry in September. He'd taken possession of his beach house close to the Cape City limits the day before, well south of Eileen's memories and the twenty-metre vessel documented as The Tenant was delivered to his dock that morning.

He left Bayville behind days earlier with no remorse and countless memories of innumerable work nights and the pleasure he'd brought to so many faceless and bodiless women. The bodies he did remember were Kathy's, Michelle's and Melissa's. At one time he thought he would forget them, but he couldn't and never struggled to dispel vivid images of them. The three were too unique: Mother, daughter and lesbian lover. Michelle and Kathy were the best of all his lovers. Melissa, however, was the most arousing and he thought of her each time he brought Eileen with him to the very precipice of their lovemaking.

He never did care about Ted Burberry and wasn't the least bit concerned that Ted had been forgotten by all who knew him or that future generations promenading through Bayville's cemetery would never read his name and be curious. Melissa Burberry was in her fourteenth week with Mr. Lim and Clint would never know that at the end of her first week, during which time she had been tutored by the other girls, she went to him asking permission to please his most preferred guests. Nor would he know Lim agreed with the provision that, if she did not, she would then please his worst.

Clint Evan's advice to her was sage and she quickly assumed the exalted position of Mr. Lim's favourite daughter. At New Year's she transitioned from a naughty girl in panties and bra to an alluring woman in chic lingerie. Now with her body coloured to a deep shade of bronze, her hair growing longer each day, she was sultry, a desired seductress to high-profile Western and European businessmen and women. She was admired and envied by the other girls and her command of Thai improved daily.

She hadn't seen her brother since her first night with Mr. Lim and wouldn't recognize him if she ever did. Lim traded him to one of the lesser houses of Bangkok's darker tourist industry to service the deviant preferences of businessmen, husbands, brothers and fathers for little more than the cost of a midday snack on the river. Timothy never thought of his sister, nor did Melissa ever think to remember him. She never thought of her mother, her father or her bedroom at midnight, though she did think of Clint Evans and how she could ever have loved him as deeply as she loved Mr. Lim who really did adore and worship her.

Clint knew Kathy received two million dollars in death benefits and that she sent Eileen Kimberly a card to thank her for her integrity and honesty. He didn't know she'd sold her eighteenth-floor condo at a substantial profit to move in with Michelle after a Caribbean cruise with Sheila and Darlene in lieu of three nights in Vegas where they planned to escape in four weeks' time, though he wouldn't have been surprised.

He didn't know Kathy had begun a career in private practice, under her own banner and never allowed Melissa or Timothy to disrupt her thoughts, despite the graphic images lingering in the darkest corners of her dreams which were fading more each night. He didn't know Kathy and Michelle never spoke of Caden or Van or that they spoke about themselves without regretting earlier years lost, thinking of their future. Nor did Clint know of his second greatest mistake in life.

He didn't know Eileen's divorce had come through or that old Kimberly honoured his original commitment to her with a cheque exceeding twelve million dollars. With the beach house and the Sea Babe gone she moved into a pied-à-terre where she would be closer to her work, refusing to live with him until they were married. What she loved most about him was his inner strength and self-reliance. He needed nothing from her but her love and never once lamented selling his business or worried about his future. When he stroked the smooth lines of her shoulders she purred and captured his hand in the nook of her neck, bringing up her hand to kiss his and wrap herself into his loving arms, dreamily absorbing the sun's midday warmth until unexpectedly complaining of feeling nauseous.

She went into the cabin to change and left him, making light of his concern, insisting she would not spoil their first evening together in her future home with her head in a toilet bowl. She drove to her condo, and once inside she went neither to her bed nor to her solarium to relax and feel better. She went to her safe and inserted the DVD she had studied so many times over the past months into her reader, standing transfixed and alarmed. She wasn't wrong. She was a fool, and went to her phone.

Randolph and her police friend arrived within minutes of one another. The trio viewed Melissa's balcony scene in Myrtle Beach, freezing the action of a man's hand pulling away her panties and the two men expressed the same concern. Notwithstanding the absence of tears running down the girl's face and the alluring gleam in her eyes, who would believe she wasn't having a good time and no judge would authorize a warrant to investigate Clint Evans based on a scar.

The video was inconclusive and, should her suspicion prove false, Evans would undoubtedly reverse any thoughts he might have of marrying her. Yet, she countered, how could she think of marrying him if, indeed, he was the man in the video who had directly caused so much tragedy and grief. She went for her handbag, passing the detective Evan's old-fashioned wrapped in tissue, reminding the detective of Randolph's annual contribution to the Policeman's Benefit Fund and surprising neither man with her typical thoroughness or candour.

Not long after the detective phoned to speak with Randolph, much to Eileen's annoyance. He was sending a cruiser to the apartment as a precaution until Eileen had time to pack a suitcase, suggesting to Randolph that she spend the night at the mansion where he would meet with them in the morning. Then the Cape City cop sat staring into his screen, reading the sickening letter and studying the composite which left no doubt who Clint Evans was or what he had done.

Reading the final page of the court transcript as the sun came up, pale from lack of sleep and too much caffeine, and seeing the photo of Kim Moon on his screen, he understood why.

He phoned the Bayville detective who sent him the wealth of information and when the conversation ended, one cop drove to Randolph Kimberly's mansion, the other went to Kathy's and Michelle's condo.

*

Clint Evans was thirty-five, released from prison ten months earlier after serving a five-year sentence for embezzlement, fraud and grand larceny. The three-year sentence handed down by a judge known for meting out maximum prison time was increased to four years for contempt of court and issuing death threats when Evans rushed at the woman, promising to kill her: one Kim Moon, who testified against him in a plea bargain. The judge believed the threat and suggested the woman use the additional year wisely.

"Do you mean to hide?" Eileen asked.

"Yes."

"He told me he was forty."

"Apparently not his biggest lie."

"You said five years, Charlie."

"He's as bad as they come. He has no conscience. He wasn't in prison a full day before he damn near beat another con to death, hence the scarring on his hand. I saw the photos, something you don't have to see. The cops up north were very helpful. The attack was so vicious the man spent a month in the infirmary and Evans did the same time in isolation. An additional year was added to his sentence with no chance of parole."

"Why me?"

"Unless he tells us, we'll never know. Eileen, this is a photograph of Kathy Burberry."

"I saw her. She's lovely. I feel so sorry for her."

"I can't think of anything he didn't do to her. What I've learned since last night would make you physically sick; however we do understand the reason why. He wanted to destroy her." Charles Bentley brought another photo from the file folder. "This woman is Kim Moon. The Bayville cops are with Ms. Burberry and her girlfriend as we speak. They believe she and Ms. Lopez will be very willing to help."

"Charlie, I watched the videos countless times. Why did I not see until now?"

"Why did anyone not see? We were all focused on the

disturbing imagery and the dialogue. If not for you, he would have gotten away scot-free."

Randolph Kimberly broke in. "Eileen, my dear, you have no reason to feel ashamed or bear the burden of unnecessary guilt. I believe we should invite the two young women to the mansion and put the past where it belongs. The rogue has toyed with them in a cruel and lascivious way. My mind is filled with horrible images of what more he might have done to you after the wedding. Invite them here at once and let's enjoy the last laugh with our Messieurs Evans, Van and Caden."
*

Johnson stayed in the hallway to finish his call. Fielding went in, adding to the women's curiosity with his self-satisfied expression. Kathy's and Michelle's reaction to the close-up of the scar was immediate. Both Van and Caden had the identical markings on their fists. When the cop told them about Clint Evans, his pathological hate for Kim Moon and his threat, Kathy asked whether the woman was in danger. He assured her the danger had passed and slid a photo of Kim Moon from an envelope. Michelle gasped and clamped hand over her mouth. The second photo was a black and white print of Clint Evans taken some five years earlier, unsmiling, his hair cut short and his eyes showing not the slightest humanity. Kathy bit into her knuckles, shaking her head in disbelief and begging Michelle to forgive her for what she had done.

Fielding put up his hand, insisting Michelle had nothing to forgive, but without their help Clint Evans could well remain a free man and live a comfortable life.

"You know where he is?" Michelle ventured.

"Yes, we do. He's in Cape City. Right now my partner's talking with Eileen Kimberly."

"How is Eileen involved?" Kathy asked.

"Until last night she was planning to marry Evans in the

fall. We assume that's why he went after your husband the way he did. We believe you and Mr. Burberry were separate issues for him. He got to Kim Moon vicariously through you. To Evans you're one and the same and he used your property, your daughter and Ms. Lopez to achieve his goal of destroying her. We assume at some point he came into contact with Ms. Kimberly, possibly while in Myrtle Beach and decided to use what he had already accomplished to greater advantage."

Johnson caught the last few words. "Eileen Kimberly is inviting you to Cape City as her guests. She assumes you want this miscreant returned to prison. First Class tickets are waiting for you at the airport. The return portion is scheduled for tomorrow and a guestroom is being prepared for you. She has also invited you to stay longer." He turned to his partner. "We're invited to the party, she wouldn't hear otherwise." He looked at his watch. "Ladies, I can't imagine two more eye-appealing women, particularly in the same room. However, and these are not my words, Ms. Kimberly believes you will both want to look your loveliest this evening." He sniggered. "Hell hath no fury, as Clint Evans is about to discover in triplicate. We'll be back for you in one hour."

Seventy-Three

Randolph Kimberly's limousine met the odd foursome at CC International and at the mansion Kathy recognized Eileen immediately, taken aback by the woman's genuine warmth. Lunch was served in a garden setting and after the elaborate meal the three cops spoke together, Randolph took Michelle by the arm to show her the grounds and Eileen sat with Kathy by her favourite fountain to hear the playful splashes of cascading water and listen to each other. They might never be the closest of friends, though more importantly there would never be hate and Kathy accepted the gracious invitation to stay longer, come to know each other and dispel the past.

Late in the day, to coincide with dinner, Eileen placed the call.

"Sweetheart, I'm sorry I didn't return your call. I felt so terrible when I got home I took a sleeping pill and didn't hear the phone ring. Then this morning I did mean to phone you until La Primera called. My best client was waiting at the gallery and would only work with me. I've been at his mansion all day hanging art and he insists we join him and a few friends for a casual dinner and poker night. It's a social opportunity we can't refuse, sweetheart. He's sending his driver to pick you up. He's very nice, if not a little stuffy," she looked over to Randolph, "so please wear a jacket and the '87 Bordeaux would be quite appropriate. The table minimum is three thousand, though five will show us in a better light. I don't want to appear inadequate in front of these people." She listened. "No is not acceptable sweetheart. He's just spent a hundred thousand dollars and he's not finished." She glanced over to Randolph again. "See you soon, and don't keep the driver waiting."

The driver was Kimberly's regular chauffeur, albeit ex-military and very capable of taking care of himself. Charles Bentley and the Bayville cops looked too unmistakeable and weren't taking chances. Clint Evans was greeted at the door by the butler and Eileen.

"Clint, you're dressed to kill."

He scanned the massive entrance. "How much is this guy worth?" he whispered.

"Roughly in the area of nine zeros, although you wouldn't think so to see him. He keeps a low profile. Come. I'm anxious for you to meet him. He's also invited other dinner guests who are anxious to see you. They're seated in the dining room."

"I'll be on my best behaviour. We can't have you losing this guy."

"I won't. He knows we'll always be friends."

The butler opened the door for Eileen and when Clint stepped through the man held out a gloved hand for the bottle of Bordeaux and followed, closing the door behind him. The men in the room pushed back their chairs and stood.

"Good evening, Mr. Evans."

"Good evening. Thank you for inviting me."

"Having you here is entirely my pleasure. Had I known of you earlier I would have insisted that we meet without the slightest delay. Before I introduce myself, may I introduce my friends? You're already acquainted with Eileen, my charming and delightful ex-wife. The gentleman standing to my left is Charles Bentley, Captain of the Major Crimes Unit in our fine city, the gentlemen to my right are detectives Johnson and Fielding from Bayville and the gentleman behind you kindly accepted to stand-in for my butler. He is also an officer of the law. Please, Mr. Evans, do sit down."

"Eileen, what's going on?"

Eileen chortled. "Dinner's going on, Clint. We're simply waiting for our other guests to arrive. Coming from Bayville you might even remember Kathy Burberry and Michelle Lopez. We would have invited Kim Moon, had time allowed." She smirked. "I see you understand. Now sit your ass down."

Evans spun around to find himself instantly pinned against the wall by the door with one arm behind his back on the verge of dislocating.

Kathy stepped in first. "Hello, Jack. Imagine meeting you here." She leaned against the wall. "As I understand by talking with these gentlemen, your assets are being frozen and after your house and boat are sold I'll be getting back my money. Oh, and Midnight Rhapsody's money, that'll be going to help out troubled children."

Michelle walked in. "Hi, Clyde." Her laughter was artificial and cuttingly derisive. "You just don't look the same with your face all scrunched up like that. You know, there's something I've been waiting to do all day. Officer, can you pull him away from the wall. I need something from his jacket." The cop looked over to Bentley who nodded. He brought both Evans' hands together, cuffed them and held him by the shoulders. Michelle pulled at his lapel and reached into an inner pocket for his billfold. She counted thirty hundred-dollar bills, put them in her purse, and tossed the billfold onto the table. "Now we're even and you're going to prison." Without warning she drove her foot violently into his groin, the force of the impact heightened by the cop not budging, causing the other men in the room to grimace in concert with Evans' distorted face and guttural scream. "From one outright bitch to another, asshole."

"No, Michelle, you're not even." Eileen stepped in, taking the billfold. She counted twenty bills, giving ten to Michelle and ten to Kathy. "You forgot the indignity of your stolen lingerie which I must assume was of the finest quality. Now you're even."

The officer shuffled a bent-over Evans into a chair at the far end of the table meant to seat a dozen couples and sat beside him. Kathy and Michelle sat between Johnson and Fielding, Eileen between Kimberly and Bentley. Each of the six courses served was superb, the officer seated by Evans commenting that he'd died and gone to heaven, despite accompanying his gourmet meal with a vegetable cocktail. The other guests were held to no such constraint. This was their party and they kept the conversation light, mostly about sailing, beach houses and travel, as Evans sat with his hands cuffed behind him, staring at a tin plate of cold mashed potatoes, a sausage and a tin cup filled with tap water.

To end the evening they drove to Evans' beach house with the guest of honour caged in a squad car, formally charged and under arrest, though he would spend the final hour of his evening in his cage glaring as the host and dinner guests enjoyed cocktails on the afterdeck of the yacht he would never sail, the highlight of the evening coming as Bentley was about to signal the squad car to leave, delaying the command at Eileen's request.

Eileen asked everyone to disembark with glasses of champagne and gather on the dock without blocking Evans' view of the stern. She had a special gift for Kathy and Michelle, an inspiration eloquently conveying the blunt message as she pulled away the silk drape covering the transom. She had renamed the yacht Evicted.

From Inside Her Bedroom

Other Mystery – Suspense - Thriller Novels
By Doug Booth:

Split Verdict
The 4th Man
The Madam
Family Lies
Mother of Pearl
From Inside Her Bedroom
The Feast of Tombola
Deferred Prejudice
The Hunt for Gilligan Rose
The Fatal Diners' Club
Silent Conviction
A Christmas Killer, Comfort and Joy
Pariah In the Mirror

***

No One to Tell (Creative Non-fiction)